STILLWATER

TANYA SCOTT

STILLWATER

A THRILLER

Atlantic Monthly Press
New York

Copyright © 2025 by Tanya Scott

All rights reserved. No part of this book may be reproduced in any form or by any electronic or mechanical means, including information storage and retrieval systems, without permission in writing from the publisher, except by a reviewer, who may quote brief passages in a review. Scanning, uploading, and electronic distribution of this book or the facilitation of such without the permission of the publisher is prohibited. Please purchase only authorized electronic editions, and do not participate in or encourage electronic piracy of copyrighted materials. Your support of the author's rights is appreciated. Any member of educational institutions wishing to photocopy part or all of the work for classroom use, or anthology, should send inquiries to Grove Atlantic, 154 West 14th Street, New York, NY 10011 or permissions@groveatlantic.com.

Any use of this publication to train generative artificial intelligence ("AI") technologies is expressly prohibited. The author and publisher reserve all rights to license uses of this work for generative AI training and development of machine learning language models.

First published in 2025 in Australia by Allen & Unwin

First Grove Atlantic hardcover editon: August 2025

ISBN 978-0-8021-6460-5
eISBN 978-0-8021-6461-2

Printed in the United States of America

Library of Congress Cataloging-in-Publication data is available for this title.

Atlantic Monthly Press
an imprint of Grove Atlantic
154 West 14th Street
New York, NY 10011

Distributed by Publishers Group West

groveatlantic.com

25 26 27 28   10 9 8 7 6 5 4 3 2 1

FOR NATHAN, SAM AND MIA

PROLOGUE

He dropped to his knees by the dam, his hands squelching into the shallows as he pitched forwards. Two semicircles rippled out, disturbing the mirror-like surface and distorting his reflection. Blood and dirt patterned his face like crude prison tattoos: dots, teardrops, stripes. His matted hair hung around his shoulders, and a layer of dried mud stiffened his clothes.

Cupping his hands, he dipped them into the quicksilver water, splashing it onto his face. The chill racked his body but, spurred on by the cold, he scooped again and again, scrubbing at his face, smoothing his hair, wiping his neck. And then his hands: he scraped at his palms, digging in with his fingernails to remove the dried crusts of blood. He plunged his hands back into the water to rinse them, then staggered to his feet. Wrapping his arms around his chest, he tucked his frozen hands under his armpits for warmth and stared blankly at the trees across the dam.

Dense fog cloaked the forest, clinging to the straight, tall trunks of the ironbarks and hovering suspended over the sparse undergrowth. Grey dawn light filtered through. The silence was absolute, a solid wall: no birdsong, not a hint of wind. The trees held their breath, as still as death. Even the water on the leaves had arrested mid-drip, frozen by the wintry night. The dam's mirror reflected nothing but the white sky.

He moved at last, leaving the dam behind to trudge past the wooden cabin on the narrow, tree-lined track. Overnight, the storm had turned it into a muddy river, carving deep crevices in the dirt. With each step, mud splashed to his knees, and he stumbled and slipped on the slick surface.

The fog thickened as he descended, reducing visibility to an arm's length. At the end of the track, where it intersected with a broader road, a rusty wire gate stood open, choked in place with mud and leaf litter from the storm. He scraped it clear so he could drag the gate across the track, and with a huff—of force, and finality—he slammed it into place. The faded metal sign rattled against the wire. He paused, staring at the single word.

STILLWATER

Then he squared his shoulders and turned his back on the sign, on the foggy track and the mess he'd left behind, and set off along the road.

CHAPTER ONE

THURSDAY, 6.11 PM

Luke held his breath as he turned the key in the ignition of his ailing Subaru. He assumed his years of steadfast atheism disqualified him for miracles, but he closed his eyes in silent prayer just in case.

The response was not encouraging: a click, then an echoing silence. The gods had spoken. Or not.

He'd ignored the warning signs for weeks, hoping he could coax the car through until his summer break. Tapping his thumbs on the steering wheel, he considered the irony: he needed the car to get to work, so that he could pay to fix the car, so that he could get to work. The circularity of it, like the cycle of life and death and taxes, would have amused him if he wasn't running late.

He gazed out at the concrete car park fronting his block of flats, searching for inspiration. His shoebox home was on the second floor of an ugly orange-brick cube, a remnant of brutal sixties design wedged into a backstreet of St Kilda that the tentacles of gentrification had yet to reach. No inspiration was to be found.

He tried the ignition again. The engine spluttered to life and his shoulders dropped with relief: perhaps the gods were listening after all.

Fifteen minutes later he reached his destination, a leafy street in Brighton a few blocks from the beach. He peered over the steering wheel at the house number, then checked his phone to be sure he had the right address. Most of his work was in group homes, not private residences. Clients like this—the exclusive suburb and majestic neo-Georgian house suggested a level of comfortable wealth—usually had permanent arrangements in place. Calling for respite was a measure of their desperation.

With his backpack slung over his shoulder, he pressed a buzzer on a gate set into a head-high wrought-iron fence and smiled into the fish-eye lens of the video intercom, noting the impressive security. The box crackled to life a moment later.

'Yes?' A male voice, clipped with impatience.

Luke's introduction was met with a long silence.

'You're late.'

He frowned. By his reckoning, he was thirty seconds early.

'My car—'

'I expected a woman.'

'You can call me Lucy, if you like.'

Another pause. Luke winced as his attempt at humour fell flat.

'Do you have ID? Are you qualified?'

Luke held his work ID in front of the camera. The logo read *Bayside Community Services Agency*. Underneath: *Luke Harris, Disability Support Worker*. The overexposed mugshot on the card made him look like a serial killer.

The gate clicked open and he stepped into a formal front garden. Manicured rectangles of lawn flanked a path lined by rosebushes, shaded by graceful silver birches. An imposing door of dark wood and leaded glass opened before he reached it.

A man in his fifties stood in the doorway. His suit was worth more than Luke's car, but it was a waste of expensive tailoring; the man's frame was so gaunt, the suit might as well have been hanging from a coathanger. Short grey hair topped a bony face, the hollow cheeks framing a hawkish nose, with the pasty skin of a life lived indoors. His pale eyes fixed on Luke in silent scrutiny for far longer than necessary.

'Right. I'm Jonathan Wylie. Phil's my son.' He threw his next words over his shoulder as he turned. 'Come on then.'

The cool sophistication of the interior reminded Luke of an art gallery rather than a home. An oversized gilt-framed mirror filled the entire wall in an entrance foyer as large as his living room. He followed Jonathan along an oak-floored corridor, past a carved staircase. Flamboyant abstract artworks and a gallery of family photographs in matching frames adorned the walls. At the end of the corridor, an expansive open-plan kitchen, living and dining area took up the width of the house. The evening sun streamed through a wall of glass at the rear, its golden haze reflecting off stainless-steel appliances and marble countertops.

In defiance of the high-end decor, the place was a mess. A smell reminiscent of hospital food soured the air. Food spills, empty packets and coffee cups dotted the kitchen counters, and a precarious pile of dishes threatened to topple into the sink. Cushions and books littered the floor of the living room. An overloaded laundry hamper sat in the middle of the dining table, like a bizarre centrepiece for a family dinner.

Phil was a big, doughy man in his mid-twenties, close to Luke's age. He pushed off a bar stool at the kitchen counter and into

Luke's space, as though he needed to get closer to check out the newcomer. His dark hair had been buzz cut, and his pale skin was pockmarked with blemishes and shaving cuts. Thick, black-rimmed spectacles sat crookedly over his nose. In his cheap green tracksuit, he seemed out of place in the plush surrounds, like an intruder—or an escaped prisoner, Luke thought.

'Hey, buddy, how you doing?' Luke said.

'I don't want it!' Phil stuck his hand into a bowl of pasta, gathered a handful and squeezed it into mush. It oozed between his fingers.

'I have to go.' Jonathan looked at his watch. 'I'm already late. I'm meeting an important client. I should be home in a few hours.'

'Ah—wait. I didn't get much from Sharon.' A few hours earlier, Luke's manager had called to explain the Wylie family's urgent need for assistance. When he refused—he'd requested two weeks' leave while he studied for his exams—she'd made a counter offer: pay for a full eight-hour shift, weekend rates, after-hours penalties. The kind of money he couldn't ignore. He expected a handover folder, a medication pack, a list of tasks.

'The place is a mess without Gabriela.' Jonathan's face twisted with irritation. 'Phil's usual carer. She looks after all this.' His vague wave encompassed the room and Phil. And Luke.

'Hey, Phil, no.' Luke caught Phil's wrist, narrowly avoiding a mushy pasta versus expensive suit situation as Phil took aim at Jonathan. 'Do you know when she's back?'

'No idea. She's been hospitalised with some kind of pneumonia, so I'm told.' A snort of contempt. 'She was here only a week ago. I hope she wasn't infectious.'

'I'm sorry.'

'We've had two casuals since then. Bloody hopeless, both of them. Look at the place.' Another dismissive wave.

Luke bit his tongue and inquired again about a communication folder. Jonathan extracted a ringbinder from a shelf and rattled off a series of instructions, all of them about the house rather than Phil. There was an alarm system—*don't mess with it, I'll leave it disarmed*—the air conditioning was automatic—*don't mess with it*—Luke could help himself to the fridge—*God only knows what's in there*.

He was glad when Jonathan left, taking his coldness with him. The room seemed to thaw in his absence.

Luke sat at the counter with Phil. 'Didn't like your dinner, hey?'

The folder informed him that Phil had an intellectual disability, autism, severe anxiety and intermittent psychotic episodes. Phil went to a day program—'school'—at a local private facility. Four afternoons a week, Gabriela picked him up and stayed until Jonathan got home; there were weekend dates where she'd stayed longer. The most recent entries were from the two casuals, who, like Luke, had picked up extra shifts.

Phil told Luke he didn't like his father's cooking because he'd put salt and olive oil on the pasta, so Luke boiled up another batch with *nothing else!*, words that Phil loved to repeat over and over. Unfamiliar with the etiquette of working in a private house, Luke had brought his own dinner: leftover stir-fried chicken and bok choy, soggy from a day in the fridge but infinitely better than plain pasta.

After dinner, while Phil sat at the table with his iPad and headphones playing Minecraft, Luke pottered around tidying. The living-room floor, the kitchen benches, the dishes. Tending to such a well-appointed kitchen was a pleasure. His own kitchenette was pathetic in comparison: the oven had never worked and only two of the burners on the cooktop were hot enough to melt butter. There was no room for the fridge, so it was relegated to the living room, next to the brown velour couch he'd picked up off the side of the road.

He flicked the switch on the impressive Gaggia coffee machine and made himself an after-dinner espresso. The aroma filled the kitchen, and his eyes closed as he took the first heavenly sip, wondering how long he could stay in this idyllic place before Jonathan returned and kicked him out. The pretence that it was his kitchen, his own fancy coffee machine and double-walled espresso cup and marble counter to rest it on entertained him.

When Phil tired of Minecraft, he directed Luke to a lounge near the front of the house, which contained an enormous L-shaped couch and a flat-screen television big enough to remind Luke that he hadn't been to the cinema for months.

While Phil watched his chosen movie—*Ghostbusters*, which he'd seen *hundreds of times!*—Luke opened his laptop to worry about his neglected study. His two exams were just over a week away, and he had two assignments due before then. He checked his bank balance on his phone, adding up numbers and calculating tax in his head, but no arithmetic was required to know that, even with this shift, he couldn't afford to fix his car any time soon.

There were other ways he could get the money. Temptation taunted him, distracted him for a few minutes. He shoved the idea back where it belonged.

As the movie was finishing, he heard the garage door open and close, and quiet footsteps in the hall. Expecting Jonathan, he started to pack away his laptop and textbooks.

A head—not Jonathan's—poked into the room from the hallway. 'Who's this, Phil?'

'Emma!' Phil bounced to his feet to fling his arms around her, pulling her into the room. 'It's Luke! Gabriela's sick!'

With a laugh, she fended Phil off. Her eyes fixed on Luke. 'Hi. Emma. I'm his sister, can't you tell?' And then, 'You're filling in for Gabriela?'

'Your father didn't tell you?'

'I don't talk to him.' Her lips pursed.

Physically, she was nothing like Phil; he figured it was a family joke. She was just as tall, close to six feet, but half Phil's width and a little younger. A mop of dark curly hair framed a narrow face. Her clothing—faded denim shorts and a T-shirt that ended above her navel—would have looked tacky if not for her nonchalant confidence. Luke suspected she could get away with wearing a potato sack, à la Marilyn Monroe.

He wondered again about the etiquette. With Emma there, he could leave, but the agreement had been that he'd stay until Jonathan got home. He pondered it while he helped Phil get ready for bed.

When he returned to the lounge, he found Emma sitting in near darkness, the glow of her phone lighting her face and her thumbs flying as she texted. She'd turned the volume of the television down, but the screen still flickered a rainbow into the room.

'Ah . . . I could probably go.' Luke propped on the end of the couch.

Dropping her phone on the seat beside her, Emma leaned back against the cushions. She gave his statement more consideration than he expected. 'What did you arrange with Dad?'

'He said he'd be a few hours. He didn't mention you.'

'Then you'd better stay. He'll freak if he's expecting you and you're not here.'

'He doesn't trust you to look after your brother?'

'I mind him all the time. It's not that.' She screwed up her nose. 'It's more that he gets fucking weird about, like, *everything*. Do what he says and you'll be fine. And they're paying you, right?'

'Yeah. Sure.' Luke sighed and lowered himself into a seat.

He detected a vague facial resemblance between Emma and Jonathan, but aside from that they could be different species. Jonathan seemed reptilian, with his cold glassy eyes and sharp tongue; Emma lounged like an elegant cat, although Luke suspected her air of aloof indifference was an act. From the corner of his eye, he could see her checking him out and felt his skin prickle. She examined his clothes, his hair, his arms. His scars.

To defuse whatever she was thinking, he said, 'Have you heard how Gabriela is going?'

'I spoke to her earlier. She's coughing up a lung. Poor thing, she sounded terrible.'

'You must know her pretty well.'

'She keeps this place running. She's the only one who can deal with Dad.'

'It's just the three of you?' The photos in the hall showed a nuclear family of four. A mother figure, tall with dark hair, holding a younger Emma's hand. It was a difficult question to phrase politely.

'My mother died a couple of years ago.' Emma waved the question away. Fiddling with the hem of her shorts, she regarded him sideways. 'You're nothing like Gabriela. How did you get sucked into this?'

'I started during the lockdowns. They needed staff, so they paid for my training. All the other casual work had dried up.'

'You like it?'

'I do.' He wondered what her real question was. It wasn't the first time his choice had been questioned. Although the job had its challenges, he liked the clients. The pay was woeful, but he figured the work helped address the karmic balance of his life. Helping others meant he wasn't worrying about his own problems:

it put things into perspective. 'It keeps me off the streets. Out of trouble.'

She chuckled, as though he were joking. 'What do you do when you're not doing this?'

'Studying. Commerce—accounting major. I have exams soon.'

'Jesus.' Emma's eyes widened. 'You don't look like an accountant.'

'Really?'

Shaking her head vehemently, she said, 'I'd cast you as a footy player. You're, what, six-three? AFL, not rugby. I mean, you look fit, but you have a neck.'

Luke turned away to hide his smile. Her answer was disturbingly precise, although it was years since he'd played football. 'What about you? What do you do when you're not hiding from your father?'

'Office admin for a casting company—at least, that's my day job. I'm an actor. I played Chantel in *Streetwise*—you know, the TV series?' The name of the show tugged at Luke's memory. 'Did you watch it?'

He shook his head. 'I don't have a TV.'

She arched an eyebrow at him, amused. 'Well, it was awesome. All about gangs and drugs and murder. I got three seasons. Chantel was mean—a real bad-arse. I got to fire guns at the range—the director made us learn how to shoot so we looked authentic—and we did fight choreography with a kung-fu guy. It was the *best*.'

'Sounds fun.' The lie came easily.

'I wasn't joking about casting you. You'd get work as an extra— you've got a look. Kind of tough. It's good pay. And you get to be on TV.'

'Not really my thing,' Luke said, thinking, *I'd rather stick a fork in my eye.*

Emma peeled herself off the couch. 'I want yoghurt. You?'

He shook his head, relieved when she disappeared to the kitchen. He needed a moment to ground himself; her confidence sucked all the air from the room.

A minute later, she flopped back into her seat, a tub of blueberry yoghurt in one hand and a spoon in the other. Slurping from the spoon with her eyes closed, she licked her lips with relish. He'd never seen anyone eat with such lascivious intensity.

'So. Who's at home? Boyfriend? Wife and kids?' Her tongue still caressed the spoon and he was impressed she could form words around it. When he didn't answer, she said, 'Don't worry, I'm just curious. I'm not coming on to you.'

'That's a relief.' He suppressed a smile. 'Your yoghurt would be jealous.'

'Funny.' Emma's eyes narrowed. 'I mean, no offence, you look alright. Good, actually. It's not that.' Luke waited for her to dig herself deeper into her hole, but she was unembarrassed. 'I just don't think you're my type.'

'I'm not a dairy dessert?'

Emma sucked loudly on her spoon. 'Funny. My last boyfriend was a narcissistic fuck-knuckle, which *is* my type apparently, so you're safe. I'm taking a break.' The words were firm, as though rehearsed. As though she needed to convince herself. A spot of yoghurt sat unattended on her upper lip, and Luke waited: on cue, she rolled her tongue over it.

'How do you know I'm not a narcissistic fuck-knuckle?'

'Heard you talking to Phil.' Another slurp.

'I've met some fuck-knuckles in my time too.' The truth of the statement made him pause. Time to change the topic. 'Anyway, what's the deal with you and your father? Why aren't you talking to him?'

With a melodramatic sigh, she dumped the empty tub on the couch beside her, fixed him with her grey eyes and said, 'You want the long version or the short?'

Luke was at the kitchen counter with his laptop and a fresh coffee, trying his best to focus on financial statistics, when Jonathan returned.

'Do you know how to use that?' Jonathan's sharp voice cut through his concentration. He paused in the doorway, his eyes fixed on the Gaggia and his mouth flat with disapproval. 'It cost a fortune; it's not a toy.'

'I'm aware. And yes, I know what I'm doing. Would you like one?'

'It's a bit late, isn't it?'

'It's morning somewhere in the world.' Luke moved around the counter and held up a cup, raising his eyebrows.

'Alright then.' With a suspicious nod, Jonathan sat at the counter. Dark bags hung like bruises under his eyes. His face was grey, his hair limp and flat on his head. If possible, he seemed thinner and more serious than before.

Luke busied himself with the coffee machine. 'Milk?'

'No.'

Luke handed him the cup, and Jonathan lifted his head enough to take a sip. His brows furrowed with surprise. 'That's quite good.'

'I used to work in a cafe. If I messed up an order, it came out of my pay.'

Jonathan nodded, as though that were perfectly reasonable and not sheer exploitation. He glanced around the clean kitchen, the cleared dining table, the tidy couch. 'What time did Emma get home?'

'While ago.' Luke knew better than to get involved in that discussion.

'So. Saturday. Can you—'

Luke held up both hands. 'I've got exams. I'm supposed to be on leave.'

Jonathan stared. Evidently, Luke's existence outside of this room was irrelevant. After a pause, he said, 'How much do they pay you?'

Luke told him and, without blinking, he offered an hourly rate that was nearly double. Cold, hard cash. His voice held a challenge, as though he were testing the boundaries to see how far he could push; as though to ask, *Is money more important than your exams?*

Luke took the humiliation on the chin. His car wasn't going to fix itself.

CHAPTER TWO

FRIDAY, 7 PM

The statuesque Victorian pub, sandwiched between similar buildings on Grattan Street, juggled decades of mismatched renovations: a frosting of iron lacework garnished its bullnose verandah, contrasting with the seventies-era billboard fastened to the facade. On the ground floor, modern bi-fold doors opened to the mild evening, spilling music and laughter out to the street. Friday night meant a crowd of pedestrians: commuters on their way out of the city, young people seeking fun, couples hand in hand looking for a cosy table. Luke identified with none of them. He dallied by his car, half a block away, fighting an invisible battle with himself.

Escape was still an option. Nothing would be easier than getting back in his car, but his conscience intruded: he'd told Caitlin he'd be there, and he'd made a conscious choice to be the kind of person who kept his word.

Caitlin, his study group's self-appointed organiser, had finally worn through his avoidance of social events; Luke wished she would apply the same dogged persistence to her academic endeavours. His reserve only piqued her interest. Their six-year age gap felt like a generational divide; most of her speech seemed to be in a foreign dialect, and her text messages were incomprehensibly abbreviated and pictorial. She joked about him being a real adult because he lived alone. He humoured her, because she thought she was funny, but he'd been an adult for a long time.

An hour, he told himself. It was an end-of-year dinner, not an all-night rave.

As he entered the pub, a wall of noise assaulted him, and he stood before a short flight of steps to orientate himself. To his right, the public bar opened out. To his left, he could see his destination—a bistro restaurant, dimly lit and crowded with tables and bodies. Shouted conversations strained to be heard over tinny pop music. The patterned carpet stuck to his feet as he crossed the floor, and the smell of fried food and stale beer curdled the air.

'Hey, man, didn't know you were coming!' Chandu beamed, his cheeks flushed; he'd had a few beers. Brendan, seated beside him, leaned over to offer Luke a mock-serious handshake.

'Caitlin insisted,' said Luke.

'She'll do that.' Chandu poked Brendan's arm. Everyone knew Brendan had a thing for Caitlin, just as they knew she had a thing for Luke.

To change the subject, Luke asked about food and looked around for the rest of the group.

Caitlin stood by the bar, giggling with another girl, downing shots of vodka. As always, she was dressed like a hippie, in clothes like scarves stitched together and a crocheted headband around her bird's-nest hair. As Luke headed towards her, she spotted him and waggled a glass in greeting. 'You want one?'

He shook his head with a smile and followed her directions to another counter to order food. When he returned to the table, Caitlin had beaten him there; she patted the seat beside her. They'd been joined by a handful of others, who had been coerced into vodka shots by Caitlin. He should know their names. He didn't.

Their gossip was reassuringly familiar. They could have been in a grey tutorial room on campus, except for the inappropriately loud laughter. Luke wondered how long he would have to stay. He hadn't been in a pub since he left Queensland, and he hadn't missed the noise, the stench of beer, the crowds.

He endured a greasy overpriced lasagne, pushing the chips aside. Caitlin pinched one from his plate with a coy grin.

'You can have them if you want,' he said.

'You don't like chips?'

'Not these ones.' His concerns about trans fats would cement his reputation as a bore. He kept them to himself.

'I forgot you're, like, super healthy.' She indicated his drink. 'What's that?'

'Water.'

'You don't drink alcohol?'

'I'm driving.' And no, but he lacked the energy to explain.

'You can look after me when I'm drunk.' Wrapping an arm around his bicep, she raised her glass with the other hand. Her touch was more welcome than he expected; he didn't push her away. A fleeting thought of giving in to her unsubtle advances—taking her home with him so he didn't have to sleep alone—was brushed away before he could dwell on it. It would be wrong. He would regret it. Reminded of his self-enforced solitude, his spirits dropped another notch.

Brendan frowned at Caitlin's flirtation. Luke hid a sigh. He felt old, weighed down by a conscience that never let up.

'Come on, let's go dance.' Caitlin squeezed Luke's arm as she got up, stumbling to her feet. She'd had more than enough to drink. 'Who's coming?'

Not a hope in hell, Luke thought.

The girls and Chandu giggled and dragged each other towards the dancefloor at the far end of the room. A few minutes later, Luke took the opportunity to slip away. He felt an urgent need for quiet and personal space; the crowded pub assaulted all his senses at once, an overload of noise and colour that set his teeth on edge and made his skin crawl. As he escaped, Caitlin detached from the dancefloor to follow him.

Despite her inebriation, she reached the door almost as he did. 'You're going?'

'Yeah. Working tomorrow.' Luke wavered. The disappointed furrow between her brows was endearing. He should extricate himself before he did something stupid.

Caitlin followed him down the steps and held his arm, stalling him by the doorway. She was close enough that he caught a whiff of her floral perfume, and drunk enough that she leaned into him. He drew her aside so a group of patrons could squeeze past.

'*Jack?*' A man's head swivelled back, a split second after he'd passed Luke in the doorway, in a genuine double take. Three inches taller than Luke, thirty years older, suit and tie. His mouth hung open, and his eyes were wide. 'Jackie? Jesus, it's you! Where the hell have you been?'

Luke's brain blanked.

The pub—noise, beer, crowd, heat, Caitlin clinging to his arm—shifted into focus a second later. He couldn't move. Speaking was out of the question.

'Jack? No—his name's Luke.' Caitlin's words were slurred. She lifted her chin and squeezed his arm, claiming possession.

'Luke, eh.' The man's gaze dropped to the scar on Luke's chin.

With a drunken wave, Caitlin pulled Luke down to speak into his ear. 'I have to go back in. *Bathroom.*' She planted a sloppy kiss on his cheek, then stumbled as she turned, knocking into the tall man, who reached out with both hands to stop her falling.

The distraction was all Luke needed. A step backwards, and he melted into the moving pedestrian crowd on the footpath. He strode as fast as he could without breaking into a run, shielded by the bodies around him. His knees wobbled, his legs threatening to buckle under his weight. Adrenaline flushed his skin, tightened his chest. Sweat cooled the back of his neck.

A minute later, he sat in the driver's seat of his car. It took all his effort, all his concentration, to fumble the key into the ignition, praying the car would start.

Click.

Perspiration trickled down his temples. He swallowed against his dry throat and tried again, peering through the windshield and into the rear-view mirror for followers.

The engine coughed to life. He released his breath and slammed the car into gear. Clutching the steering wheel to stop his hands from shaking, he drove home with one word running on repeat in his head.

Fuck.

His ragged breath echoed back at him in the darkness, as though he'd sprinted several blocks. With every beat, his heart lurched against his ribs, like a wild animal trying to escape its cage. Sweat soaked his body. His eyes darted around, searching for a target.

Reality seeped through the panic slowly, like fingers of reason. He was at home, in his bed. The glowing red numbers of the alarm clock told him it was early, even for him. Waking like this was nothing new: it was a nightmare, nothing more. No intruder in the flat, no phone call, no sirens outside. No danger.

Snippets of vision and sound from the dream—disjointed images of a film played at high speed, with overlapping frames and discordant noise—cycled through his mind. Every effort to remember chased it further away, as though the act of grasping and missing pushed it in the opposite direction. All he remembered was the fear that twisted his guts, strangled his breath, clouded his vision.

He padded to the bathroom to splash water on his face. The air cooled the sweat on his body and he shivered, leaning over the basin as he waited for the last of the panic to subside. Streetlight angled in from the bathroom window, and in the mirror his shadow looked back at him.

His hair was short, rather than long and wild as it had been in the past. Stupid, to think simple things like changing his name or cutting his hair would fool Gus Alberici. The scar on his chin stood out, taunting him, even in the dim light.

There was no way he would get back to sleep, so he went out to the living room to sit cross-legged in front of the couch. With his hands resting on his thighs, he let his eyelids droop to half-mast. A body scan to release tension from his muscles, then he centred his awareness on his breath.

His heart rate slowed, and after a few minutes his racing mind calmed, like dust settling after a gust of wind. His years of practice had started to pay off. There was peace to be found in the slow, unimpeded rhythm of his breath, where he could let the past be and let the future unfold from the present without interference. He focused on what was real and observable—the weight of his body, the cool air in his lungs—and allowed his swirling fears and doubts to come and go without judgement. By the time he returned his attention to the room around him, sunlight filtered through the sheer curtains covering the glass doors to the balcony.

The morning light picked out the greying paint flaking from the walls of his tiny flat, reflected off the scarred coffee table, highlighted the cracks in the ceiling. From the carpet, an ingrained odour of bong water from the previous tenant played at the edge of his senses. Half of the living room was taken up by his punching bag, training mat and neat stack of weights; the brown couch and an armchair squeezed into the other half. The rest of the flat was equally cramped. His bed was squashed into the corner of the bedroom so he could access the cupboard-sized bathroom. When he first moved in, he'd scrubbed the shower recess so hard that he'd destroyed the silicone and had to waste precious dollars resealing it. Despite his efforts, it still smelled of mould.

The grimy backstreet he called home, only a few blocks from prime real estate and St Kilda's thriving entertainment district, was cluttered with wheelie bins and hard waste, abandoned cars and the flapping remnants of police tape. He'd been lucky to find this pocket of affordability so close to the beach and the city. A block in either direction pushed the rental market above the poverty line and out of his reach. His accommodation reflected the choices he'd made.

He reminded himself, for the thousandth time, that this was temporary.

Calmer after his meditation, he gloved up and attacked the punching bag. Directing emotion at the bag was what a clever psychologist had once called an *adaptive coping mechanism*. After exhausting his arms and shoulders, he practised kicks—front, side, roundhouse—stretching out to kick the top of the bag. It was not as high as Gus Alberici's head, but it was a pleasant fantasy.

To complete his ritual, he went for a long run through the St Kilda Botanical Gardens to the marina, along the beach to

Elwood and back. The familiar route took an hour at a comfortable pace and flushed out the last traces of adrenaline from the nightmare.

Memories popped up like spot fires, random and unannounced, with an intensity that seared his vision and loosened his guts. He needed to manage them before the flames took hold—not with a hose, steel-capped boots and fireproof clothing, but by tending to the environment. By calming the winds that fanned them, reducing the fuel, identifying which fires he needed to douse and which would burn out on their own.

Memories, like all thoughts, are just ideas your mind throws around, the psychologist had said. *You can choose what to do with them.*

Days that began with a nightmare required respect. If he failed to heed the warning signs, his past would intrude on his present and he would unravel, undoing all the hard work he'd put in.

CHAPTER THREE

SATURDAY 7.35 AM

The Subaru had given up. Luke smacked the heel of his hand against the steering wheel and muttered a few choice words. And then he broke into a cold sweat as he wondered what would have happened had the car refused to start the night before. He'd known his luck couldn't hold indefinitely. Not with the car, and not with Gus Alberici.

He took the stairs two at a time, stopping on the first floor at the door directly below his. His knocking echoed around the open concrete stairwell, too loud for the early hour.

'Irina, *privyet*.' Luke offered his downstairs neighbour a smile to soften the intrusion. 'Can I borrow your car for a few days? Mine's dead.'

'Your accent is terrible.' Irina was Russian, grumpy and somewhere between sixty and a hundred. Her accent and suspicious scowl made everything she said sound like an accusation, although her frequent gifts of food suggested to Luke that she liked him. She was the size of a malnourished ten-year-old but clung to her belief that it was Luke who needed feeding, which he found as convenient as it was amusing. Her yellow-blonde hair was always tortured into an updo; her face had dropped into craters and folds and half of her teeth were gold. A food stain that might be mustard was camouflaged against her luridly patterned polyester dress. 'You clean it. Put petrol in.'

Luke had driven her car once before, on a rainy night in winter when she'd slipped on the stairs and he'd taken her to hospital. Irina didn't trust his Subaru because it was a Japanese car and she was paranoid about all sorts of things. He didn't like her car either. An ancient Ford Falcon that rarely moved from the car park, its sticky vinyl interior was littered with cigarette butts and unpaid parking fines from twenty years ago.

'I need to be there at eight,' he said, an unsubtle attempt to hurry the transaction.

She handed him her car keys and shooed him away with bony fingers, like a Baba Yaga from a children's book.

※※※

In contrast to Irina's dishevelment, Jonathan's clothing was impeccable—navy suit, crisp white collar, silk tie. He admitted Luke without a word, then locked the front door behind him. 'Phil is having breakfast. God only knows where Emma is.' Opening the door in the hallway that led to the attached garage, he reached into a pocket for a business card and thrust it at Luke. 'If you need me, call Natalie—my EA—on the office number. I'm in meetings until two.'

After watching a silver Mercedes sedan sweep out of the garage, Luke joined Phil in the kitchen and helped himself to coffee. Phil wanted to walk to the park, which sounded like a great idea until Luke realised he had no keys for the house and no code for the alarm system. He examined the keypad by the front door. Triggering the alarm would probably disturb Jonathan, which cooled the temptation to test his skills; he left it alone.

Instead, he convinced Phil to make do with the backyard. Wide French doors led from the living room to a covered deck, beyond which lay a rectangle of clipped lawn; the grass still sparkled with dew. Along the left side of the property, the morning sun glinted off a sapphire pool and its glass fence. A pool house stood before a row of cypress trees at the rear of the block. To Luke's right, a gate bisected a six-foot fence, providing access to the side lane that bordered the property. Inside the gate, a carport housed a black Range Rover, and he thought, *Huh. A weekend vehicle, maybe?* Drawing in a deep breath, he wondered if he could absorb the affluence of this suburban utopia by osmosis.

Phil wanted to bounce a basketball against the wall of the pool house. The childish game and the idyllic morning—clear blue skies and fluffy white clouds, a fresh breeze carrying scents of the ocean—gave Luke a brief distraction from his lingering anxiety.

An hour into his game with Phil, Emma arrived home. Emerging onto the deck, she squinted in the bright light, with last night's make-up smudged around her eyes and her hair squashed flat on one side. Her crumpled dress was brief enough to be mistaken for a swimsuit, and the stilettos that dangled from her hand looked like weapons. She asked about Jonathan's movements, then slunk upstairs to bed.

Phil wanted toasted sandwiches for lunch (white bread and tasty cheese and *nothing else!*). Luke made himself a fancier version with mustard and olives. While Phil settled in at the dining table with his iPad and headphones, playing games that involved poking a pudgy finger at the screen and shouting, Luke finished tidying, opened his laptop and tried to pull his attention back to study.

'Hey.' Emma had changed into jeans and a T-shirt. Her hair, damp from the shower, hung in wayward curls around her shoulders. A pleasant, soapy fragrance hit Luke as she passed him on her way into the kitchen. 'You tidied up. Again.'

'I get itchy around mess.'

Emma opened the fridge and stared blankly at the contents.

'Late night?'

With Emma there, study had lost its appeal; he closed his laptop, noticing details. The way her hair curled around her neck. Her chunky smart watch, too big for her wrist. A tattoo of a butterfly on the inside of her right arm.

'I went to see Gabriela, and then I went to an opening.' She stuck her nose in the air. 'What's that smell?'

'I made Phil toasties for lunch. Do you want one?'

'You don't have to wait on me.' Deflating, she leaned on the bench. He guessed she'd had about three hours' sleep. Her phone buzzed, and she frowned as she silenced it.

'It's okay. Sit down before you fall down.' Luke went back into the kitchen. He had a vested interest: it was spotless and he had a feeling it wouldn't stay that way if he let Emma cook.

'If you insist.' She flopped onto a seat. 'I'm trashed.'

'Was it a good party?' As he buttered bread and sliced cheese, Luke listened with half his attention. The opening night party Emma had attended was his idea of hell—celebrity wannabes clamouring for the spotlight, loud music, an oversupply of champagne and cocaine, and cameras clicking every second. Anticipating her needs, he switched on the coffee machine.

'Wait—do you have permission to do that?'

'Never asked.'

'Dad is super weird about it.'

'Do I look like someone who'd harm a coffee machine?'

'Maybe?' Her tone was wary.

With a laugh, Luke placed a plate and a coffee before her. 'Latte, right?'

'How'd you know?'

'I can tell. Call it a superpower.'

'What did you put in this?' Emma indicated the sandwich. 'Mustard? Olives? It's delicious.' She closed her eyes, savouring; she'd torn the sandwich into pieces, and ate each piece as though it were the last food on earth. 'Bold move, messing with the sacred cheese toastie.' Arching an eyebrow, she nudged a crumb from the corner of her mouth with a delicate fingertip and licked her lips.

Luke shook himself back to reality. 'How is Gabriela doing?'

'Improving, I think. Not sure how long she'll be.' She wiped a hand over her face. 'When is Dad back? He doesn't usually have meetings on a Saturday.'

'Two, he said. What does he do, anyway?' Their previous conversation had skimmed over this detail. Emma's angst had focused on Jonathan's pathological need to control her rather than his means of income.

'He's a property developer. His company manages building contracts—high-rise towers, city buildings, that kind of thing.' Staring into her coffee, she shook her head. 'Nothing that can't wait till Monday.'

Luke turned Jonathan's business card over in his hand. *Wylie Consulting*. It was a good name for a company. It made him think of coyotes.

'Why do you still live with him? I mean, you're old enough to—'

'I moved out with a friend for a bit, but Dad didn't like it; he cut me off financially. Acting gigs dried up over Covid. My day job doesn't pay much. I guess I have champagne tastes and a beer budget.' A wan smile. 'Don't judge. You've got a judgey look on your face.'

Luke couldn't help laughing. '"Judgemental" is the word you're after.' He tried to straighten his face and failed.

'Smart-arse.' With a huff, she stuffed the last of her sandwich in her mouth, washed it down with coffee and whacked his arm playfully. 'I'll move out when I can. It's a bad time right now. I can't leave while Gabriela's away—Phil would lose the plot.' Her face tightened, and she stopped.

He made himself another coffee and sat at the bench beside her. 'I'm not judging, anyway. I'd do the same in your position.' He gazed around the modern, expensive kitchen and again compared it to his own.

'Where are your parents?' Her habit of cocking her head when she spoke reminded him of a sheepdog, which entertained him, even as he scrambled for an answer honest enough to satisfy his conscience.

'My mother died when I was seven. My father—hmm... Haven't lived with him since high school.'

A crumb of toast decorated Emma's chin, and Luke had to restrain himself from brushing it off.

'You live by yourself?'

'Yep. I moved back to Melbourne for uni a year ago—I've been in Queensland for a few years. I've got a flat in St Kilda.'

'Nice.'

Luke shook his head. 'It's a hole. But I like living by myself.'

'So you don't get itchy from other people's mess?' She bumped his arm.

'You're on to me.'

Emma tapped a finger on his laptop—she was a sensory person, always using her hands to gesture, indicate, touch. 'What's this you're studying?'

'Financial statistics.'

'Yikes.' As though to confirm his observation, she patted his arm as she got down from the bar stool, then swiped her phone from the bench. 'Thanks for lunch. I have to go sort out some stuff.'

A few hours later, Jonathan returned. He paid no attention to Luke's rundown of his day with Phil. Luke made him a coffee and considered charging extra for his barista skills.

Jonathan stared into his cup, preoccupied. 'Did Emma come home?'

After a reassurance that Emma was fine, he fell into glowering silence.

'Jonathan, I have to go.'

'Right. Yes. Here.' Jonathan took a handful of fifty-dollar notes from his wallet and thrust them at Luke. It was what Luke's father would have called a *pile of pineapples*, and much more than promised, but Jonathan was in no mood for discussion and Luke was broke, so he took the money without argument.

'Is everything alright?' As soon as the words left his mouth, Luke regretted them.

'No.' Jonathan fixed him with a flat, grey stare. 'Nothing is *alright*. My life could not be more complicated right now. Don't you need to be going?'

Luke indicated the communication folder on the counter. 'My number is in there, if you need anything.'

'Monday afternoon.' Jonathan put down his coffee and lifted his chin. 'Can you pick Phil up from school?'

Distracted by thoughts of Emma's skimpy dress and the wad of cash Jonathan had given him, Luke wrestled Irina's Ford into his street. An unfamiliar car parked half a block from his flat snapped his mind back into gear: an Audi sedan, black with tinted windows. He slowed to scan it as he drove past. It was empty.

He considered his gut reaction as he parked the Ford beside his lonely Subaru. Audi sedans were not uncommon. He'd never seen this particular car before. It was probably nothing.

But wariness had saved his bacon many times. He stashed Jonathan's money in the glove box and his keys deep into his jeans pocket before he made his way silently up the stairs.

His front door was ajar. The imprint of a heel dinted the cheap plywood near the lock, which had smashed through the frame. Pausing to consider his options, he took a deep breath to centre himself. The door creaked as he stepped in.

A shadow in his peripheral vision made him duck to the side. His hand closed over the attacker's wrist and he swung the man into the wall beside the door. The man grunted as Luke squashed his cheek into the plaster and locked his elbow behind him.

Something hard and cold pressed against the back of his head, and he froze. The voice that followed chilled him even more. 'Let him go, Jackie. Jesus, Ed. You'll get yourself hurt.'

Ed's chuckle was muffled by the wall. 'Hi, Jack.'

'Bloody hell, Ed.' Luke pushed off the man with a shake of his head. Ed shot him a grin as he straightened, but Luke's attention was elsewhere.

Gus Alberici took a step closer, close enough that his size cast a shadow over Luke. The gun, in his right hand, dropped to his side. Luke's gaze followed it, and Gus took advantage of the distraction, chopping out his left hand to cuff Luke on the side of the head.

'Seven fucking years! Where the hell have you been?'

'I went up north.' Luke knew better than to mess with Gus when he held a gun. He put up his hands.

'Empty your pockets.'

With a sigh, Luke obeyed. Ed took his phone, keys and wallet and tossed his driver's licence to Gus, who held it up to the light, as though checking it was real.

'Luke Harris.' Gus flicked the licence at him in disgust. 'What the fuck?'

'Harris is my mother's surname.'

'And *Luke*? Where does that come from?'

'Maybe I'm a *Star Wars* fan.'

'Sit.' Gus pointed at the armchair. Luke lowered himself into the seat, keeping his movements slow and measured. Ed stayed by the door.

Gus relaxed onto the middle of the couch. He stretched both arms out along the backrest, as though to drape around the shoulders of invisible companions, with the gun dangling from his hooked right forefinger. He was a big man, six-six and solidly built; not as lean as he'd been when he played for Carlton in the eighties, but fit for a man his age. In his day, he'd been a pin-up for his football team, with his broody eyes and matinee-idol face. Age had softened his jawline and dusted his dark hair with silver, but it only added to his gravitas. As always, he was smartly dressed in a business suit and Italian shoes. He should have looked out of place on the faded couch, but he didn't. Gus was at home anywhere.

'How'd you find me?'

'Got your car rego. Your girlfriend told me your first name. You know how many green Subarus there are in Melbourne?' Gus cocked an eyebrow.

Luke left the rhetorical question alone. 'What are you looking for?' Books, kitchen utensils and study notes were scattered like confetti on the floor. They'd pulled apart the bed, emptied every cupboard.

'Place is a dump,' was all the answer he got. 'Why'd you change your name?'

'I didn't want to be Jack Quinlan anymore.'

Gus snorted. 'You'll always be Jackie to me, kid.'

Luke bit down his resentment. Gus was the only person who called him *Jackie*. He'd hated it as a teenager and he sure as hell hated it now, but only a fool argued with Gus when he held a gun.

Gus put the gun beside him on the couch and reached into a pocket for a pack of cigarettes. He tapped one out, lit it, then leaned forwards to point it at Luke. 'Start talking.'

'I was working at Il Gatto Nero, remember? After I finished school.'

'Making fucking cappuccinos. Waste of your skills.'

That was ironic, Luke thought, given how appreciative Gus had been at the time. *Another double espresso, Jackie; make it short.*

'I went up north. Townsville, Cairns. Then the whole Covid thing happened. The borders closed—I couldn't have come back if I'd wanted to.'

The clunking of the old fridge and traffic noise, filtering in from outside, competed for space with the awkward silence. A waft of smoke curled into Luke's nostrils.

'Why'd you come back?'

'I'm studying. Commerce. Accounting major.'

'Mighty useful people, accountants.' Gus cracked a smile for the first time; instead of reassuring Luke, it sent a shiver down his spine. 'They have universities in Queensland.'

'They do. But this is my home.' Luke shrugged, praying Gus would accept the lame explanation.

Gus stubbed out his cigarette on the coffee table. 'Should have told me when you left, Jackie. And when you got back.'

Luke conceded the point. 'Yeah. I know. But—'

'It's not just your disappearing act that disappointed me, but your lack of communication. Not a fucking word!'

'Gus—I'm on the straight, alright?' Luke crossed his arms and breathed through his fear. He felt like ants were crawling all over him; he battled an urge to jump out of the chair and run for the door. 'I'm studying. I've got a job.' He explained, and his legal employment became a source of amusement to both Gus and Ed.

Gus jerked his head towards the punching bag. 'You still training? You look fit. Bigger than you used to be. Nearly broke Ed's arm just now.'

Luke shook his head, managed a smile. 'Ed knows I wouldn't hurt him. I knew you were up here.'

'How?'

'Spotted your car. You've still got a thing for Audis.' He paused. 'What do you want, Gus?'

Gus lit another cigarette and sucked so hard on it the air in the room seemed to move. He blew out a luxurious cloud of smoke, then another. He waited until he'd finished and stubbed it out before continuing. 'Spoken to Quin lately?'

'What? Why?' Luke's father was known to everyone, Luke included, as *Quin*. He'd never been *Dad* or *Pop* or anything else, except to the police, who called him *Mr Quinlan*. As they had called Luke too. Many times.

Gus waited, as though his glowering silence might encourage Luke to talk.

Luke looked to Ed to see if he could glean anything, but Ed shook his head.

'He found me at the cafe after he got out of Barwon. I told him to piss off. Then the cops were looking for him: he'd skipped parole.

They hassled me at work so much I lost my job. I had to get away from his bullshit—that's why I went to Queensland.'

Gus's silence was not encouraging.

'He owes you money, right?' Quin's ability to get into debt was legendary. Money slipped through his fingers like sand.

'You could say. And his buddy, Kevin McNally. Have you seen him?'

'Kevin?' Luke raised his eyebrows. 'No. Why? You gonna tell me what this is about?'

'I might.' Gus only shared information when it suited him.

'I haven't seen either of them since I got back. They don't know I changed my name. Or where I live.'

'You wouldn't lie to me, would you?' Gus picked up Luke's phone from where Ed had tossed it on the couch and handed it to him. 'Open it. Show me.' It took Gus a few minutes to ascertain that Luke's phone contained nothing interesting. 'Your screen is cracked, Jackie.'

'I know.' The old iPhone had been with him for years. Luke was sentimentally, and financially, tied to it.

Gus scrolled through the messages. 'Who's Phil?'

'Client. That's my day job.'

'Talk about wasting your skills.' Gus snorted. 'Minimum wage, paying your taxes. Jesus. I taught you better than that.' Picking up his gun, Gus leaned forwards with his elbows on his knees. 'Let me make this clear: I'm disappointed in you. All those years, I looked after you, didn't I?'

Signs of his anger returned: flushed cheeks, pupils dilated so wide his eyes were black. Luke forced his shoulders to relax and breathed through the tightness in his belly.

'When I saw you at that pub, I wanted to smack you senseless. Fucking disrespectful, what you did. After all I've done for you.'

A solid lump had settled in Luke's chest, as though his lungs had turned to concrete. He wasn't sure where his crime ranked in the hierarchy of insults. He'd seen men shot for less. In the knee. In the head. Sometimes both. Gus's casual approach to violence was as unpredictable as his moods.

'But.' Gus wiped a hand over his face. 'I realised that would be counter-productive. I'm gonna offer you an opportunity to redeem yourself. I need you to rouse up Kevin McNally. And I don't have all fucking year. Clock's ticking.'

'Gus, I'm not—'

Gus silenced him with a glare. 'Are you seriously gonna argue?'

Luke looked down at his hands. After a beat, he said, 'I've got exams. I'll be done by Tuesday week.'

'Don't push your luck.' Tucking the gun into a pocket as though it were nothing, Gus stood up and straightened his suit. He tossed a mobile phone and a roll of fifty-dollar notes, held together with an elastic band, onto the coffee table. 'Get your door fixed.'

Luke's gaze locked on the phone, a no-frills Samsung. After his years of freedom, he was back where he started: tied to Gus Alberici by a cheap phone and a pile of pineapples.

And then he was thrown sideways in his chair as the back of Gus's hand hit his face.

'That's for the last seven years.' Gus's words were a growl. 'Keep the phone on. I guess you're back on the payroll, eh?'

CHAPTER FOUR

SUNDAY, 11.15 AM

Irina lowered herself into the chair opposite Luke and waved her fingers at the food on the table. Luke swiped a pirozhki through the sour cream on his plate, squeezed on chilli sauce and closed his eyes to enjoy it. Irina was a master of comfort food. The crust was crisp, the dough light, the filling savoury.

Irina sipped a toxic brew of cheap instant coffee and watched him over the rim of her cup. 'You're in trouble, eh?'

'It's a long story.' Luke sighed.

Irina sat back and frowned. Or smiled. It was hard to tell. 'You got your door fixed?'

He nodded. He washed his mouthful down with tea, enjoying the burn from the chilli. 'Cost a fortune. Sunday call-out fee.' The door repairman had smiled at the imprint of Ed's heel. Luke was grateful for his lack of commentary.

He'd slept terribly, tangled in his sheets from tossing and turning, dipping in and out of nightmares about his father, Gus and guns. It was a relief when the night ended, but he couldn't leave the flat until his door was fixed. He paced the living room with his hands on his head, trying to pull himself together. His usual strategies—running, kicking at the bag, meditating, reading—seemed laughable in the face of his current predicament. The idea of attending to tax law and economics was ludicrous, as though that life belonged to another person. Which it did: that was Luke Harris's life. He'd spent the morning fighting the remnants of Jack Quinlan.

He'd changed his name legally when he was eighteen. A simple form at a government office divorced him from his past. The first time he'd used his new name aloud was in a backpacker hostel in Sydney, the day after he'd run away from Melbourne to be someone else. He was heating food in the hostel kitchen when a girl sidled up and asked his name.

Luke, he told her. *Luke Harris.* He noted her lack of reaction. It was a normal name, unremarkable, unburdened with any past wrongdoing.

'Eat more.' Irina pushed the plate closer to him, interrupting his moping. He didn't dare disobey her command. He was sure she was fattening him up for slaughter.

The layout of her flat was the same as his, but there the similarity ended. Furniture and possessions were stacked to the roof in her living room; a narrow passage through her clutter connected the door, kitchenette and bedroom. Irina had moved her suburban house into the one-bedroom flat when her husband died, decades ago. She spent most of her time in the kitchen, devising ways to bolster Luke's cholesterol levels, or sitting in bed smoking, watching SBS on the new television Luke had fixed to the wall for her a few months ago.

Bolted inside a mahogany cabinet on the far wall, wedged behind a dining table stacked with boxes, which itself was behind a brocade lounge overlaid with books and a lace tablecloth, was Luke's safe.

Irina didn't mind keeping it in her flat; she had clutter to conceal it, which Luke lacked. He'd maintained a variety of hiding places over the years—and still did—but this one he considered a work of genius. The safe contained photographs, documents, old phones and USB drives, all of which required security. Now, courtesy of Jonathan and Gus, it also held a few rolls of cash. He'd kept some for expenses and stashed the rest.

Irina was not stupid. 'What's the money for?'

'Need a new battery for my car.'

'This man—how do you know him?'

'I used to work for him.' Back when he'd been Jackie Quinlan, Gus's protégé. A loyal soldier. 'All through high school. A bit after.' He screwed up his face. Talking about it made it real.

'And now? You work for him now?'

'I don't want anything to do with him. I want to finish my degree. Get a proper job. My own house. A dog.' He met her eyes. It sounded so simple.

'Then that's what you do. You tell him.' Irina waggled a forefinger. 'You tell him *no*.'

Luke bit into his pirozhki and shook his head. The consequences of defying Gus were not worth considering. He'd seen firsthand what could happen. And there was no point talking to the police, not without an airtight plan to protect himself: Gus knew a lot of people. 'Do you need anything? I'm going to the supermarket later.'

Irina took the hint and dropped the subject.

He finished the food and thanked her for the loan of her car and the security of her cupboard. She waved away his gratitude with another flap of her fingers.

The auto parts store was closed on Sundays, which put a halt to his plans to fix his car that afternoon. He procrastinated at the supermarket. Wasting cash from Gus—and Jonathan—on luxury food was a token rebellion, but he'd eat well for a few weeks.

Thoughts of Gus competed with his growing irritation with Jonathan, who'd easily convinced him to pick Phil up from school the next day. Luke wanted to kick himself for agreeing—the dysfunction of the household was not his responsibility—but Phil's needs tugged at his conscience. Jonathan was far from welcoming, but he paid generously. And unlike working for Gus, no one got hurt.

As he wrestled the Ford towards home, he deluded himself that the chance of seeing Emma again played no role in his decision-making. When the Samsung buzzed in his pocket, it broke through a distracted daydream about the tattoo on her arm.

He pulled over so he could answer it.

Ed's voice crackled from the phone. 'Jack. Howzit going?'

Luke rested his head back. 'It's Luke. Don't call me Jack.'

'You know Gus doesn't give a shit. He's all *Jackie this, Jackie that.* You're still his favourite.' Ed's humour faded. 'Just listen, alright? Word is he owes Amin Khoury a shitload of money. You need to watch your back.'

Luke shivered. Khoury made Gus look like a model citizen, and his loathing of Jack Quinlan was legendary. Gus had always brushed off the threats, but Luke wondered how far his protection would extend. Especially now.

'Ed, what does he want with Quin and Kevin? Do you know what's going on?'

'I know bits of it. Kevin stole money from him. A lot, if the rumours are true. It was a while ago. Gus reckons if he can track it down, he can get Khoury off his case.'

Luke drummed his fingers on the steering wheel. 'Why does he owe Khoury money? I mean, normally it's Gus who—'

'You think he's gonna share that?' Another dry laugh. 'You know what he'd say. *Stay in your lane, Jackie.*' Ed's impression of Gus fell flat.

Luke let the silence settle. 'There's something else, isn't there?'

'I told him I want out. Megan's having a baby. Due in a few weeks.'

'Ah . . . congratulations?' Luke couldn't find the right words. 'What did he say?'

'What do you think?'

'*Don't forget all I've done for you?*' His impression was no better than Ed's.

'He's dark on me 'cos we're not married yet. You know what he's like. Family values and all that Catholic shit. Went on and on about morals.'

'You're getting married?'

'After the baby, yeah. She didn't want to be a pregnant bride.'

'Fair call.'

'I can't change my name and piss off to Queensland like you did,' Ed grumbled. 'Megan'd freak if she knew half of what I've done. Anyway, heads-up: he's not gonna put this on hold for your exams.'

After the call, Luke sat in Irina's car thinking, moving puzzle pieces around in his head until they were in the right order. Today: study. Tomorrow: fix his car, then go to his shift at the Wylies'.

Gus would have to wait.

CHAPTER FIVE

MONDAY 5.35 PM

Emma slumped in the driver's seat of her stationary car, in sympathy with it: her battery was flat too. Her rushed lunch had been inadequate to fuel the afternoon.

Jonathan had been warning her that the car needed a service for months. She tapped her forehead on the steering wheel, wishing she could knock some sense into her thick skull—or at least find a way to sort her father's tirades into words to heed and lectures to ignore. She had no shortage of unsolicited advice to wade through. His latest crusade was her personal safety. He'd taken to quizzing her on her movements in intricate detail. Even where she parked her car for work—*Under your office, Dad!*—which led to a lecture on how dark the underground car park was at night.

She thumbed on her phone: *Have you left work yet? my car's dead need a lift.*

A few seconds later, Britt, her colleague, answered: *leaving now where are you?*

It was the first thing to go right in a forgettable day. Phil had resisted going to school in the morning, asking over and over for Gabriela; when told Luke would pick him up, he'd paced the living room stimming. Jonathan's impatient growling made the situation worse. Distracted at work, she'd sent the wrong files to her manager; a second later, her computer had frozen for a software update and she sat staring at a spinning blue circle while her error magnified. It had taken forever to rectify, and she felt like an idiot. She thought five thirty would never swing around.

As she roused herself, her phone beeped. She checked the text—Dave, again—and threw the phone across the car, as far from her as she could manage.

His texts all followed the same theme. *I'm worried about you* and *Let's talk this through* and (her personal favourite) *I know you better than anyone, let me help you.* Since she blocked him, he'd started texting her from his friends' phones.

His latest effort: *Why won't you talk to me?*

She slammed the door and stalked out to the road to wait for Britt.

Britt spent most of the drive on a call to her husband on loudspeaker, which suited Emma: there was no need for conversation. When they reached Emma's house, they communicated in a series of hand gestures. *Thanks for the lift. See you tomorrow.*

As she opened the front door, she prepared for an onslaught. Phil would be home, with Luke, both of whom required energy to face. If Phil was as heightened as he'd been in the morning, they were in for a rough night. And Luke was an unknown quantity. She didn't want to lose her shit in front of him. He'd think she was an emotional basket case.

Dave: *You're being hysterical, Emma. Overreacting again.*

The house was quiet. Soft noises in the kitchen, a clink of cutlery and crockery. Emma dumped her bag on the hall table and went to investigate.

She paused in the doorway of the kitchen, observing. Luke stood with his back to her, tending a pan on the stove. At the counter, Phil was eating something yellow with his fingers.

When he saw her, he gave a happy gurgle and sprang to his feet with his arms wide. 'Emma's home!'

'Alright! Don't squeeze so hard—oof!' Phil's affection softened the harshness of the day. There had been a few years, when she was a teenager, when the enthusiasm of his hugs had irritated her; now, she closed her eyes to enjoy the cocoon of her big brother's love. 'Feeling better than this morning?'

'Luke's here!' Back in his seat, Phil scooped his fingers into his bowl, showing her what looked like a plain omelette. *Nothing else*, she thought with a smile. 'He made egg pancake! There's no food!'

She turned her attention to Luke, who put a board on the counter and placed the hot frypan on it, then reached into the cupboard for plates. In his agency-branded black polo shirt, jeans and worn sneakers, he was reassuringly familiar. The solidity of his physical presence calmed the room.

'Hungry?' His lips twitched with a smile, as though he could read her mind.

'What is that?' Cringing, she realised her rudeness a moment too late. 'I mean, hi. I'm starving. I was at work and then my car wouldn't start and I had to get a lift—all I've had today is a sandwich.' Words ran out. She sat beside Phil, let her shoulders slump.

Luke cut the contents of the pan into wedges and pushed a plate across the counter. 'There wasn't much to work with. Call it a Niçoise frittata. You guys need to do some shopping. I've cleaned out your fridge.'

'Is that tuna?' Curious, she poked it with her fork.

'You can do anything with a tin of tuna.' Another twitching smile.

'That's—really good.' Emma tried to hide her surprise as he sat beside her with his own plate. She couldn't find any better words. Or any words, really. No doubt he thought she was an idiot. *Flighty. Emotional. Attention-seeking.* All the words Dave liked to use. She savoured the frittata, isolating the different flavours. Tuna, tomatoes. Green olives.

A soft laugh: Luke was watching her eat. 'You love your food, don't you?'

'It's a legal high. Who needs drugs?' Emma managed a smile, but she couldn't make it stick. She finished her plate and sat aimlessly, trying to rouse the energy to speak. She should let Luke go home—Jonathan, expert at getting his way, had bullied him into extra shifts during his exams—but his company was welcome. If she sat beside him long enough, there was a chance his calmness might rub off on her.

The peace in the room seeped into her; the muscles in her neck and shoulders softened. Phil finished eating and sat at the dining table with his iPad and headphones.

'Bad day, huh?' Luke slid another wedge of frittata onto her plate. 'Eat more. It helps.'

As she ate, Emma described the woes of her day. Luke commiserated on the car front. He'd had similar problems lately, which she'd known, because it had reminded her she was due for a service but she'd forgotten because she was an idiot. Luke chatted about the challenges he'd encountered when replacing his battery and how rusted on it had been. It took her a few minutes to realise he'd fixed it himself—because of course he would, he was the kind of person who got things done, he probably knew all sorts of useful skills and—

'Emma?'

'Sorry—what?' At least her phone had been blissfully silent since she got home. 'Shit. I left my phone in my car.' She looked up at Luke, her mouth falling open. 'Hey, do you think you could order an Uber for me? I'll pay you back. I need to go get it.'

'No,' he said.

Emma recoiled, shocked by the instant refusal.

Luke's face broke into a grin. 'Don't worry about an Uber. You're trashed. I'll drive you, when your dad gets home.' A furrow appeared in his brow. 'Couldn't you take the other car? The Range Rover?'

'I'm not allowed to drive it.' Praying he wouldn't ask why—she was not proud of her driving record—she was almost relieved to hear footsteps in the hall, heralding Jonathan's arrival.

Luke stood abruptly, moving into the kitchen to tidy up. She figured he didn't want to be seen sitting with her to eat.

Jonathan's voice cut through the room, an icy blast. 'Emma? Where's your car?'

'In the car park.'

'Why—'

'I need to get the battery fixed.' Emma finished the last of her frittata and stood up.

'I told you it needed a service!'

'I'm aware.'

'How did you get home?'

'I got a lift.'

'Who with?'

'Britt from work. Jesus.'

Disturbed by the conversation, Phil got up to pace. He pressed into Emma's personal space with a low keening sound.

'It's alright, Phil.' She put a hand on his arm, but Phil pushed away to continue pacing.

'Settle down, Philip.' Jonathan's harsh words made Emma wince.

In a flurry of movement, Phil ripped off his headphones, threw them across the room and bolted towards the kitchen door. His footsteps shuffled on the floorboards, and a door slammed near the front of the house.

Luke followed, with Jonathan at his heels.

Groaning, Emma put her face in her hands, fatigue like a physical weight on her shoulders. Phil's meltdown was predictable and entirely preventable. A rhythmic thumping drew her out to the hallway, where Luke and Jonathan stood outside the powder room.

'He's locked himself in.' Jonathan pushed Luke aside to rattle the doorhandle. 'Phil! Open the door!'

'Go away!' Phil shouted from within. A series of thuds rocked the door.

'What's he doing?' Luke's face tightened with worry.

'He's banging his head. He used to do this a lot.' Resigned, Emma shook her head at Jonathan. 'Did you have to yell at him? You know it sets him off!'

Another thud rocked the door, and Jonathan huffed. 'He's going to break that door! Phil! Come out of there!'

'Stop shouting at him.' A sharp tone edged into Luke's voice.

Jonathan's eyes narrowed to slits. He could barely speak through his gritted teeth. 'He needs to stop before he breaks something!'

'You're not helping. Let me deal with it.'

For a moment, Emma thought Luke had gone too far; but Jonathan pursed his lips and took a step back.

While the banging continued, Luke examined the door, the hinges and frame. A clip on the handle locked the door on the inside. From his wallet, he extracted a bank card. Fascinated, Emma watched him jiggle the card into place between the door and the jamb. With one hand on the handle and the other manipulating the latch with the card, Luke nudged. A few moments later, the door clicked open. Phil rushed out, screaming his frustration, his arms windmilling.

Luke caught him in a bear hug and made soothing noises. 'Hey, buddy. Let's go to your room and have some quiet time.'

'It's alright, Phil.' Emma went to him, took his hands. 'Listen to Luke.'

'Does he have any emergency medication? Something to calm him down?'

'I'll get it.' Emma scurried to the kitchen and rifled through Phil's medications for Ativan. She considered filching one for herself. It was a fitting end to a sour day.

In Phil's room, she talked to him about school and Gabriela and basketball and puppies, while Luke convinced him to swallow a pill and accept an ice pack for his bruised forehead. They sat either side of him, holding a hand each, until he closed his eyes.

When Phil was calm enough to be left alone, she followed Luke down the stairs to the kitchen, where Jonathan flipped through Phil's folder, snapping at the pages as though it were the folder's fault and not his that Phil had melted down.

Luke jerked his backpack from the floor. 'Jonathan. You need to call his doctor in the morning.' His terse tone contrasted with the gentleness he'd shown to Phil.

'I'll do it,' Emma said, before Jonathan could retort that he didn't take orders from Luke and wouldn't be spoken to like that in his own house and—

Luke acknowledged her words with a nod. 'Okay. I need to go.'

'Here.' Jonathan thrust money at Luke without looking at it.

'Thanks.'

Jonathan met Luke's eyes, offered him a thin-lipped smile. 'You have a diverse skill set, don't you?'

Meeting Jonathan's cold stare, Luke pocketed the money without a word and shouldered his backpack to leave.

Emma scurried after him as he strode towards the front door. 'Luke. Wait.' She lowered her voice. 'Ah . . . my phone—remember you said you'd—'

'I didn't forget.' His voice was quiet.

A minute later, she settled into the passenger seat of an ancient Subaru. The interior was scrupulously clean: not a speck of dust on the dash, no rubbish, no clutter. In the driver's seat, Luke stared through the windscreen as though lost in thought. Emma let her head fall back against the headrest, let her eyes close. Heavy silence hung in the cabin of the car.

'I know. My father's an arsehole.'

Luke started the car and pulled out from the kerb. 'Are you okay?'

'He's never coped with Phil.' She didn't want to apologise for Jonathan, but she didn't want Luke to tar her with the same brush. 'Phil's just—he's a big sensitive kid. He can't handle arguments or shouting. Dad should fucking know that by now.' Heat flared behind her eyes. She looked out the window, hoping Luke didn't comment on her distress.

Dave: *What, you're crying about it now? Why are you always so dramatic?*

Luke said, 'I shouldn't have growled at him.'

'At Phil?'

He chuckled, breaking the tension. 'No—at Jonathan.'

'Yeah, that was brave.' She managed a smile.

'Brave or stupid? They look the same.' Rolling his shoulders, he relaxed with an exhale that seemed purposeful.

Emma watched him out of the corner of her eye. The streetlights flashed past, strobing, adding to the headache she hadn't registered until now. 'You're very calm in a crisis. Even when you were telling

Dad to back off, you didn't raise your voice. I'm surprised he took it so well. He must like you.'

'It's not about liking me. He finds me useful.'

'Your diverse skill set.' She suppressed a smile.

Luke grunted something incomprehensible. He changed lanes, his gaze flicking up to the rear-view mirror, then over his shoulder. 'Where's your car? Where are we going?'

She explained.

'Why are you parked under his office?'

'Because it's free and near where I work.' Emma sighed, weary of explaining. She parked there because Jonathan approved and it wasn't worth arguing.

Luke cut her a glance.

'I just—I didn't need that, seeing Dad yell at Phil. I'm glad you were there. I've had a shit day.' Her throat closed over the words. She squeezed her eyes closed, willing herself not to cry. Blinked to clear tears. Tried not to sniffle.

Luke stopped for a red light and turned to look at her. She felt exposed in the yellow wash of the streetlights; she wondered what he saw. Straight through her bullshit, she suspected. The cabin of the car closed in on her and she shifted in her seat, conscious of how close he was. Luke took up a lot of space in the car, with the seat racked back for his height and his shoulders filling its width. He drove with the same coordinated efficiency as when he cooked—a smooth economy of movement, purposeful, precise. She wondered if he always drove as sedately as an octogenarian, or if it was for her benefit.

He parked by a kerb, and Emma glanced out the window. 'Where are we?'

Luke switched off the ignition. 'St Kilda. You could do with an ice cream. I know I could. My shout.'

She opened her mouth to protest. Landmarks came into focus: they were parked off Acland Street. A curl of apprehension in her stomach reminded her she was alone with a guy she barely knew. She didn't even have her phone.

'Unless you're in a hurry to get home?' His lips twitched, an expression she was coming to recognise. A hidden smile.

Ten minutes later, they sat a foot apart on a bench near the St Kilda marina. Emma held a paper cup of lemon sorbet and Luke had chocolate ice cream in a waffle cone. Couples and groups of people strolled along the beach path, either heading out for the night or home from restaurants. The cool evening breeze ruffled their clothes, carrying scents of the ocean and the city.

'I'm not usually a dessert person,' Luke said. 'But I have a thing for chocolate ice cream. It's comfort food, right?'

Licking her spoon, Emma wished she'd chosen chocolate. Even simple decisions seemed beyond her right now.

'What are you working on at the moment?'

'You're trying to distract me.' Her throat hurt, as though her words had sharp edges and had stuck to her insides. Work was the least of her worries, but she didn't know him well enough to go there, not yet. She gazed out along the darkened marina, where the orb-like lights glowed as the night deepened. The darkness, and Luke's stillness as he listened, loosened her tongue. She was between acting gigs, she told him. Her role as the feisty Chantel in *Streetwise* had been a strategic career move, but after it ended, it was hard to move on. For Chantel, she'd bleached her hair, performed her own stunts and had scenes that stretched her dramatic skills.

'There's an episode where I hit someone with a car and kill them. It was nominated for a few awards.' She shrugged it off. 'I'm not in a rush for the next role. I'm waiting for the right one—something different, so I don't get typecast.' Staring off into the darkness, she directed her words to the water. 'I know I'm lucky. I can turn down work I don't want—most young actors can't. I get offered flimsy stuff. Modelling work, ads, social media. It's hard to say no. But I want to have an interesting career, like Cate Blanchett or Toni Collette. I want to play amazing characters—complex characters. I don't care if they're not lead roles.'

Words ran out. She licked the last of her sorbet from the spoon and savoured the sweet sourness.

'I like that you have a plan.' Luke interrupted the silence. 'You know who you are. Takes most people a long time to figure that out.'

'Actors forget who they are all the time. You put all your effort into learning to pretend—you have to remember what's real. That's where people go wrong.' She dumped the ice-cream cup on the bench between them.

'You and Phil get along well.' He stuck the last of his cone in his mouth.

Emma blew out a breath, resting back against the bench. 'He's not hard to get along with—he's a beautiful person. But Dad's an arsehole. He treats me like a fucking princess and has no time for Phil.' Her chest constricted. Tears wet her eyes and she blinked furiously to stop them.

She paused, waiting for Luke to comment.

Dave: *You're so oversensitive.*

Luke's voice was quiet. 'It's okay. You've got a lot going on.'

She swallowed, gathered the pieces of herself together. 'Enough about me. How did you learn to open locked doors?'

'YouTube.'

'How did you get the scar on your wrist?'

He glanced at the crisscrossed scar. 'Knife block fell on me when I was a kid.'

'Your eyebrow?'

'Car crash.'

'Your chin?'

A soft laugh. 'Kicked around by bullies at school.'

'You were bullied?' Emma raised her eyebrows. It seemed unlikely.

He flashed her a smile. 'This kid was annoying me in class, so I kicked his chair and he fell off. Everyone laughed at him. Bad move, humiliating a bully in front of everyone. He got me later, with two of his mates.'

His humour warmed her, brought a smile to her face. 'So, you started it?'

'It was self-defence. Promise.'

'This is your first year at uni, but you're, what, mid-twenties? What did you do between school and now?'

Luke looked out over the water. 'I moved around up north. Worked in hospitality, security, disability care, all kinds of jobs. Finally got back to study this year.'

Emma opened her mouth to ask more, but recognised his reticence. The conversation felt unfairly weighted; she'd talked too much about herself. Dave would have cut her off before she even started.

The conversation hung between them as they drove to Jonathan's office on Queens Road. She directed Luke to park near the entrance ramp of the subterranean car park. 'Here's fine. I'll walk down—you need a fob to get out.'

'Jonathan will kill me if I let you walk down there on your own.'

With a sigh, Emma conceded the point. At this hour, the area was deserted, the darkness cut by narrow cones of white from the streetlamps. Luke flicked on a mini flashlight attached to his keyring, and they dodged the boom gate to enter the car park on foot. He beamed the light into every corner. His vigilance amused her.

'What are you looking for?'

'Monsters,' he said.

Her phone was where she'd left it, tossed onto the passenger seat. She tried the ignition again, then retraced her steps with Luke. The drive to Brighton was quiet.

Luke stopped in the driveway. 'Are you gonna be okay?'

She was about to be yelled at by her father, and there would be a hundred texts from Dave, but there was a limit to how much she could dump on Luke. 'Thanks for listening. And the ice cream.'

'My pleasure.'

They shared a smile.

'My number is in Phil's folder if you need it.'

'Thanks. I'll let Dad know.'

He said, 'I wasn't talking about him.'

CHAPTER SIX

MONDAY, 9.10 PM

After Emma had disappeared through the gate, Luke sat in his car, distracted by the lingering scent of her perfume. His efforts to cheer her up felt off target, as though he'd missed saying something important she needed to hear. Even so, the opportunity to watch her eat ice cream made it worthwhile.

The Samsung buzzed. Gus: *Got a lead on Kevin yet?*

Luke replied, *I'm on it, I'll let you know later tonight.*

He pushed thoughts of Emma aside to focus on his task. He took the M1 across the bridge and turned at Williamstown Road to head north into Footscray. As he crossed the train line, with Whitten Oval to his left, an uncomfortable knot of nostalgia gripped his chest. Following his nose into a residential area, he slowed to a crawl in a side street and parked several houses short of his goal. There was scanty light for reconnaissance; he leaned over the steering wheel to peer through the windscreen.

Colby Street had changed since his last visit. Some of the older houses had been torn down, and the new builds taking their place sported neat lawns dotted with children's toys, native trees, flowerbeds. Number forty-three, a red-brick California bungalow nearly a century old, seemed tired and unloved in comparison. Clogged gutters overhung the front porch, and the lawn was weedy and overgrown. A magnolia in dire need of pruning took up most of the front yard. Paint peeled from the gables and fascia. The letterbox overflowed with junk mail.

Luke considered the house, his options, his strategy. From memory, he plugged a number into his phone that he hadn't called in years. It went straight to voicemail.

'This is Kevin. You know the drill.'

'Kevin, it's Jack. Gus is looking for you and Quin.' He hung up. He dialled Quin's number, also from memory. It had been disconnected.

In the time he'd been in the street, nothing had moved. He snapped on latex gloves and closed the car door quietly behind him. Stopping to collect the mail from the letterbox, he felt his way in the dark around the side of the house to the rear. He passed the broken Hills hoist and went up the three concrete steps to the porch. His key turned cleanly in the lock, and the back door swung open.

The mini flashlight on his keyring came in handy again. With the beam aimed at the floor, he ventured inside and stood in silence, listening. The back door led into a laundry, the air stale with mould and Omo. Cool, musty air chilled his skin. A hallway led to the bathroom, kitchen, main bedroom and lounge. To his right, a shorter passage connected the other two bedrooms. Once he was satisfied there were no unexpected sounds within, he padded cat-like through the house, checking the corners of each room with his beam before moving to the next.

In the second and third bedrooms, Kevin's and Quin's possessions littered the floors, and the beds were unmade. The main bedroom, at the front of the house, had belonged to Kevin's mother, Gail, and was much tidier. A powder-coating of dust dulled the scene, absorbing the light from his torch. Cobwebs decorated every corner.

The kitchen was tidy; the fridge was empty. Luke turned a tap and waited for the murky water to clear. He flicked a light switch on and off.

He thumbed a text to Gus: *No one home at Kevin's old place.*

The reply was instant: *Keep looking.*

Luke paused in the lounge, remembering. The house was the only real home he knew—a constant in a lifetime of moving around. Some of his memories were precious; others he'd be happy to forget.

Streetlight peeked through the crack in the curtains, illuminating the scar on his wrist that Emma had queried. He'd earned it here, in the doorway of the kitchen. The story of its origin—the lie Quin had told at the hospital when they stitched him up—was stale from repetition. It wasn't the first scar he'd collected, but it was the first that was visible. Until then, his injuries had been private. Hidden.

He sank onto the couch and put his face in his hands.

CHAPTER SEVEN

EIGHTEEN YEARS AGO

A light flicked on, casting a yellow glow over the dark porch, as Quin fiddled with a key in the lock. Jack didn't know where he was or why. The drive had taken so long, and covered so much distance, that the ground beneath his feet felt unstable, as though he'd got off a boat. He'd lost his ability to gauge distance or weight or any other physical properties of the world. He waited behind the unfamiliar shape of his father on the step of an old red-brick house in a city that smelled foreign. It was late at night and bitterly cold. Jack hugged his chest with his arms as a woman opened the door from inside.

Quin's voice was subdued. 'Hey, Gail. Sorry, the key was stuck. This is Jack.'

Gail had blonde hair streaked with grey, a smoker's lined mouth and pale eyes that crinkled as she narrowed them. Her tracksuit might have fit her a decade ago but now clung to every detail of her soft body. Jack could see a line where the elastic of her underwear cut in at her hip.

'What's going on?' Gail wasn't looking at Quin: her attention was on Jack. Her scanty white eyebrows knotted together, as though she were trying to figure out a puzzle.

Quin flicked a glance to Jack. 'I'll tell you later, alright?'

He ushered Jack into the lounge. A wall of warm air hit Jack's face. The house smelled of lavender soap, cigarettes, musty newspapers. An old plastic telephone sat on a stand in the hall. Pink ceramics in the bathroom. Rose-patterned carpet, scuffed linoleum in the kitchen.

Gail rifled in a hall cupboard for a blow-up mattress and blankets, which she and Quin squashed into a space on the floor in Quin's bedroom. She peered at Jack with keen eyes. 'You hungry, love?'

He nodded. Words formed in his mind, but his tongue was stuck.

She made him baked beans on toast, which he ate at a laminate table in the kitchen. His eyelids drooped. It was hard to concentrate on chewing. Quin and Gail's conversation floated over the top of his head. *He's Susie's kid* and *Yeah, she was in Sydney the last few years* and *Nah, I didn't know* and *I'll get my own place* and *When's Kev out?* and *He's exhausted, Quin, let's get him to bed.*

He'd met Quin less than a week ago, in a grey government office with kind strangers hovering over him. Since his mother died, he'd lived with a foster family—more kind strangers—while they'd tracked down his family. Which meant Quin.

Michael Quinlan was not a big man, but he had a big smile. A pleasant face, shaggy brown hair overdue for a cut, an infectious laugh. He fidgeted on his feet, like a kid who needed to pee. *Hi, buddy, I'm Quin*, had been their brief introduction, followed by, *Man, you look like your mum. Bloody hell. Spitting bloody image.*

Jack was wary of him. The shape and smell of him were unfamiliar, the timbre of his voice. Mum had spoken of him occasionally, casually: *Your dad loves this song* or *Once, your father spilled a whole tub of popcorn at the movies* or *Your father puts tomato sauce on his eggs, how Australian is that?* She'd laughed about his Australianness, the contrast to her Englishness. She'd never told Jack why they weren't together, or where his father was, and Jack had never asked. It had never seemed to matter before.

'Am I supposed to call you Dad?' he'd asked, during the long drive from Sydney. It had come out wrong—too familiar, too similar to saying *Mum*. For a moment he couldn't breathe, afraid he'd said the wrong thing. He'd peered out the window to hide his reaction, watching the green and brown hills flash past.

'Call me what you want, mate.' Quin lit another cigarette.

In the morning, Quin wasn't there. Jack woke on the air mattress, which had gone flat overnight, and fumbled his way to the bathroom and then to the kitchen.

'He's gone to the panel shop,' Gail said. She gave Jack a bowl of cereal. 'He works there sometimes, when Malcolm needs him. I've gotta go to work soon.' Her brow furrowed. 'I guess you'll have to come with me. You're too young to stay home by yourself.'

Jack dressed in yesterday's clothes and got into Gail's Corolla. She worked in a newsagency, selling magazines and pens and lottery tickets. Jack spent the day doing puzzles and looking at magazines in the storeroom, trying not to think about his mother.

When they got home, Quin was eating a pie in the kitchen. Gail said, *Quin, we need to talk,* and Jack took the car magazine she'd bought him and hid in the bedroom while they argued in the kitchen.

You can't just piss off and leave him and *I had to go to work* and *So did I* and a series of other useless statements from each of them. A few minutes later the front door slammed, signalling Quin's departure.

Gail appeared at the bedroom door. 'Come and help me with this,' she said, and Jack sat with her on the couch to do puzzles. Gail was obsessed with puzzles: sudoku, word-finding, cryptic crossword and others he'd never come across. His natural ability seemed to impress her.

'Where's Quin?' he asked later, when they were eating sausages for dinner.

'Looking for a place to live.' Gail rolled her shoulders. 'Kevin will be out soon. Quin and Kevin—I mean, they're mates, but they're not good at living under the same roof.'

Kevin, her son, had been Quin's best friend since school. Quin had bunked in Gail's house since he ran away from his own parents when he was fifteen. Kevin had been in jail for the last few years and was about to come home. He'd been pulled over for speeding and the police had found an unregistered shotgun in his car.

Jack noted Gail's resigned sigh as she explained it all. 'He was lucky he only got two years,' she said. 'I wish he'd stay away from guns.'

Quin came back later and apologised to Gail. They had a long, intense conversation in the kitchen while Jack watched television in the lounge, trying not to listen. They came to an agreement of sorts, and although the details flew over Jack's head, the tension in the house eased.

For the next few days, he spent his time with Gail, either at work or doing puzzles on the couch, trying not to think about his mother, or watching television, trying not to think about his mother. His grief was like a hole, a space where she should be; an absence of feeling rather than the presence of one.

Quin came and went. Jack learned, by osmosis rather than any explanation, that his work in the panel shop was not his passion: he was a guitarist in a rock band. The band played gigs in local pubs, covers of eighties and nineties rock. Whenever Quin was home, he'd sit on the bed with his guitar, casually strumming chords and crooning. Jack recognised most of the tunes, because his mother had loved music and had a huge collection of CDs. When he told Quin this, Quin went quiet and turned his face away. Jack didn't mention it again.

When Quin wasn't at band rehearsal, playing at the pub or banging out panels for Malcolm, he was with his girlfriend Donna or at the racecourse, betting on horses. On the nights that Quin wasn't home, Jack snuck into Gail's room and slept beside her in the big bed. She was such a heavy sleeper that she never noticed him. If he heard Quin come home, Jack would get up and sneak into his own bed on the floor.

One such night, Jack waited until Quin was settled in bed before creeping in. Quietly, his voice small in the dark room, Jack ventured, 'You awake?'

Sleepily, Quin said, 'What?'

'Can I meet Donna?'

'Why?'

'Are you gonna get married? Will I live with you?'

Quin's laugh was not encouraging. 'Married? Jesus. No. We'll stay here for now, mate. I'm looking for a place. It's just taking some time.'

Jack felt his face hot and wet against the pillow, the hole where his mother had been stretched larger by Quin's words. The idea that Quin might get married and make a family for him had teased him with its simplicity. He felt stupid to have conjured the fantasy. And it wasn't an unknown woman named Donna he wanted: it was Mum, with her crisp accent and her penchant for strong tea.

Gail reminded Quin to enrol Jack in school, which was just as well because he was tired of reading the same three books. The local primary was close enough that he could walk, and for the first week Quin walked with him. They were still strangers, and their conversations were awkward and transactional. It was a relief when Quin let him go on his own.

Going to school made him feel normal. Back home—back in Sydney, rather—he'd been good at school. His mother had worked in the school library and he was the best reader in his class. Starting at a new school had its challenges, but he understood the rules of schoolyard etiquette and played it cool. The kids wanted to know all about him: where was he from, and was it true his mother had died? Instead of answering, Jack threw himself into the playground games, the faster and more frantic the better. When the kids were out of breath, they couldn't ask hard questions.

He got along well with his new teacher and made friends with the kids who played football through recess and lunch. He and Quin tolerated each other, feeling out the edges between them. Gail provided consistency in his life. And meals, importantly.

Just as Jack was starting to settle in, Kevin was released from jail.

Jack was in the kitchen eating Weet-Bix after school when Gail brought Kevin home. Kevin was taller and heavier than Quin, with thick sandy hair, solid shoulders, big hands. A full sleeve of tattoos on his left arm. He filled the kitchen doorway and stared at Jack with accusing pale eyes.

'What the actual fuck?' he said.

Jack wanted to hide under the table. Instead, he froze, the spoon halfway to his mouth.

Gail said, 'I told you, Kev. It's Susie's boy.'

Kevin continued to stare. Jack couldn't move.

'Where's Quin? I'm gonna wring his fucking neck!'

Kevin turned to find Quin behind him. With a hand on Quin's shoulder, Kevin directed him out the back door, and the two disappeared to shout at each other in the yard.

I told you he was coming and *Susie was in Sydney* and *You're such a dickhead, Quin* and *Jesus, Kev, calm down* and *What was I supposed to do? You were in bloody jail* and *Wasn't my fault!* and *I couldn't just leave him* and *What the fuck is wrong with you, Quin?* and on and on.

'It's alright,' Gail said to Jack. 'Don't worry about Kevin. They always fight like that.'

Despite her reassurance, Jack walked on eggshells when Kevin was around. Kevin was quick to slap him whenever a smart-arse reply leaked out. And if Jack annoyed him, sometimes by his mere presence, he'd grab an implement—a wooden spoon or a spatula—from the kitchen, hound Jack into his room and bark at him to stay out of his way. Jack was usually quick enough to dodge him. Not always. Because Quin was rarely there, Gail was the buffer between them when Kevin arced up because Jack had smart-mouthed him or made a mess.

'What's all this shit on the table? Hey, kid, clean up your bloody—'

'Leave him alone, Kev, it's his homework!' Gail was not averse to brandishing a household weapon herself. It amused Jack—not that he would ever show it—that she could still intimidate her son with a wooden spoon.

'Where's Quin? Leaves his fucking kid here and—'

'Language, Kev.' Gail slapped Kevin's arm with her spoon. 'Quin's out with the band. He'll be back later.'

One of Jack's schoolbooks contained a picture of a highlander in tartan—a red-haired man with a ferocious face, wielding a massive sword—that always came to mind when Kevin was angry. Jack showed it to Gail, who told him McNally was an Irish name, not Scottish. She didn't see the resemblance.

Kevin painted houses for a living. He'd apprenticed with his late father and drove an old ute with his father's name on it. The work was patchy and Kevin's enthusiasm for it was lacklustre, which meant he was often home during the day. In the evenings, he sometimes went out with Quin to the pub or band rehearsal or wherever it was Quin went. Jack was always relieved to see him go.

A few months later, Jack twigged that Kevin and Quin were up to something. They talked into the night, drinking beer and chain-smoking cigarettes. Jack, hiding in the bedroom pretending to read, listened with ghoulish fascination to the conversation in the lounge.

Piece of cake, Quin said.

We need a man around the back. Kevin was more cautious and, though Jack hated to admit it, much smarter.

The job was a 3 am hit on a convenience store. Jack pretended to be asleep when Quin snuck out and when he snuck back in.

For a few weeks, Kevin was in a good mood, and both men threw money around. Jack got new sneakers, they had takeaway pizza, and Kevin bought Gail a flat-screen television. The money burned a hole in Quin's pocket: he went to the Flemington races and blew the rest of his share on a booze-up and a poorly considered trifecta. When Kevin laughed about it, Quin threw a punch at him. Jack peeked out from the bedroom as they flung fists and insults at each other and wrestled on the floor. There was no question who'd come out on top. Kevin outclassed Quin in every way. Gail's wooden spoon intervened before any permanent injuries were inflicted.

Jack was worried that Quin's behaviour would mean they had to leave—he'd lived in Gail's house long enough to consider it home, despite Quin's ongoing futile search for affordable housing—but the next day it was as though nothing had happened. Kevin and Quin sat at the kitchen table smoking and drinking coffee together, talking about the football, while Gail cooked scrambled eggs for breakfast.

'You alright, Jack?' she said, sensing him loitering in the hallway.

'I'm good.' He sat at the table, keeping Quin between him and Kevin, fascinated by the colours in the bruising around Quin's left eye. He wondered why they called it a black eye, when it was actually purple and green.

Quin and Kevin reached for the tomato sauce at the same time and laughed at each other.

'Don't worry about these two,' Gail said, waving her cigarette at the men. 'They've been fighting like that since they were your size. Not going to stop now.'

A year later, Jack sat in the passenger seat, nursing his right wrist on his lap, while Quin drove. The stitches throbbed as the local anaesthetic wore off. The nurse had given him a sandwich, which he'd finished in seconds, and a strawberry Chupa Chup, which was dissolving in his cheek.

'Are we going home now?'

Quin fiddled with the car radio. 'Yeah. See if Kev's calmed down.' And then, 'Fuck.'

He pulled the car to the kerb and wound down the window. Jack swivelled in his seat. Red and blue lights flashed on the car behind them. Two coppers emerged and came to the driver's-side window. They peered into the interior while Quin rifled through his wallet for his licence.

'It's a seventy zone. We clocked you at eighty-four.'

Quin handed over his licence. 'Do I get a ticket?'

The officer nodded. His gaze rested on Jack's bandaged wrist. 'Kids are safer in the back.'

'Jack, get in the back.' Quin cast the words at him sideways.

The policeman waited while Jack cleared a space and found a seatbelt. 'Stay here while we sort out the paperwork.'

Quin's gaze fixed on the rear-view mirror. 'Fucking cops. Picked up for speeding, *now*?'

Jack finished his lollipop and looked for somewhere to stash the stick. He turned to peer through the rear windshield at the police car.

The two policemen got out of their car and returned to the driver's side with purposeful strides. 'Mr Quinlan, we need you to step out of the car. There's a warrant—'

'What?' Quin's feigned surprise didn't fool anyone. He floored the accelerator and shot out into the traffic, leaving the shocked policemen in his wake.

Jack twisted to watch. They were back in their car in seconds, and in pursuit.

The agitation in Quin's voice as he shouted at other drivers to get out of his way scared Jack more than the speeding vehicle or the screeching tyres. Quin's palm stayed rammed against the horn as he swerved from lane to lane. Jack clamped his hands around the doorhandle beside him and clamped his mouth shut. He was so terrified he feared he might piss his pants. Cars and houses and street signs flashed past as they sped along the suburban road. Police sirens faded in and out and multiplied.

Quin took a left-hand corner too fast, panicked and slammed on the brakes. The tyres squealed as they lost traction. The car careened onto the wrong side of the road and slammed into the driver's side of an oncoming vehicle. Metal crunched as the two vehicles crumpled, and the airbag exploded into Quin's face. Jack was thrown into his seatbelt and hit his head against the back of the seat in front.

His vision went blurry. Noise filled his ears and pain split his head. His stomach heaved and he tasted vomit. When he put his hand to his forehead, it came away sticky with blood.

The front door was wrenched open and Quin was dragged out.

The copper who'd made Jack sit in the back forced open his door, helped him unbuckle the seatbelt, then asked questions about where he hurt. Jack couldn't answer; his tongue was as shocked as the rest of him. He vomited on the wheel of the car and his legs melted under him until he hit the asphalt. He couldn't see properly. The noises around him funnelled away.

'Just as well you weren't in the front seat,' the cop said, and Jack snapped his attention to the car. The front had been crushed by the collision. The airbag had saved Quin's life. The cop had saved Jack's.

Jack vomited again, and then a woman in a different uniform told him she was a paramedic and would he like a ride in an ambulance?

'Yeah,' Jack said, as his vision turned to stars in a black night.

He was cheated. He remembered nothing of the ambulance. He remembered little of the next few days. Stitches in his eyebrow. Nurses both kind and stern. Not knowing where Quin was. A thumping headache that worsened whenever he opened his eyes. A doctor told him he had a concussion, but his scan was okay and not to worry. Jack felt cheated again: he didn't remember having a scan.

He did remember having two visitors in his hospital room. Both were women, and both had clipboards. One was a police officer, who told Jack she would be grateful if he could answer some questions. The other was a social worker, who interrupted many times; Jack figured she was there because Quin wasn't, because he was a kid and shouldn't have to answer questions from the police, and because his father had endangered his life and there were concerns about his safety . . .

The questions were easy at first but quickly progressed to dangerous territory. 'What happened to your hand?'

'It wasn't anyone's fault.' If it was anyone's fault, it was his own, for coming out of his room when Kevin and Quin were fighting in the kitchen. He should have known Kevin would grab something off the bench to throw at him. And he should have ducked the knife, instead of throwing up his arm to block it.

Quin had told him not to talk to cops. Jack couldn't resist direct questions, but he kept some things to himself. For example, he didn't say that Kevin and Quin had attempted a job together the night before, which they abandoned when they realised they'd been caught on CCTV. Neither Quin nor Jack had expected Kevin to go quite as ballistic as he did, throwing knives around and threatening to kill people.

A feisty public defender helped keep Quin out of jail. *Got a kid to look after*, was part of the argument. A community corrections order and a good behaviour bond kept him in line for a year.

Kevin's parole was revoked. He went back to prison and blamed Quin for the whole mess. Jack wondered if their friendship would survive.

Kev always calms down eventually, Quin said, with a shrug. *You know what he's like.*

Gail's house was different without Kevin. Not quieter—Quin made a lot of noise, with his constant chatter and his guitar and his inability to sit still—but it seemed to Jack as though order was restored, like the feeling after a storm when the rain has ended and the sky clears. Quin's community service, removing graffiti from walls in the city, had him out of the house every day. *Keeping my head down,* he said, which amused Jack because Quin wore high-vis overalls and an orange hard hat. He was far from subtle.

Jack wondered how long the peace would last once Kevin was released. He asked Gail, while eating breakfast cereal after school one day, how long her son would be in jail.

'Well, he'll be lucky to get parole.' She flicked ash off her cigarette. 'Two years, give or take. Lucky it was just attempted robbery this time. They couldn't prove he was armed.'

Jack held his tongue. He figured luck was irrelevant in either case, but Gail was Kevin's mother, so he cut her some slack.

Quin, arriving home with his usual soundtrack of slammed doors, dumped bag and discarded boots, overhead the end of the conversation and called out from the hallway. 'Don't worry, Jack. We'll find a place to live before he gets out.'

'Yeah,' Gail said with a sigh. 'I reckon that's a good idea.'

CHAPTER EIGHT

TUESDAY, 7.10 PM

From the doorway of the Wylies' kitchen, Luke struggled to make sense of the scene. Emma waved a tea towel like a surrender flag, a half-hearted attempt to clear the smoke in the air, while the smoke alarm's piercing beeps mocked her efforts. The stench of burning food pervaded the room, and the television news blared at high volume. Phil crawled on his hands and knees on the floor; Emma tripped over him and grasped the counter to stay on her feet.

'Phil dropped his lollies.' Her words came out as dramatic sobs. 'I forgot about dinner and it caught *fire* and I can't make the alarm stop and *I have to get ready or I'll be late—*'

'Go.' Luke turned her towards the stairs and pushed her up the first few.

Coughing out a lungful of smoke, he switched off the television, climbed onto the bench to reset the alarm and opened the windows. He found another packet of lollies in the pantry and tried to convince Phil they were preferable to the dirty ones.

'Emma burned it!' Phil paced the room, dipping in and out of Luke's personal space like a basketball player chasing the ball. 'She burned it! The dinner!'

'It's alright. We'll make something else.' The saucepan of charred food languished on the stove. Luke opened the fridge and assessed the contents. It had not been restocked since his hashed-together frittata. 'Pasta?'

'Nothing else!'

Less than an hour ago, Emma had called in tears to ask for help. She'd cried about needing to be somewhere and Jonathan suggesting she call, and Luke, disillusioned with study, had agreed just to stop her tears. It occurred to him that Emma was an actor and her distress might not be genuine, but seeing her was a pleasant distraction. Memories had played in his mind all day—not just of his scars, but of Emma asking about them.

While Phil's pasta was cooking, Luke disposed of the burnt food, scrubbed the pot and tidied up the mess. He surveyed the sorry contents of the vegetable drawer in the fridge, and the jars and tins in the pantry; he puzzled over the combination, then set about concocting dinner for himself.

When Emma reappeared, her transformation rendered him speechless. Earlier, she'd been in a state: trackpants, hair askew, flushed face. Now, her curly hair was smoothed into silkiness and neatly styled around her face. Smoky eyes and dark lipstick gave her an exotic glow. She wore a shiny emerald-green dress and silver heels, with her long legs bare. Luke forced his mouth closed and tried not to stare.

'Wow.' She cast her gaze around the tidy, quiet kitchen and at the progress he'd made on a chickpea and vegetable curry. He was tempted to say the same back.

'Where are you going, again?'

Emma blinked at him. 'I didn't tell you? I've got an audition—a call-back. Their first choice fell through and it's all a big rush.' She bounced around in her heels, as nervous as her brother.

'Break a leg,' he said, and got a fake scowl in return.

Luke gnawed on his lip as he drove away from the Wylie house a few hours later. Jonathan had arrived home before there was any sign of Emma, and he'd been surprised to find Luke on the sofa with his textbooks: Emma had said nothing about the audition. The fact that she'd lied, and the awkward conversation that ended with Jonathan thrusting a handful of pineapples at him, bothered him in a way he found hard to define. His irritation was with himself; he'd allowed Emma to draw him into the family dynamics.

A buzz from the Samsung made him groan. He pulled over and swiped the phone open.

Ed's voice: 'Jack. Heads-up. He's gonna call you. Job in your hood, some guy in Elwood.'

'I told him I'm not—'

'Yeah. Good luck with that.' With a dry laugh, Ed hung up.

Gus's call came as Luke parked at home. 'Found Kevin yet?'

'Working on it.'

'Job for you. Bloke calls himself Mouse. Thinks he's funny—he's a big guy.' A heavy sigh, enough to make Luke hold the phone out from his ear. 'Owes me five grand.' Gus went on, explaining how patient he'd been, how he'd cut the guy slack, how many times he'd delayed and so on, until Luke interrupted.

'I've got exams; I'm not—'

'Go and get the fucking money, Jackie.' The call ended, and the phone beeped as Gus texted him an address.

Luke sat in his car to ground himself. Resentment bubbled up; instead of fighting it, he gave it free rein, felt it boil in his guts and flush his face and curl his hands into fists. *Fucking Gus and his fucking demands. Back where I fucking started.* With his eyes closed, he let the anger rise to a peak and fall into resignation.

He went upstairs to his flat, changed his clothes and stuffed gear into his pockets, then drove to the address in Elwood.

The residential street was quiet, still, dark. Gus's text led him to a squat duplex, a house that had been divided into two units with a paling fence splitting the block in half. Number two, on the right, was hidden behind overgrown shrubs.

Luke trudged up the driveway, scoping for security. No cameras, but a metal screen shielded the door. He banged on it with the side of his fist. With his second rap, an exterior light flicked on. The door opened a crack, revealing a sliver of blonde hair and a single eye.

'I'm looking for Mouse,' Luke said.

The crack widened; a Rubenesque young woman in black leggings and a purple tank top stood inside. 'Yeah, he told me you were coming. He's not here. Come in. I'll get the money.' She unclipped the security screen and let him in without a care. Her lack of concern for her personal safety depressed him.

He followed her along a cluttered, dusty corridor into a living area and watched her climb onto a chair to access the top of a cabinet. She grasped a plastic supermarket bag and dropped down to hand it over.

'I need to count it,' he said.

The dining table was covered in junk, as was the kitchen bench. A layer of dust dulled the wooden floor. On the coffee table, an elaborate pipe bong had tipped on its side; the smell of burning grass transported him back to his childhood, to the seedy rentals he'd lived in with Quin. The place was a nightmare. His skin crawled.

After donning latex gloves, he swiped an area of the table to make space, piling up dishes and utility bills and a set of keys. He upended the plastic bag onto the table and groaned. 'Really?' The bag was full of small notes. Fives, tens, twenties. 'What's your name?'

'Kayla.'

Luke started his count, sorting the different denominations into neat piles, while Kayla sat at the table, too close, and watched. She was younger than him, he guessed. Her round, smooth face reminded him of a porcelain doll, complete with fake eyelashes and eyes that moved independently of her head as she followed the movement of his hands.

'What's yours?' she asked.

He shook his head. 'He's short three hundred bucks.'

Biting her lower lip, she looked up at him from under her eyelashes, put a hand on his arm and stroked down to his hand. Her smile was coy, but her face barely moved. The effect creeped him out. 'Thought you might say that. Maybe I can help. There are things I can do—other ways to pay . . .'

'What would Mouse say about that?'

'His idea. He likes it when I—'

'Get him on the phone. Now.' Luke removed her hand.

Kayla rolled her round eyes and found her phone.

A male voice: 'Is he there?'

'Yeah, babes, you're on speaker.' Kayla flicked her hair and pouted.

'Mouse.' Taking the phone, Luke growled into it. 'How well do you know Gus?'

'Who the fuck are you?'

'You're missing three hundred bucks. You want me to tell him you tried to pimp out your girlfriend to make up the shortfall? Do you have any idea how that would go down?'

Gus's holier-than-thou moral sensibilities were well known. His belief in the family unit, in filial and matrimonial loyalty, was absolute; any contravention of his rules was interpreted as a personal insult, a punishable offence.

Luke reached over the table for the keys he'd disturbed, turned them over in his hands. The keys, and the branded keychain, were new. 'Where's the Ducati?'

Silence, and then, 'No—Kayla, don't let him take it!'

'You've got thirty minutes, or I'm taking the bike as collateral—'

'It's worth thirty grand!'

'—or I can call Gus, and he'll ask which knee is your favourite.' Luke hung up.

The motorcycle was easily found. Luke unlocked the roller door of the attached garage and contemplated the gleaming red machine. It was cleaner than anything inside the house, which brought to mind a memory of Kevin cleaning his rifle. Boys and their toys.

Footsteps pattered behind him, and he turned just in time to slap a kitchen knife from Kayla's hand. She gasped and clutched her right hand in her left, backing away as Luke rounded on her.

'Are you serious?' He grasped her arm, kicked out her leading foot and followed her to the ground, sticking his knee into her back. Howling with the indignity, flat on her front, she writhed under him. 'That was stupid, Kayla.'

'I can't let you take the bike! He'll fucking kill me!'

From his pocket, Luke extracted a pair of cable ties, linked them together and secured her wrists behind her back. He hauled her to her feet, marched her inside and pushed her into a chair, ignoring her stream of profanity.

Twisting a flashy engagement ring off her finger—none too gently, given she'd tried to stab him in the back—he held it in front of her face. 'Is this real?'

Her eyes flicked aside; she shook her head. Lying.

'So—he's short-changing Gus a few measly hundreds, while splashing cash on a Ducati and a diamond ring for you.' Exasperated, Luke threw up his palms.

He scooped Kayla's phone from the table, hit redial and said, 'You're a moron, Mouse.'

'If you take my bike, I swear I'll come after you and—'

'Join the fucking queue,' said Luke.

CHAPTER NINE

WEDNESDAY, 7.40 AM

Unable to sleep, Luke had found the first series of *Streetwise* online and watched it late into the night. Chantel was a taller, smarter version of Kayla, with a personality nothing like Emma's. He couldn't fault her acting. The series was more realistic than he'd expected and did nothing to help him sleep. Dreams of girls trying to knife him kept him awake until the wee hours.

Lingering on the balcony with his first coffee, he groaned as his phone buzzed with a text. It was too early to start fielding calls from his study group.

Reluctantly, he swiped his phone open.

I have your tax textbook.

He recognised the number and his stomach did a flip. An image of the textbook lying open on the Wylies' sofa came to him. It wasn't like him to leave things behind; it felt like an omen, an indication his focus was failing.

He replied: *What's the ransom?*

A million in small unmarked bills.

He hit the call icon. 'I can buy a new one for sixty bucks.'

Emma said, 'You'd lose all your little sticky notes.'

'Hmm, you're on to me.'

Logistics for collection were arranged, and an hour later Luke knocked on the Wylies' door. He doffed his sunglasses as Emma invited him in.

'Wow, it's quiet in here.'

'Phil's at school. Dad's at work.' She let out an indulgent sigh. He followed her to the kitchen and she handed him his book. 'Here. No ransom required.'

'How was the audition?'

She wrinkled her nose. 'Hard to say. They never give you much.'

'Emma.' He met her eyes squarely. 'You lied to me. You didn't tell your father.'

Her gaze dropped; her hands went to her face. 'I panicked. I didn't know what to do—I'm really sorry. I didn't know if you'd come and I can't talk to Dad and . . .'

Watching her expressive face, he wondered if she was acting. Her distress seemed real. As she bit her lip and blinked at him, he decided he didn't care. With a suspicion that he was not thinking straight where Emma was concerned, he said, 'It's alright. But if you need help, just ask.'

Her shoulders relaxed. 'Can I make you coffee? A peace offering?'

In an odd reversal, she stood by the Gaggia while Luke settled at the counter, watching as she heated cups and ground coffee. She wore yoga pants and a baggy T-shirt, and bounced on the balls of her bare feet as though nervous. Her toenails were painted bright pink. Her phone beeped several times. She ignored it.

Emma noticed his attention. 'Are you critiquing my coffee-making skills?'

It would be weird to mention her cute toenails. 'You seem to know what you're doing.'

'It's an elaborate facade.' Emma placed his cup before him. 'They teach it in drama class. How to look competent when you have no idea.'

Luke smiled. 'Fake it till you make it?'

'That's it.' She sat beside him and pointed to the tax book. 'This is dry stuff. A genuine cure for insomnia.' Her phone beeped, and again she silenced it.

'It has its own charm.' Luke shrugged. 'Why are you looking at me like that?'

'I can't see you in a shirt and tie, balancing the books, doing tax.' Emma's cheeks flushed, as though her thoughts had wandered somewhere they shouldn't.

'Really?' He leaned back, grinned. At another beep from her phone, he said, 'Someone's looking for you.'

Emma dismissed it with a wave. 'Guess what I had for breakfast?'

'Random. Toast?'

'Chickpea curry—it was delicious,' she said. 'You'll be relieved to know I did an online shop. Food delivery this afternoon.'

'Lots of pasta for Phil, I hope.'

'I was going to text and ask what you wanted, but I realised that was presumptuous. You're not here to cook for us.'

He brushed it off. 'Gabriela will be back soon. And I really need to get through these exams.' He stretched his neck, rolled his shoulders.

The sounds of the house were different from his. The fridge had a soft, low hum, and a lawnmower had started up nearby; a magpie warbled in the back garden. Long shafts of sunlight filtered through the tall windows of the kitchen, picking out the highlights in Emma's hair.

'What are you doing today?' Luke's words broke into a peaceful silence. They'd been staring at each other rather than talking.

Smiling, Emma fiddled with her cup. 'Work at ten, then a friend's place. Dad will be home later.'

'You're talking to him?'

'Not really. We had another fight last night. He was furious because I went to get my phone, carried on about it being dangerous—until I told him you walked me in. Then he let it go. I told you: he likes you.'

Luke shook his head; her interpretation was overly simplistic. 'He's worried about you.'

She hesitated. 'He wasn't always like this. When Mum died—it's like he couldn't cope and turned into a control freak.'

'Grief does strange things to people.'

'It made me try cocaine for the first and last time, and turned Dad into a psycho. I think I got off lightly.'

With a laugh, Luke got to his feet. 'I should go. Force some of this tax stuff into my brain.'

She walked him to the door. The conversation had reached a natural end, but he dallied by the front door with his car keys in hand. 'So, my last exam is Tuesday.'

Her smile froze.

Brave, or stupid, he said, 'Can I call you after?'

'Luke, ah, remember I said I was on a break . . .'

He put up a hand to stop her. 'It's okay. You don't have to explain.'

'Jesus, you're so reasonable.' A quiet sigh. 'I have a lot going on, that's all. Let me think about it.'

'I'll see you sometime.' He flashed her a smile. The door closed behind him with a quiet click.

After changing into running gear, Luke headed out into the lunchtime bustle along the beach path. The warm weather brought out the masses, who emerged into the bright sunshine with squinting eyes as they fumbled for their sunglasses.

While he weaved around slower runners and walkers, he thought about the coppery highlights in Emma's hair and her awkward rejection. She'd told him he wasn't her type, and it was true: he was a penniless student who'd grown up poor in the west of the city, not a trust-fund kid from Brighton. Jonathan would freak, anyway. And it was probably for the best, given Gus's re-emergence in his life.

To appease Gus, he spent an hour online searching for anything that could point to Kevin or Quin's whereabouts, although he knew it was a waste of time: Quin barely knew how to use a computer, and Kevin typed emails with two fingers. The address at Colby Street was still linked to Kevin's painting business. An old Facebook profile for Quin had lax security settings and no posts for several years. Nothing in the court databases implied they'd been incarcerated.

With the Samsung in his hand, he debated whether to tell Gus what he'd found, and decided against it. He had nothing to report, which might inflame Gus's temper, and with just a few days until his exams, it wasn't worth the risk.

He opened his books, distracted by the flurry of messages from his study group, but one text stood out from the others.

Emma: *Are you free Friday night? Promise I won't keep you out late.*

CHAPTER TEN

FRIDAY, 6.05 PM

For the hundredth time, Emma cast her eyes towards the entrance and wondered if Luke would show. The bar backed onto the beach, with minimalist, modern decor; polished concrete floors and dark tables were reflected in the mirrors behind the bar and the rows of glistening glasses. Chilled music provided a backdrop for muted conversations.

Perched on a stool on the alfresco deck at the rear of the bar, she pretended she was okay as she reconnected with her friends. Shinita, her best buddy from school. Brooke and Amelia, who studied with Shinita at university. Matthew, Amelia's fiancé, whom Emma had not forgiven for introducing her to Dave. They donned jackets against the fresh sea breeze, clustered their stools around a bar table and chatted as the afternoon faded to evening. The sunset glinted off the bay, casting shadows across the table and washing their faces with bronze.

She spotted Luke at last. He waved as he made his way through the crowded space. The knot in her chest unfurled, then tightened again. Her decision to invite him had been impulsive, poorly considered. She'd kept it casual. *I'm meeting some friends for a drink, if you'd like a break from study?*

Now he was here, a series of emotions rolled over her. Relief that he hadn't stood her up. A nervous twinge that she was introducing him to old friends when she hardly knew him. A warm tingle in her belly as he approached.

Luke settled in beside her and smiled as she introduced him around. He'd rolled up the sleeves of a white linen shirt and paired it with dark chinos. His clothes and shoes looked new, and she wondered if he'd bought them for the occasion. If so, he'd chosen well: he blended in with the upmarket clientele, a perfect chameleon. Emma noted her friends' reactions: Brooke's sly side glance at Amelia, Shinita's smile, Matthew's surprise. She tried to see Luke through their eyes—a tall, athletic guy with a friendly face, short blond hair, nice clothes.

They didn't know what she did: that he'd held Phil's hand for an hour while he was distressed. That he'd made her sit and eat when she was so frazzled she couldn't articulate her hunger. That his very presence slowed her breathing and reassured her the world wasn't mad. And they wouldn't see, as she did, that his smile didn't quite reach his wary eyes.

Emma pushed off her stool and put a hand on Luke's arm to check he was real. 'A drink? Beer?'

She left him to make small talk with her friends, giving him no time to protest, as he answered the usual questions about what he did and how they'd met. When she returned, they were talking about Amelia and Matthew's engagement. Brooke's plans for another half-marathon. Shinita's trouble with her supervisor. The conversation turned to a dispute between Amelia and Matthew, who supported different teams in the recent football finals. Luke was a peacemaker, skilled at turning the conversation away from conflict. And away from himself.

Every time she stole a peek in his direction, she met his eyes, and he stifled his smile, as though he'd been sprung watching her.

Emma finished another vodka, aware of the warm flush of her cheeks and that Luke was sitting on his beer, barely sipping it. Two drinks weren't usually enough to make her light-headed, but it had been another long day. She sat back, subdued, as Luke and Matthew bantered about cricket and Shinita and Amelia talked about work. The familiarity was soothing, a slice of normality her chaotic life lacked.

They ordered bar food—a cheese and antipasto platter, bread and dips—and she caught Luke watching her as she dipped pita bread into baba ghanoush and savoured it.

'Stop it,' she said, bumping his arm.

He laughed, said, 'May I?' and brushed something off her chin.

His touch made her shiver, and she battled a mad desire to take his hand and entice him down onto the beach. To talk, maybe. Or not. As she toyed with the idea, Matthew raised a hand to point across the room. 'Dave's here.'

'You invited Dave?' Emma's fantasy fled. Her hand shook as she picked up her glass. It was empty. She wished it wasn't.

'Yeah, why?'

With a shrug, she arranged her face in a relaxed expression. She flicked a glance to Shinita, who returned a subtle eye roll. Unlike the others, Shinita knew the whole saga.

Emma's skin crawled as Dave crossed the room. Two vodkas were not enough to face him. Everything that had attracted her now seemed abhorrent. He was five years older than her, conventionally handsome in a dark-haired and square-jawed way, with an aura of confidence visible from space. A sense of impending disaster made her squirm in her seat. She turned to Luke and said, 'Umm . . .'

'Who's this, Em?' Dave stopped opposite her, his eyes tightening as they fixed on Luke.

Unfazed, Luke offered his hand to shake. 'Luke Harris.' His handshake must have been too firm; it brought a spasm of discomfort to Dave's face. 'Sorry, I missed your name. Darren?'

Emma swallowed back a laugh as Dave corrected him.

'Another drink?' Luke put a hand on her shoulder as he got up, with a faint squeeze. She nodded, looking up to meet his eyes and hoping he understood. His nod reassured her. 'Dave? Can I get you anything?'

There was no response, so Luke moved off to the bar.

One thing she could rely on with Dave: he was as stubborn as they came. He said nothing, just stared. She guessed he was waiting for an apology.

She glued her lips shut and allowed the silence to stretch into awkwardness.

When Luke returned, he handed her a glass and settled in as though nothing was wrong.

Dave leaned across the table. 'Who are you, then? What do you do?'

'I work for a money launderer. I'm in compliance mostly, some enforcement. You know, breaking fingers, tossing people off buildings, that kind of thing.' Luke sipped his beer, while Emma spluttered into her drink. Dave's mouth had fallen open; Luke laughed. 'Jesus, I'm joking. I'm studying commerce.'

'Right.' Dave gave him a wary side eye, then explained without a hint of humility that he was training to be a surgeon. 'Did Emma tell you about me?'

'Don't think so.' Luke cut her a knowing glance.

Dave dropped off his stool. 'Emma—a word?'

It was probably safe, given the number of witnesses. She cast an apologetic smile to Luke and followed Dave down the four steps leading to the beach path.

'Stop. I'm not going any further.' She planted her feet by the rear of the deck. Pedestrian traffic passed them by.

Dave stalked a few steps past her then back, wiping an angry hand over his mouth. 'What the fuck, Emma? You don't answer my calls, you block my phone—'

'I told you it's over.'

Rounding on her, far too close, he hissed into her face, 'You said you wanted a break! Now stop messing with me and—'

Emma lowered her voice, imagining she was Chantel again, and injected steel into her tone. 'I've told you a hundred times. You need to stop calling me.'

'You've been seeing this guy on the side? How long—'

'None of your business.' A step backwards, and she found the deck behind her, blocking her retreat.

Dave grasped her arm, drawing her in so his face was close to hers. His fingers dug into her arm, and fear curled her guts. Surely, he wouldn't be stupid enough to—

'You need me, Emma.' He forced the words out.

'Everything alright?' Luke's tone was casual. She hadn't registered his arrival. He leaned against the deck a few feet away, calmly watching.

'You're interrupting,' Dave said.

Ignoring Dave, Luke raised his eyebrows. 'Emma?'

'I'm going inside.' She tried to flick Dave off, mortified that the interaction had been witnessed. Shame soaked her.

'I'm not finished.' Dave jerked her back as she turned, but Luke wedged himself between them and lifted Dave's hand from her arm. Backing away, Emma shivered at the sudden tension as the two faced each other.

'Enough.' Luke's voice was dangerously quiet.

With a crimson flush to his cheeks, Dave puffed out his chest, stuck his chin in the air and poked a forefinger at Luke. 'Get out of my face!'

Luke's expression hardened; his eyes narrowed and his mouth formed a straight line. He dropped his chin and leaned forwards—into Dave, rather than away—and shifted his weight onto the balls of his feet.

Emma retreated, thinking, *Shit*.

After a pause, Dave stepped back.

'Wise.' A note of disappointment shaded Luke's tone.

'I'm going home.' Emma flounced up the stairs. She risked a glance back: Luke followed her, and Dave stood glowering by the path. When they reached the table, she whispered into Shinita's ear, 'I'm out of here. Dave's a nutjob.' She put a hand on Luke's arm. 'Did you drive? Can you take me home? I got an Uber in case I had a few drinks.'

The street was busy with the warm Friday evening, and they walked the two blocks in silence. When they reached his car, Luke stuck the keys in the ignition while Emma slid into the passenger seat.

'I'm sorry. I'm an idiot. I can't believe Matthew invited him.' She wrapped her arms around her chest like protective armour. 'I'm so sorry.'

'Not your fault. Narcissistic fuck-knuckle, eh?'

'I thought he was going to hit you.' Tears welled; she blinked them away.

With a tight smile, he said, 'So did I. It wouldn't have ended the way he wanted.' Before he could say more, a phone buzzed, and he patted his pockets to find it. 'Emma, I have to take this.' Into the phone he said, 'Yes?'

The tinny voice was clearly audible. 'That how you answer your phone these days, Jackie?'

Luke held the phone out from his ear. 'I'm busy.'

'What did you say to Mouse? He was spooked.'

With a glance at Emma, Luke said, 'Just told him to pull his head in.'

'Anything on Kevin? Quin?'

'Nothing so far.'

A grunt. 'I might need you tonight. At the gym.'

'Gus, I'm not—'

'Keep the phone on. Be ready.'

The call ended abruptly, leaving Luke staring at the screen.

Emma turned in her seat, questions churning. *Jackie?* And, *Mouse?* 'What was that about?'

'You heard?'

'Hard not to.'

'Long story. My father's not answering his phone. That was a friend of his.' He started the car and drew out into the light evening traffic.

'Are you worried?'

'Not yet.' He reached for her hand and squeezed it. Her breath caught with surprise, but she didn't pull away. The warmth of his hand was an unexpected comfort, a tether to reality. 'So. Dave. Does this explain your phone beeping all the time?'

She blew out a breath. 'I broke up with him a few months ago. I tried to, at least.'

'Can't imagine why. What a charmer.'

'Oh, he was charming at first.' Emma rested back in her seat, acutely aware of Luke's touch. Holding hands was an underestimated intimacy; it felt simple and honest, a communication deeper than words. 'But he was always critical, always angry about something. If I asked what, he was furious that I couldn't read his mind.'

'Did he ever tell you?'

'He didn't like what I wore, what I said, how I appeared in public. He thought I flirted with other guys—made me doubt everything I did.' Pausing, she questioned her sanity in disclosing all this. 'He wanted to get married. Have kids. I said I was too young, that I wanted a career first. He laughed at me. Told me I should go into teaching because acting isn't a real job. When I argued—well, you saw what he was like.'

A muscle in Luke's jaw twitched. 'Yelling into your face, leaving bruises on your arm?'

'He says I'm not listening, but what he means is I don't agree with him.'

'Let me guess: Jonathan liked him?'

Surprised, she shook her head. 'No, Dad hated him. Said he had a weak personality and wanted to marry into money. Dad's an annoyingly good judge of character. He has a way of seeing through people.'

Luke fell silent until they reached her house. Emma regretted her words, fearing she'd said something wrong. Twilight had settled, the sun dropping below the skyline in the city. He parked in the driveway and turned in his seat to face her.

Emma gazed at her hand, twirled her fingers around his. 'I'm sorry. I thought it would do you good to get away from your books. I thought you'd like my friends.'

'Your friends are great. It was fun until he showed up. And Dave's behaviour is his responsibility, not yours.'

The reassurance glanced off her; she was still ashamed she hadn't anticipated Dave's appearance. Of course he'd turn up the moment he knew where she was. 'Thanks for coming. It was good to see you.' It came out wrong, and she cringed.

Luke said, 'You know he's going to escalate after this, right?'

'Yeah. I know.'

He caught his lip; he had more to say, but chose not to. She watched his face change, a couple of fleeting expressions he was quick to dispel. Wondering how to tell her he didn't want to get involved, maybe? He was the kind of guy who'd let her down lightly. She had only herself to blame for allowing Dave to interfere.

'I should go,' she said, but his hand was still wrapped around hers, and when she went to move he held on.

'Emma, I shouldn't have intervened. I'm sorry if I caused trouble for you.'

'God, no. Not your fault.' A ghoulish part of her wondered what would have happened had Dave swung a punch. She extricated her hand and forced herself out of the car.

Luke walked her to the gate. With a hand on his arm, she reached up to kiss him goodbye, then paused with her cheek against his.

She held her breath, worried that the slightest movement might break the spell. Luke brushed her hair from her face, tucked it behind her ear. Stuck in suspended animation, in a not-quite embrace, neither of them moved. The longer they stood, the deeper the silence grew.

'Will you be alright?' His words were lost in her hair.

Emma put her hands on his chest and turned her face against his. The warmth of his breath tickled her skin. 'I'm fine.' She leaned into him, her fingers curling into his shirt. He felt solid and steady, a counterweight pulling her back to the earth while her head floated in the clouds. 'I'd invite you in, but . . . Dad's home.'

With a soft laugh, he tipped his head forwards so his lips touched hers. 'When can I see you again?'

The tension in her belly unfurled. 'After your exams. You need to study.'

'Deal. But we can talk, right?'

'Deal.' She stood on her tiptoes to kiss him, then fled through the gate before she could do anything stupid.

CHAPTER ELEVEN

FRIDAY, 9.20 PM

From the driver's seat of his car, Luke stared at the closed gate. The night deepened with Emma's departure, as though a light had gone out. Through his open window, the ocean breeze curled around his neck and made the hair on his forearms stand up. Cooling down after the warm day, the bayside suburb gave off a cloying smell of asphalt and salt air and relief. A hum of traffic carried from the highway, like a far-off swarm of uncoordinated bees.

Dave's arrogance, Gus's call, Emma's kiss: the three distractions ran around his mind, competing for space. It was a long time since he'd shared a kiss like that. A word from Emma and he would have braved Jonathan to see where it could lead. His senses buzzed, firing in all directions; he clenched and unclenched his fists, stretched his neck left and right, forced himself to relax.

He'd been close to losing his cool with Dave. Jack Quinlan was not buried as deeply as he'd hoped.

A white van slowed as it passed the Wylie house, crawling along the street as though scoping the area. It turned into the lane providing access to the side of the property. A flare of red—brake lights—was visible from the street. The van had stopped alongside the house.

Luke was out of his car before he formed a conscious thought. He rounded the corner with wary steps.

The front doors of the van opened and closed in unison as two men emerged. From the driver's side, a wiry, dark-haired man in shorts and a work shirt; from the passenger side, a bulky, bald man in grease-stained overalls. The tailgate creaked as the driver wrenched it open. The bigger man extracted a set of boltcutters and ambled to the metal gate that led into the Wylies' backyard. A chain, passing through D-shaped holes, held the two halves of the gate closed. The man snipped the chain as though it were made of cotton. It rattled to the ground; he tried to reach through the hole to turn the latch, but his hand was too big.

'Gordy.' He gestured to the smaller man. 'See if you can budge that.'

Luke, standing by the entrance of the alley, paused to process the scene. It seemed too early in the night for a burglary, and yet Gordy was rattling at the latch, leaning awkwardly into the gate with his right arm reaching through the hole.

'Dunno, Ivan. It's stuck.'

'What's holding it? Let me look.'

Luke strolled towards the two men with his hands in his pockets and cleared his throat. 'Hey, fellas. Can I make a suggestion?'

'What?' The big man—Ivan—turned, boltcutters in hand.

'Find another place to rob. I mean, take your pick.' Luke waved a vague hand. 'Any other house on the street.'

'You think you're funny?'

'And it's a bit early, isn't it? Wait until everyone's asleep, at least.'

'Piss off.' Ivan straightened. He had a few inches and at least thirty kilos on Luke. His hands were like melons, as big and round as his head. Brandishing the boltcutters like a weapon, he took a step towards Luke. 'Mind your own business.'

Luke's tone hardened. 'Leave or I'll call the cops.' He took his phone from his pocket.

'Walk away, dickhead.'

Ivan flicked a glance to Gordy. Luke didn't understand the communication between them. He touched his thumb to the screen as though to make a call.

'Really?' Luke's thumb hovered.

Ivan shifted his weight, preparing to attack, but Gordy was quicker. He rushed in with his hand outstretched to wrench Luke's phone away.

But Luke's phone was safely in his pocket, and Gordy's hand closed over air. The heel of Luke's right hand smacked upwards under his jaw, jarring his teeth into a painful bite and knocking his head backwards. Gordy crumpled with a howl as Luke's foot hit his knee.

As Gordy recoiled from the kick, Luke ducked a swipe from Ivan that would have taken off his head had it connected. He wasn't so quick with the next, and Ivan's fist brushed the side of his face. Luke darted inside the man's range, lowered his shoulder and jammed it against the meatiest ribs he'd ever tried to break. He landed a few punches, but Ivan got his hands under Luke's arms, lifting him off his feet to slam him against the metal gate. The force knocked the air out of Luke's lungs. The man's arm drew back and Luke dropped below it just in time. Ivan grunted as his fist clanged against the gate.

Gordy scooped up the boltcutters from the cobblestones, limping on his injured knee. Luke dodged his first swipe by swinging under Ivan's armpit, putting the big man between him and the weapon. He got in a solid punch to the guy's kidney. Ivan spun around, searching for his target, and ran straight into an expert three-punch combination: jab, cross, hook.

Confused, Ivan took a few stumbling steps back and swayed on his feet, putting a hand on the gate for support. Blood dripped from his nose, and his mouth hung open, but he didn't clutch his head or double over like most people would after three blows to the face.

As Luke retreated, shaking out his jarred hands, he spotted Gordy in his peripheral vision, swinging the boltcutters with two hands like a baseball bat. Luke snatched the end with his left hand, pulled the man off balance towards him and, when he was close enough, jabbed him in the face with his right.

'Fuck!' The smaller man, unlike his comrade, bent in half and yowled with pain. He melted to the ground.

'I told you to leave.' Luke kept his eyes on Ivan, who was shaking himself off. 'Time to go, fellas?' He jerked his head towards the van and weighed up the boltcutters, clicking on the catch that kept the handles together. He transferred them to his dominant right hand, with a feeling they might come in handy.

'Fuck that.' Ivan bared his bloodied teeth like a dog as he rounded on Luke. 'You're gonna pay for this. I'm gonna—'

It wasn't clear exactly what he was gonna do, because Luke saw his clumsy punch a mile away. Luke sidestepped and let it hit air, let Ivan overcommit. 'Really? Seriously?'

'You think you're funny?' Ivan, recovering, latched on to Luke's left forearm so hard that Luke could feel his bones grinding together. Ivan got in another punch, grazing Luke's cheekbone. It knocked Luke backwards, even as he struggled to break away from the man's grasp. He felt stretched, as though the left side of his body was pulled in one direction and the right was pushed in the other.

Ivan grabbed for the boltcutters. Luke swung the tool against the man's undefended ribs and he grunted, but his grip didn't waver.

Luke twisted, opening the space between him and his opponent so he could get a swing up, and smashed the tool against the man's outstretched arm. A groan of pain, and the hand unclasped: he was free.

'You broke my fucking arm!'

'I told you to leave.'

'Fuck this!' Ivan's round face contorted with pain, sucking into itself like a deflated airbag. He backed off, cradling his right arm in his left.

'Let's get out of here.' Gordy picked himself up off the cobblestones, cursing as he put weight on his injured knee. He cast a narrowed side eye at Luke and hobbled to the van.

Luke stood aside as the van reversed out of the alley. He considered the weapon in his hand, the blood staining the ground, the Wylies' gate. He thought about calling the police. But he'd have to wait for them to arrive, and they would want to know why he held the boltcutters and whose blood it was on the cobblestones and who had injured whom. They'd want to see ID; they'd ask who he was. He didn't need that kind of attention.

For a nanosecond, he thought about going inside to tell Jonathan, but Jonathan would be as bad as the police.

The Samsung in his pocket beeped.

Ed: *Boss is up to something keep your phone on.*

Realising that he'd better get cleaned up and ready for whatever Gus wanted, Luke tossed the boltcutters into his car and drove home with his hands gripping the steering wheel and his head full of noise.

He reached the safety of his flat and headed for the bathroom. His new white shirt was spattered with blood and went straight into the basin with cold water to soak. The shoes and pants would need cleaning too. He showered, scrubbing with soap and hot water to remove any blood or DNA; then he turned off the hot tap and stood under the freezing water until he couldn't stand it a second longer.

He lay on his bed and stared up at the ceiling.

It was years since he'd fought like that. When he closed his eyes, the scene replayed in his mind and body. He saw it, heard it, felt it: his kick hitting Gordy's knee, his fist cracking on Ivan's face, the sting in his knuckles, the force echoing all the way up his arm to his shoulder. The boltcutters smashing Ivan's bones.

Memories of other fights flashed across his consciousness, escaping from the deep crypt where he kept them buried. Hands on his throat. Fists in his face. Winded from a gut punch. Breathing into cracked ribs. His knuckles abraded and bleeding. Purple bruises on his elbows, forearms, shins. The hot breath of his opponent. The sour tang of blood in his mouth. The flush of exhilaration at winning; the humility of losing. The fear of pain. Of death.

And on cue, the memory of the first time he'd fought for his life resurfaced. He pressed his fingertips to his eyes, but it didn't take away the images or stop the panic from flooding his body. His chest tightened and his guts loosened and he lay immobile, at the mercy of the flashback, until it faded to a tolerable level. And then, purposefully, he brought the memory to the surface and replayed it, like a movie, as though he was sitting back with a tub of popcorn to watch. An impartial observer.

They're your memories, Jack, the psychologist had said. *You're in charge.*

CHAPTER TWELVE

FIFTEEN YEARS AGO

The suburb of Sunshine was deceptively named, as far as Jack was concerned: it was grey and industrial, a maze of decrepit housing and suspicious faces. He hated Quin's new rental the moment he saw it. The gloomy mission-brown brick accurately predicted the cramped, dingy interior. The flimsy plaster walls, painted a sallow peach, made everything look sickly. Jack missed the solidity of Gail's old house, with its double-brick walls and heavy doors. He missed the magnolia tree in the front garden and the rambling backyard with space to kick a football. He missed Gail's cooking and the smell of sausages.

He refused to change schools, which meant catching a bus to Footscray every day. They had moved on a rainy weekend in April, and Jack had walked to the train station to buy a weekly ticket and pick up the timetable.

The first time he caught the bus—alone, because it had been his idea—he was terrified. He worried he'd bought the wrong ticket, the driver would growl at him, or he'd hit the red *Stop* button at the wrong time. But after a few weeks, he settled in to the routine. He badgered Quin once a week for fifteen bucks for his fares and used the spare change Quin left lying around to buy snacks at the school canteen.

One afternoon after school, he was wandering towards the bus stop, thinking about food, when a voice stopped him.

'Hey.' A man sauntered closer. 'You're Mickey Quinlan's kid?'

The man was bigger and tougher than Quin: close-clipped hair, black jacket, bad teeth.

Jack put on a brave front. 'Yeah, he's my dad, whatever.'

'Where is he?'

'I dunno. Try calling him?'

'I've been calling for days, smart-arse. Where is he?'

Jack's bus pulled up. He edged towards it. 'I dunno. I gotta go.'

On the bus, he replayed the incident in his mind, gnawing on the inside of his cheek. When he got home, he made cheese toasties and tried to distract himself. He read some of his library book (*The Sea of Monsters*, the second in the Percy Jackson series), but he couldn't concentrate. He watched repeat episodes of *The Simpsons* on television, but that didn't help either.

Several hours later, the key turned in the lock.

'You still up?' Silhouetted in the doorway, Quin looked smaller than Jack remembered. Much smaller than the man looking for him.

'There was a guy outside school. Looking for you.'

'Who?' Quin's keys clinked in the bowl on the hall table.

Jack told him everything, word for word.

'Shit.' Quin flopped onto the couch.

'Who is he?'

'Robbo Parker,' Quin said.

'What does he want?'

'Three grand, that's what he wants.' Quin grunted. 'And if I had that much cash, do you think I'd be driving that piece of shit out there?'

'You owe him money.' It wasn't a question: it was a sigh, from a ten-year-old who understood his father's specific inability to hold on to money. Jack had heard it all before. Quin had borrowed cash, stolen it or lost it at the races. This led to a series of threatening phone calls, then a black eye or two. Quin would find the money by borrowing or stealing from someone else, and the cycle continued.

Once, Jack lost patience and asked why Quin didn't get a regular job. Like the people who worked in offices or shops or cafes or garages. Like Gail, or even Kevin. Quin's response had been lukewarm: *I'm not cut out for that kind of thing.* His casual work for Malcolm was as much as he could handle.

Three thousand dollars seemed like an enormous amount of money. The most Jack had held in his hands was a twenty-dollar note—which he had, being his father's son, stolen from Quin's wallet.

'What are you going to do?' Jack's question was serious. He could often see flaws in plans that Quin couldn't, and he was much better with numbers. Once Quin had given a debtor nearly double because he couldn't work out what twenty percent interest was. Since then, Jack had offered to help whenever cash was involved. He told Quin it was part of his homework for maths.

Quin shrugged. 'I'll borrow it. I've got tips for Thursday at Moonee Valley. If I can get some money on a quaddie, it'll be fine.'

Jack wanted to shout at his father's stupidity. Quin's poor understanding of odds and high tolerance of risk were a terrible combination.

Instead, he asked, 'Where'd you get the tip?'

'Malcolm. He knows all the trainers. His brother-in-law's a bookie.'

'Wasn't it Malcolm who gave you tips last time?'

Jack watched as Quin's brain kicked into gear and he remembered the last time he'd gone on a betting spree with Malcolm's tips. He'd lost so much money he'd had to sell his car to pay a debt.

In the morning, Jack tiptoed into Quin's room and filched a fiver to get breakfast on the way to school. A hole-in-the-wall place near the train station made a mean bacon-and-egg roll, which was a luxury, but he had a feeling Quin's finances were about to take a hit.

He ate his breakfast on the bus, thinking about what three thousand dollars would look like. Would it fit in his backpack? He'd seen crime shows on television where perps carried briefcases full of cash. Usually American money, green and sombre. Not cheerful like a pile of pineapples.

He stepped off the bus, turning to walk along the main road towards school.

'Kid.'

Shit.

Robbo Parker fell into step beside him. 'Where's your old man?'

'Leave me alone.' Jack picked up his pace.

Robbo grabbed him by the arm. 'Come on, kid. Don't make this hard.'

Jack wanted to tell him to fuck off, but fear froze his tongue. 'Let me go.' A whimper, not the roar he'd intended. 'I'll scream.'

'No you won't. You're pissing your pants too much to even talk. Just like your shit-for-brains father.'

The words goaded Jack: he struggled against Robbo as he found his voice. 'Lemme go!'

'Fuck this.' Robbo dragged him towards the kerb, bleeped a car open and shoved Jack headfirst into the back seat. There was no time to respond; before Jack could sit up, the car had pulled out into traffic.

'Sit there and shut up,' came the command from the driver's seat.

Jack flung himself against the car door, but it wouldn't open. The plastic latch flipped uselessly under his fingers. The doors were on an automatic lock that Robbo controlled by a panel in the driver's door.

'Never thought I'd need the child locks.' Robbo laughed. 'Where are we going? Where is he?'

'Let me out.' Jack's head felt light. Black dots threatened his vision.

Robbo ignored him and hit buttons on his steering wheel: bluetooth for his mobile phone. A dial tone sounded on the car speakers. Jack stopped pulling at the door, fascinated, as he heard his father's voice.

'*Quin. Leave a message.*' A long, protracted beep.

Robbo said, 'I've got your kid in the car with me and he's gonna tell me where you are, alright? We're on our way. Have the money ready.'

He ended the call and slowed for a red light. Jack recoiled into the back seat as Robbo turned to look at him, his broad face twisted into an expression Jack couldn't read. A mean smile, appraising eyes.

'You don't take after Quin,' he said. 'You look like Susie, though.'

Shocked, Jack said, 'You knew my mum?'

'She used to hang out with the band. Posh Pommy bird. Legs up to here . . .' Robbo indicated somewhere around head height. 'Far too good-looking for Quin. She was nuts, though. Freaking fruit loop.'

Thanks, Jack thought sourly. His memories of his mother were vague but sweet. And while he didn't appreciate Robbo's tone, he ached to know more. Any time he'd asked Quin about her, the conversation had been shut down.

The light went green and Robbo gunned the accelerator. 'I need a direction, kid.'

'I'm gonna be sick.'

'Spew in the car and I'll slap you into next year.'

A ringtone pierced the air. Robbo hit buttons on his steering wheel and Quin's disembodied voice filled the cabin. He sounded as though he'd just woken up. 'What the fuck, Robbo!'

Robbo turned to Jack. 'Say hello to your dad.'

Jack hugged his backpack and shook his head.

Abruptly, Robbo pulled the car to the kerb, reached into the rear and grabbed Jack by his collar, wrenching him over the centre console. Jack let out an involuntary howl of shock. 'I said, *say hello*.'

'Quin!' Jack squirmed out of Robbo's grip. 'Call the cops or something!'

'Yeah, right,' Robbo scoffed. 'I don't think there'll be any police involved, do you, Quin?'

'Give me two days!'

'You think the kid wants to wait two days?'

Turning again to Jack, he raised his eyebrows, as though it were a real question. Jack retreated into the back seat, clutching his backpack and wishing Quin had let him get a phone. He'd call the cops, even if Quin wouldn't.

'Didn't think so. Tell me where you are.'

'I'll get your money,' Quin said.

And hung up.

Fuck, thought Jack.

'The address—*now*.' Robbo glared in the rear-view mirror. 'You might as well tell me. I'm gonna beat it out of you eventually.'

Jack looked at his hands, at the scar Kevin had given him. Bloody Quin. He made poor choices when it came to friends.

Robbo grabbed his shoulder, shook him and slapped his ear. Jack blurted out the address.

When they reached the house in Sunshine, Robbo pulled up outside. 'What a fucking dump.' His assessment gelled perfectly with Jack's. 'Let's see if Daddy's home.'

Robbo marched him up the concrete steps to the front door and banged on it. The house remained stubbornly silent. Jack already knew his father had fled, because his borrowed Toyota was gone from the driveway.

Robbo grunted. 'Fucker. He's done a runner. Is there a spare key?'

Jack figured there was no point arguing. His face stung where Robbo had slapped him. 'I've got one in my bag.'

Inside, the house was cold and dark and unwelcoming. Robbo went from room to room, checking for Quin. He kept a hand on Jack's collar, dragging him along.

When it was clear Quin wasn't there, Robbo shoved Jack into a dining chair. 'Sit there and shut up.'

'I'm supposed to be at school.' The bacon-and-egg roll reappeared in Jack's throat as his stomach heaved. He gulped it back down.

'Do I look like I give a fuck?' Robbo rifled through the kitchen drawers.

'What are you looking for?'

'Duct tape.'

Jack said, 'It's in the laundry cupboard.'

Robbo eyed him suspiciously. 'Show me.'

The laundry, a poky room beside the kitchen, had a sink, an ancient washing machine and a rarely used door to the outside.

Jack opened the cupboard to demonstrate the mess of stashed tools and hardware items and cleaning implements. It came to him in a rush, as Robbo reached over him and plucked a roll of silver duct tape from a shelf, what the tape was for.

Panicking, he ducked out from under Robbo's arm and lunged towards the external door. He managed to pull it open a sliver before Robbo slammed it shut.

A fist cracked against his left cheek, knocking him back against the cupboard door. His legs crumpled under him. Squeezing his eyes shut against the pain in his face, he flopped onto his hands and knees and tried to stand.

'Get up.' Robbo's words were a growl.

Jack tried to move, but his limbs wouldn't respond. The laundry floor was dusty under his hands.

Robbo lashed out, his foot catching Jack in the chest. Jack cowered with his arms over his head. With a hand fisted on Jack's collar, Robbo hauled him to his feet, leaning down to spit words into his face. 'Thought you'd run off on me, you little shit?'

Winded, Jack couldn't answer.

Robbo pushed him to the living room and into the chair again.

Jack held his breath as Robbo tore off lengths of duct tape and fastened him to the chair. His lower legs were taped to the legs of the chair; his wrists were bound together.

'What—are—you going to—do?' Jack couldn't breathe past the pain in his ribs. Panic made his vision blurry.

'Shut the fuck up.' A backhand to Jack's cheek nearly knocked the chair over. Robbo tore off a strip of tape and plastered it onto Jack's mouth: the conversation was finished.

After another rustle in the kitchen drawers, Robbo brandished the small, sharp knife Jack used for cutting cheese.

As he turned, weighing it in his right hand, the man's face broke into a smirk. 'Shitting yourself now, aren't you?'

Jack shrank into the chair as Robbo approached, terrified as much by the man's unhinged grin as he was of the weapon. Robbo pressed the blade against Jack's throat, hard enough to sting. Jack's head floated and his vision blurred; he blinked frantically to clear it, afraid to take a breath in case he moved against the knife.

With the knife in one hand and his phone in the other, Robbo clicked off a couple of photos.

When Robbo retreated, focused on his phone, Jack sucked in a breath, then gasped as the pain caught his injured ribs. He panted in shallow, irregular gulps, as Robbo called Quin. The volume was loud enough that Jack heard the answer.

'*Quin. Leave a message.*'

'Quin, you fucker,' Robbo said. 'I've sent you a cute picture. Get your arse here with my money. I'll give you an hour.'

An hour seemed both a very short time and a very long time. Robbo paced the lounge like a caged, angry, perspiring animal, wearing a path in the already scuffed carpet as he turned the knife over in his hand and muttered to himself. He made coffee, then tipped it out because there was no milk.

Jack's imagination took off, racing with questions and worst-case scenarios. What was Quin doing? Could he get the money together in an hour? What would Robbo do if Quin didn't come through?

He's going to kill me. The thought crept up on him and expanded until it was undeniable.

Fear swirled, muddling his thoughts with rising panic—fear that this was it, that his life might be over before he got a chance to do all the things he wanted to do. He hadn't finished primary school. He'd never kissed a girl. He'd never kicked a goal in front of a crowd.

His bladder was close to bursting. He squeezed to hold on.

Pins and needles tingled his feet from being stuck in the one position too long; his hands were useless in his lap. When he swallowed, the taste of blood made him gag. Blood dripping from his nose made him sniff intermittently, which earned him annoyed backhands from Robbo. He'd lost count of the slaps.

As the hour dragged, as he squashed down the fear of his impending death, he found another focus: humiliation. He was so small and helpless that a lowlife like Robbo could overpower him. Humiliation led to resentment, a stepping stone to anger.

As he watched Robbo pacing, he started to burn. His eyes were hot—not with tears, but with fury. His jaw clenched and his stomach tightened. He wanted to spring out of the chair and hammer his fists into Robbo's face. Scratch his eyes, bite him, kick him in the nuts. He wanted to cause *pain*.

But more pressing than that, he really, *really* needed to pee.

The hour ticked over, and there was no sign of Quin.

Robbo stood over Jack, hands on hips, thinking. When he reached out, Jack recoiled, expecting a slap, but instead Robbo tore the tape off his face. Jack gasped aloud with the pain. He felt as though half his face was ripped off.

'Where the hell is Quin?'

Jack bottled his rage and panted, 'I really need the toilet.'

Robbo adjusted his jeans. 'I'm gonna untie you, you go piss. Do anything stupid and you'll pay for it.'

Jack's legs were like jelly; he sat on the toilet to recover, relishing the privacy. He ran his hands over his bleeding face and checked the bruising on his ribs. After holding on for an hour, his bladder took a while to respond.

He took so long Robbo banged on the door. 'What are you doing in there?'

Jack's hackles rose and heat flared behind his eyes. Standing, he tested his arms and legs, which were coming back to life. He considered his two options for survival, which came down to probabilities: the probability of Quin paying up in time to prevent Robbo from killing him versus the probability that Jack could get away from Robbo. The odds of either seemed slim. Facts came to him: Quin had no access to funds. Robbo had a knife. Jack was the fastest runner in his school.

Robbo pushed open the toilet door. 'What's taking so—'

Jack kicked him hard in the shin.

With a howl, Robbo grabbed at him, but Jack followed up with another kick, aimed at the man's groin.

He missed.

Robbo grasped Jack's hair and swung him headfirst out of the toilet cubicle and into the corridor wall. Jack jerked around so that his shoulder hit the wall instead of his head, leaving a dent in the plaster.

Dodging Robbo by keeping low to the ground, Jack covered the distance to the front door in a stumbling run, with Robbo's outraged shout following him. He grabbed the doorhandle as Robbo clamped a vice-like hand on his shoulder.

'Come back here, you little—'

'Get off me!' Jack flailed wildly, reaching for anything he could use as a weapon. His hand closed over the chipped ceramic bowl on the hall table, which Quin used to dump his keys and loose change and debris from his pockets. Without thinking—Jack's mind had blanked with panic—he swung it upwards.

The bowl hit Robbo's chin with a satisfying clunk. A roar of pain, and Robbo's hand left him to fly up to his face.

The bowl thudded on the carpet. Jack wrenched open the door and sprinted for his life.

Later, long past his usual bedtime, Jack stood on the doorstep of an unassuming house in a suburb he didn't know. His case worker from Children's Services hit the doorbell. She'd packed his belongings into one of Quin's bags; he had his school backpack on.

From the moment he flagged down a security guard at the train station, he'd been thrust into an unpleasant spotlight. He'd been taken to hospital, where the nurses called the police. He told his story a hundred times. The suspicious cop found it hard to believe what had happened—so much that Jack lost his temper and kicked a chair and it hit her in the leg—and she wouldn't believe that it wasn't Quin who'd hit him, because they'd arrested Quin and his mate Steve outside the house in Sunshine, where they'd beaten Robbo up, and apparently Jack's story had holes. The case worker had swooped in and growled at the cop to leave Jack alone.

Exhausted, Jack had asked could he please just go back to Gail's, but the case worker shook her head. Quin's arrest had triggered a formal process, and she knew all about Quin and Kevin and Gail and Jack's history. *You need somewhere stable to live. I've arranged an emergency foster home.*

Mr and Mrs Dewey were older than Gail, older than any of his teachers. Jack came into their care with a sulky glower and simmering anger that lacked a focus. For the first week he refused to go to school unless they let him go back to Footscray, which was out of the question. His rage was a physical presence in the house. He shouted at anyone who looked at him. His foster parents were patient, and let him hide in his room and throw his shoes at the wall—they had removed everything of value from the room—until he tired of it.

Which he did. One day he got up and put on the uniform for his new school and sheepishly ventured out to have breakfast, avoiding eye contact.

Living with the Deweys felt surreal and artificial, like he'd been dropped onto an alien planet. There were definite perks: three meals a day and snacks, a packed lunch for school, the right uniform and books. Proper shoes from a shop where the sales assistant measured his feet. Mrs Dewey—*Liz*, she insisted—took him to the dentist and a doctor for a check-up, and taught him how to cook and tidy. Mr Dewey—*Mark*—taught him how to mow the lawn and make things in the shed. Their house was larger than Gail's and spotlessly clean, but empty; their three children had grown up and moved on with children of their own. Jack had a bedroom to himself, shelves full of books, a desk to do his homework on. Liz's old dog curled up at his feet on his bed (against the rules, but Liz turned a blind eye). He had assigned chores, like washing dishes or taking out rubbish, and was thanked for doing them.

They checked he was doing his homework, praised his grades, put his schoolwork on the fridge with magnets. They asked if he'd like to play football and bought him a new footy jumper and boots. He was driven to school in the morning and picked up in the afternoon.

A sense of order and routine dictated the Deweys' lives, and Jack absorbed it like a sponge. Every day was the same. The only decisions he had to make were about how to spend his time: which book to read, whether to kick a footy, play with a friend, help Liz with dinner. The Deweys were quiet, conservative people. Boring, by some measures. No police banging on the door; no gambling or owing money. Liz had a way of encouraging Jack to do the right thing, with questions like, *What kind of person do you want to be?*

On learning that his grades were at the top of the class, Liz encouraged him to sit a scholarship exam for an academic private school. She assured him the school was excellent, and her enthusiasm cut through his wariness. *They'll let you skip ahead in classes. It'll be a great education—the best way to have the career you want. You're a smart boy, Jack. You could be a doctor or a lawyer if you work hard.*

Liz was ecstatic when the letter arrived offering him a scholarship to Rodley Grammar. Jack's wariness returned—the school was in the city and sounded posh and serious—but her kindness made him eager to please her. Shortly after his enrolment was confirmed, Liz told him that Quin would soon be released from jail.

Quin had served fourteen months of a two-year sentence for assault. On release, he went back to work with Malcolm, found a flat to rent in Footscray and immediately started campaigning for custody of Jack.

A legal process where no one asked Jack's opinion happened around him. Liz and the case worker argued, but in the end Quin won. His application was supported by his parole officer and a well-meaning lawyer from Legal Aid, who claimed discrimination against a single father and insisted that Quin had turned over a new leaf. The overstretched foster system gave up without a fight.

Jack finished primary school with excellent grades, a Most Valuable Player football trophy, and applause from Liz and Mark at the informal graduation ceremony. A month later, he moved back to Footscray with Quin, and his orderly world descended once more into chaos.

CHAPTER THIRTEEN

SATURDAY, 8 AM

The beeping of Luke's phone pierced the fog of sleep. He rolled over and swiped it from the bedside table, silencing it with clumsiness. An ache in his hand confused him until he remembered why. Lying on his back, he held his hands in front of his face. His knuckles were shadowed a dusky purple, with a few spots of broken skin. He'd pulled up worse.

He retrieved the phone from the floor and scanned the messages. The beeping was the frenetic chatter of his study group, who texted at lightning speed in a soup of emojis he usually ignored. With two days until the exam, Caitlin was panicking about statistics. He flopped back onto the bed. He'd call her later.

He had slept fully dressed, expecting to be roused at any moment, but whatever Gus had anticipated, he hadn't needed Luke's help. There were no missed calls or texts on the Samsung. Small mercies.

He padded to the bathroom and splashed water on his face, trying—failing—to avoid his reflection in the mirror. A red mark decorated his jaw on the left, with a darker bruise on his right cheekbone. On his left forearm, a cluster of purple marks reminded him Ivan had tried to crush his ulna into his radius, and there were bruises on his ribs from punches he couldn't remember. It was like that with fights. There were always unexplained injuries. Like the scar on his chin: he still couldn't figure out exactly how that had happened. All he remembered was the futility of the fight.

Last night had been the same, and his stupidity made him close his eyes with shame. He should have walked away. The senseless grind of history repeating soured his mood. The fear there was something intrinsically wrong with him—that he was condemned to a lifetime of fighting and violence—made him hang his head.

He put on running gear and ventured out to clear his mind and loosen his muscles. Ignoring the scattered pains in his body, he tried to use the run as a meditation exercise, focusing on his body, his breath, the sounds and smells of the city, the colours of the beach and sky. But his focus drifted as he ruminated on Gus's call while he was in the car with Emma. Typical Gus, keeping him on his toes. A reminder that he was on the hook.

After his run, he called Caitlin to talk through her statistics problem. She asked, plaintively, what he was doing that day, and he had no answer but managed to refuse an invitation to study with her. He didn't have the energy to come up with a story to explain his bruises.

He'd not long hung up when the phone buzzed with another call. Jonathan's number flashed on the screen, and Luke frowned at it until it stopped.

A text: *Call me.*

The commanding tone irritated him. He paced to the window with his hands on his head. After calming himself down, he blew out a breath and hit redial.

Jonathan answered before the second ring. 'I need to talk to you, now. Come to my office. Park underneath—I'll leave the gate up.'

Luke opened his mouth to argue, but the line had already gone dead.

Curiosity got the better of him, and twenty minutes later he arrived at Jonathan's office building. The modern cube of mirrored glass and steel was like Jonathan himself: cold and soulless. Most of the businesses were closed on a Saturday, and the place seemed deserted. Annoyed by the summons, and with himself for obeying, he punched the elevator buttons harder than he needed to.

The elevator opened into a carpeted foyer. The words *Wylie Consulting* were etched into a frosted glass door. Plush carpet and shiny chrome fittings lent the office an air of genteel sophistication. A reception desk stood unattended, and the lights were dimmed on a long corridor of closed doors. The hushed silence made Luke vigilant. He slowed, checking the corridor and the corners for threats.

'In here.' Jonathan's voice came from a door on the left.

He sat behind a desk in a corner office twice the size of Luke's flat. Expansive windows framed a spectacular view across Albert Park and to the bay beyond. Glass-fronted cabinets and bookshelves lined the other walls. An enormous potted palm filled the corner, fronds spreading out in tropical splendour in an otherwise frosty room.

'Luke. Sit down.'

It was like being called to the principal's office, although Jonathan was meaner than any of Luke's principals had been. Luke settled into an overly soft chair opposite the desk.

Jonathan fiddled with a pen, tapping it against the keyboard of the laptop before him. The expanse of polished desk, clear of any extraneous clutter, separated them. No paperwork, no coffee cups, just a shiny silver MacBook.

The silence was deafening.

'Something you want to share with me?' As always, Jonathan's words held an accusation. His gaze flicked to Luke's abraded knuckles.

Luke chose his words with care. 'Ah . . . okay. There were a couple of guys outside your side gate, in the lane. I asked them not to rob your house.'

'They cut the chain on the gate.' Jonathan nodded. 'And someone bled all over the place. I take it that wasn't you.' His gaze bored into Luke's face.

Another long silence settled, prickling the back of Luke's neck. 'How did you know I was there?'

Jonathan spun the laptop around, angling it so Luke could see the screen. With a touch of the mousepad, a grainy black-and-white image came to life: video footage from a camera placed high above the lane. The prickling on Luke's neck worsened.

On the screen, the van appeared, then the two men. Ivan, a blurry, bulky mass, took the boltcutters to the chain. Luke appeared, his left side to the camera.

Luke's mouth went dry as he watched the fight erupt. The kick to Gordy's knee was vicious. The force of Ivan slamming Luke against the gate seemed enough to shatter a skull. No wonder his back felt sore. Luke had dropped below Ivan's fist with a heartbeat to spare. His knuckles throbbed as he relived punching Ivan in the face. Gordy, limping on an unstable knee, then doubled over with his nose streaming—it was Gordy's blood on the cobblestones—and then the tussle with the boltcutters, and Luke's brutal blow—

'That's my favourite part,' Jonathan said. 'Clean break through both bones, I reckon. Although he's a big son-of-a-bitch. He barely noticed when you punched him.' He replayed the jab Luke delivered to Gordy's face. 'That was more effective. You punch like a boxer. And what was that kick, some kind of martial arts? Where did you learn to fight like that?'

'School.' Luke controlled his breathing. 'I didn't see the camera.' He was vigilant about video surveillance; it bothered him he hadn't picked it.

'It's hidden under the eaves. It's new. Tiny unit.' Jonathan's eyes were glued to the screen, like a kid with a video game. 'I must have watched this a hundred times.' He tapped the mousepad to play it over, a ghoulish smile playing at his mouth.

Luke closed his eyes. The violence was sickening. He resisted the urge to smash a fist into the screen.

Jonathan snapped the laptop closed. His cold gaze came to rest on Luke, who did his best not to flinch. 'So. You asked them not to rob the house. And they refused.'

'I told them I was going to call the police. That's when they attacked me.'

Jonathan chuckled without mirth.

'Look, Jonathan, I'd just dropped Emma home. I knew she was inside. I didn't want them breaking in, alright?'

'Oh, I understand.' He nodded. 'Why didn't you call the police afterwards?'

'They'd gone, and I had somewhere else I needed to be.'

'And you would have had to tell the cops the blood wasn't yours.' Jonathan tapped his pen on the desk. 'You didn't come inside to tell me either.'

'Like I said, I had to go.' Shifting in his seat, Luke asked, 'You didn't hear anything?'

'Phil was watching television. You know how loud he likes it.' Jonathan leaned forwards over the desk. 'If you saw those two men again, would you recognise them?'

'Yes.' He knew their names, too, but it wasn't the question Jonathan had asked.

'I've got the registration of the van. I'd like you to help me identify them.'

'You reported this to the police?' A solid band wrapped around Luke's chest. 'You showed them the video?'

Jonathan steepled his forefingers and tapped them against his lips, observing Luke's reaction. 'Would it relieve you if I said I have no intention of reporting it?'

Luke said nothing.

'I thought so.' The words were soft. 'Those thugs weren't there to rob the house—they were looking for me.'

'What did they want with you?'

'A little trouble I'm having with a client. Happens from time to time in my industry—sometimes I step on toes. It's better not to involve the police.' Jonathan paused. 'But they won't get away with it. You're going to help me find them. I need to stay at arm's length.'

'No.' Luke held up his palms to ward Jonathan off. 'I'm not getting involved.'

'You're already involved.'

'How?'

'The employer of those two'—Jonathan indicated the screen—'will be trying to identify you by now. You think you can break an arm like that and get away with it? They'll want revenge.'

Luke pushed himself out of the chair. With his hands on his head, he wandered to the window to think, gazing out at the tufts of cloud in the pale sky. Jonathan followed and stood beside him.

He registered on Luke's radar, despite their size difference. Luke wouldn't put it past the man to carry a weapon.

'I'll pay you for your time.'

'I don't want your money.'

Jonathan's veneer of civility vanished. 'Don't be ridiculous. Your car is older than you are and you're taking cash shifts during your exams. I know you're broke.'

'I want you to delete that video.'

Jonathan rocked back and forth on his heels, considering. 'I think we can come to an arrangement. You help me find those two, I will pay you generously *and* I'll get rid of the footage. Deal?'

Luke blew out a sigh. 'I'm not doing anything illegal.'

'You need to stay out of trouble, don't you?' Jonathan inclined his head. 'Let me guess. A juvie record you need to keep sealed?'

'I've never been convicted of a crime.' He'd been arrested, questioned and cautioned, but nothing had ever stuck. His record was clean. And since he changed his name, he'd kept well away from cops.

'Careful choice of words.' Jonathan was not fooled.

'I have exams. I finish Tuesday.'

'Fair enough. It can wait a few days.'

Luke hesitated. 'Alright. After my exams. I'll help you find them, and you'll delete that video.'

'Deal.' Jonathan took an envelope from a drawer and tossed it on the desk. 'Consider that a down payment.'

With a controlled exhale to hide his irritation, Luke scooped it up and turned to leave, but Jonathan wasn't done.

'One more thing. About Emma.'

'What about her?'

'Stay away from her. She doesn't need someone like you sniffing around.'

It took Luke a few seconds to find words. 'Are you serious?'

'What do you think she'd say, if she saw this?' Jonathan gestured to his computer. 'Doesn't cast you in a flattering light, does it?'

Luke held his tongue long enough to get out of the office. He waited until he reached his car before looking in the envelope. Jonathan had not lied about being generous. Twenty crisp hundred-dollar bills peeked out at him. It was out of proportion to the simple task; finding Ivan and Gordy was just the beginning. Gus and his rolls of pineapples were the same, a combination of push and pull, carrots and sticks.

As though the thought had summoned him, the Samsung beeped.

Have you found Kevin yet?

Luke texted, *Working on it my exams finish on Tuesday.*

Meet me at the gym Tuesday 10 pm don't be late.

CHAPTER FOURTEEN

SATURDAY, 8.15 PM

Slouched in her car outside Shinita's house, Emma watched the clock on her dash tick over. The minutes stretched out as she delayed her drive home and the inevitable confrontation with Jonathan. Shinita had tried to drag her along for a night on the town—*It'll cheer you up, Em*—but she couldn't find the energy.

She'd spent her Saturday afternoon at work helping Britt, after a power outage sent their IT systems offline. Their manager was out of town and, instead of rushing back to help, had chosen to phone in to yell at them both for not backing everything up the day before.

Stop rolling your eyes, Emma, the manager had said, which was disturbing, because how the hell did he know what face she was pulling?

At least she had her car back in working order. Instead of starting the ignition, she chewed her lip and considered the pros and cons of calling Luke. It felt too soon. She didn't want to scare him off, and a fear that she would put her foot in it made her hesitate. But there was no other way to find out what she wanted to know—other than asking Jonathan, which wasn't going to happen.

She texted, *How's the study going?*

Her phone buzzed instantly.

'I'm having a break for dinner,' Luke said, as though she'd asked the question aloud. 'What are you up to?'

'I'm sitting in my car avoiding Dad.' She slumped down in the seat. Quiet noises carried over the phone line: a clink of cutlery. 'What are you eating?'

'Salmon, rice, broccoli, edamame, pickled ginger.'

'Sounds delicious. I had a greasy pizza with Shinita. What did you do today?'

'You really are procrastinating, aren't you?'

'Maybe I just want to talk to a sane person and not a psycho.'

'I'm sane, am I?'

She laughed, but noted he hadn't answered her question. He had not, for example, explained what his car was doing under her father's office. She'd parked there for a few hours for work. His old Subaru stood out like a bad cliché among the shiny European cars. 'So . . . you've been stuck inside all day?'

A pause. 'Pretty much. I did some work with a friend from uni this morning, over the phone. She hates maths. I don't know what she thought she'd be doing studying accounting.' Another laugh.

Emma frowned at her phone, glad that Luke couldn't see her. The opportunity to drop her question casually into conversation was gone, and he wasn't going to bring it up. It was a bust. 'I should let you get back to it. Talk soon.'

When she got home, she slotted her car beside Jonathan's in the garage and tiptoed in. Jonathan had hearing like a bat, a kind of eerie, inhuman sonar; but if he was busy in his study and Phil had the television on, there was a chance she might get to her room undetected.

In the hallway, she stopped. The unmistakable soundtrack of *Ghostbusters* blared in the lounge. She found Phil on the floor and stopped to give him a hug and check he was okay.

The door to Jonathan's study stood ajar, and as she crept towards the stairs, she winced at his raised voice. Someone was getting a piece of his mind. The one-sided conversation stalled her: *You think I'm going to take this lying down* and *I told you to leave me the fuck alone.*

A sliver of the study was visible through the open door. The expansive room, with its tall windows overlooking the front garden, was lined with bookshelves. A pompous antique desk took pride of place in the centre of the room on a thick Persian rug. Jonathan's pacing cast shadows as he moved from one end of the rug to the other. He hung up the call and slapped his phone onto the desk. Emma edged closer, nudging the door a little wider as her fascination overcame her fear. Jonathan went to the safe and opened it. She couldn't see what he was doing.

He spun around. 'Emma?'

'Who were you talking to?'

'Just work.' Jonathan straightened, brushing the question off. And then came the interrogation, which she should have been used to by now: *Where have you been? Who with? Where did you park? Is Dave still hassling you?* And a new one: *Why did Luke drop you home last night?*

She kicked herself. She'd kissed Luke outside the front gate, in front of the security camera. 'We went out for drinks. It was nothing.'

'I don't want you dating him.' Like an angry, growling dog, Jonathan took an aggressive step forwards. She backed out into the hallway. 'Pleb like that, all he sees is money.'

With her hands on her hips, she said, 'And here I was thinking he just wanted sex.'

A red flush spread up Jonathan's neck to his face. His mouth dropped open. Another step towards her, and he grabbed her wrist. 'Come here. There's something you need to see.'

'Dad, let me go! What—'

He ignored her protest, pulling her into his study, then tapped impatiently at the keyboard of his PC. Emma waited, chilled by his odd behaviour. She couldn't remember the last time he'd touched her.

His voice was low. 'Watch this.'

Footage from the security camera rolled on the screen. She expected to see the front of the house, but instead, the side lane came into view.

'Since when do you have a camera out there?' Emma shivered. She'd used the side gate to sneak in and out without Jonathan's knowledge many times.

'A few weeks. Watch.'

A van, two men.

Luke.

The fight was over in minutes. Emma froze her face into a mask; she could sense her father's eyes on her and reacting would fuel his agenda, but her guts felt weird and tense and the violence took her breath away.

Jonathan replayed it. 'In case you missed the details,' he said.

'I'd direct it differently,' she said, with an offhand flick of her hair. 'Luke's back is to the camera too much of the time—he should be in focus, in the centre of the shot. The camera needs to be able to zoom. Also, that big guy obscures half of the action. It would have been better to film from a lower angle to catch—'

'You think this is a *joke*?' Jonathan smacked the desk. 'It's not one of your action scenes, Emma!'

'What's your point, anyway?' She swallowed, hard. 'What did those men want?'

'What does it matter?'

'And you're mad with Luke—what, because he stopped them?'

'My point,' Jonathan said, grinding out the words, 'is that he's not the person you think he is. You saw the way he punched that man. You think he's any better than Dave?'

'I'm not talking about this.' Emma pushed away, physically distancing herself from Jonathan and his accusations.

His voice followed her as she flounced towards the stairs. '*Listen to me, Emma! You will* not *see him behind my back!*'

She slammed her bedroom door, cutting him off. Now that Jonathan couldn't see, she gave in to her shock, leaning against the door and pressing fingertips to her eyes to stem tears. A rush of emotion—anger, frustration, despair—shook her body, as though she might explode with the pressure. It wasn't that she couldn't imagine Luke fighting like that—it was because she could. She wondered whether there were any limits to his *diverse skill set.*

His posture when facing Dave jarred into her memory, and his words afterwards. *It wouldn't have ended the way he wanted.*

And that odd phone call in the car. His explanation had been lame. She pulled out her phone, debating whether to text him.

She didn't.

Instead, she sat cross-legged on her bed and tried to calm down. Images from the video footage returned and she closed her eyes, but the violence still played in her mind. Luke had gone from kissing her to breaking a man's arm within minutes. Admitting that Jonathan might be right was like dragging fingernails down a blackboard. And he hadn't mentioned Luke being at his office: she wondered if he'd called Luke in to interrogate him. It was the kind of power move she'd expect from her father. The fact that neither Jonathan nor Luke had told her about it rankled.

She went to her bedroom window, which overlooked the lane. If she leaned in close to the glass and tilted her head, she could make out the gate. It was too dark to see any bloodstains.

After a disturbed night, she was so slow dragging herself out of bed that she missed her Sunday yoga class. Jonathan watched from the kitchen table as she moped around making breakfast. On the couch, Phil stabbed at his iPad screen with one finger, making tense, excited noises. He still wasn't himself. She sat beside him, nursing her coffee and balancing a plate of toast on her lap.

'I have to go out. You'll stay with Phil?' Jonathan scooped up his car keys.

Surprised—he was usually home on Sundays—she frowned. 'Where are you going? How long—'

'Work, and I don't know. Keep the doors locked. Don't open the front gate.'

'Why? Are you worried someone will break in?'

Ignoring the sarcastic barb, he replied, 'Just do what I say.'

She waited until she was sure he was gone and went to his study, but the handle wouldn't turn. For a few moments she stared at it, thwarted, wondering what Jonathan had to hide. He'd never locked this door before. She strode back to the kitchen to rummage in the bottom drawer for the hotchpotch of spare keys. The sixth key she tried worked.

At the desk, she felt for the sticky note attached to the underside. Jonathan trusted online password managers as little as he trusted people; he preferred to write them down on a sticky note, arrogantly confident no one would guess his entirely predictable hiding place.

She brought up the screens for the security system and clicked through the time stamps.

The camera above the garage covered the front gate. She found the moment she and Luke came into view. Their kisses looked like nothing—fleeting touches, quickly over. Without sound, it was easy to miss the solemnity of the moment.

After a pause to steel herself, she played the footage of the fight in the lane, forcing herself to watch until the two men got back in their van. Each blow made her wince.

She sat at Jonathan's desk, thinking. He wouldn't lock the study without a reason. She went to the safe and spun the dials, hoping he hadn't changed the combination. He hadn't. It clicked open.

The safe was normally home to a boring collection of documents and old boxes of her mother's jewellery. Emma had opened it a few times, when Jonathan was out, to admire her mother's old-fashioned necklaces and rings. Now, a neat stack of cash sat in front of the boxes. Hundred-dollar bills, held together with paper bands. There were ten in each packet. Fourteen packets.

'Huh,' she said.

Something black and solid disrupted the line of cash at the back of the safe. Hesitant to disturb it, Emma used the torch on her phone to illuminate the depths of the cavity, leaning in to angle the light.

She recoiled, shocked.

Closing the safe with a clunk, she retreated to the desk, where she thumbed out a text to Jonathan—*why is there a gun in the safe?*—and then, just as quickly, she reconsidered and deleted it. He'd flip if he knew she'd looked in the safe.

And he'd never tell her the truth. She'd have to find out another way.

CHAPTER FIFTEEN

MONDAY, 12.30 PM

With a light breeze brushing his face, Luke closed his eyes to enjoy the midday sun as he waited for his study group to emerge from the exam. His seat by the lawn outside the hall gave him a clear view of the glass doors. On cue, a horde of students spilled out onto the pavements and grass. Their chatter filled the air: complaints, plans for lunch, excitement about finishing.

Caitlin flopped onto the seat beside him. 'I couldn't do the last question.' She play-whacked his arm. 'You finished early, you nerd.'

'You wound me with your insults.'

She rolled her eyes. 'I just hope I passed.'

'Don't worry about it. Think about tomorrow.'

Luke's phone beeped.

Emma: *I know about the fight in the lane.*

A cloud passed over the sun; the pleasant morning faded. Luke mumbled an abrupt goodbye to Caitlin. As he walked across the campus towards the tram, he hit the redial icon. 'What?'

'You. In the lane, beating up those guys.' From the background noise, he guessed Emma was in her car. 'Meet me for lunch? Natali's, on Lygon Street. I'll be there in twenty. My shout.'

Luke abandoned his path and retraced his steps across the university campus. Ten minutes later he sat at the rear of the cafe, watching the door. His restlessness reminded him of Quin, who had always fidgeted like a child, shifting his posture and shaking his legs. Touching his face. Scratching his head.

He forced himself to be still and ordered a coffee while he waited.

Emma bustled in, five minutes after her promised twenty, and dropped into the seat opposite him. She swiped off her oversized sunglasses and squinted in the bright light. Her skin glowed, so pale it seemed translucent, emphasising the dark shadows under her eyes. He wondered what had disturbed her sleep.

'I'm sorry. I didn't ask about your exam. How was it?'

'Okay. Done.' Exams were the least of his problems.

She wore jeans and a T-shirt, expensively casual, with her hair piled up on her head. She plucked a menu from where it was wedged between the salt and pepper shakers on the table. A waiter had followed her, and after they ordered, she sat back in her chair, examining him in silence with her arms folded. His hands, his arms. His bruised face.

Luke crossed his arms, mirroring her. 'How did you find out?'

'Dad put a new video camera in the lane. You're the star of the movie.' She caught her lip in her teeth. 'That fight was fucking insane, Luke. That guy was twice your size. But—you knew what you were doing. They were all over the place, throwing punches around hoping they'd connect, tripping over their own feet, but you were calm as anything. When you smacked that guy's arm—Jesus. That was brutal. You're like some kind of ninja.'

He shook his head. 'I've never trained in ninjitsu.'

'What, then?'

'I went to a boxing gym when I was in high school.'

'A boxing gym taught you how to stomp-kick a guy's knee?' Her eyebrows arched. Luke retreated from her intensity, but she wasn't finished. 'I've done fight scenes. It's like dancing, choreographed down to each beat—but if anyone misses a beat, you get hurt. You got punched in the face and you barely flinched. Not your first rodeo, eh?'

'I watched your show. The fights were pretty realistic for TV.'

'Don't change the topic.'

Luke held up his palms. 'What do you want me to say? They were breaking into your yard. I asked them to leave and they didn't.'

'So you beat the crap out of them?'

He breathed into his lower chest and used his diaphragm to exhale. Relaxed his hands, his face. He said, 'Are you asking me to defend my actions? Is this where you tell me to stay away from you?'

Emma's throat moved with a visible swallow. Running out of steam, she let her head drop forwards. 'Dad's just worried. After what happened with Dave.'

He waited.

She shook her head, as though trying to shake away a memory. 'He only hit me once. It was enough.'

'You think I'm like him? That I'm going to slap you around if you don't do what I want?' Luke regretted the harsh words the moment they left his lips.

'No.' She swallowed again, looking up to meet his eyes. 'I'm glad you didn't lose your cool when Dave was being a dick. You would have flattened him.'

'It wasn't my fight.' He couldn't stop a smile twitching his lips. 'But I'll hold him still if you want to take a swing at him.'

'Jesus.' Emma put her face in her hands; her shoulders shook, and he couldn't tell if she was laughing or crying.

'Emma, listen to me.' He gave in at last, reaching out to pull her hands away from her face, and leaned forwards so he could speak quietly. 'I got into a lot of fights when I was younger. But not anymore, if I can help it. I don't go looking for trouble.'

'What were you doing at Dad's office on Saturday? I saw your car there.'

'He called me after he saw the CCTV footage. He wanted an explanation.'

'Why didn't you tell me? We talked that night, and you didn't—'

'I didn't want you to know. He told me to stay away from you—threatened to show you that video to scare you off.' Luke shook his head. 'I should have known he'd do it anyway.' His gut instinct, which was that Jonathan was as trustworthy as Melbourne weather, had proven correct.

Emma blew out a sigh.

'I thought it would freak you out.' Her hands were still in his, resting on the table; he gave them a little squeeze.

'It did.' For the first time, she managed a smile. 'But the more I thought about it, the more I realised you did what you had to. Even breaking the guy's arm. He was gonna do the same to you, wasn't he?' She bit her lip. 'There's a quote, which I can't remember, about not having a right to criticise if you're not in the ring.'

Luke's tension melted. 'Theodore Roosevelt. The man in the arena.'

'Yeah. That.' She returned his smile. 'Did Dad even say thank you? For stopping them?'

'I'm not sure he did.'

'Well, thank you. Did you agree not to see me?'

'I'm here now.' He squeezed her hands again.

Their food arrived. Distracted by the intense conversation, Luke had forgotten what he ordered. Emma deconstructed her panino and ate the grilled-vegetable filling with fervour before breaking the bread into tiny pieces to eat like popcorn.

With a smile, he said, 'You know it's quicker if you eat it like a sandwich.'

'I'm not in a hurry. Are you?'

'I have an exam tomorrow.' His lunch was long gone, but watching Emma eat was a great spectator sport.

'That's your last one? Then what?'

'I've got a few things on.' He needed to track down Jonathan's burglars, Gus was on his case, and his manager was about to start piling him up with extra shifts for the summer break. None of them were known for their patience. 'Emma, I'm sorry I didn't tell you. Are we still good?'

'Maybe.' She dusted off her fingers, considering. 'I feel like you know everything about me, but I know nothing about you.'

'What do you want to know?' He grinned, praying she would leave it.

She did. 'Not now. After your exams. You'd better go and study. I don't want to get the blame if you bomb out.'

It took a beach run and a half-hour of punching his bag before he could even think about study. It was hard to get Emma off his mind. The way she ate, licking her lips and closing her eyes like a satisfied cat. The curve of her eyebrows, the slant of her collarbones, her graceful neck. It took two coffees and a hefty dose of discipline to return his attention to taxation law.

For dinner, he pan-fried a Wagyu beef fillet and served it with cauliflower puree and charred broccolini, doused with extra-virgin olive oil and caramelised lemon. The satisfaction of using Jonathan's money for expensive food was as delicious as the meal.

As he went to bed—with his tax exam, Jonathan and Gus all looming over him—he had a sense this might be his last good night of sleep for a while: the calm before the storm. He'd learned not to get comfortable with peace.

Keep your hands up and your eyes open, his boxing instructor had said. *Moment you let your guard down, you'll cop one to the face.*

CHAPTER SIXTEEN

THIRTEEN YEARS AGO

Dr Bowman was a bespectacled middle-aged man who looked like he worked in a bank. His first words were a reassurance that everything they discussed was confidential, unless Jack was planning to hurt himself or others, so Jack remained tight-lipped about his fantasy of punching Quin in the face. Of punching everyone, really.

The meeting room at the school was small and airless, tucked behind the principal's office on the second floor of the administration building, with a view of the sports fields. Jack's attendance was not voluntary, but his defiance had faded to curiosity.

He'd checked Dr Bowman out online and arrived armed with information. He questioned the man's credentials: was a psychologist really a doctor? And was the man's PhD thesis, titled 'Psychosocial predictors of reform in juvenile delinquency', wasted on the rich kids in the private school?

Dr Bowman agreed that both questions were valid.

'So what are they, then?' Jack crossed his arms. 'The predictors of reform?'

'Oh, what you'd expect,' Dr Bowman said. 'Stable housing, consistent parenting, good role models.'

I'm fucked then, Jack thought.

'But also: engagement with education, team sports, outlets for expression. Trusted adults. Capacity to learn emotional regulation and impulse control. Trauma-informed counselling.'

Jack's stomach tensed. He kept his face still.

'Do you want to tell me why you're here?' Dr Bowman asked.

'You know why. Mr Saunders made me come.'

The psychologist nodded. 'And why is that?'

'I got into a fight.'

The psychologist sat back and tapped his pen on the desk. 'That's one reason.'

Jack rolled his eyes. 'But wait, there's more.'

'Children's Services gave me this.' Dr Bowman held up a thick paper file. 'Pretty big file for a twelve-year-old.'

'What's your point?'

Dr Bowman smiled. 'You're doing well in your classes—your teachers all like you. The football coach says you're a team player with real talent. Your only problem is getting into fights. I can hear frustration in your voice, Jack.'

Jack grumbled, 'I wouldn't get into fights if people would leave me alone.'

'Go on.'

With an elaborate eye roll that he knew was excessive, Jack said, 'Do I need to spell it out? I'm getting bullied because I'm on a scholarship, and the school would rather blame me than punish the kids with rich parents.'

In the three months he'd been at the school, he'd learned more about fighting than anything else. Rodley Grammar had been a fresh hell to navigate. Lush, forbidden green lawns were shadowed by heritage-listed Victorian gothic buildings, which, although they reminded Jack of BBC dramas and his mother's accent, intimidated him with their grandeur. The teachers were a collective mass of *Sirs*, with one exceptional *Miss* who copped so much flak Jack felt sorry for her. For the first time, he'd had to pay attention to keep up with the schoolwork. He'd been bumped up a few levels in maths and was in extension classes for science and English.

His classmates ranged from nerds to bruisers, but they were all rich kids with new phones who talked about ski trips, fancy sneakers and houses at the beach. The bullies knew within minutes that he was a scholarship kid from a shitty background. Their campaign started with name-calling—which amused him; their slurs were unoriginal—but quickly progressed.

They didn't like it when he hit back.

The psychologist was forced into retreat by Jack's vehemence, but Jack wasn't done. 'The definition of bullying: *repeated verbal, physical, social or psychological abuse.* He threw a water bottle at me, so I punched him. *Yeah, he made a mistake, who cares? Get over it,* they say. But it's not just that. Every day, there's something. We had a restorative practice meeting and an hour later he tore up my maths book. But apparently I'm the one with the violent streak.'

Dr Bowman paused while Jack swallowed down his anger. 'How old are you again?'

'You just said, *Pretty big file for a twelve-year-old.*'

'Not many twelve-year-olds can define bullying.' The psychologist raised his eyebrows. 'Okay. Let's go back a step. This is your first year here? And you live with your father?'

With some reluctance, he gave Dr Bowman a summary of his home situation. He figured it was in the file anyway.

'Why was he in jail?'

'Initially he was charged with attempted murder because he beat up the guy who threatened to kill me, but it got downgraded to assault. *Extenuating circumstances.* Apparently what the guy did to me was considered provocation.' Jack frowned. Robbo was still in jail. He got eight years.

'Let's bookmark that for later,' Dr Bowman said. 'Tell me about Quin. What does he do for work?'

'He works in a panel shop. Sometimes.'

'Any other work?'

Stripping down stolen cars, petty theft. 'He plays in a band. They get a gig about once a month.'

'Do you play music too?'

Jack explained he could play five chords and had no illusions of musical talent. Quin could play any song by ear after a year of lessons in primary school. He had the kind of casual, natural talent that could have been brilliance had he put any effort into developing it, but 'effort' was not a word Quin understood. He shied away from anything requiring discipline in the way most people shied away from spiders or snakes.

'You're pretty down on your father,' Dr Bowman observed, after hearing out Jack's tirade on the subject of Quin's inadequacies. 'Do you get along?'

The question surprised Jack—not because it was unexpected, but because he found it hard to answer. 'Quin's like . . . We don't fight or anything. He's just—' The right words eluded him. *Hopeless. Useless.* They sounded too negative. There was no malice in Quin's incompetence, and while it made Jack furious, he knew it was a waste of time railing against it. Quin couldn't help the way he was. 'It's like living with another kid. I have to remind him to do things. And for school, I have an email address for him that I check, and I fill in all the forms myself.'

'You forge his signature?'

'Usually they're online forms.' He'd learned to forge Quin's handwriting and signature years ago.

He retreated, unsure how much to admit: that he washed his own uniforms, cooked his own food, cleaned the flat, put out the bins. He never really knew where Quin was or when he'd be home. He visited Gail often, cautious when Kevin was there, but too moneyless and hungry to stay away. Sometimes, he tracked down Quin in whichever pub the band was playing and snuck in to badger him for cash or a bowl of chips.

Talking about it to a school psychologist would be unwise. Despite his frustration with his father, Jack didn't want to get him into trouble. There were advantages to living with Quin, which had come to him gradually as he let go of his orderly life at the Deweys: Quin didn't hound him about where he was or worry if he was late. While he'd appreciated—needed—Liz Dewey's close attention, he could imagine finding it stifling as he grew older. He'd quickly adjusted to his new independence.

Dr Bowman asked Jack about hobbies—playing football, reading, getting into fights—then what Jack was reading.

Jack said he was halfway through the sixth Harry Potter book.

Dr Bowman nodded. 'That's a good one.'

Jack's first crime, when he was seven years old, was the failure to return a library book: *Harry Potter and the Philosopher's Stone*. He failed to return it because his mother died and he had other things on his mind.

'What do you like about the Harry Potter books?'

'They're very English.' It was the first thing that came into his head. Of course, there was more to it. Who didn't like the boy wizard, in all his underdog glory?

'Your mother was English.'

Jack clamped his mouth shut.

'What do you remember about her?'

Her voice, her accent, that she'd read to him, that she'd loved books and music. She was blonde, like him. He remembered thinking she was pretty. He remembered holding her hand. He remembered she liked her tea strong. Sometimes she was great. Sometimes she wasn't. She'd been his entire world.

'We lived in Sydney, after we came back from England—I was born here, but she took me there as a baby to see her family. After she died, I came to live with Quin.'

'What else do you remember?'

Their little flat in Sydney, the rampantly green grass at the front and the red-brick steps. His first day at the new school, holding her hand at the gate; one of the kids had picked on his accent.

The timbre of the woman's voice on the line when he used his mother's phone to call an ambulance. *How old are you, sweetie? Is there an adult with you? What's the address?*

Jack said, 'I don't want to talk about it.'

'Sometimes memories won't come out until they're ready. Just tell me what you're comfortable with.'

Something in the man's manner broke through his reticence, and Jack found himself describing it for the first time. Words that had stuck in his throat for years came loose. His mother lying in bed, unresponsive. Her cigarette still alight, burning a hole on the table beside her bed. The ambulance, the serious faces and hushed voices. The paramedics crushing her chest. A woman taking him into the next room so he didn't have to watch.

Dr Bowman listened, nodded and said, 'Hmm,' in encouragement. After Jack finished, he asked about nightmares. Jack said his nightmares were not about his mother's death.

'Do you want to talk about it? The man who threatened to kill you?'

Jack looked out the window. An urge to run from the room made him squirm. 'What is there to talk about?'

'You're pretty tough, aren't you?'

Jack wasn't sure about that. He had many scars, inside and out, and some were raw from picking.

'Jack.' Leaning forwards, the man made sure he had Jack's full attention. 'What I'm going to tell you now is important.'

Despite himself, Jack sat up straighter.

'When something bad happens, you can either let it get to you—be a victim, fight reality, wish it didn't happen—or you can see it for what it is and accept it, grow around it and keep moving forwards.'

'How?' Starkly realistic, even at age twelve, Jack knew that was easier said than done. He needed to know the logistics. How did one *grow around* their mother's death? *Accept* nearly dying in a car crash? *Move forwards* from being beaten up by their father's criminal associate?

'Well, we go back and think things through. Work through the what and the why and the big feelings. I can help you with that. At the same time, you look to the future and plot a course. Plan ahead.'

Jack demurred, thinking. He needed time to consider the negotiation. The psychologist's expression evolved from thoughtful to resolute as he chose his words. Jack found it curious that people like Dr Bowman thought they had to be careful with him.

'You know none of it was your fault, right?'

'Do I?' A need to end the conversation made Jack shift in his seat. He sensed danger, as though the conversation was edging towards exposure; as though it might pick off a scab he'd been trying to leave alone.

'Do you think something you did caused your mother's death? Or the car crash?'

Jack didn't just think it: he knew it. If he hadn't been playing outside that morning before school, he would have known his mother was still in bed. If he hadn't riled up Kevin and needed stitches . . . If he hadn't insisted on catching the bus back to Footscray for school . . .

'You were a child. You had no control over the behaviour of adults.'

'Sounds good in theory.' Jack gazed out the window, hiding the depths of his guilt, his shameful secrets. He squashed them down with a scowl.

'Do you know the difference between causation and correlation?'

'I'm not stupid.' No, but he'd look up the words later.

'So, let's work through the facts of those events and see if you can prove to me you caused them.' Dr Bowman checked the clock. 'We're out of time today.' He smiled. 'You said you like to read. Do you want some homework?'

'Sure.'

Dr Bowman selected a slim book from the pile on his desk. It had a black cover, with a title in red and white: *Anger Management Workbook for Teens*. It amused Jack that the book itself looked angry.

'Seriously?' Jack rolled his eyes.

'Oh, your homework is not just to read it,' Dr Bowman said. 'I want you to critique it. Come back in two weeks and tell me what parts of it are useful and what parts are rubbish.' His eyes creased with a smile. 'I'm sure you'll have opinions.'

―✴―✴―

A few weeks later, on a cold July night, a rap on the door disturbed Jack as he washed his dinner dishes. Quin was out, at rehearsal with his band, or smoking meth with Donna, or up to no good with Kevin. The dingy ground-floor flat hummed with the racket of the ancient gas heater in the lounge, which Jack was sure was slowly poisoning him with carbon monoxide. The television was on, the volume low, keeping him company. He dried his hands and switched on the outdoor light. Two figures were silhouetted outside.

Jack opened the door. A man in his twenties, with a flat nose, close-cropped dark hair and the build of a weightlifter, loomed on the step. He wore a high-vis shirt and heavy boots, like a construction worker. Behind him was a man in a suit, older than Quin, bigger, and in much better shape.

'We're looking for Quin.'

'He's not here.'

'Where is he?'

Jack shrugged.

The older man's brow furrowed. 'I didn't know Quin had a kid.' Another shrug.

'What happened to your face?' The man had a pleasant smile and a deep, smooth voice, like a television presenter. Dark hair, heavy eyebrows. His suit was neat, his shoes polished. Jack felt scruffy and small and poor in comparison.

'Kids at school.'

'Looks like you lost a fight.'

Jack said nothing.

'I need to talk to Quin.'

'Try calling him.' Jack moved to close the door, but the younger guy stuck his boot in the gap. Memories of Robbo flooded him with fear; his voice rose in pitch, like a stupid, scared kid. 'I don't know where he is, okay?'

'He's not answering his phone.' The man in the suit focused on the embroidery on Jack's school jumper. 'How does he afford that fancy school?'

'I'm on a scholarship.'

'Sports?'

'Academic.'

'Jesus. Must have got your brains from your mother.' The man laughed, and Jack couldn't help cracking a smile. 'What's your name?'

'Jack.'

'Okay, Jackie. We're gonna take a look inside, if you don't mind.'

Jack did mind, but he knew better than to argue. Their search was brief but brutal; he guessed they were searching for money or drugs. There was no money in the house, because he would have found it himself, and if Quin was stupid enough to leave drugs lying around, that was his problem.

'Tell Quin I'd appreciate a call.' The man took a business card from a pocket. 'Grab me a pen, Jackie?' He scribbled on the card. 'This is for you. You need to learn how to hit back.'

After the door closed and he was alone in the ransacked flat, Jack studied the card. *Gus Alberici, Managing Director, Alberici Hotel Group.* Contact details were printed in black lettering beside a tasteful green logo. On the back, Gus had written the name and address of a gym, in neat letters to fit on the card. *Ask for Frank, no charge, Gus.*

He told Quin about the visit, but he kept the card to himself. He never found out what they wanted, but the next day Quin came home with a split lip.

A few weeks later, a bunch of boys at school bailed Jack up and punched him again. Enough was enough. He caught the train into the city and trudged along Elizabeth Street with his eyes peeled for the sign.

The gym was a cavernous space, the size and shape of a warehouse, dotted with oversized, sweaty men. Racks of weights and training equipment surrounded a boxing ring in the centre. At the counter, a guy with a handlebar moustache and huge biceps, like a cartoon character, stood guard. Jack loitered in the doorway, reconsidering.

'What have we here?' the man said. 'Lost grammar school boy with a black eye?'

Jack squared his shoulders. He'd had a bad day. 'I'm looking for Frank.'

The man disappeared behind a partition wall. When he came back, a smaller man in shorts and a T-shirt followed him. He was at least sixty, but his arms were ropy with muscle and his calves were cut like diamonds.

Jack held out the card Gus had given him.

'Getting beaten up at school?' Frank's keen eyes settled on Jack's bruised face. He asked more questions, rapid-fire: how old was Jack, what sports did he do, how did he know Gus, and so on. 'Well, you're too young to join up, but we gotta do what the boss says, eh?'

Still in his uniform, Jack had his first lesson with Frank, who got straight to the point and taught him how to punch a bag. Frank encouraged him to use his anger. *Name it as you go. All the things you're angry about.*

And out they came: being poor was top of the list. Not having the right shoes. Stealing from the second-hand cupboard at school. Worrying about the following year, when Quin realised how little the scholarship covered. The stupid rich kids with their stupid rich dads—

'Alright, alright.' Frank stopped him. 'Don't worry. We'll look after you.'

―――

His weekly sessions with Frank were hard work, but Jack was determined: he was sick of being pushed around. He spent his time at the gym bouncing around hitting pads, learning how to duck and block. Frank was an old-school boxer. He taught Jack how to skip, and to do push-ups and crunches; he encouraged Jack to run off his anger. *Burn it out*, he'd say. *Run it off.*

A few months later, Ed and Gus turned up at the door again. He let them in. It was only fair, given Gus had waived the fees for his boxing lessons with Frank.

'Jackie, Quin's not answering my calls.'

'He never does.' Jack had long since given up.

'He owes me money.'

'Again?'

Gus just laughed.

Jack was halfway through his dinner: pasta with ham, tomatoes and olives. It seemed rude to eat in front of them, but Gus waved him to it. 'Don't let it get cold.'

Gus peered around the miserable room: at the coffee table where Jack's homework was spread out; the pile of science fiction and fantasy novels on the end of the couch; the poster he'd made for his science project.

'You cook for yourself? Every night?'

'Pretty much.' Jack put his most burning question into words: 'Why do you loan Quin money when you know he won't pay it back?'

'Oh, he'll pay it back, Jackie. With interest. You know how interest works?'

His mouth was full, so Jack just nodded.

'I forgot. Scholarship kid. You still getting beaten up?'

'Not really.' Since he started training with Frank, hardly any of the bullies' punches had landed. It hadn't stopped them trying, but Jack's ability to avoid their fists frustrated them and amused Jack.

'They sense confidence, you know. They can tell when you're intimidated.'

'I'm not intimidated.' The assumption surprised Jack. 'Nah, I could take any of them. But I'm on my last warning. If I get expelled, I have to pay back the scholarship. You think Quin could afford that?'

'How much?'

'Thirty thousand a year.'

'Not a chance. He'd have to borrow it from me.' Gus chuckled. 'You like school, Jackie?'

Jack didn't know how to answer.

'What are your grades like?'

'I got ninety-seven on a maths test last week.' He frowned.

'What, ninety-seven is not good enough?'

'I prefer a round hundred.' It was true, and not only because he wanted perfect grades. He preferred the neatness, which he knew better than to admit.

'Smart-arse. How old are you? Fourteen?'

'Twelve.' Adults always thought he was older, because he was tall, and because he could look after himself.

Gus ruffled Jack's hair—a patronising gesture, which Jack did not appreciate—and headed for the door. 'Tell Quin I'm waiting for my money.'

The next time Jack went to the gym, handlebar-moustache man, whose name was Trevor, took him aside and handed him a cheap mobile phone.

'Keep it on,' Trevor said. 'Boss won't like it if you don't answer.'

He got his first text the next day, while he was still figuring out how the phone worked.

Like your phone Jackie?
Yeah thanks.
Keep it on. I might have some work for you.

Gus texted him randomly, a few times a week: *Do us a favour and pick up a box for me Jackie?* An address. Another address to deliver it to. Jack spent his after-school hours on buses and trains, lugging packages in his school backpack.

He knew exactly what he was doing; he could never claim ignorance. Usually it was cash, but occasionally it was drugs—powders, crystals or diverted prescription medications. He was smart enough to leave the contents undisturbed. Gus was a benevolent presence in his life, a patron, a counter to Quin's chaos. Jack wouldn't dream of stealing from him. And if the talk at the gym was true, Gus valued loyalty above all else. He was more sensitive to betrayal than honest mistakes.

The work came with an unreliable pay cheque. Out of the blue, a pineapple or two would be handed to him at the gym—a random reward system, designed to keep him hooked. Jack didn't care. Money was money.

One afternoon, another instructor in the gym loitered, watching Jack train with Frank. Hong was a tall, lanky man who reminded Jack of a cat on the prowl; the feline grace of his movements held an ominous potential, as though he could pounce at any moment. He rarely spoke, but when he did, it was with biting sarcasm and derision. Jack had never seen him smile. An unnerving tattoo of a snake peeked out of the collar of his T-shirt, curling up the right side of his neck. Hong ran classes in mixed martial arts, which to Jack looked intense and serious.

'You're Gus's new kid?' Hong leaned against a rack with his arms folded. He didn't have huge muscles like some of the men, but Jack was not fooled. Hong was tough and mean, and his lithe, flexible body was a honed weapon. 'What's your name?'

'Jack.'

'Bit of a lightweight, aren't you?'

Jack, who was sparring with Frank, lost concentration and got a smack to the side of his head. 'What?'

Frank told Hong to piss off and quit distracting the lad.

Later, as Jack was shouldering his bag to leave, Hong caught him near the door. 'Boss said you need to join my class. I don't like it. You're just a kid. But we gotta do what he says.'

'What? Why?'

'Frank'll teach you how to box,' Hong said. 'But if you want to handle yourself on the street, you need dirty tricks, not pretty footwork.'

'What kind of dirty tricks?' Despite his dislike of the man, Jack couldn't hide his interest. Dirty tricks sounded cool.

Hong flicked his eyes to where Frank was wheeling a hamper of towels to the locker room. He looked down his nose at Jack. 'Tuesdays and Thursdays at seven pm,' he said. 'Show up, or the boss'll find out, understand?'

Jack nodded. His phone buzzed in his pocket, and he had an eerie feeling that Gus had overheard the conversation.

CHAPTER SEVENTEEN

TUESDAY, 10 PM

A noxious smell of disinfectant and sweat and testosterone assaulted Luke as he made his way across the dark gym to the office at the rear. Memories of sticky boxing gloves, arduous lessons and illegal fights washed him with nostalgia. The gym had been a second home throughout his high school years. He'd grown up there. Everyone had known his name and that Gus favoured him. As he progressed in skill and responsibility, he'd gained his own notoriety. Some of the stories about Jack Quinlan held an element of truth.

He knocked twice—old habits returned quickly—before opening the office door, then took a step back as he came face to face with a bulky man with a shaved head. The man's face was bruised, and his left arm, in a blue fibreglass cast, hung from a sling around his thick neck.

Ivan's eyes widened and bulged as though he might pop an aneurysm. Luke's mind blanked with the thought, *I am fucking dead*, and he waited for something bad to happen.

'You're Jack?' Ivan could barely speak through his shock.

'No. It's—'

'Ah, come on Jackie,' Gus complained, from inside the office. 'I'm not calling you some made-up wanker name.' He leaned against the desk with a cigarette poised, ready to light. His eyes flicked from Ivan to Luke and back again, as though he sensed tension. 'You two know each other?'

Ivan said, 'No, boss,' and his eyes, unexpectedly, appealed to Luke to keep quiet.

'Jackie, Ivan.' Gus waved a hand of introduction. His attention moved to Luke's face. 'You been fighting?'

'Just a scrap.'

'What about?'

'A girl.'

Gus scoffed, shook his head with something almost like humour, and gestured to Ivan. 'Don't worry about him. You done with exams now?'

'Last one was this morning.'

Another anticlimax, as was his brief conversation with Emma afterwards. She'd been subdued after finding out she'd have to wait another few days for a decision on her audition. Concern that Jonathan had got under her skin niggled him; he shoved it aside.

The office had changed in subtle ways since Luke was last there. The computer and printer were new. Gus's chair was different. But the Carlton Football Club posters on the wall were the same, as was the old floor rug that curled up at the corners, and the musty smell was still there. Luke settled into a chair, taking care not to get comfortable. Gus sat behind his desk, and Ivan loitered near the door.

Luke scooted the chair back a little so he could keep Ivan in his peripheral vision. 'Where's Ed?'

'His missus is pregnant. He's taking tonight off.' After stubbing out his cigarette, Gus fixed on Luke. 'Tell me you've got a lead on Kevin.'

'No one home at his place. I've looked online, and I checked in with a few guys—no one's seen him.' Truth mixed seamlessly with lies. 'Are you gonna explain this to me? What do you want with him?'

'He stole from me.'

'Stole what?'

Gus lit yet another cigarette. Luke guessed he was considering whether to confide. The silence dragged.

'A delivery of cash.' Blowing out a cloud of smoke, Gus pulled a face. 'Seven years ago. My guy was rolled before he even left his street, then got picked up by the cops. Before I knew it, he was inside. He locked down, said he didn't know who took the money. I couldn't get a word out of him.'

It didn't surprise Luke. The guy probably preferred jail to dealing with Gus.

Leaning forwards on the desk, Gus fixed his eyes on Luke. 'He got out earlier this year. Told me Kevin McNally took it.'

'Okay.' Luke waited.

'The problem is,' Gus said, 'Kevin has bloody disappeared. So has Quin. No one has seen them for years.' He pointed the cigarette at Luke. 'You're gonna find them. And my money.'

Luke held up his palms. 'How the hell would I know where they are?'

'You'll figure something out.'

Luke debated the best way to phrase the obvious. 'Maybe they're dead. It's a long time to go dark.'

'You managed it, didn't you?' Gus cut him a glare. 'No. Kevin's alive. His phone is still connected, and my friend at VicRoads said he paid his car rego a month ago. It's registered to his house in Footscray. I went there. It was a bust. Or maybe he saw me coming.'

'He's not living there,' Luke said. 'The house is empty. And they're not in jail. I checked.'

'I think he did a runner with my money. And if we find one, we'll find the other.' Gus frowned. 'Quin worked in a panel shop, didn't he? And he had a girlfriend.'

Luke shook his head. 'Donna died not long after Quin went to jail. When I was sixteen.'

'Died? How?'

'She ditched rehab and overdosed the next day.' Luke had never really known Donna, although she and Quin had been on and off for a decade. Kevin had told him about her death. He hadn't seemed too upset about it.

'Kevin have a girlfriend?'

'Not for years.'

Gus snorted. 'Who were their other friends?'

'Malcolm, from the panel shop. A guy called Steve from Quin's band. I don't know his surname. The band split up years ago.' Luke grimaced and added, 'Robbo Parker worked with Kevin sometimes.'

'The bloke who beat you up when you were a kid?' Gus shook his head. 'He can't help.'

'You've talked to him?'

Silent for a good minute, Gus finished a cigarette and lit another. Luke didn't remember him smoking so much in the past. 'He's dead. And you wondered why the cops were looking for Quin?'

'What?' Luke leaned in.

'Robbo was found in his car with a bullet in his head and a hundred texts on his phone from Quin, threatening to kill him.'

'Are you serious?' Luke pushed to his feet. 'When was this?'

'Same night Kevin took my money—and in the same street. Quin shot Robbo and split. I figure the three of them planned the job together and then argued.'

'Jesus, Gus!' Luke paced a few steps.

'Calm down. Don't be a diva.'

Luke didn't want to sit; he wanted to stay on his feet, ready to bolt from the room if Gus pulled his gun. He ran his hands through his hair. 'Why didn't you tell me this last week?'

Gus pointed his cigarette at Luke. 'Stay in your fucking lane. I'll tell you what you need to know.' His heavy brows lowered. 'I was hoping the cops would find Quin, because it'd bring Kevin out of the woodwork. But my source tells me they've put the case on ice.' He stubbed out his cigarette with more force than necessary.

'No wonder the cops hassled me. Jesus.' Luke flopped back into his seat. 'Quin's not smart enough to disappear. Kevin must have helped him. And what do you think I can do, if the cops can't find him?' His day was going from bad to worse. Any reminder of Robbo Parker was enough to put him on edge. And Ivan stared at him from the doorway, strangely silent about what had happened at the Wylies' place.

'Start with the panel shop. Give them a sob story about wanting to find your old man. Take Ivan with you. He can help you out.' Gus levelled his gaze at Ivan.

Luke and Ivan made a plan to talk to Malcolm the next morning. It was civil and organised, as though they were arranging to play golf.

'So.' Gus turned to Ivan. His quiet tone worried Luke. 'Tell me you've tracked down those guys.'

Ivan flicked his eyes to Luke: *Keep quiet.*

Gus misinterpreted the look. 'It's okay. You can trust Jackie.'

Ivan said, 'I got nothing. Gordy's gotta have surgery on his knee. I gotta have another X-ray next week.'

'Broken arm?' Luke met Ivan's eyes.

'Fucker got me with boltcutters.'

'Ouch,' said Luke.

Gus flicked ash from his cigarette. 'There'll be a camera somewhere. If there's video footage of you two fucking up, you'd better find it.'

Ivan shook his head. 'No cameras in the lane. Two at the front and one over the back door, inside the yard.'

Gus snorted his contempt. 'Fuck, Ivan, I ask you to pick up a weedy cleaner and you get the shit kicked out of you! What were they, private security?'

'Dunno. But they knew we'd be there.'

'Then you were too bloody obvious. Did they have uniforms?'

'No.'

'Did you see their car?' Gus spoke as though he were dealing with a child.

'Just the three blokes. Like I said.' Ivan's face contorted with frustration. He scowled at Luke.

'What a fucking mess. They saw your faces. They'll have the rego on the van.' Gus huffed. 'Find out who they were. They're not gonna get away with this.' Jerking his head towards the door, he dismissed Ivan. 'Get out before I get angry. Jackie—stay.'

Ivan cast a grimace at Luke as he departed.

'What a cluster.' A deep line had formed between Gus's brows. He lit another cigarette. 'Keep an eye on Ivan. He's not being straight with me. If he fucks up again, it'll be his last mistake.'

Risking another reminder to stay in his lane, Luke said, 'You gonna tell me what's going on?'

Gus sucked on his cigarette, closing his eyes while he held in the precious first drag. He puffed out a cloud of smoke that hung in the air between them. 'It's a lot of years since you were in this office.' He waved the cigarette around the room. 'Things have changed. You've changed.'

'You haven't,' Luke said, before he could stop himself. 'You smoke more, swear more. But otherwise, you're the same.'

'Don't get cocky.' Gus glowered, letting out a long exhale. 'Ah, fuck it. You know what my business is. You're a bloody accountant, right?'

Suppressing a smile, Luke said, 'Not yet. And I'm pretty sure they don't teach advanced laundering until honours. Off-books finance is in third year, I think.'

'Haven't lost your smart mouth. Jesus.'

'One of your cleaners is causing trouble?' Luke held his breath. A wrong move now could halt Gus's disclosure.

'Bloke pulled the pin on me. I sent Ivan to shake him but he fucked it up. So now I have two problems.'

'What does it matter if you lose one cleaner?'

'This one is special. Balls of steel. Pain in the arse, but he can push money through like nothing else.' Gus took a deep drag on his cigarette. 'He got too big for his boots. Started demanding a bigger cut. And now he's holding up my cash flow, trying to force my hand. Normally I'd give him time to reconsider, but . . . remember Khoury? I owe him. And I'm running out of time.' Gus stopped; he'd reached his limit. He squashed the butt of his cigarette down with a forefinger, as though he were smiting a bug.

The reference to Khoury made Luke wince. 'You sent Ivan to negotiate with this guy?'

'Scare him, more like. Idiot got his arse handed to him by private security.' Silence fell. Gus surveyed the overflowing ashtray on his desk. 'Alright, Jackie. Get out of here. Keep your phone on.'

Vigilant as he walked to his car, Luke checked the shadows in case Ivan was waiting to ambush him. He wasted no time getting away from the gym, but he'd driven only a few blocks before his phone beeped three times in quick succession.

With a slow exhale, he found a spot to pull over.

Jonathan: *I need to talk to you.*

Call me.

Now.

Luke hit the call icon and Jonathan's animosity filled the car. 'I told you to stay away from Emma! I know you've been talking to her!'

His temper on a short leash, Luke said, 'Do you want my help or not? Because I can hand back that money and let you deal with this yourself.'

'Listen to me.' Contempt strangled Jonathan's words. 'The van is registered to a rental company. Write this down.' He rattled off an address in Coburg, which Luke ignored. 'We made an arrangement. You find those two thugs and you leave Emma alone. I'm paying you, remember? It's not complicated.'

Luke bit back his first response, which was to tell Jonathan where to stick his money—and his lies. He had a few seconds to decide on a path. 'Calm down. I'll find them. Give me two days.'

'Twenty-four hours, or I send that footage to the cops.' Jonathan hung up.

Resting his head back, Luke closed his eyes. For years, he'd kept his face and his new name out of the line of fire. Jonathan's video could unravel years of work; and at any moment, Ivan could knowingly or unknowingly betray him to Gus. He was walking a tightrope, balancing his fear of Gus with his suspicion of Jonathan as he inched forwards. At least Gus was a known quantity. Jonathan was harder to predict. Like in a game of chess, Luke needed to stay several steps ahead of both if he intended to win.

Dr Bowman's words, from a session when he was sixteen, haunted him: *What does success mean to you, Jack?*

Financial security. Jack had gazed out the window, thinking about Gus. *Independence. Not being bossed around. Staying out of jail. And—*

Dr Bowman waited.

And staying alive, Jack said.

CHAPTER EIGHTEEN

WEDNESDAY, 8.45 AM

The street buzzed with the everyday activity of a normal Wednesday morning: a mother coaxed two kids into the back of a car, a nurse in scrubs trudged towards the tram and a man with a toolbox greeted a woman on a doorstep. Luke sat in his car, watching normal life pass by, as he waited for Ivan to emerge. The naivety of the man—giving his home address to the guy who'd broken his arm—made Luke shake his head.

Ivan locked the door of a modest brick house and sauntered down the path. He squeezed his bulk into the passenger seat of Luke's Subaru. Neither spoke. They drove across the city towards Malcolm's workshop in St Albans.

Luke broke the silence. 'You lied about it. Why?'

'He'd blow his top if he knew we got dusted by just one bloke.'

'You think lying to Gus is a good idea?'

'You fucked us over. You knocked out one of my teeth.' Ivan grunted. 'You lied too. What were you even doing there? You know this guy he's after?'

'His daughter is a friend.'

Sniggering, Ivan said, 'The tall hot chick? Gordy and I were—'

'*Stop*.' Luke held up a hand. 'I'll make you a deal. Stay away from her and I won't break your other arm.'

Ivan retreated into his seat. 'I've heard about you. Is it true you tossed a guy off a balcony once?'

'Believe everything you hear?' Luke hid his smile. 'I didn't know you were working for Gus, alright?'

'Just as well I lied. If he knew it was you, you'd be in the shit too.'

'Gus doesn't need to know. I didn't know her father was mixed up with him.'

'Seems to me we both have secrets from the boss.'

Luke conceded the point. 'Do we have a deal, Ivan?' He sounded like Gus, which made his skin crawl.

'What Gus doesn't know can't hurt him,' Ivan said.

From Luke's car, they watched Malcolm Trigg, a heavy-set panelbeater in his fifties, hitch up his work pants where they'd dropped below his belly and amble along the alleyway beside his panel shop to have a smoke at the rear.

'That guy used to steal stuff out of my schoolbag,' Luke said. 'He stayed with us a couple of times, when his wife kicked him out.'

'What was in your bag worth stealing?'

'Money. Drugs. A phone.'

Ivan shifted with apparent discomfort. Every so often he glanced across at Luke, as though with disbelief: *This is the guy who broke my arm?* 'You don't look like a stoner.'

'Whatever.' Luke shook his head. 'Let's go have a chat.'

Malcolm took a step backwards as Luke and Ivan appeared in the alley, nearly dropping his cigarette in fright. 'Jack! Fuck, you've grown up.'

Luke flashed him a smile. 'Hey, reckon you could look at a ding on my car?'

Malcolm tutted over the knock on the front fender. Luke made up a story about wanting to sell the car and getting it into good nick beforehand.

'Could probably bang it out,' Malcolm said. 'I'll have to get the panel off. Take an hour or so. How you going, anyway? Seen your old man lately?'

'Haven't seen Quin for years.' Sobering, Luke leaned against the back of the car, as though thinking about it. 'We didn't always get along.'

Malcolm nodded. 'What happened to you, when he went inside?'

'Group home.'

'Shit. Didn't know that.' Malcolm hitched up his pants again. 'Thought you might have gone to live with Kevin.'

'I crashed there sometimes,' Luke said. 'I went to Queensland after school finished. When I got back, Quin was gone.'

'He'd probably appreciate a call.'

'His phone's disconnected. You know where he is?' Luke kept it casual.

'Hasn't worked for me since he got banged up. Must be ten years.'

'You don't know where he went?'

Malcom hiked a shoulder. 'Last I knew, he was with Kevin in Footscray.'

'There's no one there now.'

'Then I don't know. Sorry, Jack. Can't help you.'

'How's your missus?' Luke remembered Malcolm's wife as a skinny woman in black leggings who'd once fed him chips for dinner on the front porch of their house.

'Moved up to the Gold Coast with her sister.'

'You haven't heard from Kevin either?'

Malcolm shook his head. 'He used to bring his car in, but I haven't seen him for years.' He added, 'Kev and Quin, they were like brothers. Ever since school.'

It was true: Kevin and Quin's relationship had always been dysfunctional—co-dependent in a way that made little sense to others. He'd seen Kevin punch Quin in the face; he'd seen Quin smash a plate on Kevin's head. But they always made up, usually by cracking a beer. They always had each other's backs.

'I suppose they could be up at Kevin's bush block,' Malcolm said with a shrug. 'He always said he'd retire there.'

Luke shivered, as though someone had walked over his grave. For a pained moment he struggled to speak. He stared at Malcolm's lined, whiskered face.

'Where?' Ivan muscled in, taking up the conversation while Luke searched for words.

'Dunno where it is.' Malcolm's gaze went to Luke.

Luke shook his head. He arranged with Malcolm to have the dent beaten out another time.

As soon as Malcolm had disappeared inside and Luke and Ivan were safely in the car, Ivan called Gus.

'The bloke's got a bush block somewhere.' Ivan's words came out in a gush.

Luke gestured to him to put the call on speaker. For a moment he thought Gus had hung up; nothing but static came from the phone.

'He has a *what*?' Gus's voice was dangerously quiet. The long silence that followed was not reassuring.

Ivan cast Luke a worried glance.

'WHAT THE ACTUAL FUCK? HOW THE HELL DID I NOT

KNOW THIS!' Gus's voice exploded into the cabin of the car, filling the space with outrage.

Luke said, 'I think I went there when I was a kid.'

'YOU KNEW ABOUT IT? What the *fuck*, Jackie!'

'It was years ago. I don't know where it is.' He dismissed it, as he had with Malcolm.

'Well, go to his house and find an address!'

Caught up in his thoughts, Luke drove from St Albans to Footscray without a word. He parked a few houses short of Gail's, gnawing on his lower lip.

'That's the house?' Ivan said. 'Looks deserted.'

To the right of Gail's house, two new townhouses were squashed into the one block. The narrow buildings took up the entire space, unlike Gail's, which sat luxuriously in the middle of the block, like a humble castle surrounded by a grass moat. A woman with a toddler and a baby played in the nearest front yard, making sandcastles in a blue plastic clam. The woman's attention was on her children, but every so often she looked up at the street.

Luke hadn't survived this long by being reckless. It was unlikely the woman would take any notice of them entering the house; the risk was small, but it was avoidable, and delaying the search bought him time.

Paranoid, Gus had called him, many times. *Risk-averse.*

He started the car and drove away.

'What are you doing?' Ivan bristled in the passenger seat.

Ignoring him, Luke parked in the next street and called Gus. 'Too many eyes. We need to come back at night.'

Gus took a few beats to answer. 'You're still bloody paranoid, Jackie.' Voices sounded in the background and the phone was muffled while Gus growled at someone. 'I'll call you later. Keep your phone on.'

Luke scowled. Being at Gus's beck and call made his left eye twitch with frustration. He drove Ivan home, thinking about Quin, Kevin, and his feigned ignorance about the bush block.

Lying to Gus was a dangerous game.

CHAPTER NINETEEN

TWELVE YEARS AGO

With Dr Bowman's wisdom, Frank's tuition and Gus's financial support, Jack survived his first year of high school. He was looking forward to his holiday break when Quin announced they were going to Kevin's block for the summer. The bush block near Castlemaine was the only holiday destination Jack knew. He'd been there a few times, for day trips or weekends camping. In winter, it was muddy puddles and freezing cold; in summer, it was hot, dusty and writhing with snakes.

Kevin spoke about retiring there to live off the grid. *It's peaceful. Open fire, gas barbecue, tin roof. What more could a man want, other than an esky full of beer?*

A month away with Kevin and Quin would be more like a nightmare than a holiday. Jack's fantasies of beach swims and training at the gym were dashed. His arguments were met with shrugs. Once Quin had an idea in his head, he was hard to budge. 'Teach you how to shoot and all that. Some bushcraft, you know?'

The idea that Quin, a lifelong city dweller, could teach him anything about the bush was ludicrous.

They piled their supplies into Kevin's car. The esky was packed with sausages and beer.

Slumped in sullen resignation in the back seat, Jack thumbed a text to Gus: *Going on holidays with Quin don't know how long.*

Gus's reply: *Tell me when you're back.*

Kevin drove, with Quin in the passenger seat talking rubbish and the radio playing a steady stream of hard rock. With each turn Kevin took, from the highway to the B roads, the roads grew progressively narrower and more potholed. Jack felt as though he'd entered the arterial system of a large animal: if the highway was the aorta, then their destination was a fingertip capillary, an oddly claustrophobic place to be.

As they neared their destination, the steep terrain troubled Kevin's low-slung Commodore. He drove with care, easing over rocks and potholes that threatened to swallow the car whole. Jack swayed with the rocking of the car as it lumbered on, watching out his window for clues to the gold-rush history of the area. The forest was sparser than he remembered—tall straight trunks, spaced like a plantation, with an understorey of low shrubs and thick grasses. Wildflowers dotted the undergrowth with tiny spots of yellow, purple, blue. *Box-ironbark forest*, Kevin told him. Among the trees, ruined buildings, reduced to broken lines of stone, protruded from the ground like rotten teeth. Rusted tin sheds and derelict fences collapsed into themselves, defying gravity and age. Signs warned of treacherous holes where the mines had been.

Kevin slowed for a left-hand turn and stopped before a rusty wire gate adorned with a faded metal sign: STILLWATER. The letters were punched out with bullet holes: the words had been used for target practice. It fell to Jack to get out and pull the heavy gate open.

The track narrowed even further, with spiky grasses scratching the sides of the car and the towering trees meeting overhead in the middle. They emerged into a cleared area, with the cabin to the left and the dam to the right. Fallen leaves papered the red-brown ground, which the summer sun had baked to a solid crust. The eucalypts were more grey than green and everything stank of heat and dirt and ants.

Jack dragged himself out of the car, wondering what the hell he was going to do for a whole month. He'd only brought four books. The December sun was pleasantly warm for about a minute before he felt it burning his skin. He held up his phone, searching for a signal.

'Have to go to the top of the ridge.' Kevin pointed up the slope behind the cabin.

Grumbling, Jack trudged up the hill, weaving through the black-trunked ironbark trees and straggly eucalypts, with the long grass and ground covers catching at his feet. The tall trunks around him felt eerie, as though they were soldiers at attention, observing him; every time he turned his head, he caught movement from the corner of his eye—a bird or animal, or leaves falling. The quiet noises of the forest felt secretive.

He reached the spine of rocky outcrops marking the highest point and stood on a rock to survey his surroundings. He didn't know where Kevin's land ended, as there were no marked boundaries. The forest stretched out in all directions, a fuzzy blanket of grey and green on the ripples of ridges and gullies.

From his vantage point, Jack peered out over the clearing that contained the cabin and the dam, and the winding track from the road. The track continued past the clearing, heading further east through the forest to end at the cliff edge of a gully that slashed the land from north to south. Jack held up his phone and got one bar of reception.

A rustle in the undergrowth alerted him to company: a wallaby sat watching from between the trees, as still as the rocks on which Jack perched. He waited in silence until the wallaby bounded away, thinking about the ancient land, the rocks and gullies and trees. The hushed forest felt timeless and impassive, immune to anything as puny as human intervention.

Later, as they sat by the dam eating sausages in bread, Jack asked Kevin how old the cabin was. He got a grunted reply: *My grandfather might know*, which was unhelpful, as Bernard McNally had been dead for decades. The property had survived generations in the family, like the house in Footscray, untouched by wealth or improvement.

At Stillwater, Kevin's mood mellowed. He relaxed in a way he never did in the city, as though worry lifted off his shoulders and he forgot to be an arsehole. His dream of retiring there made sense. Quin told Jack that Kevin's father had loved the place too, but he'd had a heart attack and fallen off a ladder before he could retire. It prompted Jack to ask Quin about his own grandparents, but Quin turned his face away and he said, *I ran away when I was fifteen, haven't seen them since.*

The cabin was basic: four plank walls, a wooden floor, a brick fireplace and a corrugated-iron roof. They'd brought camping mats and slept on the floor. A rainwater tank leaned against one wall; the toilet was a spider-infested long-drop. Evenings were spent outside, sitting on tree stumps around the campfire, gazing at the placid dam. The first few nights, Jack startled at every sound from the forest, and Kevin teased him: *feral cats are as big as panthers out here* and *the foxes are like wolves*. But the biggest animals Jack saw were grey kangaroos, which were too shy to scare him.

Quin had brought his beaten-up acoustic guitar, and his picking, strumming and crooning provided a soundtrack to the campsite. He flicked from Midnight Oil to U2, from Cold Chisel to Bon Jovi, Guns N' Roses to AC/DC. Jack and Kevin groaned over Quin's frustrating habit of never finishing a song; his attention span meant he abandoned most songs after the second verse. Jack wondered if knowing the words to the first half of hundreds of songs would come in useful in his later life.

He soon grew bored of Quin and Kevin, whose conversation consisted of arguments and gossip and grandiose plans for the future. He stuffed food into his pockets and explored the block alone, climbing rocks and trees, swinging around branches, building cubby houses all for himself. His focus sharpened as his familiarity with the landscape grew. Within a week, he'd mapped out the steep ridge in his head: all the tracks and clearings, the best shady spots to sit and read, the hiding places behind rocks and stumps.

Next, he investigated the gully. From the cliff edge, it was about thirty metres to the base, a vertical descent made treacherous by loose dirt and rubble. He tied a rope to a tree at the top, hanging off it to make paths down, using branches and rocks as footholds to get to the mess of broken trees and leaf litter at the base. He guessed that water flowed through the gully in winter, but in summer the ground squelched and stank of stagnant water. The air was thick with flies and mosquitoes. The coolness of the shady gully was welcome, but after a close encounter with a brown snake, he scrambled to the top and scouted for another place to explore.

The area around the dam—a man-made waterhole about fifty metres long and half as wide—was more pleasant. *Been there since before my grandfather*, Kevin said, *when the gold fossickers were panning in the creek.* Nestled in the lee of the ridge, it was protected from wind and in shade for most of the day; the surface of the water was always deathly still, a mirror reflecting the blue sky. On the far side, rushes made a swamp-like sanctuary for birds and reptiles. The camp side was a muddy beach. A creek trickled down from the ridge to feed it, and another disappeared off into the gully, sluggish water oozing over the rocks and debris of the creek bed. When the heat got to him, Jack stripped off and dipped into the dam, grimacing at the greasy mud between his toes.

Near the top of the cliff, an overgrown path led to the old mine. Kevin warned Jack to stay away from it.

Never know when it's gonna cave in. It's full of bats, and they reckon it's haunted. Kevin's words were as close to humour as Jack had ever heard from him. *The last prospector never came out. If you go up there at night, you can hear him picking at the walls.*

Of course, Jack was compelled to investigate. The entrance to the mine—*it's called an adit*, Kevin said—was a hole in the side of the hill, like a cave, and high enough that Jack could walk in. The walls and roof were scaffolded with branches from trees felled nearby. It seemed as precarious as Kevin had warned.

Jack peered inside, flashing his torch into the dim interior. Kevin was right, and the stench of bat urine assaulted him. He edged in. Within a few metres, the adit lowered and narrowed, and he crept forwards. He'd expected a hole in the ground—a vertical shaft—but what he found was a gently sloping cave.

It was cool and damp inside. The adit curved sharply to the right, and once around the bend it was completely dark. He wondered how the prospectors knew where to dig. As he ventured deeper inside, he examined the scarred areas where the rock had been chipped away. To his inexperienced eye, the orange-brown rock was nothing special. When he picked at it with his fingers, it crumbled like dried-up clay.

A flurry of movement above his head flattened him to the ground: the bats had taken umbrage at his presence. He cowered, arms over his head, as their wings flapped and the air rushed around him. The ammonic smell burned his nose.

With the torch in one hand and his other following the wall, Jack pressed onwards, forced into a stoop as the ceiling grew lower. He flicked the beam around the narrow space and then, with his heart in his throat, he scrambled out. He'd seen skeletons before, in museums and science labs, but not like this.

Back at the cabin, he waited until Kevin was out of earshot to tell Quin. 'It's an old prospector, with clothes still hanging off his bones. Must be a hundred and fifty years old!'

'I wonder if Kevin knows,' Quin said.

'Don't tell him. He told me not to go in there.'

Quin did tell Kevin, who later yelled at Jack for going in and said, *Of course there's a skeleton; that's the ghost, right?*

At night, Jack listened for the ghost picking at the walls, but he never heard it, even in his imagination.

While Jack was exploring the bush and swimming in the dam, Kevin and Quin drank beer and shot at things.

Kevin's obsession with his Enfield rifle made Jack nervous. The weapon was an heirloom, an antique: Kevin said his great-grandfather had brought it home from the First World War, a story Jack suspected had been embellished with time. Kevin took the rifle apart to clean it, reassembled it and cleaned it again, polishing the wooden stock to a high shine. It was the most care Jack had seen him apply to any task.

At night, they hunted with a spotlight, casting around to find the rabbits' eyes glowing in the darkness. Jack knew they were vermin, but Kevin's dedication to their eradication was unsettling. Kevin made him fire the rifle a few times, but his lack of enthusiasm embarrassed Quin and inflamed Kevin.

'Give me that.' Kevin jerked the weapon from his hands. 'No point if you're not even going to aim.'

Jack grumbled that he'd happily shoot at targets during the day, when he could see what he was doing. In a rare moment of civility, Kevin took it upon himself to teach him. And much as he didn't want to admit it, Jack got a buzz from watching beer cans fly off the stump when he hit them.

Kevin taught him to shoot; Quin taught him to drive. Jack was only twelve, but he was tall enough to reach the pedals. He drove Kevin's car up and down the track to the road, and to the cliff edge of the gully and the dam. He learned how to reverse, how to do a three-point turn on the narrow track, how to spin the tyres in the dirt for fun. Driving gave him a glimpse of adulthood; he felt included in Quin and Kevin's world.

Another week passed, and another. By the time they packed the car to go home, Jack felt like he'd lived in the forest forever. When they arrived in Footscray, he couldn't figure out which was a dream—the block, or his city life? He'd had weeks of open sky, cool water and trees, no television, no lights, no phone. It was as though he'd hit a reset button. When he saw his tanned face and sun-bleached hair in the mirror, he barely recognised himself.

Quin didn't get much right, but the summer at Stillwater was a memory Jack didn't hate.

CHAPTER TWENTY

WEDNESDAY, 11.45 AM

After dropping Ivan home, Luke drove a few blocks and parked outside a convenience store. He went inside to buy a drink, then sat in his car. Malcolm's unknowing betrayal of Stillwater felt like a violation of his privacy—as though nothing was sacred, not even the few childhood memories he could enjoy.

Chocolate milk, another childhood memory. He closed his eyes as the sugar hit his system, thinking about betraying Ivan and the possible consequences. His conscience clamoured for attention.

Luke stared out at the parking lot. Customers entered and exited the store, carrying sandwiches in plastic triangles or brown paper bags made transparent by fried food. He'd loitered outside shops like this as a teenager, checking for surveillance cameras and security screens, assessing the confidence of various employees. Phoning Gus with information: *Knife in his back pocket. He's in the Sev on Brunswick Street. One camera over the front door.* It seemed a long time ago.

The Samsung beeped, bringing him back to the present. Gus: *11 pm on the corner.*

He'd come so far; and yet, here he was, sitting outside a convenience store waiting for his phone to beep.

He pushed Gus and his pesky conscience aside and texted Jonathan: *I have information.*

The reply was instant: *Come to the office now.*

In the middle of a busy weekday, Jonathan's building was a hive of activity. Luke parked a block away and paused to plan his tactics. The foyer was dotted with men and women in business clothes, heading out for lunch or meetings. In his jeans and T-shirt, he felt out of place. He usually took more care to camouflage into his environment. When he reached the fifth floor and the Wylie Consulting offices, he made his way to the reception area. A young woman with dark hair and perfect lipstick sat behind a glass-topped desk, typing at a computer. *Natalie Brudzinski*, the nameplate on her desk read.

Her eyebrows rose as she took in his casual attire, but her smile was warm. 'Mr Wylie's expecting you. Go straight in, Mr Harris.'

He couldn't remember the last time he'd been called *Mr Harris*, if he ever had.

'Thank you, Ms Brudzinski.' He couldn't help himself.

'Natalie, please.'

'Luke, please.' He escaped from flirting to rap on the frame beside Jonathan's open office door. His humour evaporated as he remembered why he was there. He sat opposite Jonathan at the desk and waited.

Jonathan broke the frosty silence. 'You're very efficient. I expected I'd have to chase you this evening.'

Luke didn't hesitate. 'The big guy's name is Ivan Syminski. He's a mechanic, works out of a place off Sydney Road. I've got his home address.'

'And the other man?'

'I don't have a bead on him yet.'

With a deep inhale, Jonathan tapped his pen on his desk. 'How did you find him so quickly?'

'Magic,' Luke said. 'Jonathan, I did what you asked. You can delete that video now.'

Jonathan laughed, genuinely amused. 'You don't really think it's that simple, do you?'

Luke hid his sigh. 'What do you want?'

Pushing his chair back, Jonathan got up and went to the window. He clasped his hands behind his back and rocked on his heels. Luke's attention was caught by movement outside the window. A formed flock of seagulls, silhouetted in flight against the cloudy sky, dispersed and then re-formed, as though streaming around an invisible obstacle.

'It's a great view, isn't it?' Gesturing for Luke to join him, Jonathan pointed out along the bay. 'That's one of my projects there, over at Port Melbourne. Hell of a ride, that one. You'd think people didn't want progress, the way they carry on.'

All Luke could make out was an enormous crane and the skeleton of a high-rise building. He figured he was supposed to be impressed. Maybe he was, a little.

'I built all of this from scratch, you know.' Jonathan stared straight ahead. In profile, his face seemed hollow. Every bone in his cheek was pronounced, his hawkish nose sharply defined. 'I started with nothing. My father was a gardener—kept the grass cut for rich people at a golf club and retired with nothing to show for fifty years of work.' A snort, laden with contempt. 'You understand. You're the same. You come from nothing.'

Turning to meet Jonathan's gaze, Luke held his tongue.

The words were quieter. 'I've seen the way you look at my house. And here—noting the details, the quality of the finish, the size of my desk. I can feel your envy. It's what you want, isn't it? Wealth and comfort. All the trimmings. A five-thousand-dollar coffee machine.' A soft laugh, humourless. 'It makes sense to study commerce when it's money that fascinates you. Those of us who grow up poor—we either accept it or we fight it. You're a fighter. Like me.'

'Is that right?' Under different circumstances, the assumptions would have amused Luke.

'You'll get past the money at some point. When money ceases to matter, it becomes a game, which is much more satisfying.'

'You don't know anything about me.'

Jonathan fixed him with a narrow glare. 'I know enough. I called the agency. They did their due diligence—your police check was clear. But we all know it's not a perfect system.' He rocked on his heels again. 'I know you're capable of punching a man in the face. They've done studies on it—how some people can push through the natural inhibition of antisocial behaviour, but most can't. You broke that man's arm without a second thought.'

'What's your point?' Luke was familiar with the quoted study; he'd discussed it with Dr Bowman, in the context of ethical questions raised by professional boxing and cage fighting. It seemed a long time ago.

'Ivan Syminski threatened my home. I need you to remove that threat.'

'You want me to have a quiet word with him?'

Jonathan frowned. 'Don't play the innocent. It doesn't suit you. I want you to kill him.'

Shaking his head, Luke said, 'He works for one of your competitors, I presume—another developer? You know who employed him. Why go after the messenger?'

'To return the message.' Jonathan's lip curled with distaste. 'To show him I can bite too.' With sudden agitation, he paced away from Luke, then turned, spitting his words in a harsh staccato. 'I've worked hard to get where I am—I will not tolerate this *intrusion* into my personal life and I *will not* be pushed around!'

'Jonathan.' Luke held up his palms. 'If you want him dead, you'll need to do it yourself.'

Planting his feet, Jonathan ran a hand through his hair and seethed. A spot of colour rouged his cheeks. 'No. Your skill set, not mine. You're a fixer. I knew it the moment I met you.'

The backhanded compliment hung between them. 'You've done this before, haven't you?'

'Sadly, in my line of work, these obstacles come up from time to time.' Jonathan's gaze was grey and unflinching. 'Planning issues, building inspectors, overzealous bureaucrats.' He paused. 'You know you can't refuse. If you do, I'll find someone else—but I have that video, remember. If anything happens to Ivan Syminski, who will the police assume is responsible?'

Luke rounded on Jonathan and grasped his shoulder. 'You're going to delete that *now*.'

'Don't be stupid.' A flash of fear crossed Jonathan's face, but he recovered quickly. 'Get your hands off me. Either do what I say or I'll frame you for it.'

'Who's to say you won't frame me anyway?'

'Gentlemen's agreement. I appreciate having someone like you to call on. You're no use to me in jail.'

Luke considered punching him, throwing him through the wall of glass, smacking his head into the desk. Stabbing the pen through his hand or his eye. Splintering his shin with a kick. Breaking his fingers, a couple of ribs, a knee.

The thoughts must have reached the surface: Jonathan backed away. He went to his desk to retrieve an envelope, which he tossed to Luke. 'An incentive. I'm not asking you to work for free.'

Catching the envelope in one hand, Luke paused, speechless.

'Thought so. Good choice.' Jonathan's smirk made Luke's fists clench anew.

Words were inadequate. Luke turned to leave.

Jonathan's voice followed him. 'And stay away from Emma. Don't make me renege on our agreement.'

In the safety of his car, Luke gave his anger free rein. He smacked the steering wheel repeatedly with his palms and said *fuck, fuck, fuck* until he realised how mad it was and stopped to focus on his breathing. Then he remembered his phone.

He'd hit the voice recorder a moment before getting out of the lift. Natalie's voice was quiet, but Jonathan's was clear: conspiring to murder Ivan, for no better reason than to send the message that he wouldn't be intimidated.

Luke emailed the recording to himself as a backup, then ran through his options, moving puzzle pieces around in his head. Just as the puzzle was settling into place, his phone rang, jarring him back to reality.

'Luke? What are you doing? Where are you?'

Emma's impassioned voice made him sit up straight.

'Phil's freaking out! I just got home—the emergency carer couldn't deal and I can't get Dad on the phone and—'

Luke controlled an exhale. He knew why Jonathan wasn't answering his phone. 'Why is Phil at home?'

'He refused to go to school this morning—he's all messed up! He's outside, yelling at the sky.'

'Is he safe?'

From the background noise, he guessed Emma was moving through the house. 'He's still yelling.'

Luke said, 'I'll be there in fifteen minutes.'

He pulled out into traffic, cursing his inability to stay out of trouble. There were other options: Emma could call an ambulance or the police. Was it really his job to fix everything?

A fixer. Jonathan's words rankled.

When he reached the Wylies', he pulled into the driveway and was out of his car before the engine stopped ticking. He hit the buzzer on the gate and it clicked open a few seconds later; Emma flung the front door open and he followed her through the house to the backyard. In the middle of the lawn, Phil sat cross-legged, shouting at the sky and flapping his arms around his head as though to ward off an attack of invisible birds.

'Go away!' Phil's face was pink, sheened with perspiration. His glasses perched at an impossible angle on his nose.

'Hey, buddy.' Luke flopped onto the grass. 'Whatcha doing?'

Phil ignored him to yell at the sky, frustrated that it wouldn't do what it was told and GO AWAY.

'Who are you talking to, Phil?'

No sensible answer came.

'Stay with him,' Luke said to Emma, and he went inside to check the communication book for clues. He popped out a couple of Ativan from the medication box, shoving the tablets into his pocket.

At a shout from Emma, he rushed outside to find Phil climbing up the side of the pool house. The single-storey brick building opened to the pool area; the nearest wall sported a downpipe, a rectangular window near the eaves and, now, a chubby young man scrambling for footholds. With unexpected agility, Phil scaled the downpipe, then balanced with a foot on the windowsill and reached for the eaves, stretching out in an awkward diagonal against the brick building.

'Emma—call triple zero!' Luke dashed after Phil. 'Phil, no! You need to get down!'

His words had no effect. Phil dragged himself up, his legs bending comically like a clumsy spider. He manoeuvred over the eaves and hauled his bulk onto the roof.

Luke followed Phil's path, a few seconds behind him. The downpipe, the windowsill, the eaves. He hadn't scaled a building for years. It was like riding a bike.

'What are you doing up here, Phil?' Keeping his voice as calm as he could, he held up his palms as he balanced on the sloped roof.

Phil's eyes were wide, the whites glowing around his dark irises. His glasses were long gone.

'It's me. Luke. Why don't we sit down?'

'GO AWAY!' Phil started waving his arms again.

Retreating, Luke dropped to his haunches a few metres away.

Phil sat down, hugging his knees to his chest. He muttered to himself, rocking backwards and forwards.

After a few moments, Luke tried again. 'Do you want an Ativan?' He reached into his pocket.

'NO!'

The best option was to sit in silence until Phil moved. The sun beat down on them, Phil's face glistening with the heat, and he continued to rock, staring into the middle distance; he seemed unaware of Luke's presence. Luke gazed out over the rooftops, across fences and backyards, as though sitting on a roof was a normal thing to do.

Sirens neared. For once in his life Luke was relieved, but the sound spurred Phil to his feet. Waving his arms and shouting, as though he could see things no one else could, he balanced precariously on the steeply pitched roof.

'Hey, buddy—' Luke was barely on his feet when his words were cut off. Phil launched at him, throwing his weight at Luke in a crazed run towards the edge. Luke's voice raised to a wail, but it was too late: he was knocked off his feet and they flew together into the air. Phil clasped around him like a koala, hugging with his legs and arms. For a heartbeat they were weightless; then they plummeted to earth.

A second later, the chill water of the swimming pool slapped at Luke's skin, tugged at his clothes. Clutched together, they plunged into the deep end of the pool, all the way down.

Panicking, Phil pushed Luke down, holding him with hands and feet in his desperate need to get out of the water. Submerged under Phil's struggling bulk, Luke couldn't move from the bottom of the pool. With his lungs burning for air, he tried to push Phil upwards and detangle from him. Water rushed into his ears and nose; he could see nothing but churning water.

He couldn't breathe—couldn't escape Phil's clutching hands—

Just as he started to panic, the weight lifted. A hand grasped Luke's arm, another his collar, and jerked him above the surface of the water. He came face to face with a police officer. He hauled himself over the edge to collapse into foetal position on the decking beside the pool, gasping for air.

'Bugger me.' The cop's eyes were as wide as Phil's had been. Her cap was askew, and she was wet to the shoulders from dragging him out. 'You alright?'

'Where's Phil?' Luke got to his hands and knees, still panting.

She gestured to where Phil was propped against the pool fence, with a paramedic on each arm. 'Who are you?'

Luke told her his name, and she followed as he struggled to his feet and went to Phil. The paramedics checked his breathing and talked about secondary drowning, but he wasn't worried about himself: he was worried about Phil, who'd needed an injection of sedatives. They wanted to take him to hospital. It was likely he'd be admitted to the psychiatric ward.

With sudden dread, Luke patted his pockets for his phones. His old iPhone was history; bubbles of water had seeped inside the cracked screen. The Samsung, a newer model, appeared unharmed. Luke stared at it in relief.

When he glanced up, the police officer was watching. Cops had a radar for people like him.

On the patio, Emma was explaining what had happened, speaking to a younger, male cop. She gave Luke a towel, and he rubbed at his wet head and dripping clothes. His T-shirt clung to him; he took it off to wring it out, then felt the weight of all the eyes watching him. He turned his back and realised that was worse. His scars were not pretty.

A snippet of conversation between Emma and the cops filtered through to him. Emma had recorded the incident on her phone.

'You're fucking kidding me!' Luke's words tumbled out. 'Your brother's trying to fly and you filmed it?'

'What?' Emma's eyes widened.

'Show me.' Luke groaned as he watched the footage. She'd caught him scaling the building, the flying leap into the water and Luke's undignified exit from the pool; the audio was overlaid with Emma's call to emergency services.

'You made that climb look easy,' the female officer said. It was possible she was impressed, but all he heard was suspicion.

'You should be an actor,' Emma said. 'I see more of you in videos than real life.' Her attempt at humour didn't hide her distress; her hands still shook.

Luke said, 'Can you delete it, please?'

'After I show it to Dad.'

'Delete it.' His growl was pure Jack Quinlan. '*Now*. Give me that!' He twisted the phone out of her hand.

'Jesus, Luke!'

'Hey. Give it back.' The male officer stuck out his chest and wedged himself between them. Luke tossed the phone to Emma, then stalked through the house to his car.

He put the towel on the seat. As he turned the key, Emma rushed out of the gate to knock on his window. Her face was pale.

'I didn't say thanks. Sorry about the video.'

He couldn't find a polite answer. Most of his anger was directed at himself for getting involved in the first place. He'd contributed nothing useful. But Emma's thoughtless actions made him fume— and he blamed himself for that, too; he should have expected it, he was an idiot to think he could trust people . . .

She said, cautiously, 'Luke, can we talk about it?'

'I don't want to fucking talk about it.'

He shoved the car into gear and backed out of the driveway, witnessing his own dysfunctional reaction with detachment. Lashing out and running away, as he would have done as a teenager.

By the time he got home, his body was as taut as a wire.

After a cold shower, he sat cross-legged on the floor and practised kumbhaka pranayama. In . . . hold . . . slow exhale. Several minutes later, he was calm enough to open his eyes. It had taken a long time to learn how to still his body, and even longer to stop his thoughts from swirling into negativity.

The body remembers, Dr Bowman had always said. *Start there, and your mind will follow.*

CHAPTER TWENTY-ONE

ELEVEN YEARS AGO

Jack peeked around the corner, checking the coast was clear. The school was deserted within minutes of classes ending; the building echoed with silence, as though the ghosts of students past and present made white noise beyond human detection. He shivered. The principal's secretary emerged from her office, forcing him into retreat. He waited for her to disappear down the stairs before edging towards the meeting room, praying no one would question his presence.

He pushed open the door. Dr Bowman, writing in a file on the desk, looked up and smiled. 'I wasn't sure if you'd come.'

Poised in the doorway, Jack said, 'Did they tell you what happened?'

'Mr Saunders told me.' Putting down his pen, the psychologist indicated the chair. 'Come and sit.'

Jack didn't budge. 'I'm not a student here anymore.'

'Sit down. Please.'

Another moment of hesitation, and Jack lowered himself into the chair, looking at his hands. His knuckles were healing, but his face was still a mess. He moved to speak, but bottled it back; anything he could say seemed flimsy.

'You got into a big fight.'

'I don't want to talk about it.'

'Then why are you here?'

'I don't want to fucking talk about it, alright?' Pushing out of his chair, Jack went to the window. 'I just came to tell you—'

'Breathe. Slow it down.'

With a hand against the glass, Jack let his head sink forwards until his breath misted on the surface; it was frosty outside. 'Alright, whatever. He set my bag on fire—stuck a bunch of lit cigarettes in it. So I punched him in the face.' An excellent combo: Frank would have been proud. 'But there were four of them. They held me down. Put out their smokes on my arms. Kicked me around. I got most of them back.' He'd taken a few hard knocks, but it was nothing compared to what he dished out.

What happened next was harder to admit; he kept most of it to himself. He'd been dragged to the principal's office, and they couldn't get Quin on the phone. Gail was at work and didn't answer her mobile. He even tried Kevin. In desperation, he called Gus, who descended like a thundercloud and threatened legal action unless Jack was released from his scholarship conditions without penalty. When Mr Saunders questioned Gus's authority, Jack pointed out that Gus was listed on his file as an alternative contact. There were advantages to managing his own school records.

Gus had driven him home in silence. He parked outside Quin's seedy flat, lit a cigarette, and said, *Reckon I just saved you thirty grand, Jackie. And favours come around, don't they?*

Dr Bowman drew him back to the present. 'Mr Saunders expelled you?'

'Technically I chose to leave.' Jack managed a wan smile.

'How do you feel about that?'

Jack tried to think of the right words. 'Relieved. I've had the last week off. I need to enrol at school in Footscray before Children's Services gets involved.' He wiped his sleeve against the fogged glass so he could see out, unsure how to express what he wanted to say. 'I'm pretty sure they won't have a psychologist at the public school.'

Dr Bowman chose his words carefully. 'If you'd like to continue seeing me, there are ways we can organise it. I'm here on Wednesdays, but I work elsewhere the rest of the week.'

A lump in his throat made his words hoarse. 'Quin won't be able to pay.'

'I might be able to pull some strings. For funding. Leave it with me. I'll get in touch with him to arrange—'

'You'll need to arrange it with me. Quin never answers his phone.'

'Do you? Most kids just text, don't they?'

Jack shook his head. 'I always answer my phone.' Missing a call from Gus led to an instant berating: *ANSWER YOUR FUCKING PHONE!*

He turned back to the window to hide his face, his hot eyes, his trembling mouth. It took a few moments to untangle his emotions, to make sense of his thoughts. The wash of relief—he'd assumed this was the last time he'd see Dr Bowman—held him immobile while he processed it. He bottled it away. Stuffed it down where it belonged.

'You okay, Jack?'

With a nonchalant shrug that fooled nobody, he shoved his hands into his pockets. 'Peachy. But I'd better go, before Mr Saunders catches me here.' He added, 'Wouldn't want to get you into trouble.

That would challenge our roles, wouldn't it? I'm the rule-breaker, not you.'

'Smart-arse,' Dr Bowman said.

The unexpected response brought a smile to Jack's face; he poked out his tongue as he left.

The end of his scholarship shifted his relationship with Gus, as though it had bound them together. Any gratitude Jack felt for Gus's intervention was soured with resentment; he felt dependent in a way he hadn't previously, and Gus did nothing to dispel the feeling. The day after the incident, when he knew Jack was sulking at home, Gus had put him to work.

You're off school, right? Gotta keep you busy.

So instead of resting or reading, Jack spent the week delivering messages or packages or watching men from corners, or at the gym, counting and bundling cash.

The local school in Footscray felt relaxed and familiar, and he recognised some of the kids from primary school. He slotted into his classes quietly and minded his own business. When the kids asked where he'd come from, he told them the truth: *I got kicked out of a private school for punching a bully in the face.* It helped achieve his aim of being left alone. The principal, Mrs Price, warned him of her zero-tolerance policy towards fighting. He reassured her he had no intention of punching anyone unless they stuck a lit cigarette on his arm, at which she paled. He figured she'd only heard one side of the story from Rodley.

Dr Bowman arranged to see Jack through a community health centre nearby. The neutral territory and independence from the school system meant they could both speak more freely. To Jack, it felt like a new relationship, one they'd both chosen rather than being forced together. Their formality lapsed, their language deteriorated and they shared more jokes. Confiding was easier, although there were rules: Dr Bowman made the conditions for his confidentiality clear. He didn't want to know the specifics about anything illegal, or anything that would lead to a mandatory report. They spent an entire session discussing what that meant. Jack appreciated the heads-up.

Their sessions all started the same way: 'How are you going?'

'Boss is giving me the shits. I'm waiting on a text.' Jack's phone rested on his thigh. He was purposefully vague. They talked in a code that meant Dr Bowman didn't have to breach his professional ethics.

'What's he doing?'

'He's called four times already this week.' Jack glanced at the phone, his tether to Gus. 'I'm invisible, right? Just another kid in school uniform. So, he gets me to check people out—like, what car they drive or . . . that kind of thing.' He didn't say the rest. What locks they had on their doors. Whether they had security cameras or a dog. Whether they had weapons and where they were kept.

'And you're concerned his intentions are not good?'

Jack laughed. 'I know his intentions are not good.'

'Remind me why you work for him?'

'Because he pays me and I go to the gym for free.' Without Gus, he'd be living on rice and tinned tuna. He hadn't seen Quin for three days.

'To teach you how to beat people up so you can work for him more effectively.'

'The only fights I have are at the gym.'

'Jack, you're already taller than me. In a few years, he'll be calling on you in other ways.'

Jack scoffed. 'You know way too much about criminals.'

'I worked in the juvenile remand centre for years. So many drugs, so much anger, stories you wouldn't believe. Well—I think you would, actually. Some of the kids really wanted to talk.'

'*Want* is the wrong word,' Jack said with a grunt. 'No one wants to talk about this shit.'

'You do.'

'I don't *want* to.' Jack rolled his eyes. 'But it's your job to listen to me whine about my crappy life, so I'll play.'

'On the matter of not wanting to talk about things, we still haven't talked about the man who threatened to kill you.' Dr Bowman was matter-of-fact. He brought it up every now and then, testing the waters. Every time, Jack's answer was the same: *I don't want to fucking talk about it.*

Jack's gaze flicked to the large manila folder on the desk. He wondered what was in there: reports from Children's Services, photos of various injuries, hospital and school reports, he guessed. Nothing good. He hid his tension behind a forced stillness.

'When you're ready.'

'I don't want to talk about it.'

'You remember it all. Your body remembers.'

'I don't want to fucking talk about it!' His fists balled and his eyes flicked to the door. Escape was only a few steps away.

'Breathe. You're not breathing.'

'I am breathing.'

'Slow it down.'

Dr Bowman demonstrated with a hand on his chest to show a measured inhale and longer exhale. Jack, for want of anything better to do, complied.

'What can you tell me about him? What did he look like?'

'Six-one, soft around the middle. Not much hair.' Jack breathed out. 'Bad teeth. Crooked nose. Ugly. Leather jacket like a bikie, only he isn't.'

'What else do you remember?'

'He's right-handed.' Jack swallowed past a lump in his throat.

'How do you know that?'

'He hit me more on the left side of my face.' Memories assaulted him, flashing across his vision. The crack of a fist on his cheek. Robbo's foot hitting his ribs. He put his face in his hands and tried to breathe.

'The counsellor you saw then said you weren't ready to talk about it.'

His words came out muffled. 'She treated me like a stupid kid.'

'In her defence, you were ten years old.' Dr Bowman's tone was mild. 'How should she have treated you?'

'I wanted them to leave me alone.'

'Is that why you threw a chair at the police?'

'I was fucking angry! They wouldn't listen to me! I didn't know where Quin was! Robbo would have fucking killed me!' Jack hammered a fist onto the desk and shot to his feet. His red-hot rage surged anew: heat behind his eyes, his arms and legs trembling, fire in his belly. He stomped towards the door and flung words over his shoulder. 'Fuck this. I told you I don't want to—'

'Jack. Breathe.'

He stopped, holding the doorhandle. His head was full of pressure, as though it might explode. His hand smarted from hitting the desk. Dr Bowman's kind voice felt painful, like a soft brush against abraded skin. Jack considered throwing a chair at him to make him shut up.

'I'd be angry too. You shouldn't have had to go through that. No one should.'

Dr Bowman sat still with his hands on his lap, unthreatening. Jack wanted to run, but something kept him standing there.

Trust. He trusted that Dr Bowman had his interests at heart.

Sullenly, he returned to his chair, sat down and focused on the sky outside the window.

They fell silent, while Dr Bowman considered and Jack hugged his chest with his arms.

'You must have been very scared.'

Jack's anger flared. 'I was just a kid.'

'You're still a kid, Jack.'

'Yeah, I've grown since then.' He frowned and retreated.

'You don't have to be tough in here.' Dr Bowman smiled.

Jack rubbed the scar on his neck and forced his hand away. Of all his scars, it was the one that bothered him the most.

'What would you say to him, if you could?'

Jack scowled. 'I wouldn't use words.'

'You'd want to get revenge?'

'Is this where you tell me I'm better than that?' With a snort, Jack folded his arms. 'What I would say is: I was just a kid. He thought he was so tough. Big tough guy, taking on a ten-year-old.'

'Do you remember what you felt at the time?'

Jack pursed his lips. He'd felt a lot of things.

'Let's try something.' Dr Bowman leaned forwards, his elbows on his knees. 'Close your eyes. Remember you're here now—safe. Think about what you felt back then.'

Warily, Jack obeyed.

The smell of Robbo Parker's sweat came to him.

'What would you say, if you could speak to that ten-year-old in the chair?'

'Don't piss your pants,' Jack said. He got a chuckle, which was his intention. 'I'd say, *One day you'll be tougher than this arsehole.*'

'That's your goal? To be tougher than him?'

'And smarter. Only an idiot loans Quin money and expects it back.' He got another laugh and opened his eyes, met Dr Bowman's directly. 'You know what I'd say? I'd say, *You'll be alright, because you can look after yourself.*'

'That's great, but kind of sad. You've been looking after yourself for a long time. Since your mother died, I suspect.'

'We don't always get to choose.' It was something Dr Bowman often said.

'There's a technical term for it. Hyper-independence. Kids who go through a lot can find it hard to ask for help or accept help when it's offered. As though they can only trust themselves.'

'Sounds like a useful strategy to me.' But Jack looked out the window and tucked the word away to think about later.

'Sometimes the feelings are hard to name,' Dr Bowman said. 'Like feeling helpless. Powerless. Like you have no control. Like there's no safe place.'

Jack said nothing.

'Do you have safe places now?'

He nodded. Gail's house, when Kevin wasn't there. Training with Frank. His footy team. This office.

'Good. Remember that. Remember what safety feels like. So, knowing what happened was wrong but can't be changed,' Dr Bowman said, 'makes it hard to know where to put those feelings, right?'

'Up Robbo's arse would be a good place.'

'If you like the idea of shoving your fear up Robbo's arse, go ahead and visualise it.'

Jack pulled a face and pretended to gag. 'Damn. Now that's an image I'll never unsee.'

They laughed together. A warm, relaxed feeling settled on Jack's shoulders and melted down his back, as though something that had been tightly wound unravelled and loosened and released.

On cue, his phone beeped with a text: *Need you at the gym in an hour.*

Jack was already on his feet. 'I've gotta go.'

Dr Bowman was used to it. 'See you in a month, Jack.'

CHAPTER TWENTY-TWO

WEDNESDAY, 11.30 PM

'What a dump.' Gus peered at Gail's house through the windscreen of the Audi. Flickering streetlamps cast cool white light over the concrete path, the weedy front yard, the dilapidated fibro garage.

'Looks deserted.' Luke hid his tension behind a shrug. 'And locked.'

Still rattled from the afternoon, he pulled his awareness into the present. A rushed shopping trip for a new phone had dented his reserves of cash. He'd taken the Samsung apart, dabbed each piece with paper towels and fanned them dry, wary of a delayed meltdown. It seemed cheerfully unscathed.

When he switched on his new phone, it lit up with texts from Emma. All he could think of was the refrain of his teenage years: *I don't want to fucking talk about it.*

His visit to Ivan had gone exactly as expected. He'd texted Jonathan, *All sorted*, and Jonathan replied immediately: *I appreciate your efficiency.*

Gus scoffed. 'Since when did a locked door get in your way? Go around the back.'

Luke snapped on gloves and hopped out of the car. Typical. If anyone reported a guy picking a lock and the police were called, Gus would be driving in the other direction. While Luke was *risk-averse*, Gus was *risk delegated.*

Tonight, it suited him: it saved explaining why he had keys to Gail's house. To avoid suspicion, he took his time getting inside. With his mini Maglite pointed at the floor, he checked the house was empty, then flicked a text to Gus.

Gus entered through the laundry with far less stealth. Unlike Luke's mini flashlight, Gus's 3D Maglite was a foot long, and the powerful beam illuminated the interior like daylight. Luke bristled with unexpected anger at the intrusion. Gail's house was the only home he knew; Gus was trespassing on his territory. Luke wanted to bare his teeth and snarl.

Stifling his reaction, Luke said, 'Quin and I lived here when I was a kid. The house hasn't changed at all.'

He directed Gus to Kevin's room. Gus flashed his light to the four corners and the unmade bed, illuminating the layer of dust and cobwebs on the ceilings. Kevin's clothes still hung in the wardrobe.

'The police must have searched here,' Luke said. 'Hard to tell. Quin's always made a mess. Kevin too.'

'Not neat like you, eh, Jackie?' Gus ferreted in the cupboard. He took a shoebox from the top shelf and threw it on the bed.

Luke flicked through it and the knots in his stomach tightened again. The box was full of old photographs, mostly taken by Gail. Some of them included him.

'When Gail was alive, she would have cleaned up.' Luke wandered to the room he'd shared with Quin, distancing himself from Gus.

Everything Gus touched felt like a violation of his personal space. Luke picked up a jacket from the floor, and a spider scurried away from the beam of his light.

'Has Quin been here recently?' Gus's voice carried from the next room.

'Doesn't look like it.'

Giving up on Kevin's room, Gus went to the kitchen. He opened the fridge, closed it with a grunt.

Luke said, 'Kevin's definitely not living here. There's no beer in the fridge.'

Gus shone his torch directly at Luke, who shielded his eyes with his forearm. 'I reckon he's living at his block but coming back to check on the house.'

Luke flashed his torch around the lounge as Gus came out of Gail's bedroom, carrying an armful of shoeboxes, which he dumped on the coffee table. Gus spotted the desk and moved across the room. Luke's tension went up another notch as Gus took an armful of suspension files from the filing drawer and spread them out on the coffee table. Gus relaxed onto the couch, entirely at home.

'No computer,' Gus said. If the light had been better, he might have seen the mark on the desktop where Kevin's dated PC had once sat. 'Look in those boxes, Jackie. Get the one from Kevin's room too. We might find something in a photo.'

Luke flipped through the boxes. 'They're all of people, not places.' He picked up a suspension file. 'Insurance on the house, Gail's car—Kevin's ute and tax returns for his business.'

'Bank records, more insurance, receipts . . . all ancient history.' Gus grunted his contempt, slapping the files on the table. 'Nothing here from the past decade. I wonder if Kevin does all his stuff online?'

'It's possible. Unlike Quin, he knows how to send an email.' Luke kept his tone light. 'The cops would have checked all this out, right, when they were looking for Quin?'

'Word from my source,' Gus said, 'is that the trail went cold.'

'What I mean is, if Kevin still has that block, surely the cops would have found it and searched already?'

Gus turned the torch at Luke's face again. 'You'd think so.'

Abandoning the files with sudden disdain, he stood up and flashed his light around again. He dropped to his knees and peered underneath the filing drawer. Luke glanced up from the couch to see Gus staring at an old document. In the light of Gus's torch, it was washed out and faded.

'What's that?' Luke's stomach did a flip. He was glad he was sitting down, because his legs felt like jelly and his head felt light. He knew exactly what Gus held in his hands—a document Luke had never been able to find. He'd assumed it was long gone.

'A property deed. Bernard McNally—that's Kevin's father?'

'Grandfather.' Luke could barely speak.

'It's for'—Gus narrowed his eyes, trying to make out the old-fashioned writing—'thirty acres of land in Mount Alexander Shire. Purchased in 1946. Lot three, Stillwater Road, Chewton. Where the fuck is Chewton?'

Luke's heart hammered in his throat.

'We found it, Jackie. This is it. We've fucking found him.' Gus snapped his fingers at the document. His grin was maniacal, as though the lower half of his face had split from the upper.

'Chewton?' Luke made a show of checking a map on his phone. 'Here it is. Near Castlemaine.'

He held himself together, bottling his apprehension, as they returned to the car. Gus chewed his lip. His distraction, and the darkness, were welcome; they kept his attention from Luke's reaction.

'We need to tear that place apart. I'll bet Kevin's there. I'll bet my money's there.'

'When?' Luke kept his voice casual.

'How long does it take to get there?'

Luke checked the map again. 'Ninety minutes, give or take.'

Screwing up his face, Gus said, 'Saturday. I've got other fish to fry.'

Luke wished he didn't know who those fish were. Gus's feud with Jonathan was still evolving.

Silence fell as Gus drove from Footscray to St Kilda. As he pulled up on the corner, he leaned across the car to the glove box. Luke flinched out of his way, but all he did was extract a wad of money, which he tossed in Luke's lap. 'Your work is appreciated, Jackie. Take it. Get out.'

Luke did as he was told, as though nothing in his life had changed since he was seventeen. He shoved the cash into his pocket and trudged home.

CHAPTER TWENTY-THREE

THURSDAY, 2.15 AM

Luke's night was far from over.

Instead of going to his flat, he let himself into Irina's. Her snores carried from the bedroom as he accessed his safe. After retrieving documents he'd taken from Kevin's filing cabinet previously, he stashed Gus's pineapples with the other cash. He lifted Irina's car keys as he left, then gathered equipment from his flat, the laundry and the garden shed. With his gear stuffed into an old backpack, he started Irina's car. If all went well, he'd be back before she realised it was gone.

In the Ford, he retraced the route to Footscray. Again, he entered via the rear; he left the documents from his safe on the desk. Then, with apologies to Gail, he tipped over the couch and pulled out some drawers, as though searching for money or drugs. He scattered the contents of the kitchen cupboards on the floor, messed up the bedrooms and left the back door hanging open.

Slinking back to Irina's car, he took off his gloves and used the Samsung to call triple zero and report a disturbance at the house.

Instead of going home, he went north, cutting across the dark city towards the Hume.

Driving out of the city felt liberating, as though he were a fly escaping a spider's web. He stopped to fill the tank and paid with cash, his face angled from the cameras and obscured by his black hoodie. Classic rock blared from the radio, and if not for the pit of apprehension in his belly, he would have enjoyed the drive.

He found his way without a map, electronic or otherwise. His new iPhone was on his bedside table at home, but he hadn't dared to leave the Samsung behind. When he reached the outskirts of Melbourne, he switched it off. It wasn't registered to him, and the location settings were off, but he couldn't afford a mistake now. Call it *risk-averse*, call it *paranoid*. He didn't care.

Taking a circuitous route along back roads through Gisborne and the Macedon Ranges, he emerged onto the Calder Freeway towards Castlemaine and turned off before the town to head east. The sun rose as he neared his destination, the darkness lifting in stages to reveal a white, overcast dawn.

He followed his nose to Stillwater.

After a few wrong turns, with the car covered in dust from the dirt roads, he found the entrance to the driveway. The rusty gate creaked with complaint as he dragged it across the dirt.

Irina's Ford bounced along the potholed track towards Kevin's cabin.

Still dressed in black from his break and enter with Gus, he added gardening gloves before getting out. The clunk of the car door closing echoed in the silence. A light breeze rustled the leaves of the tall ironbarks. The forest felt close and disapproving, as though the trees resented his intrusion. A chill ran down his spine as he paused by Irina's car, listening.

The cabin was silent. His footsteps seemed loud as he approached.

It was unlocked, as always. He pushed open the door and peered in.

Inside, the floor was feathered with dust. There were no discernible footprints. While his eyes adjusted to the dark interior, he forced himself to stand at the door, checking the corners and examining every lump of discarded clothing, every shadow.

Empty.

He went back to the car and sat in the driver's seat to centre himself. He'd known he would have to come back here one day, but he'd hoped it would be years later: Gus's discovery of the address had accelerated his plans. The knowledge that he was being reactive—and, therefore, likely to make mistakes—paralysed him. He gripped the steering wheel and aimed an unfocused stare at the trees. It wasn't too late to retreat. He could turn the key and drive away. He could forget all of this. Keep driving all the way back to Queensland.

Get on with it, he told himself.

Resolute, he forced himself out of the car. He recovered his backpack from the rear and set off at a brisk walk. The weather was perfect for his task: the morning was cloudy and cool. Rain was forecast in the afternoon.

He hiked uphill through the trees, his shoes crunching on the overgrown, rutted track. Years ago, he'd driven this track, over struggling weeds that had now grown into trees. Within a few more years, the track would be absorbed into the bush.

When he reached the cliff edge, he paused to let his heart rate settle. He crept along the edge of the cliff, examining the tangle in the base of the gully as he walked. He didn't have to go far. A dull gleam caught his eye and his heart leaped.

It was still there.

Luke froze, soaked with cold dread. He couldn't move, couldn't think. The enormity—the irreversibility—of what he planned hit him and he blanked.

Breathe. Breathe. Slow it down.

And then, more firmly, *GET ON WITH IT.*

He climbed down into the gully, keeping his eyes on the glints of black duco among the fallen trees and leaf litter lining the base. Memories of exploring as a kid distracted him. Back then, he wouldn't have dared make the climb without a rope. He kept an eye out for snakes.

When he reached the bottom, he staggered to a stop.

Kevin's Commodore was still there. It had landed on its side and was smashed beyond repair, almost unrecognisable as a vehicle. Trees, dead branches and uprooted bushes obscured it, like military camouflage. From above, it was blacker patches of darkness in a tangle of shadows. Only dumb luck, or a dedicated searcher, would ever find it.

A motivated searcher, like Gus.

Shrugging the backpack off his shoulders, Luke concentrated on his breathing and the task at hand.

He took out a jerry can of petrol and approached the car. Pouring accelerant on a car seemed a simple prospect, but the reality was awkward. The space was cramped, with trees hampering his movements and the nagging fear of snakes making him jumpy. Standing on a precarious branch to get better reach, and aware that spilling fuel on himself was a bad idea, he started with the chassis, then climbed through the bushes to douse the roof and the bonnet.

Consciously, he kept his attention on the task, ignoring the clamouring of his conscience. What he was doing was beyond any moral compass he'd ever tried to claim; all he could do was breathe and remind himself of the reasons why.

It was a means to an end. A domino being pushed. Evidence destroyed.

With the car suitably marinated, he moved halfway up the wall of the gully. Despite the depths of his teenage delinquency, he'd never set a car on fire before. He wasn't sure how quickly it would take or how far the fire would spread. In his rush, he'd had no time to research. There was probably a YouTube series on how to burn a car, but it wasn't something he wanted on his browser history.

For want of a better idea, he weighted a packet of matches with a stone. The first match broke in his shaking fingers. The second flared, and he stuck it inside, lobbed the packet at the car and scrambled to the top.

When he peered over the edge at the mess of branches, he thought the matches must have gone out before they reached the accelerant. But a few seconds later, a whoosh erupted and flames licked the base of the gully.

The dry eucalypt leaves sizzled and popped, and a haze of heat hit him.

He ran all the way to Irina's car, then calmed himself enough to drive along the backroads and get the hell away.

In a deserted truck stop with no cameras, he changed every item of his clothing. The clothes went into a garbage bag, even his sunglasses and shoes. He would deposit the bag in one charity bin, the backpack in another. He left the jerry can on a building site on the outskirts of Melbourne. He took nothing home except the faint smell of petrol and smoke in his nostrils.

At a self-service wash, he cleaned Irina's car inside and out. He guzzled a bottle of chocolate milk; sugar to replenish all that he'd burned through, milk to settle the acidity in his stomach.

He switched on the Samsung. No missed calls. Another massive sigh of relief.

The adrenaline faded, and his heart rate descended to normal. With discipline born of long practice, he pushed it all from his mind. This was not a memory to keep.

After the long drive home, he collapsed on his bed, wondering what mistakes he'd made, and stared at the ceiling as memories bombarded him.

CHAPTER TWENTY-FOUR

NINE YEARS AGO

As he munched Weet-Bix for breakfast in the kitchen, Jack stared out at a patch of blue sky through the crooked aluminium venetians that shielded the window. Autumn was his favourite season, the best weather Melbourne had to offer. He anticipated a cool walk to school followed by a sunny day.

A brisk rapping disturbed the peace. Jack leaned back in his chair so he could see out from the kitchen to the hall. They'd moved to this house a few months ago, which had reduced the number of people banging on the door, so he was surprised to see two shadows darkening the glass panel by the front door. Police. They weren't after him, as far as he knew.

'Quin. Cops at the door.' Jack abandoned his breakfast to shake his father awake.

'Fuck.' Quin had passed out on his bed, fully clothed, sometime in the wee hours. It took him precious seconds to regain consciousness. A stale reek of bourbon and cigarettes fouled the air. He rubbed his hands over his head as he sat up. 'Find out what they want?'

'Not my circus.' Jack returned to his breakfast.

Quin shuffled to the door. 'Hello, officers, what can I do you for?'

A burst of activity, and Quin was in cuffs. One of the coppers said, 'Hey, Jack, how's school?' as they bobbed Quin's head into the back seat of the blue-and-white. Jack wasn't sure what he hated most: that the cops knew his name, or that all he felt at Quin's arrest was resignation.

Quin was charged with theft of a motor vehicle and, given his record, was remanded in custody and likely to stay there for some time.

Jack's attempts to convince Children's Services that he was nearly sixteen and fine living by himself fell on deaf ears. He asked if he could live with Gail. He'd stayed with her frequently over the years, when Quin was on a bender or had gone missing. Kevin, surprisingly, didn't tell him to fuck off, but his criminal record and Gail's recent cancer diagnosis made them ineligible as foster carers.

Jack landed in the group residential home—the 'resi'—with his backpack, a duffel bag and a scowl. It was a few suburbs away, so he had to catch the train to school, and his bedroom was even smaller than in the series of dodgy houses Quin had rented. The only benefit was a supply of food; there was always breakfast cereal and milk, if nothing else. Three other boys shared the house, all of them stoners who drank goon bags in the park and skipped school whenever they could. A slack-jawed house supervisor was technically in charge. Jack despised them all within minutes, especially Patrick, who'd been the biggest kid in the house until Jack arrived. Patrick resented the change in hierarchy and made a single attempt to assert himself. Jack tripped him to the floor and squashed his face into the carpet.

One morning, he woke to find that his phone had disappeared while he was asleep. Jack tore the place apart in his search. He punched Patrick and smacked Jordan against the wall and held Cody on the floor with a knee on his throat, but no amount of violence revealed his phone. The house supervisor called the police, but Jack was gone before they arrived. He knew the other boys wouldn't say a word.

Gus would bloody kill him.

He went to the gym and told Trevor what had happened. He got nothing but a frown.

A few days later, as he was walking to the train after school, Gus's black Audi pulled up at the kerb and the window rolled down.

'Jackie. Get in.' Gus was wearing mirrored sunglasses.

The front passenger seat was empty, which meant Jack got Ed's usual spot. 'Where's Ed?'

'Day job.' Ed was a plasterer but, like Jack, he'd worked for Gus since he was a teenager. Jack wondered how Ed balanced his job with Gus's demands. It was hard enough to manage with school. A few months ago, Ed had offered him an apprenticeship, but Jack declined. His ideal job involved computers and numbers and clean hands; Ed's job was too similar to what Kevin did. 'How old are you, Jackie?'

Jack frowned. Gus knew exactly how old he was. 'Sixteen.'

'Haven't seen you at the gym lately.'

'Curfew at six. I can't always get there.' The curfew was because he'd broken Patrick's ribs in their last fight, which was on the list of things Gus didn't need to know.

'You're gonna be late tonight.'

Jack hid his irritation. 'Where are we going?'

'Bloke needs a talking to.'

'Who? Why?'

'Stay in your lane, Jackie.'

Half an hour later, Gus parked outside a grimy house in a quiet residential street. A patch of weeds clung to life in the place a front lawn should be; the concrete path was cracked and uneven. Jack banged on the front door. Like a revelation, he realised how much he was part of Gus's world, how familiar this situation was.

The door opened a crack, then closed with a thud.

'Paul! Open the door!' Gus said. When nothing happened, he revised: 'Jackie. Open the door.'

Jack kicked in the glass beside the door. Shards tinkled to the ground at their feet. He reached inside and unclipped the lock.

The hallway opened into a living room: cheap furnishings, worn carpet, a musty odour. Paul, thwarted in his hasty retreat through the back door, flailed and wailed as Jack caught the back of his shirt and hauled him to the lounge. Gus pointed to the couch. Jack stood by the door and crossed his arms. He knew how this worked.

A few hours later, he sat in the passenger seat again, squeezing his hands to hide their shaking. Gus lit a cigarette and switched on the ignition, his gun resting on his lap, but the car didn't move. Jack's stomach roiled with what could have been hunger but was probably the after-effect of what he'd witnessed. Adrenaline buzzed his muscles and tingled his fingers. It wasn't the first time he'd seen Gus shoot someone. He guessed it wouldn't be the last.

'You got his phone?' Gus blew out a cloud of smoke. The amount of time Jack spent in cars with smokers, he might as well take up the habit.

'Yeah.' It was Jack's job to dispose of evidence—in this case, the phone and the gun.

'Now, what did he do wrong?' Gus's tone was patient, like that of a disapproving teacher.

'He should have deleted his history. Or got another phone.'

'Smart-arse.' Gus stubbed out his cigarette. 'What else?'

'He should have kept it quiet.'

'True.' Gus nodded.

And then he smacked Jack in the face, a sharp left jab from the driver's seat that caught Jack by surprise—hard enough that his head snapped back and he saw stars.

'What?' Jack worked his jaw from side to side, ran his tongue over his teeth. Nothing broken, but the blood in his mouth turned his stomach.

'You're lucky it was just a fist.' Gus scooped the gun from his lap and twisted, pressing the muzzle against the outside of Jack's knee.

Jack froze, staring at Gus with his mouth hanging open and his stomach clenched.

'You lost your fucking phone. I needed you yesterday. You wanna end up like Paul?'

Jack's words came out in short gasps. 'One of the kids at the resi took it!'

'Can't handle a bunch of stoners, Jackie?'

Jack held his breath.

'You know what he did wrong?' Gus's raised eyebrows creased his forehead into furrows. 'He lost his appreciation. I looked after him. Like I look after you.' He glowered for a moment, then tossed the gun at Jack with contempt. 'Get rid of that. New phone in the centre console. Don't lose it, you hear me?'

Loud and clear, Jack grumbled to himself.

School finished for the year in December, and Jack was hoping for a few weeks of quiet. Patrick had gone to juvie and the house was calmer. Someone had even put up a Christmas tree. But on the first Monday of the holidays, Kevin banged on the front door of the resi.

'What do you want?' Jack's animosity filled the doorway.

'Spoken to Quin?'

'Not lately.' Quin had called a few times from jail, but their conversations were largely Jack ranting about hating the resi. Absence might not make the heart fonder, but it had shown Jack the advantages of living with Quin: privacy, freedom and independence.

'He said he'd ask you to help me out. You're on holidays, right?'

Jack scowled and crossed his arms.

'I'm going up to Stillwater to fix the cabin. Quin said you'd help.'

Jack smacked a hand against the doorframe, hard enough to make Kevin take a step backwards. He was as tall as Kevin; not as heavy, but fitter. The realisation brought him a rush of power. 'What the fuck? He can't boss me around.'

'He said it'd be good for you. You hate this place, right?'

'Convenient that you give a shit when you need cheap labour!' Jack went to slam the door. Abruptly, he changed his mind. 'How long for?'

'Two weeks, give or take.'

The next day, he threw his backpack into Kevin's work ute, which was loaded with equipment and supplies.

Kevin said, 'Got a permit? You want to drive?'

Kevin's efforts to be civil were noted. Jack fetched L-plates and took the driver's seat. Being alone with Kevin, without the buffer of Quin or Gail, was a new awkwardness to endure. He focused on the road, drove under the speed limit and paid attention to every road sign. Two weeks of keeping on Kevin's good side, biting his tongue, keeping his temper in check, seemed impossible. But fresh air had to be preferable to the resi.

Before he left, he sent Gus a text: *Away for a while to help with Quin's stuff.*

When are you back?

Two weeks, maybe.

Jack hoped the reference to Quin would be enough to placate him. Gus was weird about loyalty to family. Jack didn't complicate the message by mentioning Kevin.

After a short delay, which Jack figured was Gus weighing up the pros and cons of letting it slide or taking offence, Gus texted: *Tell me when you're back.*

They reached the gate and the long driveway track, bouncing off the potholes and crevices on the hard suspension of the ute. Nothing had changed since Jack's last visit, except that the cabin needed maintenance: it had developed a lean, and several planks had come off the walls. Jack parked the ute around the back.

Kevin went straight to the cabin to start his inspection. 'Whole thing needs restumping.' He squatted to examine the timber foundations.

Jack had forgotten how Kevin changed at the cabin. As though ten years dropped off him, his face smoothed, his shoulders relaxed and he could complete a sentence without swearing.

'Ants have got in. See, the wood's all cracked? Better if I could get concrete stumps in.' He sat back on his heels, pondering the universe, then went to unpack.

For the next week, they worked on the cabin, mostly in silence. They prised up the floorboards to expose the underfloor and removed the beams the ants had destroyed. The structure was a shell by the time they'd finished deconstructing, and they were relegated to sleeping in tents. They drove to Castlemaine and loaded the ute with timber and bags of quick-set concrete that weighed the vehicle down and made the drive treacherous. A Midnight Oil CD was stuck in the cheap stereo Kevin had jerry-rigged into the dash of the ancient ute. It played on repeat until Jack prised it out with a screwdriver. The only other CD he could find was Cold Chisel.

Jack learned, through grunts and offhand comments, that Quin had promised to help with the rebuild shortly before he was incarcerated. Jack was there in his stead, taking up his father's duty, as though it was an ancestral debt to be paid.

They propped the cabin on bricks and set the stumps, then replaced the cladding and the floor. With leftover timber, Kevin built a bench and a lock box for his rifle. They cleared out the chimney and bricked around a new hearth. The physical work—heavy lifting, lugging bags of concrete and lengths of timber—sent Jack to his sleeping bag early each night. He slept more soundly than he had in years. No resi kids to worry about. No phone calls from Gus. Just the intense blackness of the clear night sky, stars that glowed, the companionable rustling of the forest.

Kevin pronounced the project finished by cracking a beer and settling into a deckchair by the dam, looking out over the placid water as he contemplated life. Jack propped himself against a stump nearby, and Kevin offered him a beer, which he declined. They ate leftover cold sausages in bread, in silence that had never quite become comfortable.

'Head home soon,' Kevin said.

'Whatever.' Jack would be happy to spend another month reading in the sun by the dam, wading into the water when he got too hot.

Kevin grunted. 'You need to get back, don't you?'

'No rush.'

'You'll have that Italian nutter on your case.'

Jack cast Kevin a wary glance. He'd never discussed working for Gus with Kevin or Quin. He guessed their networks kept them informed. 'He'll keep.'

'Not what I hear.'

'Whatever.'

'They say he's bad news, Jack.' It was rare for Kevin to use his name. Normally he was *kid* or *you little shit* or something like that. 'Don't tell him about this, alright? This is my place.'

With a chuckle, Jack said, 'He'd like it here. Lots of hiding places for bodies.'

'Don't even fucking joke about it.' Kevin retreated into his own thoughts, long enough that Jack thought the conversation was over, but out of the blue he said, 'Quin's fucking hopeless. He should never have let you get mixed up in that shit.'

'Quin's got nothing to do with it.'

Kevin popped another beer. 'Fuck it, what would I know.'

Kevin's satisfaction at finishing the cabin made his mood unflappable. He let the conversation fade, staring at the darkening sky, as content as Jack had ever seen him.

Jack was reminded of the time Dr Bowman had asked, *What would make you happy, Jack?*

Jack's predictable answer: *Money. Lots of money.*

The psychologist had given him an article to read. Money and worldly goods, the researcher stated, could never make a person truly content. *Disposable income has no relationship to happiness. On average, wealthy people aren't any happier than the poor.*

Jack scoffed and said that he was still working on the bottom row of his hierarchy of needs—safety, shelter, adequate food—and that the idea of any income being disposable was incomprehensible to a hungry kid whose father was in jail.

Dr Bowman nodded. *You need to meet your basic needs. But after that, the statistics are clear. You don't get happier as you get richer.*

What would make me happy, then?

It's different for everyone, Dr Bowman said. *A purpose, a home, people you want to be with. Knowing who you are, doing things you want to do, having time to pursue your dreams.*

All of that, Jack said, *is much easier to do if you're rich.*

Dr Bowman laughed and conceded the point, but his words, as always, bounced around in Jack's mind long after the session ended.

As he sat watching Kevin from the corner of his eye, he wondered. To Kevin, the question of what made him happy had a simple answer: being at Stillwater. Here, everything was different. The silent dam and open sky seemed to clarify his thoughts, as though adding another dimension to life. He clutched after the idea, but it drifted away, unfinished.

During the drive home, he thought about what would make him happy. Not answering to Gus. His own house. A tidy job. A dog. And as it had before, the steel and concrete of the city made for an uninviting return, and the first thing he did was text Gus.

I'm back.

Tomorrow 4 pm on the corner with Ed.

Jack deflated with a sigh.

'You gotta find a way to get away from him,' Kevin said, as he parked outside the resi.

'I like my knees the way they are,' said Jack.

CHAPTER TWENTY-FIVE

THURSDAY, 3 PM

Luke stirred from the couch as his phone emitted a series of frantic beeps: Caitlin, texting to tell him he was on the news. She shared the link with his study group chat, who chimed in with helpful comments:
OMG is that you Luke?
Wow that wet t-shirt is see-through.
Check out the abs.
Sleeping during the day had messed with his body clock. Before answering Caitlin, he downed two strong coffees, which was a mistake; he felt wired, as though he needed to punch someone or set fire to something. Against his better judgement, he clicked on the link. Emma's video had made the mainstream news. After kicking his bag and throwing his phone at the couch, he cooled down enough to watch it again.

A career as a documentary filmmaker or paparazzo was a genuine option; Emma had captured the incident well. In contrast to Phil's awkward manoeuvring, Luke scaled the building like a seasoned professional. Phil's mad rush towards Luke was a blur. A gasp from Emma punctuated the moment they flew off the edge. The splash was nearly as high as the pool house. The arrival of the police and ambulance added a flurry of bodies and movement to the scene. When Luke emerged from the pool, his white T-shirt was plastered to his torso. With his dripping hair and a dark expression twisting his face, he looked like a grumpy cat after an unexpected bath.

Luke read the accompanying text with dread. *A disability worker turned hero when his client climbed onto the roof of a Brighton garage.* They'd attached the photo from his driver's licence. Phil's face had been pixelated. The only relief was that they hadn't published names.

He sat on the couch, stunned. He'd caught a few hours of sleep, but he hadn't eaten all day. A sense of drained emptiness, as though he was hollow, mixed with the sting of Emma's betrayal.

His thumb hovered over her number on his phone. He hit it. 'Where the hell did you send that video?'

'I didn't send it anywhere!' Her outrage matched his. 'The police asked for it—I couldn't exactly refuse!'

'Jesus, Emma! I'm all over the news!'

'If I'd known—'

'You do now!' He ran a hand through his hair, which already stood on end. He'd never liked cameras, but this was his worst-case scenario. His years of hiding felt like a waste of time.

'Luke, I'm sorry, I didn't know you'd be so—'

'So what? Worried about my privacy? Pissed off at seeing my face on the news? You have no *fucking idea*—' He cut himself off, forced his voice to a semblance of calm. 'I can't talk about this now. I'm too fucking angry.'

He hung up and put his hands on his head to pace.

I'm a fucking idiot, was all he could think.

A minute later, he swiped the Samsung open as it buzzed and said, 'What?'

'Watch your mouth.' Gus paused, as though waiting for an apology, but Luke was past apologising to anyone. 'Job for you. I'll text you the address. Ed's waiting. Guy owes me three grand. Says he doesn't have it and I say he's full of shit.'

Luke's left eye twitched.

Gus said, 'Don't fuck it up,' and the call ended with a click.

The sun hung low over the city, glinting off the tall buildings and throwing Luke's street into shadows. Leaning over the railing on his balcony, he wiped a tired hand across his eyes, thinking about how seamlessly he and Ed worked together, even after Luke's years of absence. How familiar and satisfying it was to recover a debt. How punching a smug prick felt like justice. How useful it made him feel. How Jonathan Wylie had seen through his veneer.

Sleep deprivation interfered with his emotional regulation, made his moods swing up and down. He could feel himself unravelling, like a knitted jumper coming undone. Memories intruded without warning. The bike Gail bought for him, with money Kevin had given her after a robbery. Her simple, practical kindnesses. Her funeral, when he was sixteen, which Quin missed because he was in jail. Kevin's stony silence in the car as he drove Jack home to the resi afterwards. Gail's death had bowled him over, a reminder of how he'd felt after he lost his mother. It was a reminder not to get attached to people.

Loving someone makes you vulnerable, Dr Bowman had said. *Knowing you can lose them makes you human. But without love and connection, what's the point of anything?*

Remembering his response to those words made Luke hang his head. He'd smacked his fist onto the desk, making books and files jump, then let loose with a defiant stream of denials and stormed from the room, slamming the door so hard the building shook.

It was years since Gail's death, but anger still lurked beneath the surface. She'd died of lung cancer: there was no one to blame, just her habit of thirty Marlboros a day. Back then, he'd wanted to draw blood. It wasn't fair. None of it was fair. He'd hated them all—Quin for being in jail, Kevin for his silent grief, Gus for his callous indifference. Dr Bowman for being so calm and sympathetic and wise. Gail, for dying. His mother, for dying.

And now Emma, for not understanding.

Consciously, he filled his chest with air and controlled a slow exhale. He focused on the cool breeze, the warmth of his breath.

The Samsung buzzed, and he squeezed his eyes shut and hid his face in his hands.

The phone beeped: *ANSWER YOUR FUCKING PHONE.*

Luke hit recall.

'We have a situation. Where are you?'

'At home.'

'Ten minutes, on the corner.' The line went dead.

Luke closed his eyes again. He was in no state to be dealing with a *situation*, which, with Gus, meant black clothing and latex gloves. Plastic bags and a shovel. For a few precious minutes, he was paralysed; and then, as the consequences of disobeying registered, he changed his clothes and stuffed gear into his pockets. He was half a block away when Gus's Audi pulled in at the corner. Covering the distance in a jog, he slid into the passenger seat.

The car was moving before he'd even closed the door.

Gus drove a few blocks in silence, then stopped in a loading zone with a screech of his tyres. His hand shot out to grip Luke's arm, and he cast tight words across the car. 'You've got some fucking explaining to do!'

Luke's stomach curled with fear. 'What?'

'What were you doing on Jonathan Wylie's roof?'

'I look after his son. Phil.' Luke let his breath out.

'You work for him?' Gus's eyes bulged and his mouth contorted.

'I work for a service agency. What are you on about?'

'You're all over the internet, taking a dive off his roof! You ran away to hide from Quin, right?' The assumption worked for Luke, so he let it slide. 'Well, you're not hiding now.' Gus released his death grip on Luke's arm, gave him a push and tossed over his phone. 'Take a look. There's a link.'

Luke clicked the link and endured the video footage again, wincing as though it was news to him.

'I don't like that you work for Wylie.'

Luke snorted. 'He's a glorified real estate agent.'

'He's a pain in my arse, that's what he is.'

'Didn't realise you even knew him.' Grumbling, Luke handed Gus his phone. 'How'd you know it was his house?'

'They showed the front. I'd know that McMansion anywhere. Who filmed it?'

'Phil's sister.' Mentioning Emma in Gus's presence made Luke squirm. 'The cops must have taken the footage.'

Gus wiped a hand over his face and pulled into traffic without indicating. 'Anyway. We've got a bigger problem.'

'What now?'

'Ivan's not answering. I've been trying to rouse him since yesterday.' Gus had worked up an angry sweat. His grip on the steering wheel clenched and unclenched, and his mouth twisted into an ugly frown. 'Let's see if he's home.'

It took twenty minutes to cross the city; twenty minutes of tense silence that made Luke wonder how close Gus was to pulling out his gun.

Gus crawled his car past Ivan's house. The front porch light was on.

Luke said, 'How did he come to work for you?'

Gus parked and angled his mirror to look back at Ivan's front door. 'He got in trouble with his Polish friends. Gambling debts. I helped him out and he's paying me back. But I don't know him well enough to trust him.'

'Looks like someone's home. Does he have a missus?'

Gus worked his jaw. 'Don't know, don't care. Let's go.'

It was like old times: Luke rapped on the door, with Gus behind him tapping his foot. A scuffle of footsteps inside, and the door opened a crack, held by a thin chain. A woman's face peered out.

'Hello, love,' Gus said. 'We're looking for Ivan.'

'You and everyone else.' She was Ivan's age—about forty, Luke guessed—with hair dyed a lurid cherry-red that clashed with her grey smoker's skin. Her eyes were red, too: she'd been crying. 'I haven't seen him since yesterday.'

'We're gonna come in and look,' Gus said, at which she squeaked and tried to close the door.

Luke, a heartbeat ahead of her, put his shoulder to it. The chain snapped.

With another squeak, the woman jumped back, retreating into the central corridor of the house. 'I'm telling you he's not here!'

It took only minutes to ascertain that she was telling the truth. Ivan's size limited his hiding places. It amused Luke to imagine him trying to squeeze into an air vent or through a manhole. Neither Ivan nor his partner appeared to be interested in housework: the dingy mess and sour food smells made Luke's skin crawl.

After their brief search, Gus pointed the woman to a chair in the kitchen. 'When did you last see him?'

'Yesterday, in the morning. He went to work in the office because he's got a broken arm.' Her face clouded.

'And?'

Her eyes flicked from Gus to Luke. 'Who are you? You're not Polish.'

'Who else is looking for him?'

'There's always someone looking for him.'

Luke said, 'What are you not telling us, Anna?'

She flinched as though he'd slapped her. 'How do you know my name?'

'It's on your gas bill.' He gestured to the kitchen bench, where a languishing pile of disorganised paperwork made him itch. 'We're worried about him too. Tell us what you know.' With a smile to reassure her, he leaned against the bench, pretending to be relaxed.

Anna blinked, considered. 'I think something happened to him.'

'Why do you think that?' Luke cast a look at Gus.

'I don't know.'

Gus said, 'Did he take anything? A bag, clothes?'

Anna shook her head and looked at her hands, which rested in her lap.

'Did you call the cops?'

'Not yet.' A tense shake of her head. 'I didn't want to cause trouble. Ivan doesn't like cops. If it's nothing, he'll be furious to have them on his back.'

'Give it another day or two,' Gus said. 'Maybe he'll turn up.'

She followed them to the front door, where Gus stopped. He tucked a couple of pineapples into her hand, pausing with his hand on hers. 'Forget we were here. Get your door fixed.'

The drive from Coburg to St Kilda was silent. Gus gazed straight ahead with his mouth in a firm line. A muscle in his jaw worked, as though he was grinding his teeth. He stopped a block from Luke's flat, switched off the ignition and fumbled for his cigarettes. His lighter flared, reflecting off the dark windscreen, and he blew out a cloud of smoke.

Luke studied Gus's profile. 'What do you think happened?'

Gus sucked hard on his cigarette. 'I think Ivan's dead.'

'His Polish friends?'

'No.' Gus worked his jaw. 'It's someone sending me a message. He sent me a weird text yesterday. Now I understand what it meant.'

'What? Who?'

Gus ignored the question. 'He won't have done it himself. Not his style.' He blew out a puff of smoke. 'He'll have made mistakes, though. They always do.'

Except you, Luke thought. Gus didn't make mistakes. Or if he did, he tidied them up so well no one noticed, or he paid the right people to turn away.

Gus stubbed out his cigarette in the ashtray. 'That little prick is gonna wish he'd never met me.' He blew out a long exhale. 'Saturday morning, we'll go to Kevin's block. Now get out. I need to think.'

CHAPTER TWENTY-SIX

FRIDAY, 8 AM

When Luke arrived home from his morning run, an unfamiliar car was wedged behind his Subaru. Late-model sedan, government plates, extra aerials. Inside, he could see two shapes; the front seats were occupied.

Slowing his pace, he used the hem of his singlet to wipe sweat from his face as he considered his options. Running all the way to Queensland was his first thought.

The car doors opened and two people emerged. One of them Luke recognised. He forced his hands and his gait calm as he walked towards them.

'Still keeping fit, Mr Quinlan?' The older of the two leaned against the driver's door, a grin creasing his fleshy face, while his partner moved around the car to stand nearby.

Luke returned his smile. 'It's Harris now. As I'm sure you know, Detective Sergeant Wilson.'

'Senior Sergeant.'

'They promoted you?' Luke raised his eyebrows.

'I needed the pay rise. No money on this side of the law.'

Luke turned his attention to Wilson's partner, who was sizing him up—his worn runners and sweat-soaked clothes, his messy hair where he'd removed his cap, his scars. He smiled, casting words back at Wilson. 'Are you going to introduce us?'

'Tara Packard.' She shook his hand with a firm grip. 'I saw you on TV. You were wet then and you're wet now.' Everything about her shouted 'cop', from her tailored grey trousers and white blouse to her no-nonsense shoes and practical hairstyle. She had no fear of eye contact.

'Luke Harris. If I'd known I had visitors, I'd have made an effort.'

A dimple formed in her cheek as she smiled.

Wilson cut her a look, but he directed his words to Luke. 'Can we come in?'

'Sure.' Luke gestured towards the stairs.

Brian Wilson had aged since Luke last saw him. His shiny pink scalp glistened under the silver strands of his thinning hair. A generous belly pushed against his cheap white shirt, the buttons straining with tension. His tie was already loose. Packard, twenty years younger and built like a triathlete, was neat in comparison.

At Luke's invitation, Wilson sat on the couch, his gaze roving around the minimalist space. Packard wandered to the window then checked out the bookshelves, tipping her head to read the titles. Luke took a moment to guzzle a glass of water and gather his thoughts before sitting in the armchair.

Wilson said, 'How long have you been back in Melbourne?'

'A year.' Luke smiled. Wilson was good at his job; he would already know the answers to his introductory questions.

'I like your new look. Much more respectable.' The detective turned to Packard. 'Last time I saw this guy, he had long hair and a hipster beard. How old were you, seventeen?'

'Eighteen.' Luke forced his hands to relax.

Wilson nodded towards the punching bag in the corner. 'Still train at that gym in the city?'

'Not for years.'

'Saw you on TV. You're working, what, disability care?' Like Gus, Wilson raised his eyebrows in disbelief.

He nodded. 'And studying. Commerce.'

'Seen your father lately?'

Luke shook his head. 'Not since last time you asked. When I was working in the cafe.' He sighed. 'That's why you're here? You're still looking for Quin?'

'It's gone cold, but yeah. He's still wanted.'

Packard chimed in. 'You were questioned when he skipped parole. I've read the statements.'

'Does it say that I lost my job because of police harassment?' Luke wiped a hand over his mouth. 'They came to the cafe every day for weeks, as though I was hiding him in my back pocket. Took me in for questioning three times—same questions, over and over. Harassed my flatmates about where I was, where I'd been—and they wouldn't tell me what it was about. My boss got sick of it and sacked me. I was so pissed off with Quin, I changed my name and moved interstate.'

Packard shook her head. 'There's nothing about that in the file.'

Luke snorted. 'Of course not.'

'You knew what it was about,' Wilson said. 'He shot the guy who beat you up as a kid. Left a mountain of evidence. Prints, texts, the works.'

'Yeah, I found out later. At the time, I thought he'd just jumped parole.'

'Anyway'—Wilson cut him a glare—'you haven't heard from him. What about his buddy, Kevin McNally?'

Luke shrugged. 'Not since . . . I dunno, around the same time.'

'What kind of car does McNally drive?'

'His ute, when he's working. It was his father's. White, an old Isuzu, with *J McNally* on the side.'

Wilson pulled out a worn notebook and flicked through it. 'Does he have another car?'

'A black Commodore.' Another shrug. 'Why?'

'You lived at his mother's place when you were a kid. What was the address?'

'Forty-three Colby Street, Footscray. Hasn't changed since last time you asked.'

'Does McNally still live there?'

'As far as I know.' Luke frowned. 'Why?'

The room fell silent. The sweat dried on Luke's body; his singlet stuck to him. Packard had paused in her perusal of his books and was watching him closely. He figured she was trying to read his body language and wished her good luck.

'Here's the deal.' Wilson's words were quiet. 'Couple of nights ago, someone broke into McNally's house. The place looked deserted. Uniforms tried to contact him, but no luck. It seems McNally is missing too.'

'What do you mean?'

'His phone rings out. Rates on the house and the rego on the Commodore are paid up, but he hasn't worked for a few years. The ute is in the garage with a dead battery. Neighbours haven't seen him. One said there was a couple living in the house until recently. She figured they were tenants. The utilities on the house are connected.'

'Tenants? At Kevin's place?' Luke rubbed a hand over his face. 'Can't you track his bank accounts or something?'

'Nothing in for a few years. Expenses coming out are all direct debits or paid online.'

'Sounds like he's moved elsewhere.' Luke shook his head. 'And what, you think Quin's with him?'

Wilson nodded. 'But then a few other things happened.'

'What things?'

'You jumped off a roof and a clever constable picked you as a player and looked you up. She linked you to your father and pinged me.'

He'd thought as much. 'And?'

'Did you know McNally owns a bush block near Castlemaine?'

With a smile, Luke nodded. 'Yeah. Place called Stillwater. We went camping there sometimes.'

Wilson leaned forwards. 'There was a fire there yesterday. CFA says it was deliberately lit. Traces of accelerant found.'

'What? Really? I liked that cabin.'

'No, the cabin's okay. The fire burned out half an acre of bush.'

Luke gave Wilson a quizzical look. 'So . . . what? Kevin burned some trees on his block? Like back-burning or something?'

'Could have been, I guess.' Wilson tapped his pen on his notebook. 'You haven't heard from him lately?'

'Not a peep.'

Packard perched on the arm of the couch. 'Your last contact with him was seven years ago?'

Luke shook his head. 'Actually, I tried to call him, about a week ago. He didn't answer, and he didn't call back. I figured he didn't want to talk to me.'

'Why did you call him?'

Luke said, 'I heard a rumour. Someone was looking for him.'

Packard raised her eyebrows. 'Who? Where did you hear this rumour?'

'Am I on record?'

'Should you be?'

Luke held up his hands, suppressing a smile. 'It was a rumour, alright? I called Kevin to give him a heads-up—in case he knew what it was about.'

Wilson interrupted. 'I didn't know you and McNally looked out for each other.'

'We don't. I thought he should know. I left a message on his voicemail.'

'You pulling my chain? You know I can get your phone records.'

'No need. Here.' Luke pulled out his iPhone and then stopped awkwardly. 'Actually, this is a new phone. My old phone went for a swim.'

Packard sighed, as though he were being intentionally obstructive. He unlocked his phone and handed it to her anyway. There were only a handful of calls and texts. Nothing incriminating.

'Where's your old phone?'

'I binned it.'

'Convenient.'

'If it still worked, I could show you when I called Kevin. I tried Quin, too, but his number is disconnected.' Luke held up his hands again. 'Pull my phone records, if you need to.'

Wilson cleared his throat. 'You were aware of a threat against McNally. You called him when?' Luke gave him the date. 'And he didn't answer. So, he could have been missing as far back as . . . When was that rego paid?'

'October twelfth.' Packard looked up from her notepad.

'Yeah,' Wilson said. 'I think that's enough. Come on, Tara. This guy needs a shower.'

Luke followed them to the door, surprised by the abrupt ending to the conversation. Wilson gestured Packard through but paused on the landing. Luke felt the man's hand on his arm, a few seconds after Packard had started down the stairs.

Wilson shoved a business card into his hand and spoke in a low voice. 'You working for Alberici again?'

'Who?'

'Call me when you're ready, Jack.' He took off after his partner, surprisingly agile for a man of his girth.

CHAPTER TWENTY-SEVEN

FRIDAY, 5.40 PM

Emma threw her phone on the passenger seat as the call diverted to Luke's voicemail for the fourth time. The message was simple: *Don't leave a message, send a text.* As if she hadn't tried.

'Stubborn bastard.' She directed her anger at the seagull perched on the parking meter beside her passenger window. The late afternoon sun bathed the interior; her car was more sauna than vehicle. Switching on the ignition to kick in the air conditioning, she pulled her collar away from her throat and fanned it. Her jeans and shirt had seemed appropriate in the cool morning. Now, they were another stupid choice to add to her collection.

Her phone buzzed, and she scooped it up—but it wasn't Luke, it was Phil's nurse, updating her on a change to his medication because they couldn't get hold of Jonathan and needed to let someone know. Emma rummaged in her handbag for a scrap of paper to write down the details, because in her current state there was no way she'd remember.

Closing her eyes, she leaned back against the headrest. Her neck and shoulders ached with tension. She felt like an ox wearing a yoke, dragging a wagon full of intractable problems. Hunger racked her guts, so intense it had turned to nausea. In an ideal world, she'd go home and eat microwave lasagne and hide in her room.

Resolute, she tried Luke again.

'Emma.'

Relief coursed through her. 'Don't hang up. Please.' Her words tumbled out. 'I've spent all day on the phone—I've had the video taken off all the networks—you can still find it, but it's not easy—'

'Slow down. You did what?'

'I pretended I was a legal rep for Dad.' It had been, in her opinion, a stroke of genius. 'I told them using a mental health crisis for entertainment was unethical and that he'd sue them if they didn't take it down. I can't say I didn't enjoy myself, actually. Maybe I'll go to law school if this acting thing doesn't work out.' Luke's silence worried her. 'Are you there?'

'Yeah. Thanks. That was—nice of you.' Wariness tinged his voice. 'Emma, I know you didn't mean any harm . . .'

'No. I get it.' His reaction had been an unwelcome reminder of fights with Dave—but at least with Luke she knew what the argument was about. 'I asked you for help and you ended up on TV without consent. I'm sorry. Can you forgive me? Start over?'

'I'm sorry I yelled at you.' After a pause, he said, 'Are you in your car?'

'Outside the hospital.' Now she had him on the phone, she didn't know how much to disclose. Fear of judgement—or of bursting into tears, or an unkind response that would flatten her—rendered her speechless. She wiped away a stray tear, cobbled words together. 'I had a huge fight with Dad this morning. I told him to fuck off and stormed out. He stopped my cards. I've got twenty bucks to last until I apologise.'

'What did you fight about?'

Hesitating, she said, 'You, among other things.'

The conversation she'd overheard from outside Jonathan's study had chilled her. *I'll process the money when you agree to my terms* and *Do you think I'm a charity?* and *You're the one who should be scared of the cops; I'm a legitimate businessman*, followed by a dry, humourless laugh.

In retrospect, it had been a terrible idea to confront him about it, and about the money and gun in his safe. He'd given her no useful explanation, just an earful about how ungrateful she was for his financial support.

A few hours later, the reality settled in: Jonathan was up to something.

Luke interrupted her thoughts. 'He's still insisting you stay away from me?'

'Yeah. He—ah, he went right off.' She swallowed, but her throat was dry.

'What are you going to do?'

'Go to Shinita's, probably.'

'Why don't you come here? I'll make you dinner.'

Emma opened her mouth to speak, then closed it.

The sensible option was to seek sanctuary with Shinita, her oldest and dearest friend. And yet fifteen minutes later, she parked her Peugeot beside Luke's car and peered up at a shabby block of flats, asking herself, *What the fuck am I doing?*

Luke waved from the second-floor balcony, then disappeared. Seeing him made her guts seize, as Jonathan's accusations came to mind. A fear that her fascination with Luke was more about defying Jonathan than Luke himself made her question her sanity.

Luke reappeared at the base of an industrial concrete stairwell. In shorts and an old T-shirt, he was unshaven, his hair mussed up as though he'd just got out of bed. She couldn't fault the way he looked when neat and dressed, but his dishevelment added a grungy edge. It reminded her how little she knew about him.

A flash of insight—that being here was a terrible choice—made her hesitate. She overrode it with an equal and opposite force: rebellion.

Leaning back against her car, she waited for Luke to say something to break the awkwardness.

'Are you alright?' His face clouded with concern.

All day she'd held in tears, a fine performance in which she'd pretended to be a calm, functioning adult. His gentle words broke her. Her chest seized, catching her breath; she squeezed her eyes closed, a lame attempt to stop tears. 'No. I'm not.'

He closed the space between them and pulled her into a warm cocoon. Emma pressed her face against his neck. The weight of him grounded her, drew her back to earth. She threaded her arms around his waist and closed her eyes, surrendering. Luke swayed, as though rocking a baby; his deep, slow breaths calmed hers. A gentle squeeze, and his voice was quiet in her ear. 'Come inside and tell me about it.'

He led her up the stairs, his hand clutching hers. Inside the door, she hesitated again, trying to dispel the fear that if he let go, she might float away.

'What do you need?'

She managed a wan smile and said, 'A stiff drink?'

He chuckled, his face creasing into dimples. 'Best I can do is the end of a bottle of red wine I used for cooking. I don't really drink—except when refusing is awkward.'

'Not a fan of red wine.' Emma shook her head. 'I'm not quite that desperate.' A shot of vodka would do the trick, but she couldn't say that to a non-drinker. 'I've had such a shit day.'

'I hear you.' He moved to the kitchen area, a single bench with a stove. 'Are you hungry?'

'What are you cooking?'

'Barramundi. If that's okay.'

The flat was tiny and humbly furnished: an old couch, an armchair, a small table and chairs. A punching bag, some weights. Bookshelves, neatly stacked. Everything in its place, no extraneous clutter. It wasn't just tidy but scrupulously clean—marks in the carpet where it had been vacuumed, pristine benchtops, every surface clear. The bedroom door was ajar; the bed was made. The sliding glass doors to the balcony stood open, allowing a cool breeze and noise from outside into the flat.

While Luke started cooking, Emma threw a half-hearted punch at the bag, then examined his books: fiction on one side—science fiction and fantasy, some classics—and several shelves of non-fiction, everything from history to politics, philosophy, economics and rows of psychology texts. She drew her finger along the spines as she read the titles. *Existential Psychotherapy. Introduction to Cognitive Analytic Therapy. Trauma-focused ACT.*

Watching him out of the corner of her eye, she realised he was doing the same to her, following her movements around his private space. His athletic shape, his competent hands and the way he cocked his head to listen to her were all familiar. But she sensed an unusual weight slowing his movements, as though he moved through water rather than air. Standing by the stove, with tongs in one hand, he seemed lost in thought. She caught him rubbing his eyes and running a hand through his hair.

When they sat down to eat, Emma said, 'You've had a rough day too.'

'I haven't had much sleep the last few days.'

'Come on, spill. What's up?'

Luke stretched his neck left, then right. 'It's complicated.'

'Code for *I don't want to tell you*.'

'You're right. I don't.' With a pained grunt, Luke wiped at his eyes.

'Give me the simple version.'

He thought about it, as though finding the right words was difficult. 'Remember that guy who called the other night?'

She waited.

'The one who was trying to get in touch with my father? My father and his friend are both missing. I've been looking for them.'

Concerned, she leaned forwards. 'Aren't you worried?'

'A little.' The admission seemed to cost him; he focused on his plate, pushing food around with his fork.

'Can't you report it to the police?'

A smile played at his lips, but he didn't look up. 'Ah . . . no. They've been in and out of jail my entire life. The reason they're missing probably has to do with the kind of company they keep.'

Emma waited for more, but he was done confiding. Silence fell while Luke ate and she watched him, thinking.

He looked up. 'You haven't told me what happened today.'

'I need to eat first.' She picked up her fork. He'd cooked crispy-skin barramundi, paired beautifully with a spiced couscous salad. It was restaurant-quality food, complete with a lemon-yoghurt dressing and chopped herbs. She wondered if he always ate this well. Scooping up the last of the couscous, she used her fingers to get it to her mouth.

'You know, I love the way you eat.' Luke's smile dimpled his cheeks. 'You get so involved.'

'Well, I love the way you cook.' With her chin in her hand, she examined his face, noting the trace of darkness under his eyes. Her initial impression of Luke had been one-dimensional: nice enough, nothing special. But he had the kind of face that grew more interesting the more she looked at it. Not just his scars, but the depth of his eyes, the way his smile twitched before spreading into a grin, the line of stubble that outlined his jaw.

'Finished?' He reached out for her hand.

She nodded. 'That was delicious.'

'Come and sit.'

Settling onto the couch, he rested his head back, exhausted. Emma sat beside him, and she didn't argue when he reeled her close, until her head was against his shoulder and his arm draped around her. She tucked up her feet, snuggling into him like a child. 'Tell me what's been happening,' he said.

After a deep breath, she launched in. Phil hated the public hospital, but he was still hallucinating and needed the secure ward; his psychiatrist thought it was related to stress and was adjusting his medication. As soon as it was safe, he'd move to the private hospital.

'And Dave was outside the hospital. I don't know how he found me.' She shook her head, trying to shake Dave off. He clung to her like a fly at a barbecue. 'They had to call security.'

Luke squeezed her shoulders. 'Are you alright? Did he—'

'I'm fine.' She kept her concern to herself, because it seemed irrational to suspect that Dave was following her. 'And Dad . . .' She wasn't ready to air those fears, either: that Jonathan was mixed up in something illegal, enough that he needed a gun. That the money in the safe was stolen or proceeds of crime or something worse, something she couldn't even imagine. She said, 'I don't want to talk about him.'

He laughed, his body moving against hers.

She wondered what was so amusing and turned to look at him. 'What?'

'Nothing. Just—that usually means you need to.'

A fear that he could read her mind chilled her. 'I'm worried about Dad.' The words burst out. 'I found a bunch of money in his safe. And a gun. It's something to do with his work—he's never home, and he's paranoid about security.'

Luke's arm tightened around her. 'Why would he have a gun?'

'I think he got it after those men tried to break in.' Regretting her seriousness, she bumped his arm and added, 'I guess he couldn't rely on you always being there to protect the house.'

'Guess not,' Luke said. 'What are you going to do?'

'I asked him about it, but he wouldn't tell me anything. I'm not going back there. I'll figure something out.'

The conversation reached a lull. The lights were off, and dusk had deepened around them. The breeze from the balcony cooled the room.

Luke's words were soft. 'Thanks for what you did today—about the video. It means a lot to me.'

She drew back so she could meet his eyes, which glinted in the fading light.

'People say they're sorry, but you followed up. You went out of your way to fix it.' He took a deep breath. 'You know what they say. Actions speak louder than words.'

The platitude jarred: it reminded her of her father. *Words are cheap*, he often said.

The streetlights outside cast long shadows through the open window, and in the dim room she felt as though she were caught in a black-and-white movie. Reaching up to Luke's face, she brushed her thumb over the scar on his eyebrow and confessed, 'Dad said some awful things about you.'

'He thinks I'm a low-life grub who's going to corrupt his little girl and take his money. He's protecting you.' Luke's smile didn't reach his eyes.

The summary was accurate, although Jonathan's description had been more colourful. 'I feel like a teenager. Sneaking around with a guy my father has forbidden me to see.'

A chuckle. 'Is this a long-held fantasy of yours? Bad boy from the wrong side of the tracks?'

'Funny.' She threaded an arm around his waist. 'Can I ask you something?'

'What now?'

'The scars on your back—what are they from? What happened?'

'Car crash.' He turned away. A muscle twitched in his jaw.

Liar, she thought. 'In season two of *Streetwise*, one of the characters had to sit in make-up for hours getting scars like that sculpted on. Gunshot wounds.'

'Sounds tedious.'

She put a finger on the side of his jaw and swivelled his face back. 'Don't lie to me, Luke. I'm an actor. I can tell.'

He retreated from her intensity. 'It's a long story.'

Warily, she said, 'Does it have to do with your father?'

'How do you figure that?'

'You said he'd been in jail, and something about the company he keeps.'

He gave a ghost of a smile. 'No. Nothing to do with him. I was in the wrong place at the wrong time.' With a resigned shake of his head, he said, 'I knew it was a bad idea to take off my shirt.'

The explanation was incomplete; Emma figured it was part truth, part lie. Once again, he'd changed the topic to avoid confiding. She chose to let it slide.

'Did I tell you how many times I watched that video of you all wet?' As she laughed, her chest moved against his, and awareness of how close they were made her skin tingle. 'You're always so calm. I liked seeing you all fired up. It made you seem human.'

'I'm not always calm.' Without warning, Luke pulled her into his lap so she sat straddled over him; she let out a startled gasp. She faced him in the near dark, with the sense that they were each waiting for the other to make the next move.

She leaned in, touched her lips to his, a kiss that tasted of dinner and defiance. Luke wrapped his arms around her and his mouth covered hers. His fingers tangled in her hair. Sensations saturated her—the abrasion of his unshaven face against hers, the warmth of his breath, the overwhelmingly male smell of him—and the tingle in her belly spread downwards, warning her that decisions made now were not made by her brain.

'Emma . . .' Luke's lips moved against hers.

'If you're going to say something sensible,' she said, 'just don't.'

He laughed, and she cut it off with a kiss.

And then she pulled his T-shirt over his head and he fumbled with the buttons on her shirt and she tugged at his waistband and he returned the favour and she giggled as they rolled off the couch onto the carpet and he unclipped her bra and then pretended to protest when she pushed him onto his back and she gasped when he wrestled her off and pinned her down, so heavy and solid on top of her, and—

'Is this what you want?' His words feathered into her ear.

Squirming, she couldn't tell if it was his lips or his tongue on her earlobe. The deliciousness of the moment made her close her eyes and bask. She bottled the feeling, saved it in her memory to return to later. 'What are you offering?'

'There's a bed in the next room.'

'Good idea.' Her chest rose and fell with her breath. 'This carpet's a bit scratchy.'

CHAPTER TWENTY-EIGHT

EIGHT YEARS AGO

'Stay here.' From the driver's seat of his van, Ed regarded Jack with a level of disapproval that would have made Gus proud. 'Hassan's a nutjob, and Khoury's still after your blood.' They were parked at the end of a cobblestoned alley in North Melbourne, a few blocks from the market. A light fuzz of rain misted the air. The wet alley glistened with reflected streetlight, but most of it was in shadow, an urban canyon between rows of two-storey buildings. Cold air puffed into the cabin as Ed opened his door.

'Make it quick. I've got an exam tomorrow.' And instead of studying, Jack was with Ed, collecting a debt. A few more months and he'd be done with high school, which should have been a relief. Instead, it opened a Pandora's box of decisions he wasn't ready to face.

Ed grunted and closed his door. He ambled towards the rear door of Noman Hassan's restaurant, which was tucked between a skip bin and a metal fire escape. Ed banged on the door. It opened at once. He was expected.

Three men sauntered out, surrounding Ed, who showed his palms in a gesture of peace. Jack leaned over the driver's seat so he could see more clearly, then thumbed on his phone.

'Jackie?'

'Ed's in trouble. Hassan has a sawn-off under his coat. He's got two guys with him.'

'You being paranoid again?'

Jack gritted his teeth. 'I don't think he wants to pay up.'

'Sort it out. Tell him I'll come myself if he doesn't behave.' Gus hung up.

Jack got out of the van and moved towards the men, keeping to the shadows. Hassan was a skinny beanpole, a pushover for a guy with Ed's build. Hassan's buddies hung back as Ed tried to reason with him, but Hassan's head flicked around when Jack stepped into the light.

'Jack fucking Quinlan. You taking the piss, Ed? What's he doing here?'

Jack stopped several metres away. The alley walls and roofs were spiked with CCTV cameras, but none covered Hassan or his door. With his hands in front of him, a calming gesture, Jack said, 'Just checking everything's okay.'

Hassan's hand dipped under his heavy winter coat. 'You,' he said, taking an angry step forwards, 'are not fucking welcome here. After what you did—'

'Whatever. Give Ed the money.' Jack stuck his hands in his pockets.

'You think Gus is gonna protect you here?' Hassan pulled the short-barrelled shotgun from under his coat. Like his boss Khoury, Hassan loved a dramatic flourish, and his one-handed cowboy draw amused Jack for a nanosecond, until the barrel swung towards him. 'This is a fucking insult. He can come and get his money himself!'

Ed grabbed Hassan from behind in a bear hug. Hassan's buddies sprang into action, trying to pull him off. Jack backed away, his hands in front of him as though to ward off danger, as Hassan swung around and his two men prised Ed's arms off.

Hassan broke clear.

The shotgun boomed, but Jack was already sprinting towards the safety of the van.

Another crack split the air.

A series of thuds hit Jack's back, as though someone had pelted him with stones. With his hands outstretched to break his fall, he pitched forwards onto his face. The cobblestones rose to meet him, cold against his cheek, wet under his hands. Confused, he tried to get up—and couldn't. His limbs didn't work. When he breathed in, pain seared his chest, as though his lungs were on fire—as though his body was tearing apart. Blood filled his mouth and he panicked, a primeval fear of drowning making him gasp—the world turned black and sparkly—a gurgle came from deep in his throat—

Ed's voice, raised to a high-pitched wail, echoed in his ears.

—and he closed his eyes. Gave in to the blackness.

He woke up surrounded by beeping and muffled voices and the smell of disinfectant. Waking was a process, progressive stages of consciousness. By the time he could think more than simple, immediate thoughts—*thirsty* or *where?* or *pain*—days had passed. He didn't know where his feet were. He had doped-up conversations with the nurses about his mother, who spoke like Hermione from *Harry Potter*, although she wasn't really posh at all, she was a manic depressive who'd run away from her family in England and hooked up with Quin, of all people, and died of an overdose when Jack was seven.

His lung had been punctured, he learned. Three shotgun pellets had hit the right side of his back. He'd lost litres of blood. Four hours of surgery, three days in intensive care.

'Lucky to be alive,' said the surgeon cheerfully.

He didn't feel lucky. The next few weeks were a haze of painkillers and indignity, tubes in awkward places and zero privacy. His first visitor was Kevin, who loitered in the doorway and asked if he needed anything. Ed came, then a couple of kids from school dropped by, stunned by what had happened.

One day, when Jack opened his eyes from a doze, Dr Bowman was there. 'Pretty extreme way to get out of school,' he said.

'Go on, say it.' Jack turned his face away. '*I told you so.*'

'That's not why I'm here.' Dr Bowman handed him a get-well card, inside which was an essay in neat handwriting. 'I wanted to let you know I'm moving interstate. Semi-retirement. We bought a winery near Margaret River.' His serious eyes met Jack's with genuine concern. He pointed to the card. 'That's my email address. Stay in touch, okay?'

Jack, dopey with narcotics, couldn't hide his tears. All he could do was stare out the window, which gave him a view of another hospital building and a pigeon perching on a window ledge covered in birdshit.

'Hey.' Dr Bowman put a hand on his shoulder. It was the first time he'd ever touched Jack. 'I'm going to miss you.'

Jack scowled. The pigeon pecked at something. He sensed the man getting up to leave and turned suddenly. 'Doc. Wait.' He scrambled for the notepad by his bed to scribble his email address. 'This is for you.' He handed it over, unsmiling.

'Thanks.' Dr Bowman understood. 'And call me Tim. You're not my patient anymore.'

Gus came later, after the police had given up their questioning and Jack's condition was stable. He lowered himself into a seat beside the hospital bed as though nothing at all was wrong.

'What did you tell the cops, Jackie?'

'Wrong place, wrong time and I don't remember anything,' he said.

'Good lad.'

And then Jack lost his temper: 'I told you he had a fucking gun! I've had enough of this shit—I'm not doing it anymore! You can shove it up your arse.'

'Yeah, that's enough, Jackie. Calm down.'

'I'm out. I quit.' In a flimsy hospital gown, and with a plastic tube between his ribs, Jack couldn't cross his arms to show his defiance. He settled for a flat glare.

Gus leaned back, tapping his expensive shoe on the scuffed lino floor of the hospital cubicle. 'I suppose you deserve a break, with all that's happened. Take a few months off. Get yourself well.'

Gus got up to leave. Jack spoke to his back. 'I mean it, Gus. I'm done.'

'Yeah, we'll see,' came the response.

From the hospital, he went to a rehabilitation ward. Because of his age and guardianship status, it was in an adolescent annexe of the children's hospital. The social workers arranged access to his schoolwork to ensure he got back on track. The other kids were in awe—his wounds gave him hero status—but Jack was in awe of them. They were braver than he was. There were kids with cancer, kids who'd been in serious accidents or had heart conditions. One girl in his physio group had needed a lung transplant. Another had lost a leg to a bacterial infection. And while he was jealous of them when their families came to visit, he knew he would recover his health eventually, while they might not.

Rehab was institutional, but peaceful. No phone. No working for Gus. No fighting with the kids at the resi. Nothing to do but recuperate and study. He was discharged the week before his final exams, with a suspicion the social workers had kept him longer than needed in order to supervise his study.

By late November, his exams were over. School was finished. With a need to steer clear of the resi, Jack spent a day hanging out with his class at a park in Fitzroy. His sporadic attendance at school meant he had few close friends, but his dramatic hospital admission gave him a level of celebrity. They ate fast food and kicked a footy around, but when the group headed to the pub for drinks, Jack had had enough. He could only handle so much socialising. As he dragged his feet towards home, a HELP WANTED sign in the window of a cafe off Brunswick Street—Il Gatto Nero, the Black Cat—caught his eye. The cafe was run by a waspish Italian woman named Marcella, who gave him the job when he agreed to work the early shift for cash. He started at seven the next morning.

He didn't get the perfect scores he wanted, but he did well enough. He'd applied to start a commerce degree at the University of Melbourne, but when the offer came in he wasn't ready—physically, emotionally or financially—for the transition. He deferred his place with a half-baked plan to work for a year and save some cash. After another fight with the stoners, he walked out of the resi with the same possessions he'd had when he arrived: a backpack, a duffel bag and a collection of books. He crashed on a co-worker's couch until he moved in with a girl named Lindy, who had her own flat. She was cute and taught him things about life, for which he would always love her. When that ran its course, he slept in the back of the cafe, then lived in a squat in Fitzroy until they were thrown out by the owners. He couch-surfed in a series of share houses with uni students or stoners or both, blending in wherever he stayed, a chameleon—a welcome housemate who brought leftovers from the cafe and kept things clean. Although he was technically homeless, he had the rear of the cafe to fall back on, and the summer nights were mild.

He considered asking Kevin if he could have Quin's room, but pride got in the way. He hadn't spoken to Kevin since he was in hospital. Quin was still in jail. It seemed like a backward step to reconnect with either of them, although as summer faded and the nights grew colder he wondered if his pride would survive a homeless winter.

In April, as the appeal of his nomadic life was wearing thin, he met Drizzie and Nel. He came across Drizzie on the way out of work on a frosty afternoon. She was off her head, and two guys had cornered her in an alley off the main road. One of them had his hands on her, and Jack said, *Dude, what are you doing?*

He hadn't punched anyone for a while, and he needed little encouragement to get into a fight, particularly with arseholes molesting a drug-affected woman. He smacked the guy into a wall and punched the other in the throat, and would have continued except the first guy pulled a knife. Before Jack could wrestle it from him, the guy slashed Drizzie across the chest. When they saw the blood, they scarpered. Jack used Drizzie's phone to call an ambulance and went to see her in hospital the next day, which was how he met her girlfriend, Nel. They insisted he'd saved Drizzie's life.

Drizzie loved Jack with a ferocity he'd never experienced, at least not in living memory. Nel loved him just as much, because of what he'd done for Drizzie.

Drizzie was in her late twenties, but she looked like a teenager. Her blonde hair was streaked with pink, and her skinny body was patterned with ink; her face was ghostly white and pierced. She'd been hooked on heroin for years but was trying to get clean, getting by with intermittent street oxy. To Jack, she seemed insubstantial, as though a strong wind would blow her away. Her body piercings were the most creative he had ever seen. She showed him all of them, not through any sexual motive, but because she was proud of them. Drizzie wasn't interested in Jack that way. She had no interest in men. *Never have, never will.*

Nel, like Drizzie's comedy opposite, reminded Jack of the world's greatest tennis player. Her outward hostility scared most people away. She was as solid as a powerlifter and dressed like an eighties rocker, with colourful make-up that contrasted with her dark skin. Jack saw through her toughness, because he'd worn a similar expression throughout high school. Beneath it, Nel was a protective mama bear who'd do anything for Drizzie and, now, Jack.

Drizzie and Nel gathered him into their household as though he were a younger brother. Their dilapidated flat in Fitzroy was tiny, but they found a space for him on the sofa bed in the spare room. Nel had a job in a music store. Drizzie was a special effects make-up artist but was in and out of work because of her mental health issues and love-hate relationship with opiates.

In June, his adoptive sisters bought him a cake for his eighteenth birthday. They stuck a candle in it and sang 'Happy Birthday' with tone-deaf enthusiasm. It would later be one of his favourite memories: the day he became an adult, celebrated in style with a four-dollar chocolate cake from the supermarket and the platonic love of two women.

Two days after his birthday, when he was opening the cafe, his first customer sat at a window table and asked for a double espresso and to make it strong. Hearing Gus's voice made Jack's hair stand on end.

'Bit early for you,' he said. Gus was an owl, not a lark.

'Like it here, Jackie?'

'It's a job.' He liked it enough. He was good at it. Marcella appreciated him, although she'd never admit it. It was predictable, it kept him busy and no one got hurt.

Jack prepared for the day. He filled the glass counter with pastries from the morning delivery and unpacked the milk into the fridge, then made a steady stream of takeaway coffees. At this hour, it was the regulars. Many of them knew his name, and he knew their orders without asking, which entertained Gus.

Gus tapped his cigarettes on the table, frustrated by the no-smoking sign. Jack wanted to throw something at him, but it was his workplace, so he restrained himself.

'You gonna order some food or sit there talking to yourself?'

'Another coffee. Shorter.' When Jack delivered it to the table, Gus caught his wrist. 'Where are you living?'

Jack twisted out, expertly evading him. 'Around.'

With a snort, Gus tossed a pineapple on the table. 'Keep the change.'

—✦✦✦—

Gus liked the cafe: Jack made excellent coffee and he could chat in Italian with Marcella. He appeared a few times, alone or with Ed, to down an espresso and hassle Jack.

A few weeks later, on a miserable wintry day, Jack looked up as the bell on the door tinkled and Gus took his usual table. He made Gus his espresso, then peered out the window at the rain, which splattered against the glass, drowning out the trams and traffic noise from the main road.

Gus waited until the other customers left, then made his way through the tables towards Jack.

'All recovered, Jackie?' He placed a phone onto the counter. 'Time to get back to work. You finish at three, right?'

'No. *No*. I'm not—'

'Do what you're fucking told.' Silencing Jack with a glare, Gus glanced around the deserted cafe. 'Ed will pick you up after work.'

Shortly after three pm, as though nothing had ever happened, Jack slid into Ed's van with a sullen scowl.

Ed chuckled. 'You're back.'

'Not my choice.'

'Get your head into gear. We have a mess to tidy up in Craigieburn.'

In September, winter still gripped the city with icy fingers, squeezing out any hint of warmth or colour. On an afternoon so dreary it felt as though night had fallen, Jack had all the lights on in the cafe. He leaned on the counter and indulged a moment of fatigue, thinking about the end of his shift and hoping his phone stayed quiet so he could have the night to himself. As expected, Gus's demands had quickly escalated. A few brief months, and his life belonged to Gus more than it ever had.

Back in the gym, back on the job. The thought made him hang his head with resignation.

A poster had come unstuck from the exposed-brick wall—a band he'd never heard of, probably long since given up their dreams. *Join the club,* he thought, wondering where they were now. He turned to the sound of the door opening.

'Surprise.' Quin's face creased into a grin. A blast of cold air followed him into the cafe. 'Go on. Say something.'

Jack blinked a moment. 'You want a coffee?'

'Sure. Cappuccino, whatever.' Amused, Quin glanced around at the upmarket decor. He sat at a table, out of place, like a wrong note in a tune. Jack bristled with irritation. The cafe was his territory. Quin, like Gus, was an unwelcome reminder of his previous life.

'How'd you find me?' Jack put the coffee down with a clunk and hoped Quin wasn't expecting a freebie.

'Kev knew you were here.'

It was news to Jack; he hadn't seen Kevin since he was in hospital.

Quin spotted Marcella loitering behind the counter. Despite his two years in jail, he could still muster a cheeky smile. 'Look at this: he doesn't want to talk to his old man.'

'This is your dad?' Marcella's gaze flicked from Quin to Jack and back again.

Jack ignored them, cleaning the pipes on the machine.

Quin beckoned Marcella closer. 'It's been a few years.'

Marcella said, 'You want to knock off early? Go chat to your dad.'

When he could no longer claim cleaning as an excuse, Jack grabbed his jacket from the back room and they walked a block to the park in silence. They sat on a bench, ignoring the cold drizzle and biting wind.

'What do you want?' Jack asked.

'Two years inside, and this is the welcome I get?'

Anger turned his stomach. 'I had to go to a group home.'

'Wasn't my fault.'

'Don't be a prick.'

'You're looking good. Is that a uniform?'

'Whatever. We have to wear black.' Jack didn't mind: the black jeans and T-shirt suited him and it got him tips. Customers liked his smile too. His long hair was tied in a knot. He hadn't shaved since he finished school, and his beard was a shade darker than his hair with unexpected flecks of ginger. He looked the part at Il Gatto Nero, in the heart of trendy Fitzroy.

'You still working for Gus Alberici?'

Jack turned to Quin with narrowed eyes. Quin seemed smaller, thinner. There were more lines around his eyes and mouth than Jack remembered. His dark hair had been buzzed short, but it didn't hide the amount of grey. 'Kevin tell you that, too?'

'Heard you got shot. And that you're back on the job.'

'What do you care?' Jack's phone was heavy in his pocket.

Quin shrugged it off. 'Just asking. Where are you living? There's room at Kev's.'

Jack fought back his response; he'd learned restraint, dealing with customers every day. 'No way I'm living with you two. I'm saving up. I'm going to get a degree and a proper job and have a normal fucking life.'

Late one afternoon a few weeks later, he was tidying behind the counter when Quin took the table near the window. It was where Gus always sat, and it hit Jack like a portent of doom.

Instead of fidgeting, Quin huddled into his coat and kept his eyes on the table. Jack made him a cappuccino with a shot of vanilla syrup; he looked like he needed the sugar. After work, they walked to the park, again in silence. The cold frosted their breath, but the rain held off. Quin sat on the bench and wrung his hands together.

'What's going on?' Jack shoved his hands into his pockets for warmth.

'It's Kev. He's doing a job with Robbo Parker tonight.'

Jack's stomach clenched, as though his waistband was suddenly two sizes too small. He didn't trust himself to speak.

'I fucking hate him.' Quin wiped a hand over his mouth. 'What he did to you. Kev should have told him to fuck off.' His breathing was shallow and rapid. 'I don't trust him, not as far as I could—'

'Calm down.' Jack forced his fists to relax.

'Kev's my friend. This is—it's a betrayal.' Quin's mouth was a stubborn line, the expression he wore before he threw something at Kevin or launched into a foolish tackle. It was so familiar that Jack had to turn away. While Quin got up to pace, Jack gazed around the deserted park, the swings creaking in the wind and the rain-slicked picnic tables. Needles of cold bit through his jacket.

For want of anything better to say, Jack asked, 'What's the job?'

Quin turned back. 'Robbo found out about these three blokes who rolled an armoured car. Two got busted, but Robbo knows the other guy—he got away with a hundred grand. Robbo's gonna steal it from him. Reckons he'll move it tonight. Says it's an easy job.'

Jack watched the expressions flick across Quin's face. 'Why did Kevin agree?'

'He wants to retire, up at Stillwater. This way he can do it without selling the house.' Quin sighed. 'I don't want him working with Robbo. Kev should know better. Robbo's gonna fuck him over, one way or another.'

'Last I checked,' Jack said, 'Kevin was an adult. It's his choice.'

'You don't get it!' Quin's feet squelched on the wet grass as he paced. 'He shouldn't even talk to Robbo after what he did to you!'

'You think Kevin cares?' Jack snorted.

'Well, he should! Kev and I go way back, before you were born— this is a kick in my face—in yours...'

'You want my advice?' Jack grasped Quin's shoulder and looked down at him. It was the longest eye contact they'd ever held, but it wasn't heartwarming or bonding; the desperation in Quin's eyes made Jack cringe. 'You won't change Kevin's mind. You're on parole. Stay out of it. Go home and hide under a blanket until it's over.'

Quin jerked away. 'I'll tell you what would fix this.' His mouth flattened into an ugly frown. 'Someone should shoot Robbo in the head.'

CHAPTER TWENTY-NINE

SATURDAY, 7 AM

Light slanted across Luke's bedroom from the high rectangular window, casting Emma's face into shadow. She was sprawled on her front, her cheek squashed against the pillow, her hair a wild mess. The sheet tangled around her legs. Luke propped himself on one elbow and drew his fingertips down her bare back; the base of her neck, each vertebra, the edge of her shoulder blade. Unlike his back, her skin was soft and smooth and unblemished. He shook off the memories that had disturbed his dreams. His present was infinitely preferable to the past.

Emma stirred, and he stroked her hair, tickled her neck, her ear. When at last she opened her eyes, they were bleary with sleep. It didn't surprise him that she was not a morning person.

'What time is it?'

'Early. I need coffee. You?' Luke climbed over her to get out of the bed. After pulling on boxers, he went out to the kitchenette to make coffee, smiling at her antics as she hunted for a T-shirt to put on. He returned to the bedroom to hand her a cup and sat on the bed, leaning against the wall, to drink his. Emma wrapped her hands around the cup and inhaled. She closed her eyes as she sipped.

The clunking of footsteps in the stairwell made him freeze. Irina never had visitors, and the flat opposite his was empty.

A knock on his door followed.

Emma arched an eyebrow. 'Early for visitors.'

'Stay here.' His words, cast over his shoulder as he went to the door, came out like a command.

From outside: 'Jack. Are you in there?'

Luke opened the door. 'Ed, what—'

'You've got about thirty seconds before Gus loses his shit. He's been trying to call you.'

'What?' Luke scanned the room for the Samsung. It was in the pocket of his shorts, on the floor of the living room where Emma had thrown them. He groaned. 'Battery's dead. Shit.'

'Move it. We're going to Kevin's block. He's ready to—oh, *hello*.' Ed grinned at Emma, who hovered in the bedroom doorway. 'Distracted, eh?'

'Stop it.' Luke went to Emma and took her hands in his. 'Sorry. I've gotta go. Stay as long as you want, okay?'

Emma narrowed her eyes, cautious, searching his face. 'What's going on?'

'It's fine.'

'It might be, if you hurry,' Ed said. 'Put some clothes on. Move.'

Minutes later, he followed Ed down the stairs. Gus, who'd been leaning against the side of his car, grabbed Luke by his shirt and slammed him against the wall of the stairwell.

'What the fuck is wrong with you?' Gus's face was red. 'I told you *Saturday morning* and you switch off your bloody phone?'

Luke twisted out of reach. 'It went flat, alright? Give me a break!'

'Get in the car and shut your face. I'm not in the mood.' Gus pushed him towards the car.

Luke was relegated to the back seat behind Gus. Swivelling in the front passenger seat, Ed grinned at him as Gus backed out and took off.

'Punching above your weight,' Ed said.

'Shut up, Ed.'

'Good legs. Great hair. All fluffy, like you've—'

'Shut up. Jesus.'

'That's why you're ignoring me?' Gus flicked his eyes to the rear-view mirror. 'Messing around with some girl?'

'She's a friend.'

'You like her?'

'Yes. Whatever.'

'You like her enough to sleep with her?'

'I am not having this conversation.' Luke closed his eyes.

'You like her, you marry her. That's how it should work. Kids these days fuck around too much. Lack of respect, if you ask me.' Gus was a devout Catholic when it suited him. 'Don't mess with women. Haven't I taught you anything?'

Luke left the rhetorical question alone. He wondered what Gus would say if he knew who Emma was.

'I've been married for twenty-seven years.' Gus was on a roll. 'That's loyalty. Three beautiful daughters. And I tell you, any bloke fucks with them, he'll have me to answer to.' He glared at Luke in the mirror, as though his daughters had been insulted.

Luke put his face in his hands.

It seemed only hours ago that he'd driven Irina's car out of Melbourne towards Castlemaine, although Gus took the direct route, following the navigation of his GPS. He drove out of the city towards the highway, going twenty above the speed limit.

Luke checked his seatbelt. There were rear airbags in the Audi. He mentally rehearsed bracing. Being a passenger in a speeding car still made him nervous.

He tried to get back on track. 'Do you know where you're going? I remember there's no mobile reception, other than on the ridge. GPS might not find it.'

Gus grunted. 'There's a map in the glove box.'

Ed found the map underneath Gus's gun and passed it to Luke, who distracted himself by staring at the spiderweb of roads leading to Stillwater.

He wasn't thinking about the map. Part of his mind was worried about crashing, but mostly he worried about Emma's shocked face as he left. He stared out the window, wondering if he'd screwed things up again.

Farmland flashed past as they continued north. Luke kept an eye on landmarks and forced himself to concentrate. It was still early morning when they turned into the forest. With the map on his lap, Luke studied the terrain, while Gus concentrated on avoiding potholes on the dirt tracks.

'Left here,' Luke said. He braced himself on the seat in front as Gus took the turn too fast. Fresh tyre tracks disturbed the gravel, indicating traffic over the past day.

He allowed Gus to miss the driveway, keeping up the pretence of being unfamiliar with the territory. They backtracked. Gus scowled at him in the mirror.

A fresh wave of deja vu hit Luke as they turned into the narrow track leading to the cabin. Fear of what Gus might find made him clasp the doorhandle. The gate was propped open, but fifty metres ahead a blue-and-white police car blocked their path.

'What the fuck?' Gus smacked the steering wheel. 'Cops?'

'Slow down. Chill.'

'I'm getting out of here.' Gus braked hard.

'Don't make a scene. Find out what's happening.' Luke met Gus's eyes in the mirror as a uniformed police officer signalled to them to stop, then meandered towards the driver's side door. 'Tell her we're lost. Ask for directions to the Old Mine campground.' Luke thrust the map over the centre console. Gus hit the button to lower his window. Retreating into the back seat, Luke kept his face angled down.

'Can I help you guys?'

'Yeah—we're looking for the Old Mine campground.'

'You've come too far south.' She took the map and pointed to an intersection. 'You've come up here. Go back to Main Gully Road— here—and you'll see a track for the campground on the right.'

'Thanks.' Gus pointed ahead. 'What happened? Why is the road blocked?'

'Bushfire yesterday.'

'Are any other roads blocked? Will we be able to get to the campground?'

'The fire was in a gully through there.' Her wave was vague. 'This is private property. You'll be fine getting to the campground.'

'Was anyone hurt?'

'No one lives here. It was a small burn in the gully.'

'Thanks.' Shoving the car into gear, Gus swore as he manoeuvred a jerky five-point turn on the narrow track.

He didn't say a word until they pulled over in the truck stop half an hour later. With the engine ticking over, he slapped the steering wheel. 'What the actual fuck! A bushfire? Are they serious?'

Ed searched the news on his phone. He showed the screen to Gus. 'It was yesterday morning. Burned a half-acre of bush. No damage to structures and no casualties.'

Luke leaned over the centre console. 'The cabin must have survived. He could still be there.'

Ed shook his head. 'She said no one lives there.'

'We're gonna have to wait until they've cleared the road.' Gus turned to glare at Luke as though it were his fault. As though he *knew*. Sweat prickled under Luke's collar.

'If Kevin's not there, they'll have to track him down, right?' Luke said. 'They'll be looking for him now.'

Silent, Gus considered. Luke could see his mental cogs clicking over.

Luke said, 'They'll check the house in Footscray. We didn't leave anything behind, did we?'

'What a fucking mess.' Gus started the car.

Luke retreated into the rear and closed his eyes, hoping his relief would be interpreted as tiredness.

His flat was empty, which didn't surprise him, but his surge of anger did. Bloody Gus. The idea that Emma might be curled up on his couch, watching Netflix on her phone, had kept him sane on the drive home. She'd left a note, in flamboyant cursive that made him smile, saying she'd gone to Shinita's and to call her when he got in.

His phones were on the bench, side by side. Emma had plugged them in to charge, and he would have hugged her if she was there. When he turned them on, a frenzy of beeping told him he'd missed ten calls from Gus and as many texts. Jonathan had also called and texted. *Call me.*

After a shower, he flopped onto the couch and hit Emma's number.

'Give me a tick. I need to go outside.' Emma's voice was muffled.

'Are you okay?'

'Yeah.' It took him a moment to understand her silence. 'Emma, I'm sorry. I didn't expect that to happen.'

'I was worried about you.' Emma's words were guarded. 'I went out on the balcony. I saw him push you. I thought he was going to hurt you.'

Grimacing, Luke didn't admit he'd thought the same thing. His usefulness kept him alive, but Gus's restraint would only last so long. 'I'm fine. You don't need to worry about me.'

'It's complicated, right?'

The line fell silent for so long Luke wondered if she was still there.

'Luke, I liked last night. I like you. But you and I—we have a lot going on, don't we?'

He closed his eyes, anticipating her next words.

'I have to sort out my life,' she said, which made him want to laugh. He didn't. Her life's complications were nothing like his, but they were real enough. 'I can't live with Dad anymore. But I need to make sure Phil's okay and I need to sort things out with work. I can't do that if I'm obsessing over you. And that guy—this stuff with your father—you're going to get hurt.'

'I can look after myself.'

'You know what Dad said?' Her breath caught. 'He said, *He's the kind of guy who doesn't make it to thirty.* And I told him he was wrong, but—'

'You're taking advice from him now?' The retort escaped before he could stop it; he winced, wishing he could swallow it back.

'Jesus, Luke.'

'Emma . . .' He wanted to argue, but his protests stuck in his throat and he choked. She didn't deserve his bullshit. He took a deep breath in, let it out slowly. 'You're right. You need to sort out your life.'

'Jesus, I'm a wreck, and you're just, *okay, whatever.*' Emma's breathing was audible.

'I didn't say I was okay. Just that you're right. There's too much to deal with. For both of us.'

Emma was silent; he suspected she had a hand over her phone. It was possible she was crying. And probable that it was his fault.

He said, 'Can I call you in a week or so?'

It took her several seconds to respond. 'Sure.'

'Look after yourself. I mean it.'

'You too.' They both hung on the line a little longer, until Emma said, 'Bye, Luke,' and a click ended the call.

With his face in his hands, he mulled over the conversation. Stared out the window, at the wall, at the shelf of psychology books he'd wasted time reading.

Then he punched his bag until he couldn't lift his arms. Kicked it until his feet hurt and his muscles and joints groaned. Imagined Jonathan's smug face. Gus's scowl.

With his breath still laboured, he swiped his phone open and called Jonathan, who answered instantly.

'Finally.' Jonathan huffed. 'I need to know what you did with the body.'

'What body?' Luke went to the window and pushed the curtain aside. Sweat cooled on his temples.

'I need to know—'

'No, you don't. I'm done. Get rid of that video.'

'All in good time.'

Luke bit back a response, choosing silence instead. It dragged. Jonathan, quietly: 'Have you seen Emma?'

'Are you fucking serious?' The words burst out. 'After all the shit you said about me? Did you think she wouldn't tell me?'

'Was I wrong?' Jonathan spat the question into the phone. 'Do you know where she is? She's switched off the location on her phone, and—'

'She's an adult!'

'If you know where she is, tell me now or I swear I will—'

Luke hung up.

And then the Samsung buzzed, and he had to restrain himself from throwing it at the wall. 'What?'

'Jack.' It was Ed, not Gus, his voice crackly through a speaker. 'How you doing?'

Luke wasn't in the mood for niceties. 'What's going on?'

'Megan's having some issues. With the baby.'

The context-switch derailed Luke; he felt like he'd been teleported to a different planet. 'Is everything okay? Shouldn't you be at the hospital?'

'I'm on the way there now.' Ed's wary tone told Luke there was more; he waited. 'Listen. Gus knows I'm out of action for a month. But he's on a rant—something's stirred him up. Just . . . keep your head down, okay? I've gotta go.'

Luke tossed his phone onto the couch and stood by the window. For a few minutes, he watched the street below as he worked through the events of the day in his mind. With time and space for his thoughts to settle, he found a focus. There was one common denominator to all his problems. One person.

Soon, he told himself. *Soon this will all be over.*

CHAPTER THIRTY

SUNDAY, 6.30 AM

Luke stared at the ceiling above his bed, directionless. For the last year, he'd worked almost every day. Whether it was attending classes, working or studying, there had rarely been a day he'd woken with nothing on his to-do list.

Unhealthily, he let his thoughts wander to Emma: her hands on his bare skin. Her messed-up hair. Her closed eyes as she drank coffee. All of it. He loved the madness of her.

As he sat up, a glint of gold caught his eye in the carpet near his bare foot. A teardrop-shaped earring—one of Emma's favourites. The circumstances in which it had become dislodged made him smile. He grabbed his phone to text her, then stopped.

He placed the earring on the kitchen bench, where it stared at him as he made coffee and considered his life.

After a run, meditation and breakfast, he did what a normal person would do on a glorious November Sunday: he drove to Elwood beach for a swim.

The sun glistened off the calm water, and the beach was decorated with a kaleidoscope of towels and umbrellas, a festival of colour. A bunch of children in pink rashies, yellow-and-red nipper caps and stripes of zinc cream ran up and down the sand, shrieking as they dived for batons. Luke breathed in salty air and the far-off scent of a sausage sizzle. His worries seemed far away.

He left his shoes and T-shirt on the sand and splashed out into the deeper water. Despite the warm day, the chill took his breath away, made his hands and feet tingle. The waves were mere ripples, a gentle rise and fall. He floated in surrender to the swell, pretending he had nothing to think about other than the velvet brush of sea water against his skin.

He swam a few lazy strokes between the buoys, thinking of Quin, who was scared of deep water and had never learned to swim. Kevin had teased him about it mercilessly.

Dragging himself out of the water, he returned to the beach. He couldn't risk being away from his phones, tucked into his sneaker and hidden under his towel, for too long. His breath caught as he checked for missed calls: a text from Emma lit up the screen.

Hey did I leave an earring at your place?

He thought of a hundred smart answers, jokes, banter. Instead, he texted, *Yep I found it on the floor.*

Can I come and get it?

He thumbed out a complicated reply, then deleted it and sent, *I'll be home in 30, anytime.*

He drove home, showered, made coffee and waited, all the time trying not to get his hopes up. She was coming to collect a lost item, not to revisit her decision. As though reading his thoughts from afar, Emma texted: *I'm outside can you bring it down?*

She'd parked beside his Subaru and stood by the driver's door, phone in hand. She wore a long white summer dress, which Luke guessed was borrowed from Shinita, with her hair wild and no make-up that he could discern; she looked as though she were heading off on a picnic.

'Your earring.' Luke smiled as he handed it over. It was less awkward than he expected. The brush of her hand was welcome. 'Want to come in? I'm about to make lunch.'

Shaking her head, she suppressed a smile. 'You'll suck me back in. You'll make some kind of gourmet lunch and next thing I know—'

'Omelette. With spinach and feta, toasted pine nuts—'

'Like I said.' She arched an eyebrow, then opened her palm to draw attention to her earring. 'Thanks for finding this. They were my mother's.'

Luke paused. They'd talked about her mother only in passing. He wondered if she'd glossed over it, or if he'd been too caught up in his own bullshit to ask. 'Have you spoken to your father yet?'

She shook her head.

'Emma, what you said yesterday—'

They both turned as Gus's Audi screeched to a halt behind Luke's Subaru. Gus shot out of the driver's side and slammed the door. His movements were jerky, his face twisted into a tight scowl.

Luke put a hand on Emma's arm as Gus closed the distance between them. 'You should go. Get in your car.'

Gus planted his feet. 'Jackie. We need to talk. Upstairs. Now.'

'What's going on?'

'I said *now*!' Gus's face was the colour of beetroot. His shirt hung open at the collar and the sleeves were pushed up, a worrying degree of dishevelment. He fixed on Emma. 'Yeah, you too, *Miss Wylie*.'

Shit, Luke thought.

Gus clamped a hand on Emma's shoulder, and his gun appeared in his other hand as he spun her around and pushed her towards the stairs.

'Hey—don't . . .' With his heart hammering, Luke scurried after them. Arguing with Gus when he held a gun was pointless. They clattered up the stairs; Luke had left his door open, and Gus pushed Emma inside.

He stood aside to wave Luke through. 'Lock the door, Jackie.'

'Gus, what the—'

'Shut up or I'll shoot her first and you second.' Gus pointed at the chair by the table. 'Put that in the middle of the room.'

Options occurred to Luke. He could smash the chair over Gus's head. He could dive for the gun. He could make a run for it. But with the distances and the angles, it was a bust: Gus would get off a shot.

He moved the chair.

Gus pointed the gun at Emma, who had stalled by the door. 'Look in the kitchen for duct tape. And scissors.' To Luke, 'Where's your tape, Jackie?'

'Third drawer,' Luke said.

Emma crouched to rummage in the drawer, rattling the contents with her shaking hands.

'Okay.' Relaxing his shoulders, as though his day had taken a turn for the better, Gus turned the gun towards Luke. 'Sit down, Jackie. She's gonna tape you for me, aren't you, love?'

'What?' Luke, staring down the barrel of Gus's gun, took a step backwards.

'*Sit down*.' Gus swung the gun to Emma. 'Do it properly or I'll shoot you.'

'Luke?' Emma's eyes appealed to him.

'Do what he says.'

Lowering himself into the chair, his skin crawled as Emma fumbled with the tape, her fingers slipping on the surface, the scissors dropping to the floor more than once. Impatient, Gus barked instructions at her. The tape went around Luke's wrists, behind the chair, then his legs against the legs of the chair. He wished he wasn't wearing shorts. The adhesive would tear off skin and hair, if he lived to feel it removed.

'Been here before, haven't you, Jackie?' Gus's eyes narrowed. 'Taped to a chair with a knife to your throat. Remember that?'

Luke's body remembered. He smelled Robbo Parker's sweat. Every muscle seized as he froze, paralysed by the flood of chemicals in his system. Telling Gus about Robbo had been a mistake.

Breathe.

Backing away, Emma straightened. Her voice wavered. 'Why do you call him Jackie?'

A backhand from Gus hit her across the face, cutting her off with a gasp that made Luke wince. It was out of character for Gus to hit a woman, even when angry. His temper had overtaken his morals, which sent a chill down Luke's spine.

'Because that's his fucking name! Now sit—there. Keep your mouth shut. Move and I'll shoot you.' He pointed her to the couch.

Emma melted as though her legs had given way, in a cloud of white fabric. She touched her fingertips to her lip, where a spot of blood had appeared. Her shoulders shook. She was only a few metres away, but to Luke it felt like she was on the other side of the country.

Breathe.

Luke said, calmly, 'Gus, let her go. Whatever this is, she's got nothing to do with it.'

'This is not about her! It's about *you!*' Gus rounded on him.

'What?'

'I KNOW WHAT YOU DID!' With his veins standing out like ropes and his face flushed with heat, Gus let go of all restraint. 'YOU'VE BEEN FUCKING LYING TO ME ALL THIS TIME!' His left fist smacked Luke's face hard enough to send the chair teetering on two legs.

Luke's vision blanked and his mouth filled with blood; his thoughts reduced to a single point of fact.

I am a dead man.

CHAPTER THIRTY-ONE

SEVEN YEARS AGO

Jack perched on an upturned food crate in the weedy yard at the rear of Il Gatto Nero, mulling over Quin's disclosure. Robbo and Kevin, doing a job. Quin's intensity: *Someone should shoot Robbo in the head.*

Memories pinned him in place. Reliving the paralysing fear that Quin wouldn't, couldn't, save him—that he had only himself to rely on—made him spring to his feet and pace the courtyard. The temperature dropped as the sky darkened, but still he paced, unable to stop the images flashing through his mind and the fear coursing through his body. All his work with Dr Bowman flew out the window; his back was soaked with sweat, despite the cold. A possum dropped onto the fence behind him and he startled, lashing out with a reflex fist and stopping millimetres from injuring it.

He'd never talked to Quin about the incident with Robbo. Quin had gone to jail, and by the time they were reunited it would have been awkward to rehash it. He'd dismissed Quin as uncaring, so the ferocity of his words now was unexpected. Quin had always shrugged off any conversation that touched on emotion—or numbed himself with alcohol or drugs. It made Jack wonder if two years in jail had shifted things.

Childhood memories of Quin and Kevin intruded. He'd enjoyed watching Quin play with his band at pub gigs over the years. Kevin had often driven him home, because he had school the next day and Quin's set wouldn't finish until late. They hadn't always got it wrong. As his distress cooled, Jack flopped onto the crate and put his head in his hands.

A shrill ringtone—the landline inside the cafe—cut through his thoughts. The cafe had been closed for over an hour. Fearing it was Marcella, he trudged into the darkened room to answer with his polite work voice.

'Jack? Is that you?'

Surprised, he said, 'Kevin?'

'Quin's lost it! He's had a bottle of Beam and I don't know what else—he's totally fucking paranoid! I know he told you about tonight. Did you flare him up?'

'I told him to hide under a blanket.' Jack leaned against the counter and closed his eyes. Quin's decision to bolster himself with substances was bloody typical.

Fury strangled Kevin's voice. 'He's texted Robbo a hundred times, threatening him, accusing him of all kinds of shit, and now Robbo wants to wring his neck! I should have known he'd fuck things up!'

In the background, Jack could hear Quin's voice: 'Is that Jack? Lemme talk to him!'

Kevin grunted. 'For fuck's sake, Quin!'

Quin's rapid speech was barely coherent. Jack guessed he'd smoked some meth to go with his bourbon. 'Jack, Jack! Tell Kev he can't trust Robbo! Tell him what Robbo did to you—tell him what he did!'

'Jesus, Quin. You're loaded.'

'This is so fucked—Robbo's gonna screw Kev.'

Jack held the phone out from his ear. 'Ask Kevin for some valium or something. You need to come down.'

Quin thought that was priceless and spent a few minutes telling Kevin that Jack was giving him advice on drug-taking, then realised he was still on the line and handed the phone to Kevin.

'He's a fucking liability.' Kevin's words were a growl. 'I'm gonna have to keep him where I can see him—fuck knows what he'll do if I leave him alone!'

Jack said, 'This job is toast. You need to bail.'

'Fuck off. It's my retirement plan.'

'You really trust Robbo?'

Kevin's hesitation was enough to answer the question. 'I need you to come and get Quin.'

'Jesus, Kevin! I don't have a car. Where are you?'

Kevin breathed heavily into the phone. 'I'm on my way to the job. Quin's drooling in the back seat. It's in Preston—you know where the market is?'

Jack, whose knowledge of the trains and trams of Melbourne had got him out of many difficult situations, closed his eyes. It was not impossible to get there. He tried again. 'Not my circus.'

'Come and get him or I'll fucking kill him! I'm sick of his bullshit!' Kevin choked on the words.

'Calm down. Jesus.' Jack took his phone—which, thankfully, had been quiet all day—out of his pocket. 'Alright. Listen. Here's my number. It'll take me about forty minutes. Keep him out of trouble until then and text me the address. Don't do anything stupid, alright?' He cringed, for two reasons: first, he wanted nothing to do with this shitshow, and second, it sounded exactly like something Gus would say.

※※※

After layering a hoodie and warm coat over his work clothes and stashing gloves in his pocket, Jack cut through the backstreets to the train station with his breath frosting in the cold air. He caught a train to Preston, with his face angled away from cameras and his hood up, nestled among late commuters and shift workers. Blending in meant keeping his eyes fixed on his phone.

As he hurried past the dark market to find Kevin's location, the familiarity of the situation flattened his mood: he was dressed like a criminal, skulking in shadows, anticipating violence. Just like working for Gus. He should be at home with Drizzie and Nel, watching rubbish on television. Out of habit, he pulled on gloves. Whatever Kevin and Quin were up to, leaving evidence of his involvement was a bad idea.

Kevin's black Commodore was parked in a residential street, a block away from their target's house. Jack had been unimpressed with the plan: *Robbo's watching the door from a car he borrowed—he'll call me when the guy comes out, and I'll go on foot and take the bag, then Robbo will pick me up and we'll drive to my car and switch out.* The plan favoured Robbo's discretion over Kevin's safety. There were glaring holes—did Kevin expect the guy to give up the bag without a fight?—but it wasn't worth arguing. Jack's phone beeped as he approached the Commodore from behind, and fear that it might be Gus made him stop and check, but it was Kevin, hurrying him up.

Jack rapped on the driver's window. Inside, the glow of Kevin's phone lit his face. He startled as Jack's shape shadowed his window, then opened it to growl, 'You took your time. Quin's run off.'

Jack straightened to examine the dark, deserted street. Rain misted around the streetlights, which would have been pretty under other circumstances. Only a few houses had lights on. 'Which way did he go?'

Kevin pointed into the darkness. 'He's looking for Robbo. I need to stay put. I can't risk moving yet, we'll spook—'

'Alright, I'll find him. Whatever.' Jack slapped the roof of the car to mark his irritation and set off after Quin.

At the corner, he slowed to assess the street. A handful of cars were parked along the kerb, but only one—a new SUV with dark tinted windows—was obviously occupied. Dash lights illuminated the windscreen, and the engine was idling. Jack snorted at the lack of discipline. Gus would never allow such sloppiness in a stake-out.

Quin jerked and stumbled along the wet footpath, as though he'd forgotten how to walk, moving further away from Jack with each step. At each parked car, he planted his hands on the passenger window and squinted inside. He was one car away from the idling SUV.

Jack cast around for watchers, then jogged towards him. 'Quin! What are you doing?'

'Jack?' Quin turned too quickly, swayed on his feet and overbalanced, sitting down abruptly on the wet verge. Before Jack could reach him, Quin noticed the SUV ahead. He clambered awkwardly to his feet and lurched towards it. 'Robbo! You're in there! I know it!'

The windows were almost black, but in the dash light through the windscreen, Jack saw Robbo Parker's face for the first time in eight years. Dread soaked him like a cold liquid, from the top of his head all the way to his toes. He froze, unable to force his body to move.

Quin fell against the fender of the car and pulled a tyre iron from his coat.

'Jesus—Quin!' Spurred into action, Jack was too slow to stop the first blow, which cracked the front passenger window. Quin shouted abuse as he smashed at the car. Jack caught his right arm and relieved him of the weapon. Quin wailed at the injustice, but Jack was several inches taller. And sober.

'Give it back! Come on, Jack . . .'

'Don't be a bloody idiot!'

The driver's door of the car opened and Robbo burst out. 'Quin! What the fuck!' He stopped when he recognised Jack. 'And look at you, all grown up!'

'Yeah, fuck you too.' Jack took Quin by the shoulders to drag him away. 'Get back in the car. I'm taking him home.'

With his mouth curling into a snarl, Robbo stepped in front of Jack, indicating the tyre iron in Jack's right hand. 'Give me that. I'll teach him a lesson. The shit he's been texting—'

'Leave it.' Jack snatched the weapon out of reach before Robbo could grab it. With his other arm outstretched, he barred Quin, who was snarling at Robbo like a rabid dog.

Undeterred, Robbo swung a punch at Quin. Jack yanked Quin almost out of the way, but Robbo's fist still connected. Quin yelped as he lost his feet and sprawled onto the grass. Annoyed, Jack smacked the tyre iron into Robbo's shoulder and gave him a push towards the car.

Robbo found his balance and rounded on Jack with a sneer. 'You think you're big enough to fight me now?'

'I fought you last time,' Jack said, and kicked Robbo in the knee. This time, the kick was delivered with expert precision. While Robbo was swearing and hopping, Jack swept his good ankle out from under him and sent him tumbling backwards. Robbo crashed into the car behind. Jack tried to haul the barely conscious Quin to his feet, but Robbo wasn't done.

'Jesus, you're a big fucker now.' Robbo grunted as he got to his feet. 'You look just like your father.'

Jack flashed his eyes to Quin.

'Not *him*.' Robbo sniggered. 'Your real father. The one you actually look like.'

Jack, holding Quin on his feet, blinked and said, 'What?'

Robbo, wincing as he put weight on his injured knee, laughed in his face. 'What, they never told you? Jesus! And you never figured it out? Kev said you were smart! You're fucking stupid if you can't see what's in front of your—'

Jack dropped Quin and the tyre iron and launched. He landed both fists, a perfect jab-cross, into Robbo's face, which had the desired effect of shutting him up. Images from the last time Robbo taunted him flashed across his vision—his flat face and bad teeth, his crazed grin as he held the knife against Jack's skin—and he wanted to claw out Robbo's eyes, get his hands around Robbo's throat, scratch and smash and destroy. He remembered the tyre iron and bent to scoop it up . . .

'You don't wanna hear it, do you?' Robbo, spitting out blood, recovered in time to grab Jack's wrist before he could do damage with the weapon. 'That they lied to you? That Kevin's your daddy?'

They grappled, with Robbo's back pressed into the side of his car. Straining against him, Jack lost his grip on the tyre iron, which clattered to the gutter and disappeared under the car. On the grass behind them, Quin made vague noises of protest but couldn't get up.

Robbo let go of his wrist, and for a heartbeat Jack thought he'd won; but a click made him stop in his tracks.

Robbo's words were panted. 'Get your hands off me. *Back off.*' The shape of the handgun was visible in the shadows.

Jack took a step backwards. Fear made his chest solid; he couldn't breathe. Dark spots peppered his vision.

'Yeah, good choice.' Robbo's panting turned to a sneer. 'You look even more like Kev when you're angry. Prettier, though. Not as pretty as when you were little . . .'

Again, Jack's mind blanked. Blind rage overtook fear. He sprang at Robbo, smacking the man's right hand—and the gun—against the car. He slammed his forearm across Robbo's throat, forcing him backwards as he choked for breath. The gun wavered back and forth, with Jack's hand locked on Robbo's wrist in an awkward arm wrestle.

Robbo forced his arm up, as though to smash the gun against Jack's head, but Jack caught it in both hands and wrenched it back, inching the gun towards Robbo, both of them groaning with exertion as they twisted—

A shot, deafening in the quiet street, jolted Jack away from his opponent. He tripped over Quin and landed on his backside on the grass. The shot echoed around him, repeating in his ears. His head was fuzzy with shock. Shallow gasps tore at his throat. His hands went to his face, his chest, his belly. No wound.

Robbo slid down the side of the car, melting into a puddle against the door. The gun slipped out of his hand to the kerb. Behind him, the cracked passenger window was smeared with a dark stain.

A ringtone, emanating from somewhere on Robbo's torso, played a jaunty tune for a few beats, then stopped.

Jack's phone buzzed. With his mouth hanging open and his ears ringing, he swiped the screen.

Kevin's voice was frantic. 'Was that a shot? Where the fuck is Robbo? The guy's moving—I'm going for the bag!'

'No—get out of here—we need to bail—'

But the line was already dead.

CHAPTER THIRTY-TWO

SUNDAY, 11.25 AM

I KNOW WHAT YOU DID. The words rang in the air.

Pinned to the couch, Emma couldn't tear her eyes from the gun in Gus's hand. Questions ran into each other, end to end without breaks: how did he know who she was and what had Luke done and was this maniac really going to shoot him—

Gus filled the room, not just physically but with a fury that felt alive with electricity. Emma couldn't breathe for fear the gun would turn her way.

But Luke was the one in the hot seat. Blood dripped from his nose, and his left cheek was bruised an angry red. He shook his head, as though to clear it, sending drops of blood in an arc across the carpet.

Luke said calmly, 'Gus, what are you talking about?'

Towering over him—he made Luke look small—Gus smacked him again, hard enough that the chair tipped over. Luke groaned as he hit the floor.

Gus grabbed the chair and heaved it upright. 'Open your eyes, Jackie.'

Luke spat blood out of his mouth and shook his head.

'Open your eyes!'

'Alright. Alright.' Luke's face was a mess, as though he'd smashed it into the side of a bus. Darkness stained both eyes. The left wouldn't open, and the right was a mere slit.

Emma sucked in a breath and thought, *He's fucked.*

And so was she, if she didn't do something soon.

Gus dumped the gun on the table and thrust his phone in front of Luke's face. 'Explain this. And no more lies!' He held the phone while a video played.

After the strain of focusing on Gus's phone, Luke's shoulders slumped and he exhaled. If anything, he seemed relieved.

'Okay. I can explain.' Even now, he sounded calm.

An urge to shake him violently—did he not realise the trouble he was in?—made Emma clench her hands into fists.

'You fucking lied to me! You and Ivan both lied! What the hell, Jackie?' Gus punctuated his rhetorical question with another slap, which made Luke groan.

'Where did you get the footage?' Luke forced his right eye open.

Gus jerked his head towards Emma. 'From her bloody father, what do you think? I knew you were working for him—I bloody knew it!' His fist hit Luke in the guts.

Emma's questions multiplied, like cells splitting and dividing: what the hell did Jonathan have to do with—

'It's not what you think.' Luke's words sounded flimsy. Winded, he swallowed, then gagged. 'Listen to me—'

'I'm not in the fucking mood!' Gus scooped his gun from the table.

'It was Ivan's idea! He told you there were three guys—he asked me to go along with it—I didn't know he was working for you.'

'What were you doing at Wylie's house?'

'Dropping Emma home.'

'Wylie told me that you killed Ivan,' Gus said, glowering. 'Said he paid you to do it!'

'Ivan's not dead!' Luke hung his head. 'He texted me. He's in his cousin's basement in Paynesville.'

'Why did he text you?'

'Guy came looking for him and he hoofed it. He didn't know who was after him. He was scared it might be you. I told him it wasn't, but—'

'And when were you planning to tell me this?'

'He asked me to wait. He wanted to make some calls first.'

The gun hovered, while Luke tried to retreat further into the chair. Gus seethed, exhaling through gritted teeth, but Luke's words appeared to have sunk in.

'Ivan was scared, Gus.' Luke lowered his voice. 'I didn't know he worked for you until I saw him at the gym. He'd lied to you and he asked me not to say anything—I didn't know there was a camera. And then he went on the run.'

'You both thought you'd get away with lying to me?' Gus cuffed Luke on the side of the head.

'I'm not working for Jonathan. I was going behind his back seeing Emma! He's lying to you, trying to set me up!'

Gus licked his lips, worked his jaw. 'She doesn't know?'

'She doesn't know anything!'

Gus slapped his gun on the table, stalked to Emma and held his phone out. 'Watch this, love.'

She had a few seconds to decide how to play it. Going along with Luke's story seemed safest. *I don't know anything.* It was hardly a stretch to feign distress: her eyes widened as the video played. A shaking hand covered her mouth and she gasped, let tears brim in her eyes. At the end, she flashed a horrified look at Luke. 'This is outside my place! Why didn't you tell me?'

'I'll bet there are plenty of things he hasn't told you.' Gus shoved the phone into his pocket.

'What's this got to do with Dad? Luke? What—'

'Wake up, love.' Gus's words were a growl. 'Your father's not as squeaky clean as he pretends. And nor is your fucking boyfriend.' He glowered at Luke, who grimaced as he squinted his eyes open.

'What?' She could barely articulate the word.

No one answered.

Emma sensed a crossroad looming as the mood in the room shifted. Gus paced a few abrupt steps to the left, then a few steps right; debating, she guessed, what to do next.

'Think about it, Gus. Why did he send you that?' Winded, Luke gasped the words.

Treading carefully, she tried again. 'What does Dad have to do with this?'

'Your father is playing fucking games with me!' Gus levelled an angry glare at her.

With a feeble shake of his head, Luke said, 'He doesn't know I work for you. He's screwing with both of us.' A spasm of pain crossed his face. 'He sent you that so you'd get rid of me. He's setting you up. Cleaning house.'

'Why?'

'Two birds, one stone?' Luke closed his eyes again. 'Framing you, or me. Both.'

'Why should I believe a word that comes out of your mouth?'

'Gus, listen—' Luke tried to duck as Gus aimed another punch at his head. Gus's fist connected, tipping the chair again. With a thud, Luke's left side hit the carpet and he howled, a drawn-out, agonised sound that made Emma's teeth clench. She clutched the scissors she'd secreted in the folds of Shinita's dress.

The awful noise was replaced with panting. 'You dislocated my fucking shoulder!'

'I don't care!' Gus kicked the chair, scooting it along the carpet, then reached for his gun on the table.

His back was turned for a heartbeat. Emma sprang from her chair with the scissors in her fist. There was no time to think, no time to plan—she launched onto him from behind, stabbing at the side of his chest—

The scissors bounced off, too blunt to penetrate. Gus tossed her aside as though swatting a fly; she landed on her backside on the floor.

Gus rounded on Luke again, gun in hand.

Panicking, panting, she opened the scissors out to expose one blade. Ignoring the bite in her palm as she grasped them, she jumped to her feet and swung her right arm, as though to punch Gus in the back.

The gun thudded to the floor.

'What the *fuck*?' Gus flailed, reaching for his back as he dropped to his knees. Blood spread out in a red wave, staining the side of his shirt and dripping to the floor. The blue plastic handle of the scissors stood out like an eerie antenna from his side.

Emma backed away, her mouth hanging open.

'Emma, get out of here!' Luke's words were barely audible. When she didn't move, he tried again: '*Go!*'

She spotted Gus's gun on the floor and grabbed it, then wrenched open the door and stumbled down the stairs, grasping the handrail to stay upright. A smear of blood from her injured right hand marked her passage. The sound of the door banging shut, and Gus's scream of fury, echoed after her.

CHAPTER THIRTY-THREE

SEVEN YEARS AGO

Jack shoved Robbo's body into the front passenger seat of his car, then dragged Quin by his shoulders into the rear. After racking the driver's seat back—he was taller than Robbo—he started the ignition. Rain blurred his view of the street. He couldn't find the windscreen wipers, but he edged forwards anyway, toward the target's house.

In the distance, a siren blared, then another. Someone had heard the shot and called the cops.

His hands shook as he swatted at dials and switches to find the wipers. Frustrated, he turned to the back seat, where Quin sprawled facedown.

'Quin! Where are the wipers?'

No answer. Something he hit jerked the wipers to life.

Outside the target's house, Kevin's large form tussled with a man as they fought for control of a black duffel bag. Crawling towards them in Robbo's car, the lights off, Jack leaned forwards to see more clearly. As he'd anticipated, the man didn't give up easily. He grappled with Kevin, swinging the bag like a weapon. Kevin punched him in the face, grabbed the bag's handles and wrenched it away.

Jack floored the accelerator, closed the distance and screeched to a stop within metres of Kevin. Kevin threw the bag, then himself, onto the back seat on top of Quin.

'WHAT THE FUCK?' Kevin pulled the door shut as Jack hit the accelerator again.

'Later.' Jack flicked his eyes to the rear-view mirror. Kevin's opponent shook himself to his feet and ran to a parked Toyota. Taking the corner so fast the tyres squealed, Jack covered the block to Kevin's Commodore in seconds. 'We need to get out of here—he's coming after us! And the cops are coming too!'

'What happened? Is he dead?' Kevin stared at Robbo's lifeless form, slumped in the passenger seat.

'*Later.*' Jack's hands gripped the steering wheel. 'We need to get out of here *now*!'

Kevin took the bag, and Jack grabbed Quin, who was barely conscious. Both were shoved into the back seat of the Commodore. Jack slid into the front passenger seat, and Kevin put his foot to the floor moments later.

'Go left—left again. Get out to the main road. Don't speed.' Jack checked behind them; the Toyota hadn't appeared, but the sirens had multiplied.

Kevin reached across to grab Jack's shoulder. 'Tell me what happened!'

'Quin went nuts with a tyre iron. Robbo had a gun.' Jack's words were quiet. Leaving the body in the car was bound to cause trouble, and he hadn't had time to find Robbo's phone. 'Kevin, Robbo's not your biggest problem.'

'*What?*' Kevin gaped. 'You left a body behind! How is that not—'

'The guy you rolled is called Craig.' Jack put his arms over his head. The dread of seeing Robbo paled in comparison to this. 'I know him. He works for Gus.'

'Fuck.' Kevin smacked the heel of his hand on the steering wheel once, twice and then repetitively, an accelerating drumbeat. 'Fuck. *Fuck*. Robbo told me—'

'A load of shit.' Jack tried to slow his breathing. 'I'll bet Gus organised the whole job. Craig's a bagman. He was taking it in for cleaning, right? Robbo told you a pack of lies so you'd do the hard yards while he hid in the car.'

He sat up, riding a wave of nausea. He glanced at Kevin and tasted acid in his throat. Kevin was taller than Quin. Fairer hair. Smarter. And Jack recognised something in the shape of his face: a familiarity he saw when he looked in the mirror.

If he hadn't killed Robbo already, he'd do it now with his bare hands. He could murder all of them, these people who'd lied to him his entire life. What an idiot he'd been—such a stupid kid, unable to see the truth staring him in the face. The humiliation burned.

He forced it aside and willed his brain to think. He hadn't seen any cameras. He would be nothing but a black blur, anyway. He had gloves on. His phone wasn't registered to him. Craig hadn't seen him. Nothing linked him to this mess.

Jack said, 'Where are you going? You need a plan.'

Kevin lashed out, pushing Jack so hard he bounced off the door. 'What I don't need is shit from you!'

Jack pushed back. 'Switch off your phone.'

'What the—'

'Switch it off. It's a tracking device.'

Leaning over the centre console into the back, Jack struggled his way into Quin's pockets to find his phone and powered it off.

With a scowl, Kevin did the same with his own phone, tossing it onto the dash.

Jack retreated into his seat. He needed to distance himself from this insanity; from Kevin's temper, Quin's incompetence and the bag on the back seat. He called Marcella and told her he was sick and wouldn't be in to work the next day, then switched off his phone. It bought him twenty-four hours. Drizzie and Nel would alibi him if the cops came asking. They'd say whatever he asked them to.

His biggest problem would be if Gus tried to call. He'd have to come up with something.

Quin, in the back seat, stirred and started to sing, crooning tuneless incomprehensible words.

'Shut up or I'll toss you out of the car!' Kevin clutched his thick sandy hair with his fist as though he wanted to tear it out, glaring into the rear-view mirror at Quin. 'You screwed this whole thing! The cops are gonna be looking for you! You fucking IDIOT! I'm gonna fucking kill you!'

Quin said, 'I need some water.'

The rain increased, as though Quin's plea had been answered. The windscreen fogged and Kevin switched on the air conditioning, chilling the car.

The aftermath of the fight with Robbo made Jack's hands tremble. 'Where are we going?' The city had thinned into suburbs around them.

'Stillwater.' Kevin's voice was taut with emotion. 'We need to lie low.'

'Pull over and let me out. This is your disaster.'

Kevin shook his head. 'I'll need an extra set of hands. Quin's bloody useless. If he'd just let it slide, none of this would have happened.'

Jack took a few deep breaths, concentrating on his slow exhales to release the tension in his body. They rode in silence, withdrawing into their own thoughts. The headlights cut through dense blackness and heavy rain, the windscreen wipers barely keeping up with the downfall. Kevin's face was lit by the eerie green of the dashboard lights. Jack couldn't decide which he preferred least—the chaos of Quin or the seething anger of Kevin McNally.

Kevin said, 'Get the bag. Count the money.'

Jack huffed. 'I'm not touching it.'

'Just fucking do it.'

Grumbling, Jack hauled the heavy bag onto his lap and unzipped it, then said, 'Holy shit.'

'Robbo said it was a hundred grand.' Kevin moistened his lips.

'He lied.' Jack, experienced at this task, switched on an interior light and angled it into the bag. The neat bundles of hundred-dollar notes were tightly stacked in regular rows.

By the time he'd finished counting, they were bumping along dirt roads through the forest, and his head was full of numbers. There were many reasons his head was spinning. The numbers were one. The smack on the head from Robbo was another. Fear of Gus's vengeance, of Kevin's plans; and Quin's silence also worried him.

Kevin drummed his fingers on the steering wheel. 'What's the verdict?'

Jack's voice was hushed. 'Two million, three hundred and forty thousand.' He didn't include the bundles he'd claimed for his trouble and shoved into his jeans.

Quin slurred, 'You were always good at counting,' and fell silent again.

'Get the gate,' Kevin said.

Jack didn't have the energy to argue; he got out into the rain, dragged the gate open and then closed it after Kevin had driven through. By the time he got back in the car, he was soaked to the skin.

The headlights picked out the cabin, the tyres sloshing through mud as Kevin drove around to the back. He switched off the ignition and sat in silence as the engine ticked over, rubbing his face. Rain pounded the roof; waves of water sheeted the windscreen, as though they were in a car wash. A shiver racked Jack's body.

'Robbo said my cut was fifty grand.' Kevin's chest moved with his breath, which was rapid and shallow. 'You counted right?'

Jack didn't dignify this with an answer. 'Quin knew it. Robbo was screwing with you. Short-changing you.' He moistened his lips. 'I guess that's why he brought a gun, right? In case you figured it out.'

Kevin smacked his palm against the steering wheel.

'Gus is going to freak.' Jack anticipated that Craig was already in a world of hurt. It was a huge sum of money, even for Gus.

Kevin ignored him. 'Give me the bag.'

Jack zipped it up and handed it over. Kevin opened his door and crouched against the rain as he moved through the darkness towards the cabin. He fumbled with the door latch and disappeared inside.

The headlights illuminated a narrow area between the car and the cabin door, sharply distinct from the blackness surrounding them. Kevin emerged from the cabin and trudged towards the car with the duffel bag slung over one shoulder and a torch in hand. He wrenched Jack's door open, allowing a flurry of rain into the car, and jerked his head in the direction of the ridge. 'I'm gonna deal with this. Take Quin inside.'

The torchlight danced as Kevin stalked away, shrouded by the rain. The light was soon absorbed into the blackness. Jack closed his door; getting out of the car went against all his instincts. Kevin's mood, and the knowledge that there were guns in the cabin, made the car a safer choice.

'What's Kev doing?' Quin propped himself on an elbow.

'Hiding the bag.'

With a chuckle, Quin flopped onto the seat.

'It's not funny!' Jack ran through his options. Whenever he let down his guard, Robbo Parker's face came to mind and made his muscles clench.

'What did you do with Robbo?' Quin's eyes were at half-mast. He stared at Jack with curious intensity, as though he didn't quite recognise him.

'Left him in the car.' Jack's words were almost lost as a fresh downpour pelted the roof and windscreen.

'He had it coming.'

'Is it true, what he said?' Jack turned in the seat again. Quin had slumped across the rear in a diagonal lean. 'That Kevin . . .'

'What do you think?' Quin closed his eyes. His chest moved with silent laughter.

'You think this is *funny*?'

'Is there any water?'

Jack pushed down his anger. Desperation to get the hell away rose with the minutes. Kevin had left the keys in the ignition. Jack didn't think: he climbed into the driver's seat, started the car and shoved it into gear. The wheels spun in the mud. In his impatience, he'd hit the accelerator too hard. He backed off, let the engine idle a moment, then tried more gently. The car moved forwards as the tyres gripped the wet track.

'What are you doing?' Quin's question floated in the air.

Jack didn't have an answer. He flicked the headlights to high beam as Kevin emerged from the darkness to his right. The light washed over the sodden man, the torch in his hand fading to nothing against the powerful headlights. Kevin's mouth was open with his shout as he ran towards the moving vehicle.

Kevin pounced at the car, grasping the driver's doorhandle. Jack hit the button to lock it just in time. He jammed his foot onto the accelerator and got nothing but spinning wheels.

Kevin let go and ran back to the cabin. Relieved, Jack played with the gas, edging the car along the track. Patiently, slowly, he built a little speed—but as he rounded the cabin, the headlights silhouetted a figure in the middle of the track.

Kevin, holding his rifle.

Jack slammed on the brakes.

The front windshield cracked, and a cold blast of wind and rain hit his face. Confused, his hands left the steering wheel to shield his face—had Kevin shot at him? He grabbed the steering wheel, and the car slid in the mud as he swerved to avoid hitting Kevin. The tyres lost traction and the nose of the car dug into the bushes at the side of the track. The engine stalled.

Quin's voice rose to a wail. 'He's gonna shoot us! Get us out of here!'

Jack fumbled to start the ignition, hit the clutch and smacked the gear into reverse. Again, the tyres spun. The lowered sedan was not designed for the muddy conditions.

Kevin loomed like a shadow, the long shape of his rifle at his side. A shot pinged off the side of the car.

Another shot, and the rear windshield cracked. Jack ground the gears, tried again to find traction, but the car was bogged and wouldn't budge.

'Get us out of here!' Quin's frantic yell was cut off as the rear passenger door jerked open.

Kevin grabbed Quin by his shirt and dragged him out into the rain. 'You gonna go dob on me to Gus? Jack's idea or yours?'

Quin scrambled backwards on the wet ground, like a clumsy spider. Jack threw himself out of the driver's door to hide behind the car. Cautiously, he peered around the rear.

'Kev, Kev.' Quin slipped in the mud and held up a hand, as though in surrender.

'You're such a useless prick!' Kevin's voice rose with his fury. 'I've saved your arse so many times!' He shouldered his rifle.

Quin threw his hands up in defence.

Kevin fired.

Quin cried out and Jack flinched, cowering behind the car. He was already wet to the skin and covered in mud, and the deafening gunshot sent a sharp pain through his head. He chanced another peek. It was a relief when he heard Quin's voice.

'What'd you do that for?' Quin clutched his left thigh with both hands as he rolled around.

'I'm so sick of your shit!' Kevin's panted breath was audible even from where Jack sheltered several metres away. He stalked two steps left, three to the right, left again, then turned to point the rifle at Quin. Jack held his breath. The car headlights glowed dully, reflecting off the wet trees. Kevin was illuminated in profile. With sudden disdain, he abandoned Quin to search for Jack. 'Get out here, kid! Get out here NOW! You're not gonna go running to Gus!'

Jack stayed where he was.

'Kev—get a bandage or something.' Quin's voice was drowned out by the rain.

Kevin ignored him and moved to the back of the car, rifle in hand. Jack crept around to the front, like a kid playing hide-and-seek, and peered around to see Quin.

In the darkness, he couldn't see the extent of Quin's injury. It hadn't been immediately fatal, which Jack assumed meant nothing vital had been hit. He wanted to yell at Quin to put pressure on it, but it would betray his location to Kevin. Quin pulled himself up into a half-seated position, with his hands pressed against his leg, and stared at the wound as though fascinated. He closed his eyes and slumped back.

Kevin's head flicked around, and a bullet pinged off the front of the car dangerously close to Jack's head.

A wave of fury cancelled out rational thought, and while Kevin was reloading the rifle, Jack's body acted without his permission. With an animal growl that started in his chest, he charged. Slamming his shoulder into Kevin, he tackled him to the ground with a splash of mud and freezing water. 'You killed Quin, you idiot!'

'I told him I was gonna kill him!' Kevin struggled under Jack's weight. They churned into the mud, digging deeper as they wrestled. Kevin tried to get the gun around, but Jack grabbed it by the barrel, yanking it from Kevin's hands to swing it like a club. The blow glanced off the side of Kevin's head.

Grunting with effort, Kevin slammed Jack onto his back, squelching into the mud. The rifle, slick with rain, slid out of Jack's grasp. Straddling him, Kevin wrapped his hands around Jack's throat.

Jack was gripped with fear: the madness of his anger with Robbo only a few hours ago was reflected back at him in Kevin's face. Robbo's words taunted him: *You look even more like Kev when you're angry.*

Rain bucketed down, a torrent that blinded Jack's vision to everything beyond Kevin's twisted face. Their sodden clothes hampered every movement. Panting, panicking, Jack lashed out with both hands, trying to land a punch or dislodge Kevin. The ground was too slippery to get his feet under his body to push with his hips. And even if Kevin didn't strangle him, he could drown in the puddles that collected in the potholed track.

Jack's chest burned for breath and his hands scrabbled at Kevin's, struggling to break the man's hold on him. In desperation, he clawed at Kevin's face. A reprieve at last: with an almighty heave, he broke the hold on his throat. Mud splashed as he rolled Kevin over and pinned him by his wrists, gasping as he sucked in oxygen.

'Why didn't you tell me the truth?' he panted into the man's face.

Kevin froze, his face cast into shadow by the oblique lighting from the car. He came to life suddenly, jerking upwards with his hips. Jack was thrown aside into the mud. It took him a moment to get his bearings on the slippery surface.

He turned back for Kevin and found him kneeling, holding his rifle. Still panting, Jack leaned forwards with his hands on his thighs. 'What, you're gonna shoot me too?'

'Back off.' Kevin, the rifle aimed at Jack's chest, got carefully to his feet. Left foot, then right.

Jack straightened. He took a step backwards. 'Come on,' he said. 'Enough, alright?'

The gun stayed centred on him. He felt dizzy. He could still feel Kevin's hands wrapped around his throat.

The rain eased, and there was an eerie silence. Kevin wavered, as though he couldn't quite make sense of the situation; as though he'd lost his grip on reality.

A sound behind Jack made him turn his head: Quin, moaning.

'He needs to go to hospital.' Jack could barely form the words.

'What do you care?' The gun had dipped; Kevin jerked it back up.

'Jesus, Kevin!'

'He's not your father. And he knew it!' Kevin's bitter tone made Jack shiver.

Jack's anger flared. 'Why didn't you tell me? What's the big fucking secret?'

Kevin's face didn't move, but his chest heaved. 'It's Susie's fault. She put Quin's name on your birth certificate. He said you'd been through enough. Didn't want to mess with your head. He was protecting *you*.'

'You always treated me like shit! Like you couldn't bear the sight of me! And you *knew*?'

'Because you're just like *her*!'

'*What?*'

Kevin took a threatening step towards him. Jack recoiled, put his hands up.

'Your mother! Beautiful bloody Susie! Ditched me for Quin, didn't she? And then ran off to England with you—she didn't even tell me she came back! She fucking *destroyed* me!'

The words hung between them.

'Let's take Quin to hospital,' Jack said. 'We can sort this out later.'

'No.' Kevin's hands were steady, but his breathing was erratic. 'I've had enough. Ten years I've put up with this—Quin—and Gus—'

'What does Gus have to do with it?'

'He thinks he *owns* you!' Kevin's face, twisted into an expression Jack had never before seen, was far too close. 'You don't know *anything*! All these years, I looked after Quin—after *you*—trying to keep the two of you alive! Kept a bloody roof over your heads— kept Quin in line—and now you're Gus's fucking golden boy! You're gonna rat me out the minute you can!'

Jack saw Kevin clearly, as though it were daytime and not a sodden, stormy night: blue eyes that could be his own, racked with years of rage and misery.

His voice wavered with emotion as he said, 'If Gus finds out I was anywhere near this, I'll be as dead as you.'

Kevin's eyes closed, and Jack seized the opportunity. He dived forwards, grasping the barrel of the rifle with both hands. Kevin clung on and fought back. For a breathless moment, they wrestled, until Jack yanked the weapon out of Kevin's hands. He flung it away with all his might. Kevin roared; he tackled Jack, pinning him against the car.

'Kev! Let him go!'

Jack turned his head to see Quin swaying on his knees, barely upright—but he held Kevin's rifle like he meant it.

'Kev! For the last fucking time, leave the kid alone!'

CHAPTER THIRTY-FOUR

SOMETIME

Sounds filtered through. Voices: *Luke, can you open your eyes?* The door of his flat opening and closing. Footsteps.

He ignored the sounds and focused on his breathing, drawing his attention away from his shoulder. Pain caught his lower chest: a cracked rib. He breathed into it. In and out, like waves breaking on a beach. *Pain is a construct of the mind*, Dr Bowman had said, *a subjective experience. Physical pain, emotional pain, it's all the same. Your mind can choose what to attend to, and what you attend to is amplified.*

Gus's parting words, spat into Luke's ear before he stumbled after Emma, seemed a long time ago, as though he'd been suspended in time and space and the agony of his injured shoulder. *Cross me again and I'll shoot you in the head.*

But through it all was a haze of relief. He was alive. His secrets were safe.

A hand touched his throat and he panicked, struggling against the tape that still held him, but he couldn't open his eyes. Voices surrounded him, like murmurs, as though he were underwater. He groaned as he was released; he'd been in the same position for . . . how long? His muscles had seized. Carpet under him as he was laid on his back. Something tight on his right arm. A scratch in his forearm.

Luke, open your eyes.

He tried to express his opinion, but it came out as a groan.

There were more murmurs; his left arm was pulled down, and then a sickening rotation and crunch as the shoulder joint popped into place. Then he was floating. Like he'd floated in the sea that morning. Floating, drifting, disappearing—

We've overcooked the morphine, a voice said. *He's narked out.*

There were worse things than being given too much morphine. Like nearly being strangled by your biological father. Or beaten up by your boss. The car crash, when he smacked his head and knocked himself out, that had been awful; and Robbo Parker's violence, when he'd threatened to cut Jack's throat. Memories of his mother's death were the deepest buried; he'd talked to Dr Bowman about them over the years, and they still came to him sometimes, the memory of her ashen face and the cigarette on her bedside table. But being shot had been the worst physical pain he'd—

You didn't get shot, Luke. Just beaten up. Dislocated shoulder, and your face is a mess.

He flicked his eyes open. 'Was I talking?' The words were slurred.

'Yeah, keeping me entertained.' The speaker, a solid woman of about fifty, wore a paramedic's uniform. Her eyes crinkled with a smile. 'You're sensitive to narcotics for such a big guy.'

His vision was blurry. It took a moment to realise he was in an ambulance. The narrow trolley felt like concrete under him, and he felt every bump in the road as the vehicle moved. An oxygen mask sat over his face, uncomfortable against the bruising; the air tasted of plastic. His arm was hooked to an intravenous line. A monitor clipped to his forefinger. His left arm was in a sling.

'I'm alright,' Luke said. 'I don't need to go to hospital.'

She laughed. 'You need an X-ray of that shoulder, and you need observation.'

'You put my shoulder back in?' He recognised her voice.

'Yep. Did you feel it?'

He couldn't remember. Maybe. He shook his head. 'Did somebody—how did you—'

'Your neighbour called the police.'

Luke shifted uncomfortably. He didn't remember any police. And then an electric current of anxiety jolted him upright. 'Is Emma alright? Was she hurt?'

'There was no one else there.' The paramedic put her hands on his shoulders, easily overpowering him. She pushed him back onto the trolley. 'You know who it was who beat you up?'

Luke closed his eyes. She wasn't a cop. He didn't have to say anything.

'Are you comfortable? I reckon that morphine has worn off. Your heart rate just spiked.'

'I'm fine.' It was thoughts of Emma and the police, not pain, that made his heart race.

She didn't believe him, and fiddled with his drip to give him what she called *just a whiff* to keep his pain under control.

He floated off again.

As he was transferred from the ambulance trolley to the emergency department, he realised he was an old hand with hospitals. He'd had a couple of serious admissions, and a half-dozen less serious: stitches and footy injuries and, once, a bout of influenza Gail had been worried about. He remembered coughing for weeks. Gail had put him in her bedroom and fed him soup.

Gail: his grandmother. He hated that they hadn't told him; that he hadn't been given the chance to enjoy having a family. Had she known?

Do you want us to give her a call? Your grandmother?

'No,' he said, without opening his eyes. He'd been thinking out loud again. He'd done that the last time too. He remembered telling a nurse his mother was from Guildford and she always wore Doc Martens and she'd got a nose-piercing to piss off her parents—

He heard a laugh and tried to rouse himself. A nurse was spraying something cold on his legs.

It helps dissolve the adhesive, so we can remove the tape.

That made sense. Duct tape was bad news on bare skin. He remembered the last time, because Robbo had torn it off so sharply that he lost skin from his wrists and ankles. Cable ties were kinder. Ed was fond of cable ties; kept them in his pocket for emergencies. Cable ties and a crowbar were his preferred tools. Gus was simpler: he liked his gun and his fists—

Stop talking, Luke, or I'll call the psych team, the nurse said.

He woke in a quiet room. Dull throbbing took up the space where his face should be. He couldn't breathe through his nose, and his mouth felt like he'd been eating cardboard; his tongue was stuck to the roof of his mouth. He lay still, listening. Sweat prickled his back. He put a hand to his face. A plastic splint covered his nose. With a sense that he might as well get on with it, he cracked his eyes open. The glaring artificial light seared.

He was alive.

A pastel-coloured hospital room came into focus, shades of peach and pistachio. A window on his left showed darkness outside. Sensing movement to his right, he turned his head, which made the room spin.

'You're awake.'

'Emma.' His surge of relief took him by surprise, whisking any useful words away.

She sat in a chair by his bed, holding her phone, which she set on her lap to pick up his hand. His gaze was drawn to her lower lip, where a bruise and cut were camouflaged by expert make-up.

'How are you feeling?' she asked.

'Like I've had the crap beaten out of me.' He tried to sit up, but she put a hand on his arm and shook her head. She hit a button on the electronic bed controller; the bed whirred and the head raised, bending him in the middle. The movement made him queasy.

He swallowed back bile and blood-flavoured saliva, which turned his stomach even more. 'You? Are you alright?' He searched for evidence of injury. Her right hand was wrapped in a bandage.

'Luke, I'm so sorry.' Her face collapsed without warning. Tears pooled in her eyes, and she squeezed them closed. Her lower lip trembled. 'This is all Dad's doing—he tried to get you killed. It's all my fault . . .'

'Hey.' He pulled her closer so he could touch her face. 'Emma, you saved my life.'

She pressed her face against his hand. 'I thought you'd hate me. But I had to see if you were alright.'

Luke tried to smile, but it felt as though his face would crack. A pain in his temple distracted him. 'Have you spoken to Jonathan?'

She shook her head. 'I went to Shinita's. Then I went back—I wasn't sure what I'd find, but Gus's car was gone. Your downstairs neighbour let me into your flat. I got some clothes for you. Your wallet and phone are there too. Both phones.' She pointed to Luke's backpack, on the floor near the door.

'What did you do with the gun?'

Her eyes narrowed. 'What gun?'

A laugh hurt his ribs. 'Emma.'

'It's a Glock. Not my first choice.' Sulkily, she said, 'If I see that prick again, I'll shoot him in the face.'

Luke put a hand over his eyes. The scars on his back prickled. 'Emma.'

'You think I'm joking?' The edge to her voice worried him. 'He's the one hassling Dad. He slapped me in the mouth and broke your nose.' She got up abruptly to pace. 'What if he tells the cops it was me who stabbed him?'

'Not a hope.' Luke shook his head. 'But get rid of the gun. Put it down a stormwater drain or something.'

They both turned as the door opened a crack. A nurse bustled in, pushing a trolley. 'Great, you're awake. Need to check some obs. You were out like a light when they straightened your nose.'

Luke blinked at her. It explained the splint on his face.

The nurse wrapped a blood pressure cuff around his right arm. 'Your heart rate and blood pressure dropped. The anaesthetist wants you to stay overnight.'

'I can go home,' Luke said. 'My heart rate is always low.'

'Not this low. You had a reaction to the morphine.'

'You'd make a terrible junkie.' Emma managed a smile.

'Funny.' Luke tried to roll his eyes. It hurt.

'There's a police constable outside, wants to talk to you.' The nurse scribbled notes on the clipboard at the end of the bed.

Luke said, 'I'm not really . . .'

'Yeah, I knew you'd say that. I'll tell him.' Casting Luke a smile, she left.

Luke let the silence grow. Emma perched on the bed and turned his face left then right with her fingers. Her scrutiny made him squirm. 'I look like shit. Stop it.'

'A few more scars to add to your collection,' she said. 'I wonder what your nose will look like when the swelling goes down?'

He caught her hand. 'I just hope I can breathe through it.'

'What are you gonna tell the police?'

'Nothing.'

With a sigh, Emma deflated. 'I'm gonna go,' she said. 'I'm too exhausted to badger you for answers. I'll catch you tomorrow.' She planted a kiss on his forehead.

The door swung shut after her.

Luke eased himself out of the bed and rummaged in the backpack. The Samsung was dead. On his iPhone, there were several missed calls and a single text: *This is Brian Wilson. Please call me.*

He paused on the edge of the bed to stop his head from spinning.

Getting dressed was slow and painful. After stuffing his possessions into the backpack, he poked his head out the door. A uniformed police officer was chatting with the nurses by the main desk. He waited until the man's head was turned, slipped out of the room and took the lift to the ground floor to get a taxi home.

Police tape hung loosely from his door. The chair lay on its side in the middle of the living room, with remnants of duct tape attached to it. Luke ignored the mess and headed straight for the shower.

With a hand against the tiles to support himself, he closed his eyes as the hot water found every nick in his skin, needling into cuts and abrasions. After a few minutes, the stinging settled, and he opened his eyes to watch the pink-stained water circle the drain; then he turned off the hot tap and forced himself to endure the cold blasting his shoulder, his ribs, his face. If he'd had a bathtub, he would have filled it with ice. A cold shower would have to do.

When his shivering had lasted long enough, he dried off and lay gingerly on his bed. His mattress was lumpy and old, but infinitely better than a hospital bed. The throbbing in his face returned as he stared at the ceiling. The practicalities of getting home had distracted him, but now he was alone with his thoughts.

His phone beeped. Wilson again: *Call me. Please.*

Luke switched off the phone so he could sleep. He knew exactly what Wilson had to say.

CHAPTER THIRTY-FIVE

SEVEN YEARS AGO

'Kev, I mean it! Let him go!' Quin swayed on his knees. The rifle wobbled in his grip.

With an arm around Jack's throat, Kevin swung him into the line of fire. Quin let off a shot, which missed, but it had the intended effect: Kevin abandoned Jack and stalked towards Quin, with his hands outstretched to wrest the rifle from him.

Quin fired again. And again.

With a gasp, Kevin slapped the side of his neck as though swatting an insect. Jack, his vision blurred by the rain, saw Kevin draw his hand away and stare at it. Blood mingled with the rainwater.

Like a penitent at an altar, Kevin dropped to his knees.

'Quin?' Kevin's anger fizzled to surprise. He pitched forwards onto his face, splashing into a puddle of mud.

Panting, Jack stood motionless.

Kevin didn't move.

On shaking legs, Jack stumbled towards him. He put a hand on Kevin's shoulder and rolled the limp body over. Kevin's surprise was still visible; his eyes were wide open. Blood drenched his collar and pooled above his collarbone.

In shock, Jack turned to Quin, who had crumpled to the ground. Quin's breathing was laboured, as though every intake of air was a great effort. The gun had slipped from his hands.

'He was always so fucking mean to you.' Quin's words were barely audible. 'Wasn't your fault what Susie did.'

Jack slumped against the side of the car. His hands shook as he put them to his face. Gusts of bitter wind swept the rain through his clothes, through the coating of blood and mud. His face was numb with cold. Around him, the tall trees waved their limbs, creaking with the weight of water.

Quin's face glowed in the eerie red light from the car tail-lights and the sheen of rain.

'You alive?' Jack asked.

'I don't feel so good. Can't breathe. My chest hurts.'

With unwieldy fingers, Jack felt for Quin's pulse; it was fast and weak. He tore through the rip in Quin's jeans so he could see the wound, but the more he wiped, the more it oozed, mixing with the rain to pool on Quin's pale skin.

Jack willed his brain to work. If he could get Quin into the car, he could drive him to hospital.

Inertia and shock froze him.

As his adrenaline ebbed, pain intruded. He'd taken some hard knocks. His throat was bruised from Kevin's big hands. He needed to eat. Hong had always told him that: *Eat something, after a fight, after a fright. Get your blood sugar up.* Instead, all he could do was hang his head. His entire body ached, but his soul hurt more. He felt crushed, inside and out.

Jack crawled away from Quin to vomit into the bushes. The acid stayed in his throat.

He felt himself disintegrating: he was sure that if he could see his skin, it would shimmer and shake and he would dissolve into the air. Kevin was dead. And Robbo Parker. The finality of it, the irreversibility, hit him like a sucker punch in the guts.

'Jack?' Quin's voice had faded to a whisper, disembodied in the darkness. 'Don't tell Gus. Take the money and run. You're a smart kid. Figure something out.'

Jack wiped at his face with his hands, smearing blood and snot and vomit. And tears. He hadn't realised he was crying. He sucked in deep breaths, but it didn't help. His mind and body had disconnected.

He said, 'Why did she put your name on my birth certificate?'

The silence went so long he thought he'd never get an answer. The only sound was the rain, settling around them in mists and clouds. Their breath was visible in the light from the car.

'Kev was a prick to her. Didn't treat her right.' Quin's voice floated off into the darkness. 'She was way out of his league, everyone knew it. Fucking gorgeous. He was jealous that we were friends—she liked hanging out with the band. She was smart, you know, read lots of books. But a bit crazy. She'd get all messed up in her head. Kev couldn't deal—he was an arsehole about it. I was the one who could sort her out. We never meant to piss him off, but . . . it just happened.'

'You knew I wasn't yours.' Tears wet Jack's face. It was the most Quin had ever told him about Susie.

Quin shifted. 'Not for sure. Not until you grew up.'

'You lied to me. Both of you.' Jack's head slumped. 'I don't understand why.'

''Cos we're both stupid pricks, that's why.' With a harsh sound that could have been a laugh, Quin tried to sit up but flopped back. 'Kev didn't want to know about you—he was still pissed off with

Susie. When we found out you were in Sydney, he told me to leave you there. Said he didn't want anything to do with you.' Quin closed his eyes. 'I couldn't just leave you. And later, when we figured out you were his, I told him to fuck off and leave you alone. I didn't want you to think Susie was messing around. It wasn't like that. I should have told you—but it was too fucking hard. I thought you'd hate me. I just . . . couldn't.'

Jack sniffed. He was past hiding his tears. 'I don't understand.'

'You're just like her. Same smile. Same eyes. When you were little, you even talked like her.' Quin's breath caught. After another long silence, his words were nearly lost in the darkness and rain. 'I loved her, Jack. I loved her.'

It seemed to Jack that every tear he hadn't shed over the entirety of his life erupted at once. He sucked in painful gasps and sobbed into the dark, let the tears roll down his face unchecked.

He wiped his face, trying to control his distress and turn it to useful action. He shook Quin's shoulder, slapped his cheek. Quin stirred enough to bat him away. Jack hooked his arms under Quin's shoulders and dragged him onto the back seat of the car. At least they were out of the rain. If he could get the car started, he could get them out of there.

'My chest hurts.' Quin held both hands against his chest, as though he could squeeze the pain away. 'I can't breathe.' He grasped at Jack's arm, panting.

Jack put his frozen fingers to Quin's throat. The pulse was rapid and irregular. Facts swirled in Jack's mind: Quin's blood loss; the drugs and alcohol he'd ingested earlier. 'Hold on. I'll get you to hospital.'

'No! Don't go . . .' Quin's eyes were wide; the whites glowed like a pale ring. His grip on Jack's arm loosened and his arm dropped down. His face went slack. His head rolled to the side.

Jack thought about doing CPR. First aid, like he'd learned at school. He didn't. The messages from his brain refused to transfer to his limbs. In shock, he slumped on the back seat, haunted by Quin's words.

I loved her, Jack.

The rain continued to fall, and Jack continued to dissolve. His whole life was a lie, his identity based on a puff of smoke. He didn't know how to feel about either of his fathers, both of whom lay silent. He wanted to hate them, but he couldn't summon it, no matter how he tried. He was his mother's son, after all: had she loved them both?

Numbness took the place of feeling, just as it had when she'd died.

It could have been days that he sat unmoving, cowering in the back seat of Kevin's car, or a few seconds. Time ceased to have meaning. Reality swirled around him like the rain, fluid, indistinct. When he stirred from his fugue, he was frozen in place with a layer of mud caking his clothes and Quin's glassy eyes staring up at him.

As he emerged from the car, he felt like a puppet moved by an external force, with no control over his own actions. Dawn washed the scene with grey light, seeping through a thick fog that hung between the tree trunks, hovering over the undergrowth like frosting. After the activity of the night before—the storm, and the human violence—the silence and stillness felt unnatural. The torrential rain had washed away the loose surface of the dirt track, etching deep crevices and new, deeper potholes. The Commodore looked as though it had been joy-ridden through a war zone.

Quin was right: he should take the money and split, but it wasn't so simple. He couldn't run around with a bag of cash, and he knew enough about money laundering to know he couldn't handle it himself. Not yet. He needed to distance himself. To plan.

It would have to wait.

Without conscious intention, he retraced Kevin's footsteps from the night before. Through the fog, he trudged to the cabin and past the motionless water to make the short, sharp climb to the mine. He clicked on Kevin's torch and ducked his head to enter, his breath catching at the acrid stench of the bats. When he was a few metres in, they flew out with a rush of wings that would have terrified him if he wasn't numb from head to toe.

The skeleton was still there. Kevin had tucked the bag behind it in a niche in the wall. Most people would stop well before this point, and certainly once they saw the old prospector; it was a good ruse, but it was too close to the entrance for Jack's liking. He'd already decided the money needed to stay hidden, apart from the few bundles he stuffed into his pockets for expenses.

He continued inside as far as he dared, to the point where the air tasted stale and claustrophobia made his skin crawl, and found another niche, where the prospectors had carved into the wall in their search for the elusive mother lode. Brushing away the spiderwebs, he pushed the bag to the back of the space.

His progress was interrupted by dirt trickling onto his head, followed by a creaking sound.

He flashed the torch around to see rubble fall down the wall on his right.

In panic, he sprinted for the mouth of the tunnel, as dirt and rocks cascaded onto the path before him. After more than a century of resistance, the heavy rain had eroded the mine's stability.

The saplings that held the entrance snapped under the weight of the wet earth as he reached it. Dodging the rockfall, he dived out into the light. Rocks and rubble piled into the hole, like an hourglass filling.

Clambering to his feet, he stared at the blocked mouth. The burial of the money felt like an act of God. The message was loud and clear.

'*Anything else?*' He turned his face to the morning sky and shouted his frustration like a challenge—at his dead fathers, at the universe, at all the gods he couldn't convince himself to believe in. 'Anything else you want to fucking throw at me?'

CHAPTER THIRTY-SIX

MONDAY, 10 AM

'You,' Emma said, with the disapproval of a prim schoolmistress, 'are a terrible patient. I can't believe you just walked out.' Sitting cross-legged on the end of Luke's bed, she bit into a jelly snake and stretched it until it snapped. She held out the packet to offer him one.

'How did you know?' Luke leaned forwards to select a red snake. 'Know what?'

'That these are the only lollies I like.'

'They're a crowd-pleaser. You're not special.' He got another scowl.

Luke bit into the snake and instantly regretted it. Two of his teeth were loose. Eating sticky sweets was a bad idea if he planned to keep them. He pushed the morsel to the back of his mouth with his tongue. 'Emma, I'm fine. I needed my own bed.'

Emma had arrived in a grump after finding him missing from his hospital room. He'd been lying in bed, contemplating calling Wilson and all that would follow. Having Emma perched on his bed eating jelly snakes with her characteristic relish made his physical pains almost bearable. He wondered if she always sucked on them quite so hard.

Emma put the packet down. 'So. Dad is laundering money for Gus.' She sat with the statement, thinking. He was surprised how well she'd taken it. 'And you're helping both of them?'

'I was. Sort of.' He resisted the urge to say, *It's complicated.*

'Are you worried they'll come after you again?' Emma leaned in. 'Gus was furious with you. He knows where you live. And Dad hates being foiled—fucking hates it. What are you going to do?'

'I'll deal with it,' Luke said.

'Mr I-Can-Look-After-Myself.'

Luke blew out a breath. 'Gus will calm down in a few days. And Jonathan is running out of people to fuck with.'

His iPhone buzzed on the bedside table, and he reached for it. After a moment of hesitation, he touched the screen to answer.

'Are you home?' said Brian Wilson. 'We're coming up.'

It was too late to protest: the line went dead. Resigned, Luke put on clothes and opened the door, ignoring Emma's pleas for explanation.

'Bloody hell. You're a mess.' Wilson stepped into the room, followed closely by his partner. He peered at Luke's face, at the sling, then at Emma. 'Is this why you haven't returned my calls?'

Luke brushed off the question with a shake of his head. He introduced Emma, pointed the cops to the couch and took the chair. Emma perched beside him on the arm.

Wilson raised his eyebrows and met Luke's eyes. 'You happy for her to stay?'

'Oh, I'm staying.' Emma's officious tone made Luke smile, despite the knot that twisted his guts. He took her hand, interlaced his fingers with hers.

Wilson spent another moment examining Luke's face. 'Let me guess. Amin Khoury? Zoungas is still in prison, so not him. I figure you're still working for Alberici, so unless you pissed him off . . .'

Tara Packard looked up from her notebook. 'Alberici was in the emergency at the Epworth yesterday. Minor stab wound to the chest.'

Luke said, 'Isn't that confidential?'

She hiked a shoulder. 'Thought you might already know. Maybe it was the same person who beat you up.'

'Who said I was beaten up?'

Wilson silenced Packard with a raised hand and took a deep breath. 'Listen, Jack—Luke. Remember I told you about the fire at McNally's block? Well, we found his car there. Crashed into a gully. Burned to a crisp.'

Luke said, 'What do you mean?'

'The car was incinerated. And—ah—there's no nice way to say this. There were human remains inside.' Wilson paused to swallow. 'We think your father was in the car when it crashed. His wallet was found near the scene. We believe McNally was in the car too.'

The air puffed out of Luke's chest.

After all this time, it was a relief, a release of a long-held tension. He felt rain pelting down on him, mud splashing against his skin, Kevin's hands on his throat. He saw Quin's dead eyes, the red glow of the car's tail-lights. Kevin, lying in the mud. With his hands pressed to his face, he closed his eyes and relived the feeling of dissolving into tiny pieces, of dissociating from his physical body.

Every step had been difficult: hauling Kevin's body into the car, getting the car to start, freeing the bogged wheels. Launching it over the edge of the gully without killing himself in the process.

Scrubbing the blood off his hands in the icy water of the dam; the long, painful walk to the highway to hitch a ride to Melbourne. The rush of relief that he hadn't missed a call from Gus. Drizzie painting over the marks Kevin had left on his throat. Back to work in the cafe the next day, as though nothing had happened—and lying to the police, over and over—

'Are you alright?' Packard's voice came from far away.

Emma squeezed his hand. He grounded himself in the present: Emma's hand in his. His breath. The seat underneath him.

The past intruded: *We're both stupid pricks*. They'd made so many mistakes, both of them. Messed up his life from the minute they entered it. But memories flashed past: Quin teaching him to play the guitar when he was eight years old; Kevin showing him how to cut in around a doorway.

Wilson rubbed his chin. 'It's all with the coroner. It'll take a few days to get formal identification. I wanted you to know before it hits the news.'

Luke held himself together, kept himself still on the chair instead of getting up to pace as he wanted to. 'I don't understand. How did the car crash?'

'The investigation is ongoing.' Wilson glanced at Packard. 'You knew Alberici was looking for McNally. You tried to warn him.'

Luke rubbed a hand over his face and kept his mouth shut. He'd never said it was Gus looking for Kevin: that was Wilson's assumption.

'There are a lot of anomalies.' Wilson sighed heavily. The bags under his eyes betrayed a lack of sleep. Luke figured he'd been working nonstop since the fire.

'The other day you said the fire was deliberately lit.'

Wilson and Packard exchanged another loaded look. 'Yeah.'

'You think someone killed them and set fire to the car? Why?' The answer was obvious. Burning the car was a simple way to destroy evidence. Fingerprints, DNA, injuries. Cause of death. An antique rifle. Seven years of decomposition.

A wave of nausea made him close his eyes and wince. Screwing up his face hurt. The room fell silent.

Wilson was the first to speak. 'Like I said: there are anomalies. If you know something, now is a good time to tell us. I don't know what it's got to do with your injuries, but I'm guessing they're related, right?'

Luke swallowed back a mouthful of bile. 'Not even close.'

'At some point, we'll need to talk through your movements over the last few days.' Wilson kept his tone neutral. 'Just to get everything straight. For the record.'

'Sure.' Luke leaned into Emma, who put her arm around his shoulders. 'What about arranging a funeral and all that? What do I need to do?'

'I'll give the coroner's office your details.' Wilson paused; he opened his mouth a few times, as though trying to find the right words. 'Given the suspicious circumstances, I'm concerned you might be in danger.'

'I'm fine.'

'Jack, if he can get at—'

Luke held up a hand, irritated. 'It's Luke, and I'm fine.'

'I'm sorry for your loss,' Packard said, with genuine feeling.

Luke sensed Wilson and Packard communicating without words. He appreciated their humanity. Not all coppers were arseholes. Most of them were just doing their job, protecting society from people like him.

Emma walked them to the door, and he heard subdued words discussing follow-up calls and contact details.

She returned to kneel in front of him, prised his hand from his face. 'You knew.' Her tone was cautious. 'You knew he was dead.'

Luke met her eyes. He felt as numb as he had seven years ago, but at the same time an enormous weight had lifted. If he could hold it together just a little longer, it would all be over.

'You're a good actor. They bought it. But why did you lie?'

'Because I shouldn't have known.'

'You know why they bought it?' She wiped away a tear he hadn't noticed. 'Because you're honestly upset. This was out of your control. It was Gus, right?'

He touched his forehead to hers. 'You should be a cop.'

'I thought about it, but the uniforms suck.'

Her humour warmed him, as though she'd reached inside and hugged his heart. 'I need to get something. I won't be a minute.'

He moved gingerly down the stairs and knocked on Irina's door. He pulled out a shoebox from the safe in her cupboard, avoiding her questions to return upstairs to his couch. Emma sat beside him.

Spreading the contents of the shoebox on the coffee table, he selected a photo. 'This is Quin. That's my mother. It's the only photo I have of them together.'

On the back of the photo, in faded ink, his mother's handwriting: *Sorrento 1996*—the year before he was born. Emma held it up to peer at it.

Susie Harris leaned against the driver's door of a yellow Mazda hatchback. Keys dangled from one hand, and her laughing face was half-turned, as though something out of shot had caught her attention. Tall and willowy, she wore a floral dress with black Doc Martens, and her long blonde hair was held back with a colourful scarf. Her face glowed, radiant in the sunshine, and her smile could have lit up a Hollywood screen.

Quin also leaned on the car, by the front fender, with his hands shoved into the pockets of his black jeans. He wore a faded Nirvana T-shirt, scuffed sneakers and a cheeky grin. His dark hair was thick and shaggy. He looked like he belonged on the cover of a hard rock album.

'That's your dad.' Emma tilted her head to the side. Luke kept his mouth shut. 'Your mum was gorgeous.' She bumped Luke's shoulder. 'You look a lot more like her than your dad.'

'So I'm told.'

He found another photo, with the same inscription on the back: Kevin and Quin, drinking beer at a table in a dimly lit pub. Quin was laughing, while Kevin stared straight at the camera with a reluctant smile. For Susie, Luke realised, behind the camera.

It seemed ridiculous that anyone believed Quin was his father. He wondered if Emma would notice.

'Your dad is kinda cute,' said Emma. 'He looks like a joker. Like, he's always got this big grin. Not a guy to take life too seriously.'

'Yep. That's Quin.' Kevin's smile seized Luke's stomach. He'd never liked having his photo taken, and Luke was the same. Seeing them—Kevin, Quin, Susie—at this time in their lives, before Jack came along and complicated everything, brought up a whole new set of emotions. They seemed happy, at least on the surface.

'What else have you got here?' Emma smiled as she rummaged through the items on the table. Two passports were bundled together with an elastic band. 'Oh, that is adorable.' She chuckled over the baby photo on the passport. 'So—you were Jack Harris?'

Luke nodded. 'Quin changed my surname when I went to live with him. I changed it back when I was eighteen, and my first name too. I couldn't stand being called *Jackie*—it drove me nuts.' He wasn't Quin's son. He wasn't really Kevin's either. Changing back to Harris had been an obvious move.

Emma put the passports down. She threaded her arm into his. 'Tell me about your dad. Talk about him. It'll help.'

He closed his eyes. Parts of the story he could never admit, but her presence was welcome. They curled up on the couch, entwined.

'I first met him when I was seven,' he started.

CHAPTER THIRTY-SEVEN

TUESDAY, 8 AM

The mashed morsels of hard-boiled egg floated to the surface of the spinach soup. Luke added a dollop of sour cream and stirred, fascinated by the textures in his bowl as the soup emulsified. Irina knew what she was doing: a meal designed to keep peasants alive through a Russian winter was just what he needed. He picked out the flavours. Carrots, onion, potato. Dill. The earthy flavour of the spinach. A rich chicken broth. He could taste the care Irina had put into it.

It was rare for her to visit his flat. His dysfunctional stove had sent her into a flurry of Russian complaints as she heated the soup. She mashed the egg with a fork and an excess of vigour, then waggled a forefinger and ordered him to sit. 'No more fighting. Eat. Rest.' She slammed the door on her way out. Her grumbling was audible all the way down the stairs.

Emma had kept him company until late. They'd snuggled on the couch, nursing his injuries and talking about Kevin and Quin until he ran out of words. She peered at the map on his phone as he showed her where Stillwater was, describing the long driveway, his childhood visits there and how he knew every board in the cabin. *Middle of bloody nowhere,* was Emma's assessment. It was after midnight when she left for Shinita's and he fell into bed, depleted.

In the morning, uncertainty rose as he wondered where he stood. His relationship with Emma felt precarious—unsealed, as though it had exposed edges where the fabric might fray. The flat was empty without her, but as he savoured his soup and pretended he wasn't procrastinating, he was glad for the privacy. What he needed to do was best unwitnessed. His conscience pinged: it was never as simple as right and wrong. Every choice, every decision, came with a price.

Attack is the secret of defence. Hong's mantra. Jack, being a smart-arse, had always quoted in return: *Defence is the planning of an attack.* (Hong's answer, delivered with a thump: *Defend this, you skippy little mutt.*)

He stood on the balcony with a mug of coffee. A Toyota sedan was parked across the street. Wilson's watchers had a good view of his Subaru and the front of the stairwell.

It was time to start calling the shots. He counted down from five, then hit the call icon on the Samsung.

Lowering the pitch of his voice, he shaded it with his mother's accent and introduced himself to Natalie as Vijay Patel from AUSTRAC. He stated that suspicious transactions had been flagged on Wylie Consulting accounts; he asked for Mr Wylie to call him back as soon as possible. He left the phone number for the Melbourne AUSTRAC office, which would be a dead end if Jonathan tried to call back.

Next, he dialled a number he'd retrieved from his safe. He copied Ed's accent, with a nasal twang and vowels so Australian they made him cringe.

'Mr Khoury?'

'Who is this?' Amin Khoury spoke the clipped English he'd learned at Oxford.

Luke paused. 'There's something you should know. Gus Alberici is about to go under. The cops are on to him.'

'Tell me who you are or I'm hanging up.'

With a laugh, Luke said, 'If I was you, I'd listen. He's in trouble. I know he owes you.'

'What do you want?'

'I'll let you know. I'll be in touch, eh?'

After he hung up, he drummed his fingers on the balcony railing, thinking. The sky was deep blue, with tufts of cottonwool cloud drifting lazily across it. He released his breath with purpose, then made his third and final call.

The voice that answered was wary. 'Brian Wilson.'

Luke said, 'Are you sitting down?'

'Give me a sec. Need to find a private spot.'

Luke concentrated on breathing rather than his urge to hang up. 'If he finds out I've talked, I'll have a bullet in my head within hours.'

Wilson said, 'I'm aware.'

Luke's head floated with a sudden fear he'd lost his mind. Everyone he knew who'd run to the cops about Gus was dead. He was relieved Wilson didn't try to spin bullshit about protecting him or offering immunity. The best Luke could hope for was to remain anonymous long enough that Gus couldn't hurt him.

This could be the single most important call he ever made; he wished there was a way he could add fanfare to it. A drumroll, perhaps. It was nearly ten years since he'd first considered betraying Gus.

Speechless, he searched for the right words. 'Jonathan Wylie is cleaning for Gus. He's about to start panicking because he thinks his operation is blown. My guess is he's already trying to cover his tracks.' He told Wilson what he knew of Jonathan's involvement, then fell silent.

'Your girlfriend's father?' Wilson's laugh was humourless. 'Does she know you're snitching on him?'

Luke winced, which hurt his face. He didn't want to think about how betraying Jonathan would affect his relationship with Emma. There was no easy way to express what he wanted to say: it had nothing to do with her. It was about Jonathan trying to wipe him off the board. And, more importantly, it was about Gus. 'She doesn't know anything. Thinks her father's a saint.'

'I guess she thinks you are, too?'

Time to change the topic. 'Gus owes Amin Khoury—rumour is that Khoury needs to recover his debt. Gus will be scrambling. Today.'

'Okay.' Wilson's pen scratched on a notepad.

'And you're right about Kevin McNally: Gus was looking for him.'

A sharp exhale. 'Do you know why?'

'No.' Luke paused. 'Brian, you can't give this to financial crimes. That's where Gus's insider is.'

The phone line was silent so long that Luke thought Wilson had hung up. 'Don't worry. I know what I'm doing.'

'Yeah.' The sheer lunacy of the conversation turned Luke's stomach.

'I need names. Dates. Evidence.'

'Later. When I know it's not going to blow back.'

'You need to disappear while I check it out.'

Luke's chuckle reassured no one. 'There are cops outside my front door. I think I'm okay.'

As he ended the call, he conceded that Wilson was right: if he had any sense, he'd go into hiding. It sent a chill down his spine. Wilson would go straight to those he thought he could trust, and as soon as he did, Gus would know.

Luke went inside and dropped to the floor in front of his couch, sitting cross-legged with his hands resting on his thighs. The gravity of what he'd done seeped into him. All his careful planning, his restraint, his focus, had brought him to this moment.

But as Hong would have said: *No plan survives contact with the enemy.*

CHAPTER THIRTY-EIGHT

ONE YEAR AGO

Luke reached the top of the water tower and sat on the wooden platform beside the tank with his legs dangling, squinting into the hot sun. He held up his phone, searching for a signal. Around him, the undulating landscape stretched out in a patchwork of green, stitched together by fences, roads and windbreaks. The brightness of pasture deepened into cane fields to the south, with patches of near-black bush, mountains and national park beyond. The sea was a distant haze in the east, indistinguishable from the clear sky, as though the horizon were a figment of his imagination.

He paused, in awe of the view, as a warm well of gratitude rose in his chest.

A cluster of buildings nestled at the base of the hill he'd just climbed. Encased in acres of bush, the Shamata Retreat comprised a long cabin of dormitories, a kitchen, an outdoor pavilion and a series of gardens. A diverse collection of people called it home. Their reasons for being there varied, but they had one thing in common: they all sought peace.

The path that had brought him here stretched out before him. Like Yvonne fingering her mala beads, he touched each stage with his mind. Arriving in Sydney after twelve hours on a bus. His first job as Luke Harris, in a cafe near Kings Cross. A pilgrimage to Bondi Beach. Bus trip north to see Byron Bay. Martine, the German backpacker, with her casual attitude to sex, which kept him in Byron longer than he intended. Spending the last of the money he'd filched from Kevin's heist on a beat-up Land Cruiser in Brisbane so he could continue north. Long roads, hitchhikers, backpackers. Seasons wet and dry. Working security in pubs, tearful drunk girls and aggressive drunk guys. Cafes, restaurants. Months crewing on a yacht, taking over the kitchen when the chef quit. The panic of a worldwide pandemic. He was in Port Douglas when a friend said, *Hey, they're hiring at this home for the disabled, they'll pay you to do the training.*

The fishing boat out of Cairns, after he tired of working the roster. Yvonne, when he bought a bowl of rice and tofu from the van in town, over a year ago: *I run a meditation class on Tuesdays. Everyone's welcome.*

The food van was his now; he drove it to town every Wednesday and Friday. He made chickpea burgers and mushroom tacos and broccoli frittata. Vegetarian didn't have to mean boring.

Angling his phone just right, he got two bars of reception. Every week or so, he wandered up to the water tower to turn it on, just in case. Only a few people had the number.

Two texts, both from Nel.

Hey Jack I've got a job in Daylesford wanted to let you know we're moving out of your uncles place.

Then: *Jack can you let me know you got my text.*

He stared out at the view, thinking. Remembering. It seemed a long time ago that he'd tossed the keys to Nel and said, *The house is empty—you and Driz can stay there as long as you want; he's moved overseas or something.* They'd jumped at the chance of free accommodation. It was a weight off his mind to know the house was secure.

In those awful weeks after Kevin and Quin died, as he lied to the police and Gus and everyone else in his life, he made his plan to escape. By the time he got on the bus to Sydney, he was so trashed that he slept most of the way.

He flicked a text to Nel: *Gotcha, no worries*, and added a random emoji because it would make Drizzie laugh.

The phone pinged instantly. *When u back?*

Soon.

It was a ten-minute walk down the hill. He took care, on the lookout for snakes, but his mind was distracted by the shift he'd felt inside. Threading through the raised vegetable gardens, he fell in beside Yvonne. It was late spring and the garden was full of life and colour.

'Was it important?' Yvonne hoisted a basket onto her hip.

'Yes.'

One of his first lessons: skilful speech. Speaking only what was true and necessary. On his first day, Yvonne had suggested he try a week without speaking. His internal dialogue had driven him mad; days later, during a morning meditation, he realised it had calmed. There was no need for his mind to comment on everything, adding a layer of judgement and opinion. The world was complex enough.

He followed her inside to deposit the baskets of produce in the kitchen, and they went to the small meditation room at the rear of the hall.

The wooden-walled room was a few metres square and serenely bare: a pile of cushions in one corner and in another a squat table, which bore a single incense holder. A memory of the scent filled the air. Yvonne sat cross-legged by the table, with her back against the wall, and gestured for Luke to sit too.

He did as instructed and bowed his head, waiting for her to speak.

She was a compact woman, lean and muscular like a gymnast. Luke figured she was about sixty years old. She was Canadian and had once been a heavy-vehicle driver for the army. Silver hair sprouted from her scalp, which she still shaved regularly, although she was no longer a nun. The technicalities went over Luke's head: she was in charge of the retreat and was the spiritual leader, but as far as he could tell she was not affiliated with any larger institution. The retreat occasionally hosted visiting monks and nuns, who had stricter rules than Yvonne, but her simple attire—loose cotton trousers and a T-shirt—and her lack of religious trappings made her seem, to Luke at least, more devout.

Sometimes, he wondered if he'd joined a cult. He looked as though he belonged, although he'd shaved his head out of practicality, not religious observance.

'You're thinking about leaving.'

He hadn't realised he was so transparent. 'Yes.'

'How long have you been with us?'

'Fourteen months and six days.'

Yvonne's face creased with a smile. Another of her lessons: *Be precise.* 'Have you learned what you needed to?'

He considered. *Be honest.* 'I still have a long way to go.' A bubble of irritation rose in his chest, which he noted, made space for, and labelled. It was jealousy—of Yvonne. Her expert, simple acceptance. Her capacity for stillness, to which he would always aspire.

'Are you ready to leave?'

Luke hesitated. He often lay awake, wondering if he should stay forever. The conditions were not luxurious—a mattress on the floor and cold showers—but life was simple. There was little to worry about.

'What will you do?'

'I deferred a place at university. I'll have to reapply—it's been a few years.' Luke took a breath. 'I feel . . . Staying here is the easy choice. I, ah, I left a mess behind. There are things I need to fix. People I'll have to face.' He looked at his bare feet. For years, he'd run away from what he'd done. The sense of unfinished business nagged at him.

'The right course is not always easy, is it?'

He shook his head.

'Sometimes, we have to choose a harder path,' she said. 'Every choice you make leads to other choices and, in combination, these define your path and your character. Ask yourself: which path brings you closer to your goals?' With her hands in front of her, she touched each fingertip to its partner, a relaxed steepling. 'Hakini mudra. To clear your thoughts for sound decision-making. Meditate with me.'

Copying her position, he straightened his spine and focused. Her presence made meditation an effortless pleasure, as though her stillness were infectious.

When he opened his eyes a few minutes later, Yvonne was waiting for him. She leaned forwards, hinging at the hip. 'What are you making us for dinner tonight?'

'Chana dal. Sweet potato and spinach curry. Panko-fried eggplant. Coconut sticky rice with mango.'

Her smile was tinged with sadness. 'I have selfish thoughts about you staying.'

The next morning, he woke at dawn as always and went out for his daily run.

The morning was golden, a haze of soupy humidity, but it was early enough that the air was cool. He jogged along the driveway of the retreat to the road, then turned into the forest to the south, his eyes on the rainforest floor. There weren't many things he was afraid of, but snakes were one. He knew every bump of the path. Every tree root, every dip, every hill and tree.

By the time he returned, Yvonne's yoga practice had already started. He splashed water on his face and crept into the pavilion to take a mat at the rear.

He dropped to his knees on the mat for virasana, hero pose; such a deceptively simple asana. He stretched up his spine, tilted his pelvis, adjusted his neck and shoulders. Felt the warm stretch in his quads, allowed his hips to loosen as he sank into them. Hong had scoffed at yoga—*catnip for white girls*, he called it—but Luke found that, as with many things, yoga was easy to do badly and difficult to do well. Most of what he'd learned was not about flexibility or strength, but about balance and breathing. He'd never dreamed there were so many ways to breathe.

The class settled into savasana, corpse pose, the final relaxation asana. Yvonne's gong sounded, and he sat up, cross-legged, for the first meditation of the day.

His concentration wandered from his breath to memories: the first time Dr Bowman had taught him about meditation, and the light-bulb moment when he understood that he could observe his thoughts without responding to them. Without believing them, even. Distracted again, his mind started to plan . . . If he left the retreat, he couldn't return to hospitality or security work. He needed to delay running into Gus until he had a clear strategy. He couldn't stay at Gail's house. He'd need a day job.

After the meditation, he went for a shower. The tiny mirror told him his hair was growing back, fuzzy gold growth over his tanned head. He still looked like a stranger. Shaving off his long hair had been a final release of Jack Quinlan.

When he arrived in the kitchen to start prep for the day, Yvonne was at the table, nursing a mug of tea. She indicated the seat beside her. 'Have you decided?'

Still, he hesitated.

'I have.' Her smile was kind, but her words were firm. 'Luke, I don't know what you're hiding from, but get out of here. Go and live your life.'

CHAPTER THIRTY-NINE

TUESDAY, 1.30 PM

An interrogation was not an ideal way to start an overcast Tuesday. Despite Emma's denials, Shinita was convinced that Luke was responsible for her injuries. Emma's offhand comment—*If Luke hit me, I'd have more than a split lip to worry about*—led to a rant about her poor taste in men.

After a few days of peace, a flurry of texts from Dave had taken her by surprise: *I need to talk to you* and *Just answer me, you're being ridiculous!* By the time she'd blocked this new number, her fingers shook and her eyes were hot. And she was late for work.

On arrival, she was drawn into a terse conversation with her manager, who had noticed her recent absences and distractions. *This is your first official warning, Emma.*

And then, the call she'd been hoping for, from her agent, made her head spin. Los Angeles. A supporting role in a Hollywood production. Action comedy, her own stunts, *They love your Aussie accent* and *How soon can you move?*

A rollercoaster ride had taken the place of a normal day. A sense of lawless freefall, that her life barrelled uncontrollably up and down, with sudden turns that wrenched at her guts, made it impossible to focus. The rollercoaster peaked, as high as it ever had. Breathless with the view from the top, she bottled up her effervescence—put a cork in the champagne—while she met with Phil's psychiatrist in her lunchbreak.

Phil had moved to the private hospital, an oasis of calm after the noisy public ward, with a plan for two weeks of observation while his medications were stabilised. He was chirpy during the meeting—mostly, Emma thought, because Jonathan was not there.

Dr Balachandran, who'd known Phil for years, wasted no time. She filled Emma in on Phil's progress, asked about Jonathan's whereabouts, then got straight to the point. 'It's time to think about Phil moving out of the family home. He doesn't get along with your father, does he?'

'Where would he live?' The suggestion caught Emma by surprise. 'You're not talking about an institution?'

'No, supported accommodation. Like a share house, with a carer to supervise.' The doctor smiled. 'Phil is an adult. His disability doesn't mean he can't grow up and make his own friends. I worry that he can't do that living at home. He's told me about the tension in the house.'

Emma mumbled something about discussing it with Jonathan, who had texted that he was caught up with work. After a big hug from Phil, she sat in her car and fought a series of emotions. Abandoning Phil to go to LA played on her conscience. Leaving him alone with Jonathan worried her, but the idea of him living with strangers seemed worse. It was enough to send her rollercoaster plummeting downhill. She needed to talk to Gabriela about it. And Luke.

As she drove back to work, gnawing on her lip, her phone pinged. Jonathan's latest message displayed on the screen on her dash: *CALL ME NOW.*

She hit redial and steeled herself for an argument as the call connected over the speaker. 'Jesus, Dad! I've just left the hospital. Dr Balachandran said—'

'Tell me later. Now, I need you to go home and—'

'I have to go back to work!' She hadn't heard his voice since their argument three days ago, when she'd stormed out; so much had changed since then. His involvement with Gus—his attempt to get Luke killed—seemed impossible, as though it had all happened in a dream. The reality had yet to sink in. She teetered on the edge of bringing it up, then retreated. No good had come from their last confrontation.

'Listen to me.' Jonathan's voice was hushed. 'Go home. I need you to empty out the safe. Hide the money and the gun—in your car or something, out of sight.'

'What?' Emma edged into an illegal park a block from Jonathan's office. 'Why don't you tell me what's going on, Dad?'

'Just listen.' Erratic breathing buffeted the phone. 'Leave the documents in the safe. The deed for the house is there—it's in your name.' The phone was muffled briefly, and then Jonathan's voice returned. 'And whatever you do, stay away from Luke. You can't trust him. You don't know—'

'I'm not doing anything until you tell me why.'

'I'm expecting the police to search the house. I'm sorting things out here, but I won't be home until late.' The urgency in his voice made her shiver.

'Dad, what have you done?' Aside from laundering money and trying to get Luke killed so he could frame Gus . . .

A dry, humourless laugh. 'Nothing you'd understand. But unless you want me in jail, do what I say.'

The call ended, and Emma peered through the windscreen, thinking about her rollercoaster ride. Another dip. The entrance to Jonathan's building was within her line of sight. She'd been planning to park underneath and was already late for work. A burst of honking reminded her that she had stopped illegally near a corner. As she indicated to pull out, a speeding black Audi nearly clipped her fender.

She swore at the driver, a moment before the car screeched to a halt in the loading zone outside Jonathan's building. Gus Alberici shot from the car, slammed the door and marched into the foyer.

Her guts seized.

She flicked a text to her manager to say she was held up, which would almost certainly get her fired, and drove home with her hands tight on the steering wheel.

CHAPTER FORTY

TUESDAY, 3.25 PM

Cross-legged in front of his couch, Luke focused on his exhales. Remembering Yvonne's voice, he paused in the stillness at the end of the breath, where the space between his heartbeats could lengthen; a moment of peace before the cycle started again. It took several minutes to ease into the exercise, by which time the ache in his shoulder distracted him, as did the whistling through his blocked nose.

Memories intruded: the madness in Gus's eyes. His white-knuckled grip on the gun. The vein in his temple.

Each memory came with a bodily sensation and an emotional response. The pounding of blood in his ears, drowning out all other noise; the sick anxiety in his guts and the acid in his throat; the black spots in his vision and the rigidity of his muscles as he froze with fear—was it Gus, or Robbo Parker, or Kevin lurking in the memory?

He gave up.

Instead, he worked through the shoulder-stability exercises he'd sourced on YouTube. A few minutes later, the buzzing of his phone disturbed him.

Gus.

He debated the pros and cons of answering, considered his strategy. He swiped it open.

'Jackie, I need you. Ed's out—his missus just had the baby.'

'You've got a fucking nerve!' Sitting up, Luke let his rage boil over. 'Quin and Kevin are dead! The cops found their bodies at the block and THEY KNOW IT WAS YOU!'

Gus's anger flared. 'What the hell—'

'The cops know you were looking for Kevin! You were after them! And I was *helping you!*'

'Calm down! Jesus, take a breath. I didn't kill them.'

'I don't believe you!'

Gus scoffed. 'You still upset about our little misunderstanding, Jackie?'

Holding the phone at arm's length, Luke glared at it as though it were Gus himself. It took a few moments to find words. 'You broke my fucking nose!'

'You lied to me! You know that pisses me off!'

'If you didn't kill them, who did?'

'Quin never did shit for you, anyway! Bang-up job he did as a father—'

'At least he never beat the crap out of me!' Luke's throat tightened as a truth he'd never admitted clunked into place: that at times, Gus had filled the gap where a father should have been. Acknowledging he'd ever seen Gus as a role model was too much. He forced it down like a lump of dry bread.

The words echoed, stretching into awkward silence.

Luke broke it harshly. 'What do you want?'

Gus's tone sobered. 'Shit's hit the fan. Someone's been talking to the cops. I'm waiting on a call from my man inside.' He grunted. 'Khoury's on the warpath. Wants his money yesterday. I'm going to Kevin's block to find that cash—we need to tear that cabin apart. It'll be there somewhere.'

'I'm not in any state to—'

'I'll pick you up in fifteen.'

'There are cops outside my flat.'

Gus's heavy sigh showed what he thought of that. 'Get up to the corner then.'

'No! I'm not—'

'Stop fucking whingeing, or I'll come to your door and make you! I'm not in the mood for this shit!' Gus hung up.

Again, Luke sat with the pros and cons, arguing with himself. He wasted a few minutes deluding himself that he could refuse. If he wasn't on the corner, Gus would storm up the stairs with a gun; the cops would be ten seconds behind. If Gus was serious, they'd be too late.

He dragged himself to his bedroom to change and stuffed equipment into his backpack. Pacing the living room, he called Emma to tell her he was leaving his phone at home.

'Don't go.' Her gulp was audible. 'He's just as likely to—'

'I'll be okay. He won't be able to search thirty acres before dark.' Luke bristled with the need to protect his territory.

'Luke, wait. Listen.' Emma's voice was hushed. 'Dad called me. There's a gun and a stack of money in the safe—he said to hide it in my car. I'm sitting in his study staring at it.'

Fisting his hands, Luke said, 'Why is he pulling you into his bullshit?'

'The police came to his office. He's worried they'll search the house.' Emma could barely speak. 'I know he's an arsehole, I know what he did to you, but—'

'Don't hide it in your car. They'll find it. Don't touch it without gloves.' Luke pulled his thoughts together, moved puzzle pieces around in his head. 'Okay. Here's what I want you to do.' He gave concise instructions.

'Are you sure?'

'Yes.' A warm flush—that she trusted him enough to ask his advice—distracted him until he remembered it was about hiding evidence. Not a healthy basis for a relationship.

'What do I tell Dad?'

'Nothing.' Luke couldn't hide his contempt. 'Just do what I said. Then go to Shinita's and stay there.'

It was mid-afternoon, and the stairwell was in shadow. On the first landing, he climbed over the railing at the rear and dropped to the ground, out of sight of the street. The backyard of the flats, an uninspiring patch of weedy grass, was bordered by paling fences. He climbed into the yard behind, ignoring the pain in his shoulder, and rounded the building to the street parallel to his.

After all these years, sneaking through backyards like a teenager. He tried to find humour in it, but as he trudged up to the corner all he could manage was resentment.

Gus stared at him as he eased into the passenger seat of the Audi. 'Look like you've been hit by a truck.'

'Whose fault is that?' Luke's face was stiff. The stitches on his nose had started to itch. 'You're lucky I'm even talking to you.'

'And you're lucky to be walking. Don't push it.' With an irritated grunt, Gus pulled out into traffic.

Luke watched him sideways, wary of his mood. Gus's scuffed knuckles were white on the steering wheel. His sleeves were rolled up, his collar loose, his jacket and tie on the back seat of the car. As he drove, his jaw worked from side to side as though he was trying to chew something unpleasant. Luke waited. If he gave it time, Gus would confide.

'I reckon it was Wylie who ratted on me.' He turned to scowl at Luke. 'He's always thought he was smarter than me. Weedy little prick.'

'Have you asked him?'

'Don't be a smart-arse, Jackie.'

Luke hid his sigh. He adjusted his seatbelt. Gus always drove too fast, with a flagrant lack of respect for road rules.

'I'll smack it out of him. And the money he owes me. He doesn't know what's coming. He set you up—told me a bunch of lies. I don't like that he came between you and me. Tell me you don't want revenge?' As he changed lanes without indicating, Gus flipped a middle finger at a honking driver. 'You still chasing his daughter?'

'I wouldn't call it chasing.'

'What would you call it?'

'I don't know.'

'Figure it out, because you'll be having a difficult conversation with her soon.' A snort, full of contempt. 'When she asks what happened to her daddy, and you have to decide where your loyalties lie.'

Luke peered out the window. Suburbs passed them by as they weaved through the afternoon traffic. Heading north, out of the city, again. The mention of loyalties ground against his conscience: relief that his plan had worked and Gus thought it was Jonathan who'd dobbed him in was tempered with sadness for Emma—who, despite all Jonathan had done, would beg for her father's life if it came to it.

'If Jonathan ratted you out, he's shot himself in the foot, right?' Luke turned in his seat. 'He'll be investigated. He was cleaning for you. The cops will know.'

'Probably thinks he'll cut some kind of deal.' Gus wiped an angry hand over his face. He checked his phone, taking his attention from the road for a few seconds, then jerked the steering back as he veered out of his lane. 'Nothing. My guy is taking too long. Someone's covering their tracks.'

Luke gripped the doorhandle. 'When did you find out?'

'An hour ago. I get a call if anyone flags my name. It's that detective. Wilson.' Tossing the phone onto the console, Gus lit a cigarette and glowered. 'Remember him? He wanted to charge you with attempted murder for what you did to Zoungas.'

'I remember.'

Silence settled in the car. With his face turned away to avoid the worst of the second-hand smoke, Luke watched the scenery fly past. He tried again to focus. The sounds of the tyres on the road, the wind whistling around the car mirror, the colour of the sky. The smell of smoke. The heat of Gus's presence.

There are things you can control and things you can't, Dr Bowman had said. *Don't waste your time on the latter.*

As the tyres hit the first gravel road, Gus said, 'You asleep, Jackie? Get that map out. I don't want to miss the turn.'

The map was underneath Gus's gun. Luke paused, distracted by the weapon. In his mind, he played out a hundred different scenarios, which all started with him pointing the gun at Gus. But it didn't matter what happened next. Either the car would crash and they'd both die, or he'd end up with twenty-to-life for murder. Gus wouldn't go down without a fight.

The last time he'd sparred with Gus was the night after Jack threw Ric Zoungas over the railing of his first-floor balcony. Jack had spent hours in a windowless room staring at a grey wall, repeating the words, *No comment*, with emotionless detachment, while Brian Wilson pretended to be his friend but dropped words designed to terrify him: *attempted murder* and *custodial sentence* and *remand in custody*. Jack was seventeen, which meant they had to wait for a guardian from Children's Services before Wilson could formally question him, but it didn't stop him trying: *off the record, Jack* and *I know why you did it, but I need it in your words* and *It would really help me out, you know*.

Later, after he was released without charge, Gus had picked him up on the corner. Jack had never been more grateful to have the protection of an elder. He'd settled into the passenger seat with a groan of relief.

The car ride was silent until they reached the gym. Gus ushered him inside, rolled up his sleeves, told him to glove up and pushed him into the ring.

Stupidest thing you've ever done. Gus aimed a punch at Jack's face, but in the ring, Jack was at home; he ducked around it and parried. *Gonna tell me what the hell got into you?*

They sparred for a few minutes until Jack warmed up, with Gus goading him to *Punch it out* and *Come on, Jackie, get it off your chest*. Neither held back; it was not their style. Then, between trying to land punches, Jack explained with panting breaths what he'd seen. Why he'd done it. How he'd do it again in a heartbeat. He laid into Gus's mid-section as the anger he'd felt earlier in the day flashed back.

Enough. Gus caught him in a clinch, arresting his momentum. *I reckon Zoungas got off lightly. If I'd been there, he'd have a bullet in him. There are lines we don't cross, aren't there, Jackie?*

Jack had no words to express his gratitude—not just for getting the charges dropped, but for the understanding. Gus had his back. His lectures about loyalty were not just bluff. And punching it out was exactly what Jack needed.

Pulling himself back to the present, Luke glanced over at Gus and slammed the glove box closed.

He directed Gus along the back roads, again pretending to consult the map. The bush closed in around them as the roads narrowed to tracks and the afternoon deepened.

The gate stood open, decorated with police tape. Gus drove through, far too fast on the potholed road; he didn't slow until the cabin came into view.

'The door is at the back. Go around there—to the side.' Luke pointed.

Gus killed the ignition, and they sat in silence as the engine ticked over. On their left was the cabin; on their right, the glass-like surface of the dam. The forest surrounded them, still and soundless, as though it had paused to observe the newcomers. The back of Luke's neck prickled.

'Come on.' Gus reached over for his gun then got out, tucking it into his waistband. Luke followed. The sound of their doors closing echoed. 'It's not locked?'

'No. Kevin said if someone needed to shelter here, they were welcome to it.'

Gus gave him a curious look. 'Charitable type, was he?'

'No. But he was weird about this place.'

'It wasn't me who killed them, Jackie.' It was hard to be sure, but there might have been a note of sympathy in Gus's tone.

'Tell that to the cops.' Luke stalked towards the cabin.

Pausing in the doorway, he noted details. The floor was scuffed with footprints; the table had been moved, the lock box was open and empty, and the cupboard doors hung ajar. Two folded camp chairs leaned against the wall. The billy sat at the side of the fireplace where it always had; the lantern hung from its hook. Everything was covered in dust and cobwebs. A huntsman spider had taken up residence in one corner.

'Doesn't look like the police did much of a search.' Gus stooped to enter and moved past Luke, turning a full circle as he examined the interior. 'That's a freaking big spider, eh?'

'Just a baby. Should see the wildlife in the long-drop.'

Gus grunted. He checked his phone for a signal. 'One bar.'

'You'll get better reception on the ridge.' Luke wondered how discreet Wilson planned to be. It wouldn't take much delving to figure out who he'd been talking to. Wilson had been at his flat, twice. He would have made notes. Packard might have talked in the corridor. In the staffroom.

'Move that table over to the wall.' Gus gestured. He took the camp chairs, one in each hand, and flipped them open. 'Alright, Jackie. Let's get started.'

'What?'

But Gus had already left the cabin. Following, Luke held his questions. Gus trudged back to the Audi and clicked the remote to open the boot.

A step behind Gus, Luke stopped in his tracks as the interior came into view.

He said, 'You're fucking kidding me.'

Gus said, 'Hello, *Jonathan*.'

CHAPTER FORTY-ONE

TUESDAY, 6 PM

Emma parked beside Luke's Subaru and scooped random items from the footwell of her car to hide the bundles of banknotes, stuffing the supermarket bag full. An empty water bottle, a discarded jacket, a broken phone charger, food wrappers. Who'd have known that having a messy car would come in handy?

With a deep breath for fortitude, she gathered up her keys and the bag—and then gasped as her door was wrenched open from outside. A hand gripped her arm and yanked her out of the car.

'This is his place, isn't it?' Dave grabbed her by the shoulders. Emma clung to her bag and found that, instead of fear, relief flooded her. For a terrified moment, she'd thought it was Gus.

'Get off me!' She tried to break his hold. 'Are you following me?' When he didn't let go, she pushed his chest; he stumbled back and then rallied. He slammed his body into hers, pressing her against the car, and she thought, *Shit.*

A flash in her peripheral vision, and he was gone.

Steadying herself with a hand on her car, Emma tried to make sense of what she saw.

Dave was sprawled facedown, his cheek squished into the concrete, with Tara Packard's knee on his back. She snapped handcuffs on his wrists behind him while he writhed, protests tumbling out in an incoherent stream. Packard hauled him up to a sitting position, held her ID in front of his face and told him to shut up or he'd spend a night in a cell. As she straightened, her keen eyes flicked around the parking lot to the stairwell and the street, as though checking for further dangers.

Emma said, 'I think I love you.'

'You alright?' Packard dusted herself off. 'Who's this guy? Is he the one who rearranged Luke's face?'

With a nervous laugh, Emma shook her head. 'No. Jesus. He wouldn't stand a chance.'

Packard's eyes narrowed. 'Oh. I thought he was a part of . . . all this.' She waved a vague hand.

'He's just my ex. He's stalking me.' It clicked into place. 'You're watching Luke's place? Are you supposed to be undercover?'

'Had to step in, didn't I?' Packard nodded towards Dave. Her warning had worked; he sat in sulky silence. 'What do you want me to do with him? I can call uniforms, you can make a statement, get an AVO, all that.'

Shaking her head, Emma dismissed the idea. She dropped to a squat in front of Dave, so she was at eye level. 'Dave, this is Tara. If you come near me again, she'll toss you in jail. You should see what she's like when she's angry.'

'Don't make me angry, *Dave*,' Packard said, deadpan. 'But let me see some ID. So I know who I'm dealing with.' She ferreted in his pockets for his wallet, found his licence and snapped a picture with her phone.

'Pretty sure this is not police procedure.' Dave's words were a mumble.

'Oh, you think?' She threw his wallet in his lap. 'I'm gonna uncuff you, and you're gonna drive away. Stay away from her. There won't be another warning.'

Dave grumbled something about police brutality but, at another glare from Packard, slunk away to his car.

Still grasping the bag of Jonathan's dirty money, Emma glanced up at Luke's balcony. She forced her body language to relax.

'Go on up.' The cop jerked her head to the stairs. 'I'll sit in my car and watch nothing happen. He's still recovering, eh?'

Emma nodded. 'I'm just dropping this off. Ah—thanks.'

'Pleasure was all mine,' was the dry response.

CHAPTER FORTY-TWO

TUESDAY, 7.25 PM

Over the years, Gus had delegated a variety of tasks to Jack. Some were victimless, if ethically unsound; some were less palatable. Jack's second-most common complaint (bruised knuckles came first) was getting blood on his clothes, particularly when he was living at the resi and it was hard to get to the laundry without questions being asked. Gus's instructions were simple and direct. *Get him out. Hold him still. Clean up the mess.*

Nothing had changed.

As he hauled Jonathan out of the boot of Gus's Audi and marched him into the cabin, Luke searched for sympathy and came up empty. Jonathan was restrained, with tape over his mouth and cable ties on his wrists. After pushing him into a chair, Luke pulled off the tape. He knew it would sting.

'*You.* You look like shit.' Jonathan's eyes bulged. 'Now it makes sense. I knew you reminded me of someone. What is he, your fucking godfather?' He descended into a rant at Gus: *You're gonna pay for this* and *If you think this is a good way to get money out of me—*

Luke dug in his backpack for tape and fastened Jonathan to the chair, tuning out the tirade. His skin crawled; memories of being in the same position distracted him.

Gus paced, thumbing his phone and waiting for a call to connect. Leaning against the table, Luke folded his arms and watched Jonathan, who ran out of abuse and fell silent. Jonathan's gaze flicked around the cabin, as though searching for an escape, and settled on the huntsman in the corner. He shuddered.

'Emma's fine,' Luke said, breaking a long silence. 'She's staying with friends.'

Jonathan's eyes narrowed.

'No luck.' Abandoning his attempts to connect, Gus stood over Jonathan with an aggrieved sigh. 'I'm disappointed in you, Wylie. Trying to renegotiate when we were doing so well. And talking to the cops—that's just plain stupid.'

Again, Jonathan's eyes bulged, goldfish-like, in his gaunt face.

'You owe me a hundred and forty grand, plus interest for the two months you've been fucking with me.' Gus flicked a glance to Luke. 'What's that add up to?'

'Your usual terms?' Luke closed one eye and cocked his head to calculate. 'Interest is seven zero eight seven. And fifty cents.'

'Let's call it ten.' Gus leaned over Jonathan, casting a shadow onto his face. 'Where's the money?'

Jonathan said, 'I'm not gonna—' but he was cut off by Gus's fist in his face.

'Try again.' Another punch.

'Alright!' Blood dripped from Jonathan's nose, past his mouth to his chin; his head slumped forwards. 'It's at home. There's a safe in my study.'

'How do I know you're telling the truth?'

'You'll have to trust me.' Jonathan's teeth were outlined in blood as he sneered. 'You'll need the combination. So, if you want the money . . .'

'Jackie, get his phone. It's in the glove box.' Gus threw Luke his car keys.

Luke escaped the cabin, relishing the reprieve. He found the phone and trudged inside to toss it, and the keys, to Gus.

A split second later he thought, *Should have held on to the keys.*

Gus demanded a passcode from Jonathan, and after scrolling through the contents, he put the phone on speaker. A dial tone cut in and out, the connection patchy.

'What are you doing?' Spitting blood out of his mouth, Jonathan maintained his outrage.

'Calling your wildcat daughter.'

The call connected: Emma's distorted voice was an irregular, incoherent staccato. 'Dad—are you—I've—where—I—'

'Listen to me, love.' Gus kept his eyes on Jonathan. 'Your father's here with me. There's something he wants you to do for him.'

Jonathan shook his head wildly, flinging blood and snot from his nose. 'Leave her out of it. Don't—'

With the phone in one hand, Gus pulled out his gun with the other and held it against Jonathan's knee. 'Tell her the combination. I'll give her an address to deliver the money to. Tell her to do what she's told or I'll come after her next.'

Emma's voice: 'I—this line is—'

Luke said, 'Gus, she can't hear you.'

'She knows the bloody combination!' Jonathan's wide eyes were fixed on Gus's gun. His chest moved in shallow, panted breaths. 'Emma, do what he says, alright? Get him his money!'

'Do you get a better signal if you hold it higher?' Luke said.

Emma: '*Luke?* Is that—'

Gus rattled off an address in the city, repeating it three times while Emma interrupted with versions of *I can't* and *What?* and *You're cutting out* until, losing his patience, Gus squeezed the trigger.

Jonathan screamed like an angry cat, his howls filling the cabin.

'Did you hear that, love?' Gus spat his words into the phone. 'Now do what you're told.' He hung up.

The echo of the gunshot faded. Blood oozed down Jonathan's leg, soaking his trousers and pooling around his ankle. A low moaning, as though a ghost haunted the cabin, came from his pale lips.

Gus paced in anger, hands on his head, veins popping out and his shoes clacking on the floorboards. 'She'd better get that address right.'

Luke kept his tone neutral. 'What now?'

Gus paused, looking around the cabin. 'We wait for confirmation of delivery, and for my guy to call. And we find Kevin's stash. Start over there—pull up the floorboards, see if there's anything underneath.' He tapped on the wood panelling by the fireplace. 'I'll pull these down.'

Luke prised up the floorboards he'd installed as a teenager, with nothing but a screwdriver for the job. Without proper tools, it was slow going.

'Should have told me I'd need a crowbar,' he grumbled.

Gus grunted at him to get on with it. The search was punctuated by Jonathan's groans of pain. Gus soon tired of the noise. 'Tape him up, Jackie.'

Luke took his time with the search, racking his brain for solutions. Dusk fell quickly. One moment it was daylight, and the next they worked in darkness. He lit the lantern, which cast a flickering yellow glow over the cabin.

After an hour of destruction, the floorboards were piled at one end of the cabin and the wall cavities exposed. Jonathan had been relegated to a corner and the table was outside. Luke examined the underfloor, using his torch to illuminate the packed dirt under the joists, while Gus poked the broom handle inside the chimney.

'Nothing.' Gus straightened, tossing the broom aside. His ability to flick from calm to fury and back again kept Luke on his toes. 'He must have buried it somewhere. Anywhere around the cabin he might use?'

Before Luke could answer, Gus's phone buzzed.

'About bloody time,' Gus said, but his triumphant smile faded as he realised the connection was even worse than the last. The crackling, indistinct words brought a spasm of frustration to his face. 'Fuck this. I'm going up on the ridge. Which way, Jackie?'

Luke's stomach seized. He pointed vaguely up the hill. 'You'll need a torch.'

Gus hopped across the floor joists to the door, flashing a narrow cone of light as he stalked away.

Luke counted to ten, then crouched before Jonathan. 'Listen. Our only chance of staying alive is to get out of here before he comes back.' He pulled the tape off Jonathan's mouth, then cut through the fastening around the man's legs and the cable ties that held his wrists. 'Can you walk on that leg?'

'You think I fucking trust you?' Jonathan lashed out at Luke with a clumsy fist.

Catching Jonathan's wrist, Luke said, 'I'd leave you here and let him shoot you, but I don't want to explain that to Emma. So shut up and do what I say. We're gonna disappear into the bush.'

'And then what?'

'I'll figure something out.' Options ran around his head. None of them were good. He wasted a second wishing he still had Gus's car keys; what a stupid mistake. Hauling Jonathan to his feet, he wrapped an arm under his shoulders and dragged him out across the destroyed floor.

Night enveloped the forest, a wall of blackness ahead. The sky was a deep indigo smeared with backlit clouds and spotted with stars; the moon, partially obscured by clouds, cast a ghostly white light. Luke paused to get his bearings. Ahead of him was the open expanse around the dam. As his eyes adjusted, the glint of moonlight on the smooth surface marked the boundary of the water. He dragged Jonathan to the right, into the gloom of the forest. Unseen obstacles—stumps and fallen logs—banged their toes and shins, and the ground covers caught at their feet like vines. Every time Jonathan put weight on his injured leg, he gasped with pain.

Twenty metres inside the tree line, Luke found what he was looking for: a fallen ironbark trunk he'd played around as a kid. It wasn't much of a shelter, but it would have to do. The sparse forest provided little in the way of hiding places. He dumped Jonathan behind it. 'Keep your head down. Your face will glow if he shines a torch this way.'

'How are we going to—'

'Quiet. He's coming down the hill.' Luke pushed Jonathan's head down until he was flat on the ground. He peered over the log, watching Gus's torch bob towards the cabin and waiting for the inevitable scream of fury.

'WHERE THE FUCK ARE YOU, JACKIE?'

Luke's body seized and he cringed, crouching with his eyes squeezed shut. If he'd stayed in the cabin, he'd be dead.

'YOU CAN'T HAVE GOT FAR!' Silhouetted in the doorway, Gus flashed the torch around the clearing—to his car, underneath it, to each side. Systematically, he examined the tree line. A few steps forwards, and the torch focused on the ground, as though looking for tracks.

Or blood.

Luke's breath caught, and he thought, *Fuck*.

Examining the ground with each step, Gus flashed the torch forwards. Jonathan's bleeding wound had left a subtle trail of breadcrumbs. Barely perceptible black drips on the leaf litter; just enough to give Gus an indication of the direction they'd gone, and the log was the only possible hiding place . . .

'Don't make a sound.' Luke whispered the words into Jonathan's ear and crept away, keeping low, with a handful of trees between himself and Gus. Things he could control, and things he couldn't: he couldn't stop Gus from finding Jonathan, but he could be ready to attack when he did. He'd have one chance to overpower Gus and get the gun.

And then what?

He pushed the thought out of his mind. His shoulder twinged, a reminder of his injuries. Of his mortality.

With his torch in one hand and his gun in the other, Gus's eyes were fixed on the ground. Each step took him closer to Jonathan's position.

'You think you're smarter than me, don't you, Jackie? Thought you'd get away with it.' Gus stopped, wiped his face with the back of his hand. 'After all I've *fucking done for you!*'

Like a cat, Luke slunk behind a tree a few metres away from Jonathan, keeping his body close to it. His best bet was to circle around and get behind Gus. He crouched, searching with his fingers on the ground for a projectile. They closed over a solid stick; he drew it out, wincing as the leaves rustled.

'Where are you, Wylie? Losing a lot of blood, aren't you?' Gus's shoes crunched on twigs underfoot. Three metres from the log, he stopped, listening intently to the silence, then returned his focus to the ground.

He moved forwards again. Two metres away.

Luke pitched the stick. It hit a trunk behind Gus with a hollow clunk.

'What the—' Gus spun around.

Taking advantage of the distraction, Luke flitted to the next tree, trying to place himself out of range of the torch. He froze behind the trunk while Gus's light moved in a slow, systematic grid around the tree the stick had hit.

'You're not gonna get away, Jackie. I know you're there.'

Turning a full circle, Gus returned his attention to looking for Jonathan's blood trail. His light hit the tree Luke hid behind, then dropped to search the ground. Luke held his breath as it passed over the toe of his black sneaker. The beam continued on to play over the fallen trunk, illuminating the ridges in the rough black bark, the faded lichen, a cobweb.

Gus took a step forwards.

Luke let out his breath and started a countdown. Five. Four. Three. Two—

'What the *fuck*?'

Gus's light flashed towards the cabin as the hum of a car engine reached them. Distant at first—near the gate, Luke guessed—it drew nearer with a steady, consistent crescendo.

Luke froze, holding his breath. He'd been a nanosecond from launching onto Gus. Beating a hasty retreat behind the trunk, he flattened against it as Gus turned and broke into a jog, heading back towards the cabin.

'Jonathan. Stay put.' Luke's heart hammered in his throat. *Cops*, was all he could think. Gus had disappeared out of sight behind the cabin.

Tyres crunched on the track as a vehicle gained speed.

Luke ducked from tree to tree until he was level with the front of the cabin. Gus had stopped in the middle of the track, illuminated in the beam of the car headlights. Luke shielded his eyes, trying to identify the vehicle—a large SUV. Black.

A Range Rover.

Before his thoughts could make sense, the driver floored the accelerator, heading straight for Gus.

Gus leaped out of the way, getting off two shots as he dived to his left. One pinged off the bonnet, and the second hit the driver's window. The driver lost control, and the vehicle ploughed into the trees on the passenger side and stalled. Gus, on his feet in a heartbeat, smashed at the driver's window with his gun. He wrenched the door open.

Gus reached in and dragged Emma out by her hair.

With a gasp, she tumbled to the dirt; she found her feet and punched Gus in the back. The gun dropped to the ground as Gus clutched at his side. 'You split my stitches, you little—'

Emma aimed a kick at Gus's leg, then scooped up the gun, but Gus recovered and wrestled it away. With a frustrated cry, she twisted out of his reach.

In a mad sprint, Luke charged towards them, but he was too late to intervene as Gus smacked Emma across the head. She dropped to her hands and knees, then scrambled towards the car and dived through the open driver's door as Gus let off another shot.

Launching himself onto Gus's back, Luke clung on with a hand clenched around Gus's wrist to control the gun. Gus roared, swinging wildly in an attempt to fling him off, while Luke hooked a forearm against his throat. A tearing pain in his injured shoulder made him groan. Panting with the effort, he knew he couldn't hold on for long.

'Get off me!' Gus twisted, swapping his gun hand so he could get his right hand up to Luke's left shoulder. He squeezed. The pain blanked Luke's vision. He fell backwards, rolling out of Gus's line of fire as a crack from the gun sent dirt flying up near his leg. His left arm was heavy, numb; he tried to get up and had to roll onto his front and use his right.

He said, 'Come on, Gus—I can explain.'

'Why should I listen to anything you—'

Luke found his feet and rallied, cutting off the conversation as his hand caught Gus's wrist just in time to send the next shot wide. With a grunt of effort, he twisted the gun out of Gus's grip, sending it flying. Gus stooped, looking for his gun in the dirt, giving Luke an opening for a right hook that caught him in the jaw and sent him reeling sideways.

They spotted the gun at the same time, on the ground five feet away, glinting dully in the red glow of the tail-lights. As one they dived, hands outstretched. Luke got a hand to the weapon, but Gus knocked it away. They scrabbled again, on their hands and knees. Gus was closer—

'STOP!' Emma projected her voice with all the authority and volume of her training. Her tone made both Gus and Luke freeze.

She stood by the car with her feet planted squarely and her arms held straight out in front. The gun she'd stolen from Gus was comfortable in her hands. Her posture was perfect and her face was calm.

'Stand up. Both of you.'

When they didn't, she took a step forwards and reset her posture.

'I said, STAND UP!'

Luke moved first, warily. He sensed Gus getting to his feet a metre away.

'You're not gonna shoot anyone, love.' Gus dusted dirt off his suit.

'Don't call me *love*. It's not 1950, arsehole. Move. That way.' With the gun still gripped in both hands, she jerked the barrel to the right.

Gus obeyed, putting more space between him and Luke.

'Where's Dad?' The gun wavered from Gus to Luke and back again. Her eyes gleamed. 'I heard you shoot him!'

With his hands in front of him, Luke kept his voice down. 'Emma, he's alive. He's in the forest.' He watched her face; her eyes tightened as his words sank in. 'I'm gonna pick up the gun, okay?' He flicked his gaze to the ground. It was almost in reach.

Her chest moved with a breath. She nodded. To Gus, she said, 'Don't you move. Not even a—'

Gus lunged for his gun, knocking Luke aside. As Luke stumbled to regain his footing, Gus scooped the weapon from the ground; he swung it in a wild arc and got off a shot that moved Luke's hair.

Emma fired, another crack splitting the night. She stepped forwards and another shot followed.

Gus Alberici froze, arrested in time and space for a heartbeat, then sprawled onto the dirt.

'Arsehole,' Emma said. The gun slipped from her grip as she dropped to her knees.

CHAPTER FORTY-THREE

TUESDAY, 9.30 PM

The moon, peeking out from the clouds, cast the scene into shadow. Gus lay where he'd fallen, facedown. Emma swayed on her knees.

After the echo of the shots faded, the dark track was still and silent. Crouched down, with one hand on the ground to steady himself, Luke was momentarily disorientated, wondering if he'd imagined the sound. His senses returned with a thud.

Stumbling to Gus, he kicked the gun away from his hand, just in case.

He squeezed the man's shoulder, rolled him onto his back and dug his fingers into his throat for a pulse. An expanding stain of blood on Gus's chest soaked his clothes, dripped into the dirt.

Emma got up, on shaky legs, to kneel at Luke's side. 'Is he dead?'

Luke's head was full of noise. Reality blurred with memories, like watercolours seeping together. The past felt close, as though it walked with him in a parallel time. He was eighteen again. Kevin's wide eyes stared at him. Quin's weak, thready pulse under his fingers. Gus's face looked peaceful, as though he was thinking, but Luke had never seen it so still.

Emma's breath came in short, shallow gasps. Her hands shook as she clutched at Luke's arm. 'I thought he killed Dad. I was so fucking mad.'

'It's okay. We'll sort it out.' Luke pulled her to her feet, wishing he believed his own words. She fell against him. Her composure had vanished and she shivered, leaning on him for support.

'Emma!' Jonathan limped towards them, grimacing with each step as he dragged his injured leg. 'Are you alright? How the hell did you—'

'Later. I'll explain later.' Her voice was muffled by Luke's chest. 'And no. I'm not fucking alright.'

Luke looked over Emma's shoulder as Jonathan stooped to pick up the gun she'd used. He bristled. 'What are you doing?'

His face stiff with pain, Jonathan examined the gun. 'This isn't mine. Where did you get this?'

Emma's shoulders heaved. 'It's his. I got rid of yours. Like you said.'

Jonathan squinted along the barrel of the gun. He pointed it at Gus's body.

And fired.

He turned to Luke. 'Get her out of here. Call the police and tell them some crap so they come. And hurry up. I need to get to hospital.'

'What? Dad—'

Jonathan held up a hand to silence her. 'You were never here.'

'But—'

'Don't argue with me!' Jonathan's eyes glowed, wild with intensity. His pale face shone with perspiration. 'I've got good lawyers. They'll get me off. But you—*you* need to get out of here.'

'What about, *Thanks, Emma, for saving my sorry arse*?' She pushed at his chest, and he fell backwards onto his sorry arse, on the ground beside Gus.

'Thanks.' He delivered the word with a scowl.

'Emma, he's right.' Luke spoke quietly into her ear as he coaxed her to the car. Her token resistance was more confusion than rebellion.

In the passenger seat, she put her face in her hands and let her shoulders slump. 'Shit, Luke. What have I done?'

'Breathe. Count in to four, out to eight. It'll be alright.'

'How can you be so fucking calm?'

'I'll panic later,' he said. 'Stay here. There's something I need to do.'

In the cabin, he recovered his backpack. Kevin's wallet and phone, which he'd kept hidden for years, were tucked inside. He'd switched on the phone a handful of times, always from the house in Footscray, to set up and monitor the direct debits for the utilities and to keep an eye on Kevin's bank balance. After wiping them clean, he planted them in the glove box of Gus's Audi.

On his way back, he approached Jonathan, who grimaced as he wrapped his jacket around his leg. 'You'll deal with the car?' Jonathan gestured to the Range Rover. 'You can't take it home. The bullet holes—and the tyre tracks . . .'

'I know a bloke. I'll sort it out.' Luke swallowed his distaste. 'You don't have to do this. Get in the car and I'll drop you at a hospital. I can clean this up.' He jerked his head towards Gus's body.

'Done it all before, right?' Jonathan shifted his leg, a spasm of pain crossing his face. 'No. They'll link me to it anyway. This way it's self-defence.'

'Ship has sailed, right?'

In Gus's pockets, Luke found three phones. Gus's personal phone he put back. One was Jonathan's, which he restored to factory settings and tossed to the ground. The other would require disposal.

Jonathan's face twisted with distaste. 'You're up to your fucking neck in this.'

They exchanged a long, measured look. Luke stared at the injured man, considering his options.

'Don't worry, I'm not going to snitch on you.' Jonathan snorted. 'I'd be dead if you hadn't pulled me out of there.'

'True.' Luke checked that Emma was still in the car, out of earshot. He leaned down to speak into Jonathan's ear. 'You're doing the right thing by Emma. I respect that. But I don't trust you.' He dropped his voice lower; his words were barely a whisper. 'You think you'll get off lightly here. And the financial crimes—a slap on the wrist, a few years in minimum security. But conspiracy to murder is another matter altogether. I recorded you.'

Jonathan gave him a thin-lipped smile. 'Insurance, right? What about Ivan? I still have that video.'

'Don't worry about Ivan.' Luke gazed out over the top of Jonathan's head, taking in the dark scene. 'I'll keep that recording to myself—if you keep my name out of this. Mess with me again and I know where to send it. Do you understand me, Jonathan?'

With a bitter laugh, Jonathan gestured to Gus's dead body and said, 'You sound just like him.'

CHAPTER FORTY-FOUR

WEDNESDAY, 7 PM

Luke took a chair out to the balcony and wedged it between the glass door and the metal railing. He put his feet on the railing and leaned back, phone in hand. Emma was with Phil. Malcolm was working on the Range Rover; he was waiting on a call.

As he closed his eyes to feel the sea breeze, anxiety was there, waiting. He wondered if a day would come when he wasn't worried about the consequences of all he'd done. Most of his day had been spent destroying or hiding evidence. Emma's clothes, his clothes, his backpack. Everything that might link them to the crime scene was gone.

His game of dominoes was almost over. Not all of them had fallen as planned, and the game could still be swept from the table by an unseen force. But at least with Jonathan under police guard in hospital and Gus dead, he was unlikely to collect a bullet.

He leaned over the railing and waved as a car parked by his Subaru, then went inside to open the door.

'Jesus, it's hot in here.' Wilson tugged at his tie as he stepped inside. Sweat beaded on his ruddy face after his climb up the stairs. He carried a manila folder.

'It's cooler out here.' Luke took another chair from the living room out to the balcony. 'Where's Packard?'

'She deserved a night off.' Wilson leaned on the railing, examining the humble view, and placed his file on the ground. 'I hope you have no ulterior motive for enticing me out onto your balcony.'

Luke rolled his eyes. 'Jesus. Let it rest.'

'I know Alberici greased palms to get you off.' Wilson grimaced. 'Half the station wanted to give you a medal. We knew Zoungas was dealing drugs, but we didn't know about his other business. What a sicko.'

Luke met Wilson's eyes. 'I will never unsee what I saw on his computer.' It was the closest he'd ever come to admitting his involvement. 'You didn't come here to dredge up ancient history, though.'

'You know why I'm here.' The chair creaked under Wilson's weight as he sat. He rubbed his face. 'Alberici's dead.'

'I saw it on the news.' Luke crossed his arms. 'What happened?'

'Body was found at McNally's bush block. Jonathan Wylie sitting beside him, holding a smoking gun. Anonymous on a burner phone called it in. Wylie says Alberici bullied him into cleaning money. Abducted him, held a gun to his head, all that jazz.' Wilson wiped his face again, smearing sweat. 'There were tracks from another vehicle—there was another player, unidentified. McNally's wallet and phone in Alberici's glove box. The cabin was torn to pieces. I don't know what he was looking for.'

'Are you supposed to tell me all this?'

Wilson snorted. 'Wylie's lawyered up. He's not saying much.'

Luke said nothing.

'You're a known associate. Your name is on the list—at least, Jack Quinlan's is. They'll check everything. Phone records, banking, all that. They're working on warrants as we speak. Get yourself a lawyer.' Sobering, Wilson said, 'I know you weren't directly involved. Tara was outside. You were here all night, out of action. Your girlfriend visited in the evening, then came back just before midnight, stayed till morning.' Wilson paused. 'Did she tell you what happened with her ex?'

Luke nodded. 'Tell Packard I owe her a beer.'

'You said Alberici killed McNally. And Quin too, presumably.'

'Yeah.' Luke couldn't hide his note of disappointment. His original plan to frame Gus for Kevin and Quin's murders had seemed such a perfect revenge, but Gus would never feel the burn.

'Hard to prove. Circumstantial evidence, unless you want to go on record.'

Luke shook his head. 'Not a chance.'

'There's more.' Reaching for his files, Wilson took out a folded document encased in a plastic pocket. 'I found this among McNally's paperwork in Footscray.'

Luke took the document, then raised his eyes in disbelief. 'Is this for real?'

'It appears so. The dates and signatures check out.'

'That's not Kevin's writing—it's Quin's.' Luke slapped the document down. 'Is this some kind of joke?'

'No joke. We matched it to other documents in the house. McNally was dyslexic—could barely write. Looks as though Quin wrote it out for him.'

Luke picked up the document and scanned it again. On a form from the post office, in Quin's childish, sloping characters, Kevin's will was simply written.

. . . nominate as executor Michael Quinlan—all assets to Jack Quinlan date of birth 15 June 1997 . . .

A broad smile spread across Wilson's face. 'Why would McNally leave everything to you?'

'When was this?' Luke turned over the document to search for a date.

'Dated 2011. Witnessed by Kevin's mother. I don't know who Donna Truro is, but we checked out the signatures. They're legit.'

Luke stared at the document. For a psychotic moment, he felt Kevin's hands on his throat again. The document felt heavy in his hands, weighed down by four dead signatures.

'Here's something else I found.' Wilson rifled through the file again. 'This is McNally's first booking photo. He was nineteen—got done for petty theft. Look.'

Luke swallowed past a lump in his throat. Kevin's hostile face stared back at him.

'Kinda looks like someone, doesn't he?' Wilson reclined with a satisfied smile. 'He was your father, right? Did you know? Did Quin?'

'What does it matter?' Luke's voice was thick. 'They're both dead.'

Wilson's face settled into an unreadable half-smile. 'He did the right thing. The house in Footscray is yours. And the bush block. You'll need a lawyer to sort it all out.'

Luke put his face in his hands. Relief spread like warm liquid down his back, melting him into his chair.

'You alright?'

'Just . . . surprised.' As lies went, this was an easy one.

Wilson packed up his file. He held out his hand to shake Luke's. 'This is it, okay? Stay out of trouble. I don't want to hear the name Jack Quinlan ever again.'

'That makes two of us,' Luke said.

CHAPTER FORTY-FIVE

THREE WEEKS LATER

Straddling the bluestone retaining wall, Emma sat with one foot on the sand and one on the walking path. Half of her on a shifting surface; the other half on stable ground. The beach was dotted with people enjoying the mild evening, although the cool breeze would soon send them inside. She put her jacket on and returned her attention to Luke, who was busy unpacking paper cartons.

The bruising on his face had faded, and a narrow pink scar replaced the stitches on his nose, which had returned to a normal size and shape. He'd changed in the past few weeks. The calmness she'd so admired was still there, but now it was unforced; he no longer feigned relaxation for the benefit of others. It was a subtle change, but Emma had learned to see through his acting. Gus's death had lifted a millstone from around his neck.

Mirroring her position, Luke sat facing her. Between them on the broad wall, he laid his containers of food. 'This one first,' he said. 'Kingfish sashimi. Fresh wasabi.' He brandished a pair of chopsticks.

'Why are you so obsessed with food?' It was not food-court sushi: he'd gone to a fancy place in the city. Emma tasted the sashimi, her eyes widening as the wasabi cleared her sinuses and hit the back of her head.

'Good question.' Luke's brow furrowed as he considered. She didn't interrupt to explain that it had been entirely rhetorical. 'You never know which meal will be your last. Imagine if you died, and your last meal was a crappy five-dollar pizza?' He looked down at the gourmet spread between them. 'Also, my diet as a kid was about eighty percent sausages. I'm making up for it now.'

Emma smiled, abandoning her chopsticks to pick up the sashimi with her fingers, and voiced her biggest concern. 'You're sure Phil will be okay?'

'It's a great place. They know what they're doing. I've worked in lots of houses—not all of them are as organised. Or as clean.'

'That's what Gabriela said.'

'Do you know when you're leaving yet?' Luke stuck food in his mouth, as though to make the question offhand. She saw through it.

'Few more weeks. Visa issues to sort out.'

'Are you . . . financially, is this all going to work?' Again, Luke pretended it was a casual question. 'I mean, Jonathan will get time, for sure. His assets could be seized as proceeds of crime. It'll be a big mess.'

Emma shook her head. 'I've had a lot of meetings with accountants and lawyers lately. I'm fine, Luke.' He said nothing, so she went on. 'He had good separation of his business and personal assets. The house is in my name. So is the beach house.' She'd never told Luke about the beach house; his eyebrows rose. 'He set up trusts for Phil and me—although I can't get at mine until I'm twenty-five.' She hiked a shoulder. 'But I'm not going to starve.'

'What about the house, while you're overseas?'

'Amelia and Matt are going to house-sit.' The arrangement had fallen into place, as though by fate. 'Stop worrying about me.'

'You'll miss Jonathan's trial.'

'He doesn't want me there. He told me to change my name.' She picked up another piece of sashimi, examined it at eye level and shoved it in her mouth. It was so tender that it dissolved on her tongue. 'How do you rationalise this stuff? A few weeks ago, I could have sworn he hated me. I thought I hated him—and I still do, for what he did to you. But I should be the one going to jail. He's giving up his freedom for me.'

Luke looked out to the beach, hiding his reaction. 'Parents protect their young. It's their one job, right?' The words were thick. He shook his head, as though to shake the feelings away. Then, predictably, he changed the topic. 'What will you change your name to?'

Emma smiled. 'I thought I'd take a leaf out of your book and use my mother's name. Rossetti.'

'Emma Rossetti.' Luke nodded. 'I like it.'

'You'll come and visit me, right?'

'If I'm not in jail.' He paused, as though he had more to say, then shrugged.

For days after Gus's death, she'd moved in a soup of fear, convinced that she or Luke or both would be arrested; but as the weeks passed and Jonathan's lawyers did their magic, her fear had settled to a dull baseline of anxiety. Luke seemed unfazed. She wondered if his relationship with the fat detective had anything to do with it.

Luke pulled the lid off another carton. 'Sesame-seared tuna with ponzu sauce.'

'You're changing the topic with food.'

Laughing, he scooped up a piece of tuna. 'There is also the small matter of what to do with the money. I figure it's yours now.'

When she'd handed the bag of money to his downstairs neighbour for safekeeping, Irina had grumbled, *Tell Luke he needs a bigger safe.* 'What are my options?'

Luke leaned back on his hands. 'You could turn it in. You could spend it, although you'd have to be careful not to alert the ATO. You could donate it to charity—same proviso. Or you could clean it.'

'Can you do that for me?'

'What do you take me for, a criminal?' A laugh. 'No. I'm not laundering money for you.' His gaze flicked out to the beach. 'I'm done with all that.'

Liar, she thought.

'Fine.' She stuck a piece of tuna in her mouth. It was hard to frown around something so delicious.

'Don't look at me like that. I'll hold it for you, until you figure out what to do with it.'

'At Irina's?'

'No. I'd hate to get her into trouble. I have other hiding places.' He flashed her a cheeky grin and gestured to the next carton. 'Shredded slaw with miso dressing and fried tofu.'

The sun set over the bay, casting a bronze haze over Luke's hands as he laid out the food. She sat back, watching him: his hair that needed a trim; the shape of his shoulders; his precise, competent movements. He'd not once tried to dissuade her from leaving, which, after Dave's contempt of her career, was refreshing; but a small part of her wished he would show a little regret. Luke's focus on the practicalities of her impending departure was a distraction. It meant they weren't talking about their relationship, whatever it was. The past few weeks they'd stuck together in an unspoken, desperate enmeshment—partners in crime—but any discussion of the future seemed off-limits.

She said thoughtfully, 'We know a lot of each other's secrets, don't we?'

His lips twitched. 'Guess so.'

She held up her hand, with her fifth finger out and the other fingers bent. 'Pinky swear. I'll keep yours if you keep mine.'

'What are we, five years old?'

'You want me to cut your palm and draw blood?'

With due solemnity, he wrapped his little finger around hers. 'You think I'm gonna spill your secrets?'

'You wouldn't dare.' She gasped as he pulled her forwards, off-balance, and kissed her soundly on the mouth.

'I'm gonna miss you, Emma Rossetti,' he said.

CHAPTER FORTY-SIX

FIVE MONTHS LATER

Luke dug the shovel into the earth and scooped a load into the wheelbarrow. On the next pass, it hit resistance. He tossed the shovel aside and used his gloved hands to uncover a series of rocks, then hoisted them one by one into the barrow until it was full. Another load, one of hundreds he'd trundled out over the past week. Grasping the handles, he pushed the barrow out into the bright light. Equipped in heavy work gear, a hard hat and a head lamp, he looked like a miner—which he was, although it wasn't gold he sought.

The adit's collapse had been less complete than he'd feared, but every time he entered a nagging fear of being buried alive kept him on his toes. After clearing the entrance, he'd reinforced the walls with rock and hand-cut saplings, but he was realistic about his engineering skills. The sooner he could get the job done, the better.

He dumped the load onto the expanding pile, with a glance up at the afternoon sky. The waning sun cast long shadows through the trees. He rolled his shoulders and stretched his neck, fatigued after the day's labour. Merlin, his rescue greyhound, peeled himself up from resting in the shade to press his snout against Luke's thigh for attention.

'One more load.' He rubbed the dog's ears. 'Back to sleep. Good dog.'

Adjusting his head lamp, he turned the barrow and trudged along the packed dirt path into the adit. Earlier in the day, he'd nudged the old prospector from his rest. Another day, perhaps two, and the job would be done.

The shovel snagged. He dropped to his knees and dug with his hands.

'Hello,' he said, as he unearthed a duffel bag crusted with a layer of dirt. He sat back on his heels and waited to feel something: excitement, joy, closure. A wash of relief was all he could summon. He put the bag on the barrow and wheeled it out into the light.

'Guess I'm done,' he said to Merlin, who wagged a hopeful tail.

With his equipment piled on top, he navigated the barrow down the steep track, bumping over exposed roots and rocks with Merlin on his heels. Near the base, where the track met the driveway, two headstones poked out of the bushes, small enough that they'd be easy to miss. The silver etching glinted in the angled sun.

Michael Stanley Quinlan 1973–2022

Kevin John McNally 1973–2022

Buried under each headstone was a plastic canister of ashes. The year of death was inaccurate, as were their death certificates. Luke figured they wouldn't be bothered by the detail.

At this time of day, the sun angled sharply through the forest, casting the cabin and the dam into shade. As always, the water was smooth and silver, motionless and soundless. A cool breeze had sprung up, but while it feathered the rushes on the far side, it didn't raise even a hint of a ripple.

A dented Isuzu ute waited behind the cabin. The duco on the side held the imprint of *J McNally*, but it was just a memory; the colour had long since worn off. Luke hefted the wheelbarrow into the tray and stacked his equipment beside it.

He dusted the dirt from the bag before taking it inside the cabin. A week ago, he'd replaced the floor, and the air was scented with fresh wood. Against the wall, a camp bed nestled; a table and chairs took up the far corner and a comfortable chair waited in front of the fireplace, beside Merlin's sheepskin bed.

Sometimes, he heard Kevin's voice, asking what the hell had happened to his cabin—criticising Luke's choice of timber, his joins, the new furniture. Sometimes he heard Quin humming the Rolling Stones as he rummaged in the esky. Sometimes he saw shadows, their shapes. The house in Footscray was similarly haunted; he saw Gail in the kitchen and smelled sausages frying. It didn't bother him. He knew he wasn't mad, and he didn't believe in ghosts. It was just his memories keeping him company.

He heard Emma's voice too. The image of her retreating form as she disappeared through the security doors at the airport was burned into his memory. The doors closed, and she was gone, as though she'd only ever been a figment of his imagination.

On the table in the cabin, he cut the bag open with a knife. The plastic banknotes were cheerfully clean, in contrast to the disintegrating bag. As he stood back to stare at the money, a spark of optimism loosened his muscles. He could fix up the house in Footscray. Buy a ticket to LA to see Emma. No more stressing about bills. He could finish his degree in peace.

Laundering it safely would take time, but he could be patient when he chose.

From the esky under the table, he took two cans of beer and trudged to the graveyard. He held a can in each hand. With a melodramatic flourish that would have amused Emma, he tipped one onto each grave.

'Thanks, I guess,' he said. 'Rest in peace, you pair of old crims.'

He stuffed the money into a clean bag, shouldered his backpack and clipped Merlin into his harness in the ute. At the end of the driveway, Luke stopped to close the gate and straighten the freshly painted sign. The radio blared classic rock, and as he bounced on the potholes of Stillwater Road, he sang along with a smile. He knew the words to the first half of every song.

ACKNOWLEDGEMENTS

I would like to acknowledge the Traditional Owners of the land on which this book was written, the Wadawurrung people of the Kulin Nation. I pay my respects to their Elders, past and present, and to all First Nations people as the original storytellers of this land. I've made my home in Doonmarnwaring, which means 'a place where the warri (salt water) and lakorra (clouds) meet' and I give my thanks to the countless generations who have cared for this beautiful country.

It's harder to write acknowledgements than thousands of words of fiction, because I know there are people I'll miss, and for those I do remember to name, a brief mention on an acknowledgements page is far too little. I sincerely hope I've thanked everyone I need to along the way.

So here's the list. For my agent Tom Gilliatt of a4 Literary, I have just one more question . . . I'm not joking—the questions will never end. Thank you for seeing the potential in Luke's story and being a tireless champion of *Stillwater* from the very beginning. Thanks to

Jane Palfreyman and Ali Lavau for their brilliant editorial advice; to Cate Paterson, Angela Handley, Kate Goldsworthy, Bella Breden, Anabel Pandiella, Matt Hoy and the amazing team at Allen & Unwin for bringing it all together. To the team in the USA, thanks for navigating time zones and Australian slang: David Forrer at Inkwell Management, and Joe Brosnan, Jenny Choi and the team at Grove Atlantic. Many thanks to my two talented cover designers—Luke Causby and Eric Fuentecilla. Writing and publishing are very different worlds, and I've been blessed with the most supportive bunch of people to help bridge the gaps.

Thanks to the very helpful Luke from the Victoria Police Media, Communications and Engagement Department for his advice on police procedure. Any errors (and liberties taken) are entirely mine.

To my first reader, Sarah Catania, a special mention—you have the attention to detail a great editor needs, and I hope you got a chuckle out of Merlin. Thanks also to my book club for reading an early draft and discussing it as though it was a real book! That was weird. Good weird. We're not just about wine and cheese after all.

A massive thanks to the authors who read advance copies, including Hayley Scrivenor and Mark Smith. Your kind words and support mean so much to me as a debut author.

I've been writing for a long time, secreted away by myself, and it's been a revelation to join a thriving community of writers. I've met amazing groups of people through my PWE course at Victoria University; at Varuna, the National Writers House; through the Write Here on the Surf Coast Saturday group; and in the stellar 2025 Debut Crew (a shout-out to Madeleine Cleary, our fearless leader, and the Melbourne Side Crew). Your encouragement and lively discussions, and the sense of inclusion in a community, have added an extra layer of enjoyment to this year.

ACKNOWLEDGEMENTS

Thanks to Andrea, Darren and Nat for your unwavering belief in me—this is what family is for. And also to my extended family and friends—I know it's taken a long time, but you knew I'd get around to it one day.

To Nathan, Sam and Mia—thanks for listening to my monologues, and for the endless cups of tea and coffee, beach walks, late dinners and wine. Thanks for giving me the time and space to play with my imaginary friends.

And, lastly, to you, the reader—thanks for being here. Without you, books wouldn't exist. Keep reading!